Mr. Vanderbilt's Photographer

Steven Gittelman, Emily Gittelman and Andrew Wells

SUFFOLK COUNTY VANDERBILT MUSEUM

Copyright © 2014 by Steven H. Gittelman

No part of this publication may be reproduced, stored in a retrieval system, or transmitted, in any form or by any means, electronic, mechanical, photocopying, recording, or otherwise, without the prior written permission of the copyright owner.

All rights reserved.
Printed in the United States of America
First Printing, 2014

ISBN 978-0-615-93463-1
Library of Congress Control Number: 2014935033

Suffolk County Vanderbilt Museum
180 Little Neck Road
Centerport, NY 11721
(631) 854-5555
www.vanderbiltmuseum.org

To William and Molly Rogers,
for their generous support of this work and of the Suffolk County
Vanderbilt Museum, and to the Robert Bronner family
for their trust in sharing their father's legacy with us.

SUNDAYS AT THE MUSEUM WITH EMILY

I would be John the Gardener and she would be the seaplane pilot's daughter—or—Rosemary Warburton, Mr. Vanderbilt's stepdaughter. We would stay in character from the moment we piled into our 1931 Model Ford until we left the museum. It was all about a dad and his daughter … perfect summer days …

Contents

Acknowledgments vii
Foreword ix
Prologue xiii
June 1931 1
Eagle's Nest 15
New York (and Centerport again) 30
Slowly to Sea 35
Into Tropical Waters 45
Jamaica 56
The Galapagos Islands 66
Tagus Cove 73
August 78
Letters Home 84
Tahiti 90
Bora Bora 102
Samoa 106
Pago Pago 112
Consuelo and Earl Depart; Others Follow Suit 116
Pago Pago and Apia 122
The Fiji Islands 128

Viti Levu 139
Dredging 142
Noumea Harbor 145
To Australia 149
Brisbane 152
The Carlton Cabaret 155
Alone in the World 163
The Crash 172
Cairns and a Cuckoo 176
Timor 184
Bima 192
The Commodore's Birthday 197
Surabaya 206
Far East 212
Muntok 216
Penang 221
Ceylon 228
Canals and Cairo 240
Greece 254
An Unexpected Realization 261
Delphi and Naples 266
Monte Carlo 273
Epilogue 285
Index 289
About the Authors 305

Acknowledgements

WE ARE THE lucky ones. Rarely are authors trusted with such richness of primary sources. Years ago Robert Bronner, the son of Bob Bronner, approached the Suffolk County Vanderbilt Museum with box after box of his father's writings and photographs, we all knew the importance of putting it into an accessible form. We received two diaries, hundreds of pages of letters as well as hundreds of fine negatives. Mr. Bronner was also generous with his time, spending hours with the principal investigator describing his father in great detail. All illustrations have been generously provided by the Bronner Family except in a few cases as indicated.

Others assisted us in our work. Elaine Trimarchi read the early drafts and encouraged us to complete the work. She liked it. Gretchen Oldrin Mones, a trustee on the Vanderbilt Museum Board of Trustees, provided detailed editing. Pat Keefe, Director of Public Relations at the museum, provided precise and energetic editing of the final draft. Maria Grudzinski and Nancy DePaolo provided much needed clerical support; compiling, scanning and preparing the many photographs, preparing indexes, assisting in research, and checking the final proof. We thank Katie Cullen for assisting with the index and illustrations. And Anthony Ferguson for assisting with illustrations.

We thank the Board of Trustees of the Suffolk County Vanderbilt Museum for resolving that this volume should be written and supporting our efforts throughout the process.

We are also grateful to Dr. William and Molly Rogers for providing the financial support required to publish the work through funding from the Rogers Fund.

Foreword

IT IS RARE that an author has the richness of primary source materials that we have had in the writing of this book. Robert Bronner felt a distinct sense of responsibility toward his father and leaving him to join Vanderbilt on his voyage around the world. It generated a feeling that he had abandoned someone in need. Bob, as he chose to be called, wrote a continuous stream of letters from the first day until the last, maintaining a long distance dialogue that spoke of a gentle love between two men.

Bronner was a talented artist whose photographic skills grew exponentially on the voyage. It is his exceptional skills that created the hundreds of vivid photographs that were loaned to us by his family, which help us to recreate the photographic image of this voyage. Vanderbilt hired Bob Bronner and Al Gilks to document the voyage and it would seem that his choice was unimpeachable. Perhaps only a Vanderbilt could summon such talent.

Bob's daily experiences as a specialized member of the crew of the *Alva* were memorialized by his daily diaries. We could not have asked for a better trail, a time capsule, if you will, of an experience that could never be recreated.

Alva Vanderbilt, William K. Vanderbilt II's mother, used the keeping of diaries and logs as a means of educating her three children. Willie K. was required to keep a daily log of the voyages that he took with his family. We can thank Willie K. for his travelogues that he wrote as the *Log of My Motor* series which represent the first travel guides ever made available by the American Automobile Association. It should come as no surprise that Willie wrote a sequence of books about each of the significant voyages he took on his later yachts. In 1929 he documented his trip around the world in his yacht *Ara*, and in 1933 he published "*West Made*

East with the Loss of a Day," his own book on the voyage that Bob Bronner documented for us so well.

The archives of the Suffolk County Vanderbilt Museum are rich with scrap albums of articles kept by Willie K. There one can find the original log of the *Alva* on this journey. But sadly Willie K. left us none of his personal communications, no personal letters, nothing that gives us a sense of his personal voice.

In writing this book, we chose to employ selected quotes from both Willie and Bob. The story line regarding both men is as they presented it. We took the liberty to create a bit of dialogue to connect the trails left by these two men. The dialogue between Bob Bronner, Al Gilks, and some crew members was added to flesh out events and situations.

Bob Bronner's son, Greg, generously loaned all of the Bronner materials and provided us with his own memories of his father. His loving memories were quite moving and rather beautiful. We feel particularly fortunate and privileged to tell the beautiful story that follows.

"Inasmuch as this is my second voyage around the world to the westward, I have lost two days of my life[;] to recover them I ought to make two circumnavigations to the eastward. But what would I do with them if I had them? If one could only gain two decades as easily!"

— Willie K. Vanderbilt II, as written in his memoirs—
"West Made East with the Loss of a Day," a recounting
of his second circumnavigation of the globe.

Prologue

IT WAS quite a gift for a small boy. He picked up the Ingersoll and held it out to show his father.

"I know," the man said, smiling.

The boy turned it around and looked directly into the lens.

"It goes the other way," his father explained.

The boy smiled knowingly at his father, saying what his expression had already revealed.

"I know."

"That's it."

"Dad, it snowed last night, can I go out?"

"Don't go breaking it now, that's brand new." But the boy had seen the long grin on his father's face. He'd never gotten a Christmas gift like this. Not to say that he hadn't gotten gifts before.

With his father watching over him through a frosted window, the boy snuck up on an ancient tree whose seminal branches appeared to have given up the ghost. The snow was soft and gentle, too shallow to have caused the tree to lay down its limbs.

The boy looked through the eyepiece, his breath fogging the air as well as the barely visible image. With a sense of perspective and composition beyond his years, Bob Bronner clicked the shutter, collecting the image.

Christmas 1911

June 1931

HE HANDED the tickets to the official at the bottom of the stairs and approached a lineup of behemoths. Bob had heard their plaintive wail from a distance, reverberating off the hills, but he had never challenged them up close. Young Robert Bronner, scrawny and balding, stepped out toward the platforms. Of the five sweltering, dripping, steaming giants before him, the largest was to be his charger for the distance between Los Angeles and Chicago.

Struggling with the all-pervasive effects of the Great Depression, the *Limited* wasn't the train it used to be: now often too hot and overcrowded—hard conditions in hard times. The engine dwarfed him, they all did, not just the one assigned to the train famously named *Los Angeles Limited*. He counted the wheels of the engine: four wheels in a leading truck, followed by eight mounted to drivers—each taller than a man—and four more trailing.

It was hot as hell and his duffel felt leaden. The Los Angeles heat was up to its sullen windless tricks; proving no less formidable than the skin-searing steam spewing from the engine. Bob's shirt was plastered miserably to his torso. And that dripping, sweltering steamer was suffering a misery of its own. Loads of horsepower were tied up in that enormous assemblage of steel, named *Mountain*; a double-entendre that also referred to the immense mountain chain bisecting the route.

The conductor bellowed the familiar cry *"all aboard,"* and Bob focused on the remedial mission at hand—get on, and get a seat. A plume of steam, white with moisture, hissed forth from *Mountain*, engulfing the platform and, as Bob would later describe it, scaring "the bejeebers" out of him. Weighed down by the noise, the heat and the scalding wetness, he dragged his pitifully overfilled duffel to the nearest set of steps leading into the first of many long, green cars. Finding this to be a mail car with no place hospitable for a traveler, he continued on down the platform where four more Pullman-green cars followed. He guessed that they were ninety feet long if they were an inch, and he struggled on, stricken, as the ticket master rejected him, waving him to the back of the train. Although he travelled at the call of a Vanderbilt, he was riding on a ticket sent to him by post, and had no sense of the living arrangements under which he was destined to spend the next four days.

The dark-green Pullman sleepers each had their own name emblazoned in yellow print—*Dahlonega, Nolando, Lake Champlain, Lake Crystal* … and each had windows spread apart just enough that Bob could see, in his mind's eye, their luxurious travelling compartments: spacious sleepers, fancy dining cars, and majestic observatory decks.

As he continued down the platform, and the long line of cars trailed on, he found out that his tickets were not the kind that he had dreamt they would be: for eventually, six crowded coach cars substituted for the Pullmans. The coaches were a Union Pacific tactic for saving money during bad times. It was intended that passengers would find them tolerable, and for a price fitting with the era. The Pullmans and their upscale fare had gone the way of the Depression. The *Los Angeles Limited*, once a rising star, was losing its Pullman-green.

Bob threw his duffel up into the first coach car and pulled himself up the tread-beaten stairs. His hair was thinning, and he could do with a few pounds, but some might say that he was tall and handsome. If he hadn't been struggling clumsily through the coach, he might have piqued the interest of some of the young women already assembled inside. Instead, as he moved down the aisle with his duffel brushing precariously against irritated passengers, just about everyone glared as he awkwardly forced his way from one end of the car to the next—then repeated the process in the next car—and the next. In the fourth car, there were two empty seats in the same row, adjacent to the aisle, but on opposite sides. There he would attempt to make a home among the coalescing smells of people who had given up on the West, and were headed back where they, or their parents, had come from.

Just as Bob settled into his lucky find, an elderly couple (who evidently had found the stale cabin air intolerable) were assisted onto the

JUNE 1931

train and laid claim to the seats Bob was occupying. He was not one to protest—though common courtesy might have been suffering these days, he would never stay seated while the elderly and frail stood.

Upon relinquishing his seats, he considered the ramifications: four miserable days of the oppressive heat without a place to sit and rest. Sitting over the handle of a rocking suitcase—head drumming against the hard cabin wall or a window pane—the same glaring girls stepping around him, disgusted, as he lay like a vagrant in the corridor or vestibule. Fortunately for Bob, his good nature was soon rewarded. The conductor had found four hapless souls who, unable to afford tickets, had snuck onto the train and were unceremoniously dismissed. Bob was a man of riches now. He claimed a seat for himself and one for his personal cargo.

Hoards of people waited on the platform—carpetbaggers and women and children with dust across their faces. Two years into the Depression, it was hard to gauge what anyone had or didn't have, but everyone wanted a second chance. Bob had just been given one—a seat, a ticket, and better yet, employment as a photographer. Not just any photographer—Mr. Vanderbilt's photographer.

Bob ran a handkerchief across his brow and breathed deeply. The butterflies in his stomach were unrelenting, and the big moment was fast approaching. He was already on the train now. Before long there would be no turning back. Where was this adventure going to take him? What he knew was that he was expected in New York, at Mr. Vanderbilt's house, in a town called Centerport—wherever that was.

Clunk—the sudden jerk of the train as it pulled its way out of S.P. Station. Bob was glued to the spot. In his mind he'd played through the morning's tasks a few hundred times. He'd pictured himself boarding the train taking a car out to the station, leaving his father that morning, and packing the contents of his room: his clothes, his books, and his camera equipment. He thought about the journey from Brooklyn ten years ago when his father, a widower with two young sons to care for, decided to take the family out of New York to the greener, and decidedly warmer, pastures of California.

With the last of their money, they had bought an old, banged-up Kissel car at a police auction. The car, which had seemed to have a life of its own, was once owned by a bootlegger, and lent considerable glamour to the expedition. Hauled up in the back of the rickety little

The second-hand Kissel car driven by the Bronners on Bob's first cross-country journey. (1920)

vehicle, Bob had completed his first major photography project – a child's photographic journey as he trekked the seemingly endless miles from the East to West Coast.

He'd learned a great deal on the way: not only about photography in general, but also about his own aspirations as a photographer and an artist. Perhaps it was the drive west that inspired him to pursue a career in film; seeing the potential for pictures and photographs to breathe life into the record of human experience.

Not long ago, he'd been fetching coffees and running errands at MGM, a job he felt lucky to have. Hardly anyone worked these days, and to have a home and steady work, at a movie studio no less, that was like a golden ticket right there.

He had kept his head down and it had paid off in the form of a promotion—assistant photographer. More responsibility had given him more opportunity: to learn his art and to be around important people, to wonder whether the lady in the passenger seat of the flashy car was a movie star or the wife of a movie star. Anyone dressed up those days was probably somebody, and it was fun to dream.

At MGM, with a job and a steady paycheck, Bob could dream about anything. He could dream about becoming a photographer someday; of

The Los Angeles home built by Jack Bronner: His retirement refuge, and a symbol of hope for new beginnings for his two young sons.

working with the film crews on motion pictures, or going to the theater to see his work—something of his own, on the big screen.

The thing about dreaming, though, is that you can easily get carried away. And Bob had. He had been working on the lot—doing the best he could—which seemed the only way to make a difference in life. Then had come a sudden tap on the shoulder, and the sound of a warm, familiar voice.

"Son, how would you like to take a trip around the world with Mr. Vanderbilt?"

It was Al Gilks—Bob's friend and immediate supervisor—a union shop photographer, a man with a career, a man Bob trusted.

Perhaps it was Al's voice behind him: the soothing sound of the man who now served as his mentor on the team at MGM. Or it might have been that Bob was ready for an adventure. Maybe he was just conditioned to say "yes." In the fulfillment business (a fancy word for errand boy), polite requests had been voiced as questions—"Would he get some film cans?"—"Would he get a cup a coffee?" But this tap on the back was different. It was still a "Hey you!", but the tone had changed. As if the man asking was smiling as he voiced the words. Conditioned or not, wishing to please or not, when Bob Bronner heard those words, he simply answered—"Sure." And that was that.

Immediately afterward, he had wondered what on Earth had compelled him to "accept without a moment's thought?" To agree so quickly to something he knew nothing about. One word and suddenly his whole future had been tossed into uncertainty. He could hardly back down now. A trip around the world with Mr. Vanderbilt was what the man had said. But who was this Mr. Vanderbilt? Bob had put his life and career in the hands of a complete stranger.

People didn't just go around the world in those days. Regular people, like Bob, stayed home and worked – if they were lucky enough to have a job that is. They didn't fight for leisure; they fought for labor, or just the chance of it. There was a war going on outside of MGM. People – whole families – sheltered under makeshift housing, were scavenging just to get food. That was the norm; at least that was what the newspapers roared about. Bob couldn't actually say he had felt it, or seen it face-to-face. He knew there was trouble, just not his trouble; not as long as he'd remained ensconced at MGM—gradually climbing the ladder of studio photography. Now he had done it.

The headlines told of a whole world turned upside down by the Stock Market crash two years ago and there was no telling where it was going. The national income had suddenly fallen by 50%, and by 1931, almost one-in-five Americans were unemployed. Most of the rest were underemployed and living in hand-to-mouth desperation. Bob was phenomenally lucky.

They said that every day, in every city, hoards of people lined up outside of the grocery stores, in breadlines, waiting for a handout. The soup kitchens were overrun too, and suddenly everyone was buying cartons of apples for $1.75 from the Pacific Northwest – "Buy an apple a day and ease the Depression away." It didn't work for most.

Over at MGM, a sprawling film lot, there was none of the depressing mess of the outside world to contend with. Never were disillusioned men seen loitering about, even if they apparently were everywhere else. If for no other reason, things were nice on the lot, or out by the gas station, because MGM was doing better than most other companies out there. The big executives were busy churning out films and hiring: movie stars, camera crews, directors, writers, and guys like Bob

Jack Bronner with his two sons; George (left) and Bob (right), "The Three Must-Get-Theres" at a stop along their cross-country trek. (1920)

Bronner—hired to get the coffee, and promoted into career apprenticeships. The big-wigs lived in another world, certainly not Bob's, but Bob's had been good enough.

What sense was there in giving it all up? Word was that this Vanderbilt had been into motorcar racing as a young man, had run into some trouble, and hadn't been much heard of since. No matter how big Vanderbilt's yacht was, Bob felt pre-claustrophobia at rubbing elbows in such close quarters.

He'd heard about those gangsters and mobsters out in Chicago and New York. There were people out there who loved to destroy people. Bob strived to be good. He fell short sometimes, but he still helped his old man to look after himself. Sometimes he resented it—not his father, but his brother's leaving, and the extra burden that put on him. It was hard enough growing up without a mother; one loss was enough to fracture a family. Then the trip out to Los Angeles years back—leaving friends, and the only home they'd known, for the land of opportunity and uncertainty. But he was one of the lucky ones.

Bob stretched out as best he could, but it wasn't good enough. He tried hard not to violate the boundaries between himself and his fellow passengers. This journey would be a rough one; he knew that now. He'd mulled what kind of state of desperation he might witness in every town and hamlet they passed through.

In the San Bernadino Valley he caught the first glimpses of farmers—dirty, and toiling out in the baking sun. In the towns, as the train rushed through Nevada and on toward Salt Lake, there were real tell-tale signs of trouble: a multitude of folks, mostly young men, were camped by the tracks at the edges of towns – their faces blurred and distorted in the rectangular windows of the *L.A. Limited*. The depression wasn't as palpable at sixty miles per hour. Bob drifted in and out of sleep, allowing the wires that paralleled the tracks to lull him into drowsiness—never-ending strands that sagged and peaked—sagged and peaked.

The first day they passed through California, out into the Mojave, and onward to Nevada. It was too hot in the daytime and too cold at night. As they pulled into Omaha, Bob sent his father a telegram from the station with news of his progress. He couldn't be there with him, but he had promised to stay in touch every day, and he had every intention of keeping that promise.

On board the
"Los Angeles Limited"
June 30, 1931

Dear Dad:
    Just pulling into Omaha, Neb. And it is hot. We expect to get into Chicago tomorrow A.M. 9:30, then the New York Central to New York. Be in N. Y. the second.
    Today is terribly hot. Last night was cold at an elevation of 8000 feet. Have to give myself a wet towel rub down for everything is all over dirt. My back feels like sand paper.
    With love,
    Bob

The days passed slowly. The conductor confirmed that they would pull into Chicago by 9:30 a.m. the following morning, and then arrive in New York the day after. Bob occupied a little corner and sat down to read and plan. He had brought along an old newspaper clipping someone had given him—something to keep him occupied. There was little else to do aboard an overcrowded train. The children had started out in good spirits, and he had found it amusing enough to watch them for a while:

teasing each other and playing with the few little toys they had. But they were quiet now.

Associated with the newspaper article was one prominent image of a stately looking older gentleman with pattern baldness. A bushy, grey half-ring of hair was all this man had left, but it gave him a distinguished look, which he'd complemented in this particular photograph with a black tuxedo jacket and white bow tie. The caption read, "Cornelius Vanderbilt—*The Commodore*. May 27th, 1794—January 4th, 1877," and was followed by an article about the northeast railways.

The sun's rays flickered over the top of the pages with the rocking of the coach car. Bob dropped the paper into his lap, allowing the blazing waves to wash over him in full force. He squinted hard, teasing the colors to bleed and morph beneath his eyelids. He fell asleep.

He woke up early in the morning, July 1st, still feeling hot and uncomfortable. The *L.A. Limited* was on schedule as they approached Chicago, where passengers going further east had a one-hour layover. Bob treated himself to a rub down with a wet towel the instant that he had access to water and a bit of privacy; soothing his sandpaper-like back by ridding it of all the dirt he'd picked up sitting in the train car.

The stop in Chicago gave him enough time to buy something to eat, and explore the environs. He saw several parts of the city, walking down the lakefront along Michigan Avenue, but he was careful to avoid getting himself lost by wandering too far. He had half-expected to see gangsters in the street carrying Tommy guns, but to his slight disappointment, Bob was not a witness or bystander to any bank robberies.

"The only thing that disappointed me was the fact that we were not greeted by machine guns or fire-crackers," he wrote to his father, after the next rumbling railway slog had gotten well underway.

The train was going at seventy, sometimes eighty, miles per hour. They were on the New York Central Railway now—or to be exact, the *Twentieth Century Limited*—leaving Chicago at 1:15 p.m. and flying past the Studebaker factory in Elkhart, Indiana, a little later that afternoon.

The *Century*, as they called her, was a marquee train—a creation of the Central to combat the fast traffic of the Pennsylvania Railroad on the New York to Chicago route. The river route, all nine hundred and sixty-one miles of it, would be negotiated in some sixteen hours. It

Jack Bronner outside his family's south Brooklyn home, in a family photograph labeled "Sickness." It's not clear what Bob's father's "sickness" actually was. (1910)

would be flat, but glorious, travelling at sixty miles per hour all the way until Harmon. There the grey *Mohawk* would be connected to the butt of an electric engine for the slower, underground haul to Grand Central Terminal.

Bob had read that the competition between the Pennsylvania and the New York Central was something of a legend out East. Often two trains would be engine-to-engine on the approach to Chicago. The Pennsylvania travelled only nine hundred and one miles to reach the same destination, but theirs was a hillier route, taken at a decreased speed. The train ran all Pullman, with no affect of the Depression evident.

As they continued to fly through forests and valleys (the "regular Eastern scenery," as Bob called it), they ran into storm clouds. Although

Bob Bronner, right, with his baby brother, George, as a front-car 'passenger.' (1909)

it was still hot, the air was more humid and the rain – "Hurrah! Here's hoping for rain" – looked imminent.

Progress was fast. New York was rapidly approaching as he sent off the third note to his father. The rain now coming down in streams. He was only a boy when he left New York City with his father and brother (and they'd only lived in Brooklyn anyway), but Bob still remembered a powerful hold that the city had on people, and how the energy drove them forward. His eagerness was reaching its peak, and (as it happens with forms of sudden self-reconciliation) the purgatory of his long-neglected emotions rattled and pinched within him.

The passengers that had stayed on past Salt Lake, Chicago, and a couple of other spots along the track, were notably lacking in enthusiasm—either looking forward to New York so as to get on with their lives, or to find a new beginning after the promises of the West had failed them. They would look to pick up on the energy of the city. For now, they were a lackluster lot, drowsiness and boredom having taken their toll. Bob sat inconspicuously among them: also exhausted, also delirious, also carrying all his belongings—but as a man of great prospects.

As they reached Harmon, the train came to a halt and the big *Mohawk* remained panting at the nose. A large electric beast, lacking in grace or charm, could be seen passing the train and then anchoring at the front. From that point forward the glorious *Mohawk* was to be a passenger as well—the electric power took over.

They didn't enter New York at ground level. Just as the sun was gaining strength, the light was suddenly cut out, wrapping them in darkness as the train was towed underground toward the terminal. Only the occasional distant light, anchored to the tunnel walls, was visible—beady eyes peering out of the stillness, diffusing and contracting periodically in the shadows cast by the approaching cars. The train emerged into a shallow-ceilinged cavern—the welcome room for the incoming *Centuries*. The platforms were now running alongside, and to Bob's amusement, a red carpet was laid out to welcome the now awakening passengers.

"They're giving red-carpet entrances in New York City now," Bob giggled to himself under his breath.

The excitement of Grand Central Terminal was contagious and the passengers began stirring in unison. The platform was at the same height as the train floor, making it easier for everyone to get off, dragging possessions and relatives alike. Only a few were met by greeters.

Bob couldn't help but crack a smile as he stepped down onto the red carpet and started off. He struggled at first to free his worldly goods from the entanglement of legs, luggage and railroad furnishings, but he found a gap and was soon underway.

A smaller electric engine was poised to move trains in and out. The big, steam *Mohawks*, configured like their *Mountain* cousins, were prohibited from building up a head of steam in the cavernous, and poorly ventilated chamber.

The early morning arrival had been right on time and the flow of passengers was in one direction. Strangely, there were commuters disembarking onto the same platform, making for an eclectic combination of arrivals: those at a turning point and others at their daily routine.

Bob went up a sequence of stairways that appeared to switch back on themselves, but instead emerged into a totally unearthly world—the great terminal's bright concourse. He stopped to give his eyes time to adjust. It was dawn and the sun had cleared the sky of stars, replacing them with a profusion of bright pencil points that streamed into the terminal through a looming cathedral window facade, striking the marble floor and reflecting onto the ceiling. The hall he entered was as big as any he had ever seen. He tried to take it all in as hustling commuters nudged him from all sides. The ceiling appeared cerulean blue in the reflected light, with thousands of stars spanning overhead in a profusion of gold leaf—constellations reborn under a daytime sky. In the center of the terminal was a grand, gold-leafed clock with four faces. Beneath the ornate, opal masterpiece was an information booth. Bob walked up and asked where he might obtain a ticket for Centerport, Long Island. The response was a kindly one—"You will have to take the Pennsylvania Railroad, at Penn Station, on 34th Street."

Nearby was a bust of Cornelius Vanderbilt—*the Commodore*. Bob recalled the article he'd read: Generations earlier this pioneer of a man had made the New York Central a powerhouse. It was his grandson, William Kissam Vanderbilt, who had undertaken the reconstruction of Grand Central Terminal some thirty years previous. That man's son, William Kissam Vanderbilt II, acted as direct liaison to William J. Wilgus, railroad engineer. It was rumored that young Willie K. had been the eyes and ears of his father. This great cathedral to railroad power was the true home of the William Kissam Vanderbilts.

As he made his way out of the terminal, right into the heart of the city, Bob was struck by how New York had changed in the years he'd been away, and since the first Vanderbilt rule. The more he looked around, the more he recognized—or thought he did. Tremendous changes had taken place, and as he stepped outside he saw the face of this progress: where there were once thirty stories, now there were sixty. Everything was bigger and louder, and ever more incredible.

When he dreamed of Manhattan as a kid, seeing the skyline from the roof of another building or from the shore by the river, Bob always imagined it as a kind of paradise. After all, Manhattan was where the rich lived—where men like William Kissam Vanderbilt II enjoyed fabulous parties, and made millions of dollars by building, buying, and selling. To him it was a land where opportunity floated in the air. The sad reality was that New York was not a haven by any stretch of the imagination. The city was (he could smell it all too well) effectively a sewer now. Families lived on the streets. People were desperate for work, food, housing – anything.

Bob had been given directions to *Shelton Towers*—a large hotel not too far from the station. He also had instructions to travel out to Long Island the following day, assuming he hadn't fallen ill.

"Mr. Vanderbilt doesn't want anyone carrying illness at his estate," he remembered Mr. Gilks stating emphatically.

Bob took a moment to get his bearings. The *Shelton Towers Hotel* was at Lexington Avenue and 49th Street. He tracked signs to Park Avenue and followed the line of traffic toward 49th. He had a rough recollection of the city grid, and he felt a certain satisfaction in that: he almost felt like a native again, with that sense of indefinite belonging. He turned onto 49th Street and headed east.

He recalled what he had learned about the hotel. The *Shelton* was 34 stories high, and at the time of its construction, was the tallest hotel in the world—holding one thousand two hundred rooms. Apparently, the designer, Harmon, had received various awards in architecture for his work.

Bob arrived quickly. The inside of the hotel was just further confirmation of his phenomenal good fortune. The butterflies in his stomach lulled and then soared as he took in the details of the hotel's amenities – reading rooms, solariums, roof gardens, a swimming pool, and three squash courts. The establishment apparently took pride in now offering board to "mixed-occupancy transients," inaugurating the development of Lexington Avenue as "Midtown's avenue" of moderately priced hotels.

Bob excitedly checked in at the front desk, and to his surprise, received new marching orders from the smiling receptionist. He was to meet "Alfred Gilks—principal photographer," that afternoon in the hotel lobby. They would make their way together to the Vanderbilt Estate in Long Island. Newly excited at the prospect of meeting his notorious employer, Bob picked up his bag and followed the porter over to the elevator. His room was on the twentieth floor.

Out the window, it looked like a mile down to the ground. He had to crane his neck to see down over the tops of the buildings across the street. He'd been thrust up into another world. He was living a dream, and the opportunity of a lifetime was ahead of him.

Eagle's Nest

"You could hardly expect him to be anything other than eccentric or at least idiosyncratic," stated Mr. Gilks, "having been born into one of the wealthiest and most prestigious families in the world."

They were on their way out of the city on an early commuter train, across Long Island's open farmland. The windows were all wide open, fighting the July heat, and allowing smoke and soot to pour into the car amid a lot of coughing and brushing at shirt sleeves.

A local woman, in an adjacent seat with her two children, had noticed a watch tucked into Mr. Gilks' breast pocket and, wide-eyed, leaned in asking him for the time. Having wanted to make a proper impression to their employer, Mr. Gilks and Bob had dressed for the occasion—Gilks in a grey double-breasted suit, a white shirt, sharp jacket with gold tie, and grey fedora—all suffering under the soot. Bob was more modestly dressed: slightly weathered brown suit pants, white shirt, bow tie, and checkered newsboy cap. Mr. Gilks sat facing him, intent on further inflating his already well-piqued curiosity.

"And all this money was made by one man?" asked Bob.

"For the most part," Mr. Gilks replied. "*The Commodore*, Cornelius, was the ultimate curmudgeonly tycoon of the northeast. He died as the wealthiest man in America. When he did, it was his son that inherited the mass of the wealth; this was William Henry Vanderbilt. William Henry went on to create his own money too; which would have greatly surprised his father, who called him 'Blatherskite'."

"Blatherskite?" Bob repeated, quizzically.

Cornelius Vanderbilt, the original Commodore, built his railroad empire from the ground up, amassing a 105 million dollar fortune. This was more money than the US Treasury possessed and worth 1.15% of the U.S. economy in his day.

"A person who talks at great lengths, but makes no sense," Mr. Gilks explained, with a grin. "'Any fool can make a fortune,' the Commodore had said, but 'it takes a man of brains to hold on to it after it is made.'"

"So William Henry was a fool," Bob presumed.

"His father obviously thought so, but William Henry actually managed to double the family fortune and expand their railroad empire. He worked himself into the grave to do it mind you, but he passed a healthy sum on to each of his children; most importantly his two eldest sons: Cornelius II and William Kissam."

"And William Kissam is our captain—Willie K. Vanderbilt," Bob assumed.

"No, no, this was his father. Actually, William Kissam I was largely propped up by—"

Another loud whistle cut Mr. Gilks short. Bob jumped. Gilks immediately stuck his whole head in and out of the window before grabbing for his suitcase.

"This is it," he said abruptly, as if having completely forgotten his earlier train of thought.

"Those whistlings always scare the bejeebers out of me," Bob said emphatically, his fingers curled and stiff.

Having not gotten much rest, Bob and Mr. Gilks had taken the Long Island Railroad out of Pennsylvania Station early that afternoon. Bob felt surprisingly reinvigorated once they'd reached the small Victorian station, but was growing increasingly nervous as he got closer and closer to the personal residence of his new employer.

They were picked up at Greenlawn station by a chauffeur who drove them directly to *Eagle's Nest*. The car was a Lincoln Town Car, quite new, but strange in its own right—it had leather fenders. The gravel kicked up from the country roads seemed strangely silent as the latter absorbed the rattle that they would have otherwise made. This time, Al Gilks was content to sit up front in silence and stare at the road ahead. From the backseat Bob felt rather odd. There was a partition separating him from the driver and Gilks. Although the window in the partition had been rolled down halfway, the effect was the same. He felt like he was in the world of a millionaire. Bob took in the details of the run-down, little town. Centerport looked as if it ought to be a thousand miles outside of New York City—somewhere up in Maine maybe, with more traditional seaport towns. Many buildings were boarded and the streets were far from clean. There were a few people about, but only one motorcar. As they left town, several dejected looking men and women ambled wearily along the roadside.

After a steep climb and several hard turns through densely wooded bends, the entrance to the anticipated deep retreat finally revealed itself. The town lay in complete contrast to the sophisticated magnificence of Willie K. Vanderbilt's estate. *Eagle's Nest* looked right out of a fairy tale. The home was extravagant, but seemed somewhat out of place: being covered in stucco, more appropriate in Los Angeles than the variable climate of New York.

Bob saw two large, intimidating statues of eagles in front of the gate to the property. "What are those?" he wondered aloud.

"When Mr. Vanderbilt first visited the property, an eagle came soaring out of its nest, so he gave it the name *Eagle's Nest*," The driver volunteered helpfully. "Those statues used to decorate the old Grand Central Terminal before the renovation."

Since the driver was seemingly willing to play tour guide, Bob asked him another question. "Has Mr. Vanderbilt lived here for long?"

"A bit more than twenty years, I believe. He built the place himself. It was all just woods when he bought it."

Surrounded by navigable water on three sides, it was a perfect retreat, thought Bob, for a wealthy man who either loved sailing, or sought refuge from the stresses of city life.

"When he first came out here," the driver continued, "he wanted to get away from folks, have a place where he could enjoy some solitude. The first building was just seven rooms. But construction expanded over time, especially after he married the second Mrs. Vanderbilt."

As the motor was shut off and Bob stepped out of the vehicle, he was taken aback at how *Eagle's Nest* could be so startlingly magnificent, and yet still invoke a kind of serenity. The estate was immense and grandiose, and yet from up the hill you could still hear the breeze coming off the water, and the waves lapping at the shore. Unlike the Vanderbilt residences he might have imagined, if anything, this was a place to live. And live well.

* * *

As Mr. Gilks was off being re-introduced to Vanderbilt, a valet showed Bob to a storeroom for his equipment and then passed him off to various others: cooks and maids, eager to give him a tour of the facilities. Over the course of the afternoon he accumulated a list of strict rules to be followed at Mr. Vanderbilt's orders: onboard the *Alva*, Mr. Vanderbilt was "the Commodore"; there would be no spreading illness; no excessive rowdiness; regular showering; the crew would wear naval attire; no exception to posted duties; no travel on the 13th of any month; no animals; no bartering with cigarettes...the list went on. He was eventually dismissed to wander the grounds, but told to stay out of the kitchens and the boathouse, and given strict orders not to disturb the family in the main residence.

Alone, outside the marine museum, Bob looked out over the golf course toward the bay; his camera slung over his shoulder as he leaned on the folded tripod. As he took in the surroundings, he began to set up the shots in his mind. Leading down to the harbor, evoking Willie's love of the sea, was a long wharf lit by gas lamps. It was a charming setting. A gardener had described it to Bob as Mr. Vanderbilt's safe haven—away from the chaos of the city, societal pressures, and familial pressures that faced him there and in Newport. It was also a starting point for numerous sailing adventures, with its own private harbor, all invoking a lifestyle that was ostentatious certainly, but apparently not for a man of his stature and means.

In 1913, Mr. Vanderbilt had added a quaint French Norman-styled four-storey boathouse, and transformed *Eagle's Nest* into a haven for marine collections accumulated on his various yachting expeditions.

"Mr. Vanderbilt comes back with a ton of these things after every trip. Says it beats the hell out 'a scrap-bookin'," the custodian proclaimed, as Bob admired the various presentations of fish just inside the main doors of the marine museum. He'd found the door left open, and his curiosity

The front view of the marine museum at Eagle's Nest, where Willie K. housed a large, private collection of specimens accumulated on his voyages.

had gotten the best of him. "Don't let any of them fishes bite ya." With a smirk, the custodian walked off toward an open janitorial closet.

Just as Bob was feeling confident that most people had forgotten he was there, he stepped back outside to find Mr. Gilks hustling up toward the main residence. He seemed to look through Bob at first, then—as if a light suddenly flickered on in his head—his eyes lit up purposefully and he approached hurriedly, as Bob turned to face him.

"Come with me. Mr. Vanderbilt is asking for us in the drawing room."

Inside the main residence, Bob followed Mr. Gilks through a downstairs door left conspicuously ajar; a smoky haze wafting through the crack. They entered a small study, decorated in dark tones: hardwood walls partially covered with maroon drapes. Underfoot, a blue-green carpet evoked the color and texture of the ocean. Bob hadn't had time to stow away his camera, and it was still slung sluggishly over his left shoulder. The large tripod, now tucked tightly under his right arm, had the potential to be menacing in the small study that was filled with statues, antiques and other rare voyage memorabilia. Even in the day the room was mostly dark—lit by lamplight—with two burning electric fixtures mounted in the upper left and right corners of the far wall. On the left was a large desk. On the right, two cozy armchairs faced a grey stone fireplace. In the corners to their immediate left and right were two beige globes—several feet in diameter—mounted in wooden frames.

Bob moved to position himself to the right of Al Gilks, in the back-right corner of the room, closest to the door. Inside the small study, a middle-aged man of diminutive stature leaned over a cluttered desk, looking over some large maps. Bob immediately assumed he was Mr. Vanderbilt. He was older than in the photographs that Bob had seen, but was still sturdily built; only about five and a half feet tall. He was dressed casually for the summer weather: a loose white button-down shirt, checkered shorts and simple loafers. Not yet acknowledging their presence, Vanderbilt began to pace back and forth, working to generate a solid blue haze with the smoke from his cigar.

Bob looked over to the right of the desk. Displayed there was a framed photo of a younger man, standing in front of an enormous captured manta ray. The ray was twice the man's height when strung up on the deck. It was hung by its face. A man in a sailor's outfit and another man in a bowler hat stood at either side, stretching out the ray's armlike appendages to reveal its full span. One man stood in the forefront, smoking a pipe and looking off to the side, seeming remarkably indifferent,

Mr. Vanderbilt's son-in-law, Frederic Cameron Church, stands in front of a Giant Manta Ray, captured off the coast of Florida, in an epic battle during which the ship's rod toyed with breaking before hauling in the largest "devil fish" ever recorded. (1925)

if not slightly bored. Bob felt a sudden shock to see that something so monstrous existed in real life, and felt a pinch of anxiety at the thought of photographing writhing beasts like these as Mr. Vanderbilt took them on like Captain Nemo.

Mr. Vanderbilt looked up toward the doorway, suddenly registering their presence.

"Ah! Good, Mr. Gilks. I remember you mentioning earlier that you'd like to see how we went about documenting the specimens on our first voyage. Correct? I've considered this request, and I'd be honored if you allowed me to show you a private exhibit of mine. I thought that your assistant might like to come along as well." Vanderbilt grabbed for his hat. "Indulge me slightly, if you will. Rosamund has convinced me to play the showman."

With a cigar still in hand, Mr. Vanderbilt led the way from the drawing room out into the cold, fossiliferous limestone hallway. He pointed out portraits of his mother and father that graced the upper walls of the small foyer. There was also one of himself as a child, and others that might be called "instant relatives": paintings of nameless subjects deemed to be important.

The noontime sun shone brightly as they broke into the arcade that joined the rest of the house to the nursery wing—built to house Rosamund's mother and her two children. Across the courtyard was a bell tower. Bob paused to look at it and noticed an extremely large and old-looking bell hanging inside. Vanderbilt noticed and stopped to look at the tower briefly. "My son sleeps in the bell tower. I may not be able to keep him in at night, but I most definitely can wake him up in the morning!" Mr. Vanderbilt exclaimed with a broad smile. They laughed.

Vanderbilt led the way through a small, formal boxwood garden. The sun beamed at their faces. Bob and Gilks used their right hands as visors, while Mr. Vanderbilt strode on unaffected. To his left, Bob spied

This photo faces out of the arcade into the courtyard. To the left is the nursery wing, where Mr. Vanderbilt's step-children and mother-in-law slept. To the right is the bell tower which Mr. Vanderbilt's son, Willie K. III, used as a bedroom.

an unusual mural of what looked like the sun, but in his haste to keep up with Mr. Vanderbilt, gave it little thought.

Some steps led up to a pair of dark, towering wooden doors. At either side, several large pots with ferns inside were positioned equidistantly—at head height.

With a small grin, Vanderbilt opened the heavy wooden doors. Bob noticed that they were now in a grotto underneath the nursery wing. The only light shone from a large, glass rectangle imbedded in the floor, which glowed a phosphorescent blue. It took Bob a few moments to realize that it was made of glass thick enough to walk on. The glowing orb of Mr. Vanderbilt's cigar was the beacon that provided them with the man's location. Above the floor, glowing blue, Mr. Vanderbilt appeared as an apparition in the dark. Bob's eyes were fixed on the luminescent blue square as Mr. Vanderbilt searched with his right foot, feeling for something on

The entranceway to the *Habitat*. Unlike the marine museum up the hill, this was a unique display, rarely shared.

the floor. A subtle, undetected cue caused an expanse of light to open before them.

Two shining black orbs, and row upon row of sharp white teeth—a Great White shark, poised to attack. At the bottom of the still scene were the partial remnants of a shipwreck, accurate in detail down to the placement of barnacles and shattered beams. Beneath that was crisp white sand, marking the waterless ocean floor, dotted here-and-there with deepwater crustaceans. Another shark appeared to move about in the tank as well; his gills alight and his muscles rippling. The second shark, with its mouth agape, terrorized the small schools of fish in nearby tanks.

Of course it was all a bit of showmanship. The sharks were elements in dioramas. Bob would never have expected such lifelike three-dimensional artistic reproductions to be hidden beneath a wing of a railroad millionaire's home, but he was more than familiar with showmanship. After all, he had been an employee of Metro-Goldwyn-Mayer. He was, nevertheless, impressed. Vanderbilt showed them a sequence of dioramas, each lit magically as he depressed a hidden pedal in the floor and then re-depressed it to return to darkness.

They moved from one scene to the next. Bob's reaction was multi-faceted; awe, with a gutting tinge of exposure to the personal. Each diorama explained a chapter in Vanderbilt's expeditions: most detailed scientific explorations, but some delved into the familial. Three of nine dioramas were dedicated to scenes of beach and craggy rocks. Bob sensed that in these scenes Willie was preserving his own history.

"The Galapagos," Mr. Vanderbilt exclaimed. "The introduced species on the Galapagos were brought there by man and represent a severe threat to the future of the indigenous species. It would be a shame to lose what is there."

A different diorama depicted Long Island waterfowl: a throwback to Willie's childhood days in Oakdale, at *Idle Hour*, his father's estate. An odd scene introduced goats braying to a foreboding moon. Another included the Vanderbilt family hunting lodges in Canada. It was more than a natural history tour, it was all notably personal. It struck Bob as odd that he might, in some fashion, end up immortalized himself in some later addition.

After having walked through the underwater exhibits, past all different kinds of fish and sharks, the lights came on. As they did, Bob was overcome with a strong urge to start swimming up to the surface as quickly as possible.

* * *

After a spirited discussion with the group about the ship's features and assembly, Vanderbilt had taken a long gaze at the odd-looking mural Bob had noticed before and then dismissed himself to his study.

"A sundial," Bob realized.

Bob and Al Gilks then went down to the docks. At Mr. Vanderbilt's request, Bob had been sent onboard the *Alva* where he would stay overnight. He would work with Mr. Gilks to determine what equipment they would need, and to make sure that everything already there was in working order.

Mr. Vanderbilt had explained how he and his wife had visited Kiel, Germany, in March of that year, where they took possession of their newly constructed vessel, traveled back across the Atlantic to New York. They had recruited a mixture of construction workers and seasoned sailors to fill out their manifest. The couple had traveled back and forth from New York to Germany three times while the ship was being built. Mr. Vanderbilt was proud of and heavily invested in the project. They had discussed the ship's problems as it was being constructed—hovering around the office of Krupp-Germaniawerft talking with the naval architects and laborers. The ship was launched in Kiel by Mrs. Kenneth G. Gastleman, the wife of the acting naval attaché for the United States Navy in Berlin. It was a suitably formal event, the ship being named for Willie K's mother that morning, leaving on the waves amidst cheers. That was on November 18th, 1930.

The ship Bob saw in the mouth of Centerport harbor was what looked like a brand new vessel. She was two hundred and sixty-four feet and five inches in length, with a water line of two hundred and fifty-nine feet and two inches. She had the capacity to store enough supplies to adequately provide for more than fifty people for one year.

The power of the ship's engines was also tremendous—"Two Krupp-Diesel engines—two thousand one hundred brake horse-power—one hundred and fifty revolutions per minute -a maximum speed of seventeen knots. An average of fifteen knots," detailed Ruid, a German quartermaster who had been designated to show Bob to his room.

The *Alva*: Vanderbilt's eleventh yacht and the culmination of his ocean dreams, under construction at Krupp-Germaniawerft, in Kiel, Germany. (1930)

Bob toured the ship that would be his home for over a year. There were two chart rooms where Mr. Vanderbilt and his other crew members would review their progress. The lower room was next to Mr. Vanderbilt's bridge-deck cabin, and served not only as a functional room for the ship's navigation, but also as a delightful, livable room, with two extra-large windows for ventilation and light. There was a spacious chart table, a sofa, and various navigating instruments: a state of the art compass—a Sperry Master gyro compass—and an automatic dial-telephone switchboard. Below the lower chartroom and the bridge-deck cabin, down a companionway ladder, was the wheelhouse; occupying the central section of the flying bridge, where watchmen would keep a keen eye. A variety of complicated instruments was available to help with this critical function; all gibberish to Bob who had no experience with seafaring or navigation, but Ruid was mighty passionate about it all.

There were two clear-view screen windows in this area, with whirling circular panes, keeping the glass free of moisture whatever the weather conditions. There were also engine-room revolution counters to help track the ship's speed. An automatic *Tyfon* fog signal with controls for the ship's bell and a whistle were set up next to the steering-gear controls to facilitate control and monitoring of the ship's progress.

Mr. Vanderbilt had also installed multiple telephone systems on the *Alva*, reasoning that, in case of an emergency, it would be dangerous for him to be "anything but instantly accessible." With only one line, a busy signal might flash and prevent him from being reached quickly enough. He had several independent lines installed about the ship: one between decks from the bridge to the stateroom, one to the wireless room, another to the engine room, one to the quarter-deck stateroom, and one to the crow's nest.

Mr. Vanderbilt had also installed the latest dredging equipment aboard the ship in preparation for the work that he intended to do in the South Seas—to collect fauna and flora from sea bottoms at considerable depths. The possibility of discovering a new species of plant or animal was a legitimate one. The key piece of equipment was an oblong iron frame with a bag net attached to the end. The apparatus was not standardized, but Mr. Vanderbilt had gone ahead and developed a framework of his own design, which he created at a small blacksmith shop in Northport. The objective of the design was that the dredge itself should ride on the bottom of the sea, with the mouth of the net facing in the direction of movement at all times, regardless of impending obstructions. A heavy bar was attached across the open end of the frame, and was intended to be strong enough to break away any small obstacles. A steel runner was positioned under it and kept parallel to two small bars. A bridle shackled to the crossbar led to a swivel and a wire cable. The framework was heavy and demountable. For the sake of storage, the entire contraption had to be taken apart and stowed. A net fit into the framework at a ten foot by four foot-six inch opening. When expanded for the dredging process the net's funnel reached nineteen feet, its mesh growing finer towards the smaller end.

In order to collect samples, Mr. Vanderbilt had also developed a means of attaching a receptacle—a long, cylindrical glass jar—drawing the net tightly around it so that small fish and crustaceans that found their way inside would not break the assembly. The mouth of the outer net had a smaller net shaped inside it to prevent the escape of the large specimens. On the other hand, the lower end of the large net had a silk net of fine mesh sewn into it, in this case to prevent the smaller crustaceans and fish from escaping. The dredge was safely stored aboard the ship, on deck and well-protected from the weather: close to the fourteen-foot promenade deck that ran down the starboard side, and the port-side deck that protruded four and a half feet.

On first appearances, the discrepancy in the size of the decks made the ship appear lopsided, one deck being more than three times as wide as the other. But Vanderbilt had been keen to point out that, "Both sides are not seen simultaneously, nor is the asymmetry structurally apparent. Instead, the design of the ship cleverly conceals the imbalance."

There were lounge chairs at one end of the promenade deck, with even a space for playing games. Officers had their own portion of the deck on which to relax when they were off duty, and had access to recreations such as shuffleboard and exercise equipment such as punching bags and quoits.

The crew's quarters, where Bob would be housed, were well-lit and roomy. "The Commodore was adamant that the crew be made comfortable," stated George, another enigmatic crewman who'd been giving Bob his tour. "In his words, 'no man should have to steal up in the middle of a tropical night to sleep in a lifeboat, because his quarters below are unlivable.'"

The crews' area featured shower rooms: with both fresh and salt-water baths, and four washrooms with state-of-the-art plumbing.

When Bob first saw the place he knew that his true home aboard the ship would be the photo darkroom and film-storage chamber. He would be working with the very latest 35-millimeter and 16-millimeter moving picture cameras; both color and black-and-white photography equipment. They even had a camera on hand for underwater scenes. The dark room and film storage room had been carefully constructed, designed to manage the problem of dampness, which, in a tropical climate, could wreak havoc on undeveloped film. More than that, the room was designed to become immediately sealed in the event of a fire. All that he would need to do was to leave the room and seal the door. The room would fill with carbon dioxide, cutting the oxygen supply to the fire and thus extinguishing it almost instantaneously. The apparatus and equipment would all be protected.

As Bob finished his tour and returned to the deck, other crew members were busy loading on the first supplies. Down in the kitchen Bob had heard from the head chef, Albert, as the supplies started pouring in.

"One thousand two hundred and fifty quarts of Water-Gordon milk and cream; bottled and pasteurized under extremely controlled conditions to minimize the bacteria count. These products will remain sweet for at least four months," he proclaimed with pride.

Copious supplies of chilled vegetables and fruits were also loaded onto the ship, along with shelf upon shelf of other general supplies to keep the crew comfortable—linens, blankets, glass, china, cutlery, pots and pans, shoes, clothing… and every utensil, every good, was inventoried and labeled. As far as Bob saw, they couldn't have been any more prepared. This voyage would be nothing short of pure luxury.

New York (and Centerport again)

THE *ALVA* was due to set sail on Tuesday, July 7th. After having spent the night of the 4th aboard the ship, Bob returned to New York to make his final preparations before leaving town. They headed out from Long Island early that morning to avoid the rush of people coming in after the holiday. It was a smart move, as the city looked particularly busy that afternoon.

Buzzing from his recent adventure, Bob sent a telegram to his father from the *Shelton* with the details of the last couple of days. With a wide-eyed smile, he recalled the showcases of animals and fish, the large room with the strange lights, and the buttons in the floor that lit up each window. He was sure that his father would feel his enthusiasm.

Back in New York, he was left to reflect on the day at *Eagle's Nest*—his first encounter with one of America's wealthiest citizens. Thankfully, he had a few days to prepare, to collect his thoughts, and to relax. He planned to keep a journal of his travels. He felt as if he was turning a new page in his life. He began to daydream of boasting about fabulous luxuries in years to come. *Could he too perhaps live to reap the comforts of extravagant wealth?* Bob imagined that Mr. Vanderbilt lived very much like a king. True, he had no conception of the life of royalty beyond what he had read in books and newspapers, but if he had had to describe the life of a king, he would have described the life of William K. Vanderbilt II. And then there was Mrs. Vanderbilt—a graceful and sophisticated woman, like the elusive Hollywood movie stars. Alongside her husband, she appeared to be living a true-life Hollywood romance.

To try and contain his excitement, and pass the days before departure, Bob took to swimming in the mornings in the hotel pool. He and

Mr. Gilks had been put up at the *Shelton* again, and told to await further instructions. They had to gather supplies of course, but in the meantime there was little else for Bob to do other than see the sights and catch up with his father—who had sent a telegram to the hotel desk to let Bob know he was doing fine back in California. Despite the excitement and the considerable distractions, Bob was still worried about his dad and very keen to stay in touch.

"Received your wire," he telegrammed back. "Glad to hear all O. K. there."

He told his father about the afternoon on the *Alva*, and about remaining overnight to help put the necessary equipment in its proper place. He had made first introductions with most of the crew and his roommate, "Taxidermist, a fine fellow." He knew his father would be pleased to hear these details, and that his son was safe. With a smile, he added a note to his letter about his new roommate—"I hope he doesn't try to skin or stuff me some night, when he has a nightmare or takes to walking in his sleep."

With considerable enthusiasm, he told his father about the staterooms on the *Alva*, "like the ones on the *Berangaria*[1] or the *Isle de France*[2], and other high-class ocean liners"—at least, that's what he imagined, based on the pictures he had seen of such luxury liners. It was hard to imagine the *Alva* being anything less than elite, if not in a class of its own. He described the radio system, which fitted the ship for entertainment, and other needs—news updates and the like. He also wrote about the showers and the gym, knowing his father would be impressed with those features as well.

"The *Alva* is an absolutely up-to-date ship," he concluded, "all-steel hull, smooth; teak wood decks and trimmings. It has the most complete wireless and radio sets of any yacht made; all navy style."

Bob and Mr. Gilks had a lot of shopping to do the following morning, in final preparation for the departure on the 7th. And they had to move quickly. Bob had his orders to be on the job early the following day. He had to be ready to board the ship again from Centerport harbor, and shoot some pictures around *Eagle's Nest*. The official plan was to sail by three in the afternoon on Tuesday.

---

1. Sic: In his letters to his father, Bob refers to the RMS Berengaria (formerly the SS Imperator)—an ocean liner built for the *Hamburg American line*, completed in 1912—as the "Berangarin."
2. Sic: The "Isle de France" that Bob refers to is actually the SS Île de France, launched in 1926.

William Belanske, the sole scientist (of sorts) to make the journey, is shown here working in his studio on various fish taxidermies.

They had spent much of the 4th arranging a place on deck to show pictures, and had about twenty reels of silent subjects and eight reels of sound, along with a top-of-the-line projector set to display them on. Nevertheless, they were always in need of more supplies. They spent their last free afternoon in New York running about from place to place in search of other pieces of equipment they might have need for.

Bob used much of the afternoon to indulge himself in the spirit of the sea—buying two lightweight duck suits for life onboard the ship. On his tour of the *Alva*, he'd seen that much of the crew was dressed in navy attire. Even if he was only the photography assistant, he'd decided to spend a little money beforehand in order to be properly dressed, and equipped, for life at sea. Maybe he was getting ahead of himself, but he'd be sailing with the *Alva* for a full year after all, and he imagined he'd be something of a seasoned sailor by the end of it.

Bob then spent considerable time searching New York for a shop that sold pith helmets, with no luck. He eventually gave up, frustrated, but figuring that he'd try again when they dropped anchor at Newport News, their first port of call along the eastern seaboard.

Meeting up with Mr. Gilks, they discussed whether they'd found all the things that they required. Satisfied with a hoard of sailor attire, extra pants, and various other odds and ends—from shower products to film and camera accessories—Bob and Mr. Gilks returned to the *Shelton* to pack away their spoils.

Leaving New York for good this time, they walked to Pennsylvania Station in order to catch the same train out to Greenlawn. They arrived in Long Island late at night, but still in time to meet a few other members of the *Alva*'s crew, who were waiting at the harbor to be taken out to the ship. Although it was a warm night, they stood on the pier draped in a heavy fog. The fog thickened as they got closer to the waterfront, and when they boarded the water-taxi to go out to the *Alva*, only the driver seemed confident that he knew the way.

The small party of eleven, huddled in the little taxi-boat, pushed off for the *Alva*, laid out in the sound about five miles from shore. They had to go through narrow channels, sand spits, and past many buoys to reach it, and when even the pilot himself admitted that he'd lost his bearings, it wasn't long before everyone on board was offering up different opinions about which direction they should be headed. Amidst the confusion, the little boat had run into one of the sandbars, and everyone had to go over the side and push her back into deep water. On the next attempt they saw a light and headed for it, only to run aground again. Everyone got out a second time and helped to shove the boat off, this time surely headed for open water.

Bob sat quietly, taking his cues from Mr. Gilks, and not wanting to get into any kind of dispute with his shipmates. But after the second grounding it took fifteen or twenty minutes before they saw anything resembling the *Alva*. Everyone was getting tired; Bob feeling the weight of the day's city walking in his crooked knees. When something loomed up in front of them, someone was suddenly shouting out to throw the boat into reverse to avoid running aground again—or worse. After that final debacle everyone was ready to forget the *Alva* for the night, to chalk up their navigational issues to the fog, sleep on the coast, and wait until morning. With most very ready to bunk down, some right there and then, finally someone aboard saw the light buoy they had been looking for, for the last hour or so. The boat shoved off again and rounded the buoy, heading toward, and finally bumping into, the *Alva*. It was midnight by the time everyone arrived, and it was another hour or so before they'd gathered their belongings, quieted down, and organized themselves into their bunks.

Bob leaned back in his cot, breathing a sigh of relief. He adjusted himself in his new bed, enjoying the crisp sheets and the smell of freshly painted walls as he drifted to sleep.

Slowly to Sea

THE FOLLOWING afternoon, Willie K. and his wife Rosamund left their home, saying goodbye to a small, teary party of relatives and friends on the dock. This voyage—the *Alva* herself—was their shared dream; their shared pursuit of something, a bounty, that their newfound love and Willie's money promised to realize.

Despite the long night, Bob had gotten up at 6:00 a.m. He planned on getting to work almost immediately, only to learn that the equipment he wanted to unpack had not arrived yet. He promptly ordered the water-taxi to go ashore and bring it out, working all day to get the last of it on board and properly stowed away. He caught glimpses of Mr. Vanderbilt on the shore, already dressed in full navy attire, chatting and shaking hands, as he and Rose prepared to board the ship themselves. Rose's two children stood alongside to see them off.

"We can't wait any longer. We desire to see endless waters, star beams in lonely regions, streaks of dawn over fairy islands, and swift-gliding outrigger canoes," Mr. Vanderbilt could be heard proclaiming.

By 4:30 that afternoon, with everything finally in its proper place, the propellers turned and the ship made its departure.

"Hoist the launch! Heave up the anchor!"

A veritable captain of the sea, qualified by the Navy to captain vessels of any size, Vanderbilt called out orders to his crew and took the big, brass handle of the engine-room telegraph in his hand, throwing it forward with a cry of "Slow ahead!" They headed out westward in Long Island Sound, attending to the wireless reports of a heavy fog blanket shrouding the entire Atlantic coast line from the Virginia Capes northward.

The poor visibility that afternoon made their progress slow, even though they were still in very familiar waters. Squinting through the fog, keenly marking their progress, Bob remained on deck as they made their way past New York, hoping for a workable view of the city. Blanketed in smoke and fog, it looked more like a phantom city than the New York City familiar to him. The Empire State building, which he had visited only a day or so before, was only partially visible—one side covered in cloud. In the end, it was too dark to take even one photograph.

They dropped anchor on the flats, close to Governors Island, three hours and thirteen minutes later. Switching off the main engines, they spent the first night in the Upper Bay of the East River.

Again, Bob sent a telegram to his father to let him know they had started out successfully. "It is a beautiful ship," he wrote again, while praising the staterooms and private tile baths—"All real hard wood trimmings and silver fittings." He also decided to write about Mr. Gilks for the first time; "A prince of a fellow if there ever was one." A sentiment he'd expressed to his father on numerous occasions.

Sitting with Al later that evening, (Mr. Gilks now insisted that Bob call him "Al"), Bob wrote in his diary to pass the time and traced the first leg of the trip—marking up a map so he could keep a visual track of his travels. He handed Al a cigarette from the pack his father had given him to share with the other men. Al wasn't used to the brand (with its paper, combination tipped design and all white color), and basically had to be instructed on how to place the thing in his mouth. His failed attempts to light the wrong end gave them each a good laugh.

The second night's sleep was much more refreshing than the first, but when Bob awoke on July 8th, it was clear things were not quite going according to plan. The official plan had the *Alva* stopping in Havana, Cuba and Colón, Panama, for a day each, then perhaps three days in Panama in general before heading through the Panama Canal. But when Bob telegrammed his father that morning, they had made no progress. They were still at anchor in New York harbor, opposite the 69th Street ferry in Brooklyn, near his old hometown. After so much anticipation, the delay brought Bob's anxiousness to a boil. For most of the day he paced back-and-forth along the port-side deck, neurotically passing cigarettes from hand to mouth. The Commodore, however, appeared to be making the most of the delay.

When he had turned in with Rosamund the previous day, Bob had heard him mention that he was particularly keen to give the ship a good once-over, in search of loose bolts, as it were. That morning, Rosamund and the Commodore painstakingly examined the rooms of Consuelo—the Commodore's daughter, named for her paternal aunt. She would be accompanied on board by her husband, Earl. They planned on flying to the equator to board in Panama, in order to take part in the leg that would see *Alva* make the trip down the canal, out to the Galapagos, and on to the islands of the South Seas.

When dinner was announced by the sound of a bugle—the mess call, as it were—there was much shuffling about. Within fifteen minutes, the upper class—the Vanderbilts, Michelle and Pierre Merillon, and their guests- Dr. Lane, first mate Reddington Robbins and others—assembled in an upstairs lounge to drink a toast to the successful commencement of the cruise, but not before retiring to their staterooms to dress. Everyone downstairs participated in a sumptuous meal, but the "early to bed" proposal upstairs wasn't even a thought on the lower decks, and general rowdiness ensued. Bob and Al were instead busy trying their best to capture a decent shot of the New York skyline, despite the fog.

"Do you have a shot yet?" asked Gilks, impatiently.

"No, not yet. The fog is drifting to the left, if we wait it out just a bit longer we might get the full cityscape," Bob replied, optimistically.

"We're getting too far away, and the ship's about to veer. It's now or never."

"I think I got the Chrysler building," Bob proclaimed with some enthusiasm. "Oh, the fog's lifting now. Let's get another."

"Too late, we're turning," Al pointed out, extremely frustrated, as they lost sight of the city.

When the ill-favored weather finally dissipated several days later, the crew was busy finding its connection to the world back home: there were regular radio broadcast updates from the officers (or sometimes from the Commodore himself), and the on-board newspaper that some of the wireless operators were made to compile at the Commodore's insistence. Routines were beginning to take form, partially fueled by the captain's notion of acceptable sets of activities that the crew should be participating in—as a matter of staying sane over a year at sea. After posted

The year-old Chrysler Building made a brief appearance through the fog, over the rail of the *Alva*, which lay at anchor waiting for the fog to lift.

duties had been taken care of, the fitness equipment, the games room, and recreational fishing off the stern were all popular choices.

Struggling to adjust to the rocking of the ship in the confines of their photography room, Bob and Al were busy unpacking and stowing away cameras, projectors, chemicals, flares, films, and other equipment that still needed to go into the special storage and development rooms. They had taken care of a lot of it before setting out, but there was more still to do, particularly with the inflammable content. They spent the majority of the day below deck.

Bob had been organizing and testing equipment for hours. Mr. Gilks had retired to his quarters, leaving him to his own devices in the tiny photo-darkroom. Hardly any sound reached the confines of the isolated, narrow studio—the buzzing in Bob's ears was complemented only by the soft lull of the open ocean. He had been just about to retire when,

There was no need for anyone to be at the helm, as the *Alva* warned away all on-comers. Al and Bob took the opportunity to stow equipment and prepare for sunnier days.

suddenly, a deafening ringing filled the lower deck. Bob jolted up from his hunched position, scared that he'd ignited one of the flammable containers and desperate to remedy the situation. He'd need to leave the room immediately and seal the door, so that the room could fill with carbon dioxide and put out the fire. *But where was the fire?* He looked back over his shoulder, staring out the door, waiting for someone—sailor, quartermaster, oiler, Al, anyone—to come charging in and tell him to *"get out now!" "Get out immediately!" "A fire already?" "Son, what did you do?"* But no one came. And still he saw no smoke. So, he hadn't set off the alarm? He listened carefully. No—the ringing was throughout the entire ship. *Were they then in danger of colliding with something—a communications tower maybe, or another ship? Or of running aground?* Bob stood, briefly, waiting for some informed crewman to pass by and tell him what to do. After more than half a minute with no one passing by, Bob made his way into the lower passage, and up the stairs toward the main deck.

About halfway up the stairwell he could finally hear voices—people calling out orders, and others screaming back-and-forth at one another. He emerged onto the main deck to find frantic crewmen running all around—some carrying axes, and two pulling large hoses. The ringing was from the fire alarm, and deck hands (some looking bewildered) had run for the fire extinguishers, axes, and hoses, which were laid in racks at various points around the ship. Others, including the starboard and port launchmen—Eric and Erich—and most of the other German crewmen—were busy preparing the lifeboats, systematically untying them from the side deck.

Bob walked swiftly over to a lifeboat that had already been untied and was being set on the pulleys for descent. At the thought of abandoning ship he realized that all of his possessions were still in his duffle, by his bedside. He seriously considered running back to get them, and he might have done just that if he had been given a few more seconds. But, almost in synchronous fashion, the crew stopped dead, and stood at attention. After a few moments the ringing stopped.

The Commodore emerged from the portside promenade along with the ship's boatswain, Heinrich Hamann—a short, fat, easy-going fellow. Without speaking, he inspected the fire racks and checked the positions of the crew, while Heinrich inspected the assembly of the lifeboat pulleys. Vanderbilt was holding a stopwatch by a long string, grasped in his right palm. Looking around, Bob realized that most of the senior crew and upper class were nowhere to be seen. And then finally he understood.

Heinrich, the boatswain, gave Bob a quizzical look as he spotted him standing idly in the middle of the deck. When the Commodore decided that all was in order, he congratulated the men on a successful fire drill, and dismissed them to their regular duties.

* * *

After the commotion had died down, and after he'd returned to seal the film-storage chamber, Bob went looking for Al, who had been suspiciously missing during the whole affair, probably having been given prior notice of it. Bob was convinced that Al had thought it would be a howl and a hoot to keep him in the dark about the drill, and he was definitely going to give his boss a friendly chiding for pulling such a stunt. After some searching, Bob finally found Al just inside the doorway of the lower chart room, where several of the senior crew and upper-class passengers were congregated.

Bob stood outside the doorway. The senior crew seemingly hadn't taken notice of his presence. Instead Bob heard them discussing plans for the voyage, the dialogue starting from somewhere in the middle.

"What week will it be then?" asked William Belanske to no one in particular. "We'll of course be leaving port at various invitations, and that must be accounted for."

"Having left on the 7th, regardless of the delay, I would expect slightly more than a month from then," proclaimed a middle-aged man across the room, whom Bob recognized as Reddington Robbins, the ship's first mate.

"Tahiti by the second or third week of August then?" asked Belanske.

"Yes," the man responded.

"What about stocks for that stretch? There will be a larger crew this time, and we'll be adrift for weeks after we leave the South American coast. If we aren't careful we'll be eating like the locals by that point. We can't expect a resupply in Galapagos—unless we want to eat the boobies."

They all laughed. Bob chuckled, not really knowing what they were laughing about.

"Indeed, as Mr. Belanske said, the crew should be well-fed. They should also be well-paid. I want to make arrangements to send part of their salaries directly home. They should also have regular access to the radio, and postcards for peace of mind. And an extra ten dollars a month for good behaviour." It was Mr. Vanderbilt, standing behind the chart counter, who carefully outlined these details to his senior crew.

An opulent-looking young man gave him a sideways sort of look.

"The Commodore is of course not just any employer, but the men must be kept somewhat respectable," Belanske piped in, smirking. "And tobacco! Tobacco, Red. I'm sure Mr. Merillon agrees. We must have extra cartons of cigarettes. They make an ideal gift in almost all cases."

"Two hundred and fifty thousand," said Mr. Vanderbilt. "That's the order. The crew can purchase them at half the New York City price, but we're telling them not to use them as barter with the locals—that we'll deduct it from their pay if they do. We won't, in the end. But we can't have the whole crew using cigarettes for trade. We'll run out in no time."

"Two hundred and fifty thousand?" the young, opulent looking man (who was evidently Mr. Merillon) repeated, amazed. "How did you manage that?"

"Not at all difficult. In fact, it's been ideal, with all our new storage space, to fill up on most everything before even leaving home port. Suppliers, especially the local ones, are very pleased when you buy in bulk—eager to give you discounts and the like."

"In fact, just last week I was in town doing some shopping. The other shoppers took no notice of me at first, obviously making a point not to stare—so I had this shop basement, with all the bargains, all to myself. The young saleswoman comes up to me and asks, 'Can I help you?'"

"Yes. I'll have two dozens of these bracelets, please. I also want three dozen bead necklaces, and four dozen earrings and assorted finger rings."

"She gave me one of the sternest looks I've ever seen. Quite amusing. Then I walked over and purchased alarm clocks, and mirrors, and magnifying glasses in quite the same manner. The other customers must have been thinking that I had gone completely mad, until I explained to them all that I was buying these things for the natives of the South Sea Islands."

Everyone in the drawing room laughed along at that point.

"Have we considered what will be done if someone falls ill?" asked Mr. Merillon. "Confined to their quarters," a man standing by a bookshelf responded quickly. "In isolation, ideally."

"That rule will unfortunately have to go for everyone," Mr. Vanderbilt clarified.

He stood up straight and moved toward the middle of the room with his arms partially outstretched.

"Mr. Gilks, have you met Mr. Belanske."

Al Gilks and Belanske shook hands.

"Mr. Belanske is our taxidermist. He'll be preserving the finest of all the new aquatic species we discover. The same ones that you'll be photographing Mr. Gilks," Mr. Vanderbilt explained.

"Keep in mind, the primary focus of the expedition is science," Belanske explained. "We all may be getting on in years, but this is more than a leisure cruise. You are here, foremost, in the name of science."

"Very exciting indeed," Mr. Gilks said emphatically. "Very exciting."

"Science is about detail, Mr. Gilks," Belanske stated with a heavy emphasis. "Never stop reiterating that fact to your assistant here."

He glanced at Bob, having noticed him standing in the doorway.

"Beauty has a value in and of itself; a photographer obviously understands that fact. But for others, like the Museum of Natural History, who will likely want to see details of our discoveries, it's about careful meticulous cataloguing. Attention… to… detail."

This Belanske fellow had more of the fast, enthusiastic manner that Bob had expected of Mr. Vanderbilt. Instead, surprisingly, it was Mr. Vanderbilt himself who consistently made Bob the most at ease. He was a gentleman, not snobbish, but a gentleman still. *"The Commodore,"* as Mr. Belanske had called him, was generally non-confrontational. Bob thought of the twenty year-old Vanderbilt, racing in cars through Long Island and Europe, and drew a despairing contradiction. He was obviously passionate. And now he'd supposedly found purpose in the wonders of the natural world, keen to share it with anyone who was interested.

Bob realized that people were now looking at him. Mr. Merillon was giving him a deep stare that made him somewhat uncomfortable as he became aware of his clearly inappropriate attire. Bob, clumsily, bowed out of the doorway.

"Sorry for intruding," he said, head tilted forward. "Very sorry. I'll be going."

"Son," Reddington Robbins called to Bob as he turned to leave, "Well done on punctually abandoning ship. Don't forget the cameras next time."

They all erupted into laughter.

* * *

The *Alva*'s progress was steady, and at last, by the evening of the 9th, they passed the Diamond Shoal Light Vessel off Cape Hatteras, moving out indefinitely into open waters. They sailed around Frying Pan Shoal Light Vessel, which stood forty-six miles south of Masonboro Inlet, marking the shallows around Frying Pan Shoals. Its four legs acted as a waypoint for blue water fish—tuna, king mackerel, and dolphins—with dozens of species of tropical fish moving about the waters off the coast of North Carolina.

The Commodore dealt with phone calls from the bridge throughout the night, telling him it was time to change direction. Periodically, he would leave his cabin, climb up to the bridge, look around, make an entry in the rough log, squint at the clouds, and then swiftly return to his bunk. Bob caught many of these performances while he leaned in the dark against the starboard rail, enjoying a late-night cigarette.

Bob snaps a well-timed photo of a school of porpoises, following playfully off the bow.

The *Alva* continued sailing down the Atlantic seaboard. The Commodore considered Cape Canaveral a "particularly nasty place," where the shoals extended far out from the coast, making navigation particularly difficult, especially with all the squalls and thunderstorms going on closer to the shore. As they passed a deserted-looking *Breakers Hotel* in Palm Beach, a school of porpoises began following the ship, playing around the prow for five to ten minutes at a time, then disappearing, and promptly returning. Bob and Al spent most of the day taking movie shots of the porpoises and, occasionally, of the Commodore.

Into Tropical Waters

THE FIRST real stopover for the *Alva* was Miami, just off the mainland. The Commodore had his own private island there—Fisher's Island—which he'd bought in 1925, bartering off a luxury yacht to the island's then owner. In the past he'd used it as a home base for his yachting expeditions, but the huge propeller blades of the *Alva* were too large to fit to the dock. So while the Commodore stayed on his private island, the *Alva* would stay in Miami, and the crew could go ashore. They planned to sail for Havana at noon the following day, so this would be their last port in the good ole U.S. of A., and the men were making use of it—pouring jovially off the decks into the sunny Miami streets.

Coming in the night before, they could see the Gulf Stream from along the shore—a light-green phosphorescence about a quarter of a mile wide that carved straight out through open ocean, as if a river ran through it. A few men had stood leaning forward on the rails, taking in a full sunset as color palettes—waving, solid, continuous motifs—the tangent rays rushing against the sky, reflecting into the waters, and refracting into the depths. With the sun setting at their backs, and the horizon advancing on them, the atmosphere lit up in reds and pinks that dimmed until the blue-black ocean at port side was all-black, and then the sky itself—black—as the horizon collided with the soft glow from the *Alva*.

Bob and Al had again been occupied with taking pictures of the ship and the fish lingering around the hull. Though there was a breeze blowing as they moved inland, it was a sticky one, and was not nearly enough to dry the sweat off Bob's face and neck. Down in the darkroom, Bob had to strip to his shorts, still perspiring profusely. Morton, the ship's electrician, was keeping him and Al company. The electrician was keen to follow the process as they developed some early prints of the eastern coast.

The Alva base on Fisher Island, Florida.

The Gulf Stream was lapping the ship's sides as they moved out of port, and although the same stormy weather followed them—with a lot of lightning and thunder—they were still making good progress, because the sea remained tentatively calm. Bob and Al could work on developing the latest films, handling the more delicate equipment without the risk of damaging it.

"Give me good old California instead of this air," Bob moaned.

"This ain't nothing kid, trust me," said Morton.

"I can't even imagine a place more humid than this," said Bob, sweat pouring off him in streams. "There's more water than air."

At that moment, Anton, the first assistant engineer, passed by the darkroom; he stopped to talk when he noticed the small gang assembled inside. He stood in the doorway with his arms across his chest, smiling devilishly.

"Listen, you just let me know you're up for it and I'll tie a buoy to the bow and throw you over the back with it. That'll cool you down nice and good. There're sharks, sure, but you wouldn't be much of a meal for them anyway."

Morton cut in. "Wasn't it you boys last time tha…"

"I dunno what you're talking about," Anton said expressionlessly, looking away over their heads at some drying prints of the Florida coast. Among them, a gorgeous poolside snapshot from the Fisher Island Estate.

Morton sat smirking. Bob looked back and forth at the two of them, deciding not to ask.

"Don't you gents have any work to do?" asked Al, slightly irritated. Bob saw that the heat was definitely getting to him. Al took a dry sleeve to his brow then pinched the sweat from his eyes with his thumb and index finger, blinking hard from the stinging.

"Hey, she ain't sinking, is she? So, we're doing our job, and be thankful," Anton bellowed defensively.

"Yeah, I've triple checked everything by now: even the switches and navigation bits that were always working. There's only so much work you can make up for yourself. Same routine tomorrow." said Morton. "Listen, life at sea is mostly slow. You've got to get used to putting your feet up." As he said this he leaned back in his chair and put his feet up on another table by the side wall.

* * *

When the *Alva* left Miami on the afternoon of the 14th, en route to Havana, a sizeable crowd came to the dock to see the ship off. Bob stood on the starboard deck, camera in-hand, and felt like something of a celebrity as he watched the crowds waving them off. The docks in Miami would be his last busy photo session until their next landfall. When they were at sea for several days at a stretch there was, naturally, less to photograph. In general, there was a lot of down time. Later in the trip there would be more prints to develop, but they hadn't taken enough pictures yet to build much of a backlog.

They said goodbye to the American coast that evening, and were told that they would be in Havana by daybreak. Given some free time, Bob got to wandering about parts of the ship he had yet to explore. In the operating room, the on-board physician, Dr. Lane, was busy managing the medicinal supplies, still stowing them away in various lockers, while familiarizing himself with the space. Bob recognized the doctor as one of the men from the lower chart room a few days earlier. He took a step back at first, suddenly remembering that this man was on board, realizing that he still hadn't met the doctor, and quickly connecting the dots in his mind. He wondered how he had missed him all this time, being that the infirmary was right across the hall from the darkroom.

"The biggest challenge will be getting clearance through all the quarantines applied to the territories we're visiting," he explained to Bob, having ardently encouraged him into the clinic, clearly intent on chatting him up. The doctor didn't seem as busy as he was used to being: he shuffled items from one shelf to the next, and once done immediately began transferring them back to where they'd originally been.

"The Japanese territories—they're the worst. You're lucky if they let you so much as come within a mile of the shoreline. And Africa—let me tell you, the way to not get sick in Africa… is to not land in Africa."

He turned and looked at Bob, wide-eyed and unblinking, challenging a response.

"Didn't everyone get their shots already? I had to get a physical—official doctor's approval and everything."

"Sure, inoculations for typhoid, vaccinations for smallpox. But those are really just the start of it. Truly, the most important thing is that we have all your dental records on file—in case there's no other way of identifying your body."

He turned to Bob with the same challenging stare as before. After a few seconds of not getting a response he picked up a flat steel case, looked inside, moved to place it on a shelf, quickly looked back inside again, and then stared blankly.

"How many times do I have to tell those boys in cabin crew to stay out of my supplies? You tell them, will you? You tell those boys to stay out of the bandages and rubbing alcohol, otherwise the stuff is going under lock and key, and I swear it won't come out unless someone's lost a limb! You tell them, will ya? Will ya?"

"Sure. Will do," said Bob.

* * *

The *Alva* had pulled to dock in Havana at seven in the morning. Bob and Al went ashore at noon and hired a car to get around, trying to find a photo store to stock some basic supplies. They tried four different places, each time taking no less than fifteen minutes to get the vendors to understand what they wanted. Bob would give it his best effort—"Cuatro by cinco, Panchromatic film," and made a sign with his fingers like scissors cutting and then say, "Cut film." The clerk would then say, "Si, si," and run into the back and return with about six dozen of all kinds, except the right kind. They eventually gave up, hoping for more luck at the next port, where the locals would hopefully speak English.

Later that afternoon, Bob and Al decided to start a new project and rode out to Miramar, known to tourists as "the American section." The area was marked by refined homes and boulevards in more of a European style. Al stopped off to see a friend, and Bob was left to take the car around and shoot some pictures. In this instance he was obviously the assistant—left with the car to fend for himself. He smiled about it. It was a "learning experience" for him, after all, and unsupervised in the streets of Havana, he had his first opportunity to let loose. He made it his mission to take in every detail.

Havana was like two cities, one within the other. There was old Spanish town near the harbor, outlined by the original fortifications, and the new city, which spread for miles out along the coast. The *Malecón*, a wide, swerving esplanade, traced the portion of the northern coast that cut through the city.

The streets in the old town were often so narrow and congested that only one car could pass at a time. The sidewalks were similar—pedestrians could usually walk only in single file, otherwise risking stepping precariously into the street. "That's why the natives carry all their bundles in a basket on top of their heads," Bob would later write to his father. The narrow alleys and high buildings kept shoppers hidden from the sun for all but a brief period at either side of high noon. Where the streets were wider, sidewalks were usually hidden underneath large arcades. Many graceful electric trolley cars roamed the city core, past open-air businesses, inviting in locals and American tourists alike.

The new city featured large modern buildings and wide boulevards, specifically designed to accommodate the motorcar and an ever-burgeoning populace. A wide thoroughfare called the *Prado* boasted the capitol building, along with many other stately edifices.

Havana was new, independent, and prosperous; a now-popular travel destination—especially for wealthy Americans.

Bob ended his day at the beer garden, where the beer companies were giving away free beer for advertising purposes. "Good beer, too," he wrote gleefully.

Here in classic perspective, Bob preserves the capitol building, completed in 1929, as part of his documentation of 1931 Havana.

A few hours later he returned to Miramar to get Al. The *Alva* was supposed to sail at three that afternoon. After their struggle to get the film they'd needed (which had eaten up much of their time for fun) Bob and Al were rushing back to the ship. They got there only to find out that the plans had changed.

Special charts had been hung in a common area of the deck where everyone could see them, showing every part of the ship in different colors and specifying each man's duties. As they returned, a notice posted overtop stated that they were now staying overnight. The Commodore and his wife had gone ashore.

With their boss out, Bob and Al seized the opportunity to get away. They quickly joined up with a crew set to return to the streets. Running with the artist, taxidermist, engineer, electrician, and first mate—Bob and his little gaggle of friends gleefully set out to paint the town red.

"This way, I know a place," Morton called out.

"Why didn't we hire another car?" Bob asked. "They cost next to nothing. And between the six of us even..."

"Would have set us each back a whole fifteen minutes in wages," Red sarcastically figured.

"Nah, you won't want to be driving" Morton explained.

"In this heat, you'll be tripping over yourself in no time. Skinny boy like you," Anton said with a challenging flip of the chin.

"Not a chance," Bob said smiling. "None of that tequila for me; but get us there quickly, will you? I want another beer."

"Haven't you been out boozing today, already? Jeez kid," Anton said, laughing.

"The boy's out to paint the town red," Belanske quipped, laughing along.

Morton looked around at the names of each of the businesses they passed, finally stopping and leading them into a surprisingly clean little establishment called "Sloppy Joe's."

"We should save some time," Walter Maguire, Belanske's taxidermist assistant (and Bob's roommate) suggested. "Mr. Belanske and I want to visit Moro Castle. It's the old fortress at the entrance to the harbor. We should all go. It's all the way across the bay, so we'll need some time to get there and back."

"You're going to make Bobby boy carry that camera all the way over there? Forget it," said Anton, emphatically.

"No. Listen here, Anton, we didn't go last time, because a bunch of guys were busy chatting up the local scene, and I'm not skipping out on it again," Belanske said doggedly.

"Siete cervezas!" Al Gilks proclaimed to the Hispanic bartender throwing a handful of Cuban pesos onto the counter. "Bob, set up a shot, will you?"

The bartender handed Al a glass as Bob set up the angle.

"To the Commodore!" a few of the crew cried out from a corner table, clinking their glasses as the camera flashed.

* * *

Evening had quickly become late night, which in turn had become very late night. Moro Castle was long forgotten. No matter, since no one, including the taxidermists, seemed to remember or otherwise care. Much of the group had settled eagerly into a wide-boothed corner

Gilks takes advantage of a bit of brew on tap in a Havana establishment. The always proper, and often dapper, Gilks was respected by Vanderbilt as 'near equal' and always referred to as "Mr. Gilks."

table at Sloppy Joe's. Mac, Belanske, Morton and Al had been there most of the night. At first, they chatted among themselves, then as the night progressed, they got into a mix of choice words with other tables of American sailors, until Morton and Belanske started chatting up more of the locals: consuls and other government officials, and some business men.

 Bob had been in and out of the bar most of the night. His stomach was unsettled pretty much from the get-go, but he wasn't going to let the others know that. Instead, he used his wanting to see the lights of Miramar at night as an excuse to get some fresh air. He'd met Anton out front on one occasion, and the engineer had chosen to go exploring with him. Bob figured that he was eager to get away from some of the others, like Morton, who had been getting louder as the night went on.

"Don't pay attention to that one there," he told Bob, "unless you're up for it." A not particularly attractive Cuban girl, perhaps in her early thirties, Bob thought, looked at them devilishly and beckoned them over to her, motioning with her fingers. Looking briefly, Bob saw her disheveled hair and a dress that was showing a whole lot of leg and bosom. She was smoking a cigarette and it seemed as if she almost swayed from side-to-side.

"Don't tell me that's not your thing," Anton said, nodding his head at the girl, while smirking at Bob.

"Funny. Hell, Vanderbilt himself couldn't pay me for that."

The girl had noticed them nodding in her direction and began walking toward them.

"Oh God, she's coming this way. Don't look, just keep walking," Anton said, unable to keep from laughing. "I think she likes you."

They began to walk fast. And then faster still. Bob quickly looked over his shoulder. The girl was following them at a brisk pace now, smiling as Bob turned and looked her in the eye.

"Oh damn, get inside the bar."

Inside, there was general rowdiness all around. Apart from a table of German crewmen from the *Alva* who kept to themselves, choice words were being flung all about.

"The *Alva* is top of the line! She'll outpace and outhaul any ship in that harbor!" Bob heard Mac cry out.

"Please!" was the response, with scattered laughter, "That big tourist ship wouldn't last five minutes against any one of those military vessels with a real navy crew."

"Try competing in hauls against one of those wooden Cuban fishing boats, maybe," another man called out. "They're tough, but you might just take them!"

There was even more laughter.

"Blasphemy!" Anton cried out.

"Oyyyy!" the crowd cried out, showing their pleasure at his return.

Bob walked up and faced into the bar among a crowd, not once turning around. He waited for some time, leaning against the bar as others who had been waiting before him (and many others who hadn't) were served.

"¿Qué tomará?" the bartender finally asked.

"Ah...tequila," Bob responded, realizing he didn't know the word for beer.

The bartender poured it and Bob paid him, then he slowly turned around to eye the scene. Everyone was gone—all except the German men, who gave him a weird stare until one nodded toward the door.

Bob left the tequila on the counter, getting a frustrated glare from the bartender. He went outside to find Anton talking with some trim-looking sailors from another ship. Mac, Belanske and Al talked among themselves. Morton leaned clumsily against the left door of the establishment, talking up the same girl that had followed Bob and Anton. Some taxis approached and the other Americans said farewell, filling every last seat.

"Honestly, why didn't we get taxis?" Mac asked again.

Morton was standing up as straight as he could, but having trouble. He was still talking to the Cuban girl. She smiled at him, leaning her head to the side, and subtly swaying her naked leg while using the toes of her heeled foot as a pivot. She touched his arm. He paused and touched her disheveled hair.

"¡HOLA!"

"¡Eh, Hola! ¡Gringos!"

The group finally quieted down and looked for who was calling to them. A sizeable group of Cuban men, at least a dozen, were standing in the middle of the street about fifty yards off. The girl jumped as she noticed them.

"¿Fernanda?" one of the men to the left called out.

Morton looked at her, confused, and then back at the group of men. They were all staring at him. There was the briefest of silences before one of the Cuban men screamed out and threw a bottle of tequila in their direction that Al just barely dodged before it shattered against the back wall.

"Run!" Anton cried out.

Suddenly they were all running down the street—a gang of angry Cuban men in hot pursuit. Mac had apparently had more to drink than he had let on, and ended up on his knees—two, then three times. Bob was starting to feel his stomach turning as well—saved temporarily by having left his tequila on the counter.

"Taxi!" Anton cried. By some miracle, there were two together turning a corner in the otherwise deserted streets. As they were stopping, he opened the door and threw Mac and Morton in, one after the after, while Bob waited on Al and Belanske, trailing behind, all of whom jumped into the second cab.

The confused drivers, beckoned on by their belligerent wailing, quickly raced away, with the furious gang only yards behind.

* * *

Back on board *Alva*—a little worse for wear after the events of the previous night—Bob, Al, and the rest of their renegade group set to work again, knowing that they were inevitably under some scrutiny.

En route to Kingston, Jamaica, the Commodore spent a great deal of time looming in the darkroom, where Bob and Al shared the pictures they had taken of his Miami estate. As much as the Commodore might have enjoyed tales of their mischief, Bob knew not to overstep his bounds. On a whim, the Commodore could dismiss him, crushing his dreams with brutal finality.

With tequila and beer still pouring off them in cold sweats, he and Al presented photographs as formally and unassumingly as they could within the clumsy confines of their little equipment room. Much to Bob's relief, the Commodore was delighted with the pictures and encouraged them to take even more. He made no mention of their antics from the night before, word of which had spread around the ship absurdly quickly.

"Did you visit Moro castle?" he asked.

"No sir, we didn't make it in the end," Bob explained.

"Pity," replied Mr. Vanderbilt, turning to leave. "I'll see you on the upper deck for cigars—once you're feeling fit, Mr. Gilks," he said, a glimmer in his eyes clueing Bob in to a thinly veiled grin, as he left them, walking briskly toward the stairwell.

Bob turned toward Al Gilks.

"It sure gives one some ambition when a man like him gives encouraging words and compliments. Now I want to show him all the more what I can do. If only all business men were like that," Bob said happily.

Al turned and smiled at him. "Hand me the case from Havana," he requested.

Jamaica

THE CLIMATE transformed as the *Alva* finally moved down into the real tropical waters, and with the change came new phenomena that delighted and fascinated the crew. At night, sometimes until ten o'clock, heat lightning flashed across the sky, lighting up the hazy cloud formations in shocks of vivid blues and greens. Many of the crew again stood out on the deck: chatting, smoking, and taking in the scenes until late into the night.

The *Alva* arrived in Kingston on the 18th. Jamaica was an English protectorate, run by the locals, who mostly spoke very good English with a true accent: "Heggs and 'At a Lice. Now laugh, doggone ya!" Bob wrote in a letter to his father while sitting on the deck—quite amused with his own interpretation. He had been very satisfied to find out how well he could communicate with the Jamaicans—who could usually also speak with the real English accent and perfect enunciation. As the police and customs officials boarded the ship he was impressed to see how the locals seemed to have full control of public offices—"big black 6 ft. Bobbies and traffic cops."

The *Alva* dropped anchor in Kingston harbor at one that afternoon. Al and Bob went ashore. Some consideration was given to renting another car and going into the hills to photograph some real native life, but they started out having quite a job of getting the equipment down the gangway and into the motor launch (as the waters were very rough), and the sky was getting quite dark by the time they got to heading out. When the pair reached the town market, large crowds of locals were shopping and dickering for bargains.

Al Gilks changed a ten-dollar bill and in return got a pocketful of pounds, shillings, sixpence and two pence pieces, and was left trying to figure out what they were worth in U.S. dollars. They might have short-changed him a half-penny, but he would hardly have known it. From the pocketful he got in return it looked to him as though they gave him twenty's worth, or more, and cheated themselves.

The crowds were really bustling, making it difficult to set up a good shot, and the weather was ominous, so they decided to shoot the market on their way back, and just get as far out as they could in the meantime.

The road was laid with gravel and the town was twenty miles behind them. As they rode along on their return, they passed by the locals still walking home from their shopping in Kingston that morning. The road was lined with them—some having to walk twenty or twenty-five miles with big baskets, and gallons and gallons of water or booze on their heads. When the rain started, they began running, still carrying everything. Women and children, many barefoot, scurried in droves in the opposite direction, somehow not falling, even though many carried bundles that looked about equal to their own weight.

The party drove through tropical vegetation that covered the better part of the country side: bread fruit, coconut palms, bananas, coffee, some rubber and tignum (iron wood) trees. In the rain, it was impossible to shoot or photograph a thing, so they headed straight back to the market. The town, however, was closed up, without a soul in sight, even though a little over an hour earlier the crowds had been jammed up shoulder to shoulder. There was nothing to film now in the deserted streets, and after a short look around without any sign of activity, Al and Bob returned despondently to the *Alva*.

Back on board the ship, Mr. Vanderbilt and his party enjoyed the view for a while longer before setting sail again. Everyone was tingling from their experiences in Havana and Kingston, but by Monday, July 20th, having been at sea for almost two weeks, they were back on open waters. The wind had increased the previous night to force seven, with all ships in the area reporting high, heavy seas. At midnight, emerging mightily from a bad squall and rough winds, they arrived in Colón, Panama.

Bob spent longer than usual trying to write up a letter to his father. It was the roughest weather they had experienced, and his pen banged and streaked hopelessly across the page. During the worst of the storm, the sea was all but coming up over the decks. He had to strap himself in bed that night, and he was already feeling seasick.

At lunch a particularly heavy roll-over upset the dishes while the crew was seated at the table. Bob's drinking glass was the first casualty—landing in his lap before it hit the floor.

"Did that getchya Bobby boy?" Anton chuckled.

"Urgh, I'd wager a penny that if the glass had been empty it never would have turned over," Bob groaned, while trying to dry himself with his handkerchief.

"Oh, the life of a sailor!" Anton cried, raising his glass with a hearty laugh.

Bob and Al were up on deck all morning shooting while the sailors told stories of their adventures. They started up the gangways where the rails were covered with salt brine.

"I can now imagine how a salt mackerel feels," Bob thought out loud, "feeling salty all over. Ha!"

"At least your adventures are giving you a solid, practical knowledge of such things," Al replied.

Indeed, Bob had made a great effort to shed all apprehension about the trip, beginning in Havana, and was starting to enjoy the little things: the experience of eating while seeing the knives, forks, and cups move in front of his eyes; to be in the stateroom to see the clothes hanging out from the wall stand at a forty-five degree angle; and to be so layered in salt that all his clothes were permanently speckled white.

The *Alva* would start through the canal the following morning, where the crew expected to have the chance to catch up with correspondences, to pick up letters from friends and family, and send out the next installments.

It was a rough trip from Kingston, but it was apparently, at least according to the Commodore, something experienced sailors considered normal for that area.

"The trades seem to blow strong all year round," Mr. Vanderbilt had said. Force five or six is what they were used to encountering.

Bob was simply proud to have contained his seasickness thus far. The wet, barren wilderness was unrelenting. And even though they were in the harbor, it was hard to sleep that night.

By daylight, they were ready to shift their position to the flats. When the hook was up, the Commodore moved the ship out from its temporary anchorage. At 5:30 a.m. the canal doctor and custom-house official arrived on board. The ship was mostly silent, with much of the crew still in their bunks, and from his cot Bob could hear the roused Commodore talking to someone on deck.

"Early hours seem to mean nothing to the authorities here," Bob heard the Commodore complain, seeming more than a little disgruntled at having to haul himself out of bed at someone else's behest.

After the check and breakfast, everyone went ashore to explore. Al and Bob went swimming in the *Hotel Washington's* pool, and had a big spree in Colón that night with the same gang as in Havana. The little party were firm friends now. They crept back aboard the ship that afternoon around 6:30, not drunk (Bob insisted); they'd certainly had a good time though.

Changing their clothes and freshening up, Bob and Al set out again, this time to Panama City and Old Panama by train to catch up on some of their work. The rain was following them everywhere, and they didn't manage to shoot any street scenes in Panama.

They went to shoot the ruins of the cathedrals and convents, built in the late sixteenth and early seventeenth centuries, and later ransacked by the pirate Henry Morgan. All around, the vegetation was dense and for the first time, Bob began to feel like a real adventurer—lost in the wilderness. He carried the camera equipment, dodging lizards, spiders, and crabs scattered all about the pathway—it was unsettling, and every moment of it thrilled him.

"Are there any poisonous animals here?" Bob asked Al, as they stumbled along an uneven, rocky path, Bob lugging some of the heavier camera equipment. The overhanging treetops cut out much of the sky, making it hard to judge just how far they'd trekked into the flora-dense Central American jungle.

"I would imagine so," Al replied.

"Wonderful," Bob replied, smiling.

Al was several paces ahead, trying to guide them toward a set of ruins that occasionally appeared from between the brush. Rounding a corner he jumped back, almost knocking Bob—with the equipment—off his feet.

"Whoa, damn me, what is that?" Al cried out.

"Where?" Bob cried back.

"There, on the tree!" Al called back, pointing hesitantly, while leaning away.

A green, throaty lizard, with a long, straight tail held itself vertically against a tree trunk, with one eye fixated on them.

Here Robert masterfully captures the ruins of the old city of Panama—built in the seventeenth century, and later ransacked by the pirate Henry Morgan. By 1931 they were overgrown by dense vegetation.

"That? That's just an iguana," Bob told him.

"Oh. Right, right—fine. Let's get moving then. We'll have to hurry on now. The ruins seem to be further than the men in the market suggested," Al called out.

* * *

Signs posted on the bulletin board announced to the crew and passengers that no livestock were to be allowed on the *Alva*. "Birds, parrots, monkeys, and dogs are prohibited," the Commodore had written. His first mate would explain how Vanderbilt had always found them a nuisance in the past. "He's decided that animals litter the ship, make terrific noise, and smell bad," Reddington explained to a small group who were visibly unhappy with the rule. Panama was the first stop where crew had come across a lot of indigenous fauna, and many men had been keen on keeping

To Bob, these early arches represented a real triumph in engineering, albeit from a different era, but simple, rustic, and magical.

their own: iguanas, turtles, snakes, golden frogs, even monkeys. But the Commodore wouldn't have it. Not even cats or dogs were allowed. Fish, and the occasional landed bird, would be the only exception.

The ship weighed anchor and proceeded to the oil dock for refueling.

The next port equipped for this purpose would be Brisbane, Australia—a long way off. Although the dock was dirty, and the heat hardly bearable, they stayed tied in that uncomfortable spot for most of the day, with the passengers ashore, while the Commodore and his crew were at work.

By the evening, they were clear and back to the anchorage, the last of their supplies ready for departure. They were ready to sever relations with the waters of the Caribbean, and their radio communication confirmed that two more passengers would be ready for pickup the following day. Willie K.'s daughter, Consuelo, and her husband Earl would be joining the company. Two other men joined the stewards' department that day as well, replacing one who had left the ship at Kingston and another, a

German, who was headed back to Hamburg by tramp ship. Both the departed members were from the original construction crew. They had been among a few dozen men, mostly Germans, hired by the Commodore's representatives to man various positions aboard the *Alva*. Despite their earlier beliefs, they had ultimately found that building ships was more to their liking than sailing around the world in them. A large, multinational crew still remained however—about fifty: Americans, Canadians, Englishmen, Germans, Swedes and Dutchmen.

"Are you two men used to life at sea? Life on a ship?"

"Yis, sir."

"Yis, sir, the other repeated."

"And you understand that you'll be travelling for almost a year? And once we return to the United States, you will have to find your own way back to Panama. The *Alva* will not be returning to Panama. You understand this?"

Bob, listening by the portside railing, predicted the response.

"Yis, sir."

"Alright, fine then. We're short two stewards. Does anyone speak Spanish in the steward's department?" the Commodore asked of Evans, the second mate, who was standing nearby.

"I'll check, sir."

The two Panamanian men stared straight ahead.

"I imagine each of you have all your necessary belongings, because we're not staying any longer. Well? Do you?"

One of the men looked at the other.

"Yis, sir—all things." The other replied.

"Alright then. Louis, show these two to Gustave, he'll work something out."

Bob wasn't sure who Vanderbilt had meant as there were, in fact, two stewards on the *Alva* named Gustave. He figured that Evans might have been confused as well, but if he was, he didn't speak up.

The welcome assembly soon cleared off.

"Yis, sir." And this one was right into Bob's ear. It was Morton.

"That'll end well—I'm just sure of it," he joked.

Bob didn't give much of a response as he adjusted the tripod, so Morton wandered over to the far side of the railing. As he did, one of the docking ropes started to loosen only feet away from Bob's head. Bob stopped what he was doing and stared at it as it sagged.

"Hey! Scram!"

He turned to see the portly, and apparently grumpy, boatswain, Hamann, approaching the port side, followed by the port and starboard launchmen—the Erics—who rather ironically, also looked very similar—two thin, blond, blue-eyed German boys.

"If you don't have enough pictures of fishes by now, then it's too late—we're leaving port," Hamann stated, wryly. "You can't stand around right now; you're in the way."

"Where did those boys get to? Eric!"

"Ay, Herr Hamann!" both called out.

"No you, portside Eric!" he bellowed at one.

"I am portside Eric."

Hamann paused, and stared half-angrily half-confused, clearly trying to figure out if they were playing games with him.

"Okay. You. Draw in the lines."

Bob had gathered his equipment, and lugged the whole unpacked assembly over toward the stairwell to the lower decks.

"Hey! Scram!" Morton called out as Bob struggled down the stairs with the unfolded tripod. "Dinner?"

The following day, Thursday, July 23rd, the Commodore and Rose excitedly awaited the arrivals. The *Santa Barbara* appeared at noon and made fast to the pier, with the entire party there ready to welcome the young couple. Unfortunately, a tropical downpour began almost immediately. Consuelo and Earl were whisked from the dock over to the *Alva*, luggage in tow. Their "fine but dull" flight from New York had made them particularly excited to land and step out into the lush Canal Zone, and they were noticeably unenthused with the weather that welcomed them.

Writing to his father later that day, Bob realized it could well be a few weeks before he would be able to correspond again. They were going to leave Panama to explore the surrounding islands, and the next mailing point would be in Papeete—in the Society Islands of the South Sea Islands group—Tahiti.

The *Alva* had to make slow progress through the Canal, the gates closing behind her at three-thirty that afternoon. Four electric mules, attached to the ship with wire hawsers, hauled her through three successive locks. Gatun Lake was eighty-five feet above sea level, and it was twenty-eight miles across to the deeply excavated Culebra (or Gaillard Cut), some seven miles long and three hundred feet wide. Bob remained below deck through much of the journey. It rained constantly.

They crossed over the Continental Divide and entered Pedro Miguel Lock, progressively dropping thirty feet to Miraflores Lake, and then through two more locks, down another fifty feet total, to the Pacific Ocean.

The next morning, breakfast was served earlier than usual. They'd arrived in Balboa (a district of Panama City) at ten the night before, where they dropped anchor accompanied by sheets of lightning and peals of thunder. The crew was mostly up early because they'd been given leave to visit the city. The ship would sail at 5 pm, according to a note on the bulletin board, which had become the main center for communication between the upstairs and downstairs companies. Everyone was allowed to set ashore well before the departure time, giving plenty of opportunity to visit the many piers, markets and boulevards. This was their last civilized port of call before weeks of open ocean on their way to the far side of the world.

[1]On board the Alva

Thursday, July 23rd, 1931

Hello Dad:

We are now pulling out of Cristobol[2] harbor to go through the Canal.

Al and I went to Panama by train yesterday and shot movies of the old ruins of Panama cathedrals, churches and convents buil[t] in 1540 or 1610 by the Padres and ransacked by Henry Morgan, the pirate, in 1640 or so.

Also saw the towns of Panama and Balboa. Both very beautiful places, but it seems that wherever we go to shoot it rains on us[;] we didn't get any street scenes of Panama.

I think it may be a few weeks before you hear from me again as after we leave here we start exploring Islands. The first mail point for me to send you letters will be Papeete, Society Islands in the South Sea Islands group. We will be there for about three or more weeks, I have been informed.

---

1. Since the L.A. Limited Bob had already sent dozens of letters to his father, Panama to Tahiti being the first real lapse, with no mailing point in-between.

2. Sic: Cristobal harbor.

July 23, (2)

We expect to stop first at the Galapagos Islands on the Equator on the Pacific side after we leave the Canal, and I understand this is not a mailing point.

Al and I expect to be quite busy from now on, especially myself. Will have to shoot pictures by day and develop them at night.

The Commodore's daughter came aboard from New York at last stopping place, a[s] has the mail for the crew.

Well, Dad, there is not much to write about now and I have got to get to work now and prepare to shoot the Canal and locks from the boat. I will keep adding to this as we go through and give it to the [p]ilot as he goes ashore at Balboa.

We are just about through the Canal and sorry to say we couldn't get many shots of it as it began to rain again, and became too dark with over-hanging clouds as we got past the first set of [l]ocks. It is all very interesting, though.

July 23, (3)

We expect to be in Balboa in the morning and that will give me a chance to mail this.

In the first Locks (Gatum) we were lifted up three steps—a height of fifty feet. The water fills into these in about ten minutes and then the gates open and we go into the next one and are lifted up again.

I certainly have plenty of work to do. I have about four dozen negatives to be developed and have to make a half[-]dozen prints of each. Oh well, it's a great life when you can't weaken.

Here in the Canal Zone the Government runs everything, and all the employees of the Zone get everything they need from the government. All of it is duty free. We bought a lot of things from the Commissary for one-third less than you can buy them in New York or Hollywood.

They sell cigarettes for eighty cents a carton. I had to get in on some of that. I'm going to turn in now for I have a hard day ahead tomorrow.

Love, Bob

The Galapagos Islands

BALBOA WAS adorned in a Spanish style, chalked with an American liveliness, raised considerably by the presence of a United States Fleet in port. Before they'd hauled anchor, the *Alva's* crew had a fortuitous encounter with the Commodore's uncle—George Vanderbilt—who was in town with his yacht, *White Shadow*.

In snippets of conversation, Bob had heard about the Commodore's past life. Something about the way his eyes drifted, and the way he spoke so wistfully, betrayed his guised, but habitual, reflection on past phases of his life.

"I'm not romantic in the way that young people are—believing in one love, one chance at everything," the Commodore alleged to a small party sitting out on the forward boat deck in wicker chairs and beach recliners.

Bob was off on the far end of the promenade, filming Balboa harbor. As the man behind the camera, he felt more invisible as the days went on. The senior crew often spoke very frankly in his presence; irrespective of whether he was the intended audience or not. All the while he documented every detail in film, photo, and mind. During off-hours, he was the well-liked boy photographer. During work hours, he was a fly on the railing.

"Where did we lunch in Havana? Ah, yes—a little '*Restaurant de Paris*'. Morro stone crabs—delectable. We drove for hours through the ancient colonial sections of the city, and then over some splendid roads through tropical scenery, and in again through modern boulevards. Some buildings were even reminiscent of American skyscrapers—blotches, really, on an otherwise very charming city. "We finished off the day with a jai-alai fronton. Have you heard of this sport? A brilliant Spanish game—very swift."

Rose sat to the Commodore's right, allowing her husband to do the full recounting of their trip thus far. It was obvious that he was very happy with her. She was pretty, charming, elegant, of petite stature; a partner to him—an equal. But their love was almost of the somber sort. Rosamund was clearly ambitious, making the most of her good manners, quick-wit, and refined sensibility.

"Well, I'm glad to hear that the trip thus far has been treating you well, despite the rain," said the Commodore's uncle.

"These voyages for Rose and me, they're almost—cleansing."

Mrs. Merillon smiled at this remark.

"Leave it to weeks of endless rain to make one feel purified," he quipped.

Bob knew that their romance had begun in secret. Their trips helped to ease the frustration of years spent in hiding, longing for a renewal of sorts. Rose was nothing like the glamorous Mrs. Vanderbilt that the crewmen described. She was attractive, yes, but without her husband's charisma. She never tried to push herself into the limelight—she even seemed to prefer the wings. The first Mrs. William Kissam II was apparently markedly different.

"Jamaica was quite a sight, despite the rain. Endless banana plantations, pastures, and tilled acres—driving over roads that unfolded cool views of the distant Blue Mountains. Not a bustling place like Havana, though. Groups of loitering men all around—city and countryside—idling while the hours away. A pity really."

Consuelo, Earl, Rose, Mr. and Mrs. Merillon, and Al Gilks were all apparently aware that their presence was necessary, but it seemed as if most of them had long stopped paying much attention.

"These canals are a monument to the greatness of their designer—a real triumph of modern science in medicine and engineering. The man's name was William Grawford Gorgas, I believe," Willie K. told the group. The company all silently acknowledged the comment. A long silence followed.

"Are we interested in dining in the city tonight?" George Vanderbilt suggested.

"Well...unfortunately we've just come from lunch at the *Century Club*, and we spent considerable time afterwards wandering about," the Commodore replied. "Actually, I'm afraid we may be off soon. The weather has already put us quite behind schedule."

The forward deck of the *Alva*.

* * *

On Saturday morning, July 25th, almost three weeks into the voyage, the *Alva* was headed for the Galapagos Islands. There was a long journey ahead, without much opportunity of touching land. The water supply was cut down and rationed. Once they had left Panama, the crew was informed that it would be allowed to wash only at meal times. There were two months at sea ahead of them before they would reach decent fresh water. Among other things, it meant that Bob would have to stop developing negatives for a while, even though he still had a large pile to work through. He was going to be busy for a long time after they passed Brisbane.

For the first time since leaving New York the Commodore and his guests were wearing coats. The climate was changing, and regular cool breezes called for different attire. With calmer seas and cooler air, Bob now felt like a different kind of adventurer. No longer did he imagine himself as a storybook pirate cruising the Caribbean, hunting for treasure under the burning sun. In the cooler climate, he felt like a true explorer, a man traversing the oceans in search of strange, new civilizations.

At noon on the 27th, the thermometer registered a temperature of seventy-nine degrees and, for the first time, the air was dry. It was a relief for Bob and Al to be rid of the tropical heat, as it was a lot easier working with the equipment—much less nerve-wracking when their hands weren't dripping with sweat.

In general, everyone seemed more relaxed. Doctor Lane and Earl—Consuelo's husband—organized a boxing tournament in the mess room that evening and everyone, including the Commodore, found themselves cheering and jeering. A young and charismatic man, Earl was quickly making many friends among the crew. He had been an intercollegiate boxer during his senior year at Yale, and he bore his passion in such a way that made him both personable and agreeable. By virtue of his athleticism, Earl had become the nominal physical director—a vocal proponent of exercise regimens that were keeping much of the crew conditioned and fit. He was often seen on deck early in the mornings, or in the gymnasium skipping rope, shadow boxing, riding the bicycle, rowing or punching bags. At six feet five inches, he would have been able to hold his own among even the hardiest men aboard.

The Galapagos Islands were a very tranquil place.

"I can't pretend that I'm not delighted to be back here," Vanderbilt said, standing amongst a crowd of gatherers. "These islands are a marvel of the scientific world, and a most important stop for the *Alva*. This place holds so many memories for me," he told the small group that had assembled on the bow, as the famed islands appeared over the horizon.

"So far from the oppressiveness of Manhattan and city life," he mused.

On his second excursion to the South Seas, Vanderbilt had many memories to share with his guests, and as they looked out at the various species of fish busily skirting about the ship, he beamed with enthusiasm as he told the story of the capture of the Manta ray—harpooned after a battle that lasted for hours.

He went on to recall childhood episodes: poring over maps of the area, wondering whether he would ever make his own voyage to the mystic islands, far off the South American coast. He was now on his third visit, with a growing knowledge of the place from reading stories by early navigators, accounts of pirate adventures, Darwin's own account of the area, and William Beebe's *Galapagos—World's End*. He found the islands familiar—five large and ten small—lying almost directly on the equator, about six hundred miles west of Ecuador.

The Galapagos were famous for a host of reasons, but perhaps, in recent years, most notably for the near extinction of their iconic tortoises. These were the same creatures Charles Darwin had written about in 1834. Native to the volcanic islands, the tortoises had been hunted for their meat for centuries, used by the locals and whalers to make soup. By the early twentieth century, their population had declined dramatically.

The islands did not have especially tragic associations for the Commodore, though. Because here, while on an earlier trip to the islands, he had fallen in love with Rose.

With the likes of William E. Belanske, curator of Willie's own Marine Museum, and one Capt. Charles Thompson, Willie K. had set sail southward on the *Ara*, his choice yacht of the twenties. Also along for the ride were Mr. And Mrs. Barclay Warburton.

Rosamund Lancaster Warburton was a darling of the society papers by virtue of her sweet and lovely nature and camellia-like complexion. The importance of Rose's presence on the trip was made instantly apparent when Vanderbilt postponed their journey so Rosamund could attend her grandfather's funeral. Though her husband was on board, the passion that Rosamund and Willie shared couldn't be kept secret for long. They were soon inseparable aboard the two hundred and twelve foot yacht, "Which, relative to the *Alva*, suddenly seems quite small," Vanderbilt noted. It wasn't long after they returned from the magical isles that Rosamund obtained a divorce and the lovers were married.

"Seeing these islands now, for the third time with Rosamund, I can remember even the particular sensations of falling in love—that is, the first excitement of pursuing a beautiful woman."

Rose smiled.

Bob was beginning to develop a more complex impression of Willie K. Vanderbilt.

While the Commodore and his party set about their usual, leisurely endeavors. Bob and Al set out almost immediately to explore. Bob learned that the islands were uninhabited—nothing but volcanic craters, one still smoldering as they passed by it. The ground was terribly hard to walk on as it was all lava and shale. They got some good shots of seals, but the creatures came close to pushing over their camera as well as the

THE GALAPAGOS ISLANDS

Sea iguanas were to be found everywhere among the volcanic isles of the Galapagos. Their dark color helped them blend into the volcanic sands and rock of the inhospitable islands.

little speedboat they had taken out to shore. Trying another approach on land, the pair managed to corner one small group. They got a couple of good shots before three of the seals worked up the courage to charge past them, escaping and knocking over the camera equipment in the process.

Later, Bob and Al were invited to go fishing with the Commodore and his party, ostensibly to get more pictures, and as soon as they put the hook in the water they had a big Grouper (or Mackerel) on the end. They caught several large sharks from the yacht, and could see them swimming around the boat most of the day. They also saw a Manta, or "Sea Bat", jump out of the water and flop down with a sound that was like the crack of a .45 gun. The fish was about fourteen feet across, weighing at least five hundred pounds. Once he'd seen it, the Commodore could hardly contain his excitement, and pestered Bob to take as many pictures as he could.

By the 28th of July, the *Alva* had arrived in Canary Bay, docking at about nine in the morning. There was some drama this time, of a different variety, when the Commodore called several of the crewmen to investigate why the ship was swinging around instead of staying still. After some investigation, one of the men discovered that they had lost the stern anchor, the chain parting and causing the thing to disappear into the murky water below—about twelve fathoms deep. At the Commodore's suggestion, the crew began trawling the sea bed to try and locate the anchor. Bob and Al joined in the rather arduous exercise, dredging for it all afternoon, finally hooking it at 4 pm. The event held everyone up—Bob and Al in particular—who were supposed to have had the smaller boat available to go to Guy Fawkes Island and take more pictures of the seals. When they got there at 5:30 p.m., the light was already too weak to shoot anything.

Later that night, Al proposed a short demonstration—a display of some of the pictures he and Bob had taken so far. It helped to raise everyone's mood after a long and rather trying day. The Commodore rewarded all with a drink and a "Well done, boys!" and had the ship's makeshift orchestra play tunes, which were complemented by the romantic setting and the starry sky.

The Galapagos Islands drew men of science and those like Willie K. Vanderbilt who, with his scientific pursuits, was searching outwardly for justification.

Tagus Cove

BY THE 29th of July, the *Alva* was well on her way towards Tagus Cove, on Isabella Island, passing mantas and at least six whales, which spouted every so often to everyone's great excitement. The Commodore was quick to note that they were passing through what must have been a good feeding ground for the gigantic mammals—there was hope for specimens aplenty.

Although the anchor was dropped in the mid-afternoon (affording Vanderbilt and his party ample opportunity to go fishing), Bob spent most of the time up on deck, enjoying the effects of the Humbolt Current, which wafted up from the Antarctic and cooled the surrounding region. He was taking every advantage of the first days in weeks that brought neither rain nor stifling heat. The fairytale Galapagos offered chill winds, crisp air, blue skies, endless waters, and an astonishingly unparalleled disconnect from Western civilization. The most startling effect was not in sight, but sound. When the *Alva* dropped anchor, the stillness observed was inimitable. There was a continuity of sound in every lapping wave, every breeze, every distant flapping of wings, that hung on the air, uninhibited, as the distinct sounds trailed off in echoes from the shore, then into a subtle humming, then languidly into imperceptibility.

The Commodore later took a small party ashore to try to capture some live birds—including penguins and flightless cormorants—as specimens for the museum.

A little higher up the shore, Earl stepped in to help Bob and Al in herding yet another group of sea lions—three this time—into a position where they could be suitably photographed. *Flash! Flash!*—some quizzical sea lion expressions—and back to regroup, as everyone joined together, to climb the crest of the hill back to the cove.

As they headed back to the *Alva*, Vanderbilt was surprisingly somber. In their chitchat, he considered the number of ships that had visited the island since his first voyage there in 1926—"mostly yachts and tuna-fishing vessels from Southern California," he figured. But still, the native wildlife had seen enough to now be weary of human visitors.

"It's a sad commentary on the havoc civilized man inflicts on the primitive world," Vanderbilt mused out loud to his little shore party.

As the discussions about the newfound weariness of the local fauna continued, the group passed by a small volcanic depression that had formed into a salt lake on the cove's surface, one of many alien features that mesmerized the first-comers during the short excursion.

Despite the hype that had led up to their arrival in the Galapagos, the Commodore planned to up anchor at six that night, after only one day at Tagus Cove. His eagerness to move forward both surprised and disappointed Bob, who had thought that they might spend up to a week in the enchanted isles. The Commodore seemed all too ready to move past what he considered "quite familiar," leaving Bob to wonder how the place could be so easily dismissed considering the nature of the voyage, and the need for preservable specimens to add to the marine museum.

Bob listened in as the Commodore discussed his plans with the taxidermist and his first mate.

"Tagus Cove has, unfortunately, lost much of the charm it had five years ago. On former visits, we found squawking penguins, scurrying sea iguanas, vociferous sea lions, blue-footed boobies, pelicans, herons, and man-of-war birds," Vanderbilt listed. "I regret that the *Ara* and *Alva* have contributed to this decline in some small way, but I have always instructed the crew not to destroy life. We have only taken specimens for the museum."

Bob's attention drifted back to the shores. He leaned onto the portside rail and watched some gulls swoop and dive through the mist by the shore.

Then the orders were given, and the *Alva* set off.

The *Alva* was on a strict schedule, and everyone was getting restless with the overwhelming majority of their time being spent at sea. A few had worked off some energy on the promenade deck, with another boxing match refereed by Earl—an opportunity for crew members to blow off some steam.

On Friday night, Bob met with the second mate, Louis Evans, to enjoy some grape-nuts and real cream—opening up a speakeasy, and smuggling in the cream and grape-nuts, because they weren't being served such things for breakfast anymore. In fact, everyone was beginning to complain about the food, which was without question getting worse. The *Alva's* once plentiful storerooms no longer contained fresh fruit or cereal (except corn flakes), and some of the boys had taken to stealing—going around and picking up whatever they could find to eat in the privacy of their cabins late at night. Bob generally refrained from breaking the rules, but still needed an occasional reprieve as much as the next man.

With his regular gang—the taxidermist and the artist, plus a couple of the second mates—everyone managed to have a few laughs. And they needed it too. The upcoming leg of the trip would last for eight or nine days. They would cover some three thousand miles before they reached their next stop, the Marquesas Islands.

On the morning of July 30th, they were trolling in the direction of Fernandina Island, with the idea of catching tuna and possibly some edible fish to fill the larder for the long journey. Approaching inhospitable shores around the black-lava island—where many sea iguanas dwelled among the rocks of the extinct volcanoes—they managed to spot a humpback whale.

The Commodore was delighted to see the animal cruising along the surface "in lazy fashion," and turned the ship to meet it.

"It's either inquisitive or unheedful," he cried out, excitedly.

The *Alva* was swung around so that they could stay close to the whale. Only when it came within thirty feet did Vanderbilt's nonchalance fade at subtle suggestion from others, as many began to think of the "terrible teeth and jaws of the sharks" that infested the surrounding waters. They opened up the motor and decided to flee—to the great relief of many of the guests.

Vanderbilt then (in the most frenzied furor Bob has witnessed from him thus far) picked up a harpoon and became determined to snag a manta ray—but none appeared. Instead, they spotted a school of mackerel and, as fast as the crew could get its lines over, they were ready to haul in a batch, filling the ship box to the point of overflow with fifty sizeable mackerel, several groupers, and five yellowtails. Considerable time was then given to deciding how best to store the haul.

With their daily work becoming increasingly relaxed, the next night the little group met in Al's cabin for more laughing and good times. They listened to the phonograph and drank a couple more Bacardi highballs between them. They couldn't manage to get any water, though—it was still two months before the *Alva* would be able to resupply on fresh water, so it was being rationed at a premium to the lower orders. The *Alva* was beginning to have something of a hierarchy at play. The focus of the *Alva's* luxury, of course, was on the upper-class passengers. The water was also turned on in the guest's quarters. Bob stole a bath down in Al's cabin, because Mr. Gilks was considered of higher rank (the equivalent of an officer rather than a crewmember), and he was given hot water most of the time.

After lunch, Pierre Merillon, Earl, and the Commodore took the ship over to the Narborough[1] side of the straits, and moved along at three or four knots until someone shouted out, "There she blows!" seeing the same whale that had been following them earlier that afternoon, repeating his morning act, again on their starboard side, but some way off. The Commodore quickly went to the bow of the ship armed with a harpoon and an elephant gun. Pierre and Earl remained seated, waiting to hook on to a tuna, but certainly curious about what was happening with the whale. Suddenly, another whale appeared on the port side, moving quickly towards the ship, straddling the surface and shooting out water with "malice in his eye," as Vanderbilt would later recall. "Something had to be done with a whale of that size approaching"—his tail could easily smash the boat and rock her toward capsizing.

The Commodore dropped the harpoon and picked up the elephant gun, giving the whale a ball in the middle of the back, while yelling more orders—"Hard over right rudder!" He ordered the officers to turn the ship and haul—"full speed ahead"—in a different direction, as fast as the motor could take them.

"The gunshot probably didn't do more than tickle him," Earl said, laughing off the rush of adrenaline.

Willie K. kept the elephant gun close at hand as they pulled into open ocean, staring blankly out to sea for long periods. All the while: Rose was typing up her husband's notes, Consuelo was putting stamps

---

1. Fernandina Island, Galapagos, is also called Narborough Island.

The bow of the *Alva* as she charges out over open ocean.

in her album and playing solitaire, Earl was exercising, Dr. Lane was keeping a quiet eye on the ship's company, Mrs. Merillon sketched and helped Pierre with his log notes, Belanske and Mac mulled over methods for various taxidermies, Reddington kept the ship's course steady and true, and Bob and Al idly considered how best to keep busy without any water to develop new negatives. It was a quiet and comfortable life for them all, as they rolled along.

August

"Day to day, I feel like I'm running a small town. I have to watch every little detail. Otherwise, who will? I've lost almost eighteen pounds being at sea. Eighteen! Can you believe that? Yet still I'm greeted with, 'What! Aren't you going to the gymnasium today?' If not by my wife then my son-in-law—who's such an enthusiast for exercise. Then there's the sleeping issue—I'm a light sleeper you see. The slightest thing tends to wake me. But even more, it seems that I'm always in demand. It's true: I designed the ship to make it easy for me to access the bridge whenever I was needed. Every night, before I go to bed, I leave an order in the upper chart room—"Call me at 6:00 a.m.—Commodore." But in bad weather, or if there's anything unusual at play, the watch officers call no matter what the hour. I'd be lying if I said this lack of sleep wasn't becoming a problem. It's, of course, my role as captain; but still, I'm terribly overworked."

It was midday and Vanderbilt was enjoying a reprieve on the quarterdeck—sipping cocktails and chatting with his guest, Pierre Merillon. The sun was particularly strong that afternoon, so a few deckhands had been appropriated to fetch two chairs and a large umbrella.

"I can now manage the early rising without experiencing too much discomfort. A matter of getting up and jumping into a pair of trousers, throwing on a sweater, and dashing a lot of cold water over my face."

Indeed, Bob had, on a few occasions, seen this early morning routine. Up on the deck, Vanderbilt would glance over at the barometer, then he would go to the bridge, to be greeted by his second-in-command (whose watch ran from four to eight), while also acknowledging the quartermaster at the wheel, and the sailor who was responsible for mopping up the deck and wiping down the rails with a chamois (the ship was scrubbed down every day and touched up as needed). He had coffee, bread, and butter made available as the sun was rising. He would gather up his notes, putting everything together to determine their direction and course for the day.

Later, he would usually have a chance to shave and prepare for breakfast (barring any emergencies with the ship). And finally he would go about entertaining his guests at breakfast, in the late morning and into the afternoon. After dinner, they played either backgammon, Russian bank or contract bridge (a game that was apparently invented by Willie K's younger brother, Harold), while listening to music on the radio—this according to Al anyway—Bob rarely saw Mr. Vanderbilt much after the mid-afternoon.

As for Bob himself, it was a comfortable life, for the most part. But as the weeks went on, there were times when things went less than smoothly, and tensions with the crew would surface. August saw the first occasional bickering.

"I can't take these terrible meals much longer. The bread is stale and the rest is just inedible. And we're barely given anything to drink to wash down that awfulness," Morton moaned to the usual gang as they returned from a late dinner.

"If the Commodore knew what was happening with the food he wouldn't allow it," Bob said, passionately. "I've heard how he talks about these things. He insists that the whole crew be as comfortable as possible. Someone's just got to let him know, that's all."

"Well, then you can complain to him," Anton responded, cheekily.

There was a short, temper-driven silence.

"Can't they just turn on the showers once?" asked Mac. "Just one time, that's all—for thirty minutes or something."

"If you were allowed more than a few sips and drips of water at mealtimes then Mr. Merillon wouldn't be able to have his three baths per day," Anton explained, sarcastically. "You're lucky that the Commodore is such a stickler for sickness, otherwise you'd be eating your meals with oil all over your hands."

"Didn't you manage to wash up at one point?" Morton asked Bob.

"Yeah… Yeah, Al has water in his room."

"Oh…right… you bastard. I thought the showers had been left on at some point, and that you'd gotten lucky, or something. Figures."

The engine room of the *Alva*.

"Bobby boy—Ha! He's the real sneaky one. Won't steal so much as a grape from the kitchens, but takes a whole bath from right under Vanderbilt's nose," Anton said, with a broad smile.

Bob smiled slightly in response.

"The Commodore likes him—so he flies under the radar. He's too worried about all those Germans that keep abandoning at port to bother considering 'the official class and rank' of his photographers," Morton assessed. "And yet he's still on my back constantly—always worried that the ship is going to sink."

The electrician had gotten into a daily routine of checking, and rechecking, every little thing that had power running to it, while the Commodore hovered in the wings.

"The Commodore's not nearly as hard as ole' Benson, I tell you" Anton alleged. "The Chief is definitely the one that keeps this ship running, I'll give him that, but the man never stops. I'm even starting to feel bad for those two German boys. They built this ship, but he treats them like real lackeys—second and third assistant engineer alright—Ruid, and the other one. There have been times when they've known things that I sure didn't, but I'll never let Benson know it… And neither will any of you for that matter."

Bob had met Benson C. Martin, the chief engineer from Nova Scotia. He had been with the Commodore for twenty-seven years. Everyone liked him. He had snow-white hair, a ruddy face, and pleasant smile. He was also straight as a ramrod.

"As soon as the ship arrives in port, he sets his force to overhauling pumps, or whatever else. He'll be calling out to me before I can even so much as take a look at the coast: 'Hanson, take down the grinding valves.' 'Hanson, the traps have to be cleaned.' 'Hanson…' 'Hanson…' And he's the one with a continuous eye on the water supply. It's easier to get a twenty-dollar gold piece out of him than a pitcher of fresh water."

"We could still go swimming off the stern," Bob suggested to Anton. "Hey, you offered it, didn't you? Throw a buoy off the stern you said. Sounds like fun if you ask me."

"We're getting to that point, I'll tell you—we're getting there," Anton groaned.

* * *

A new month brought them more rolling seas and inspired an even greater longing for a steady run of time on dry land. Downstairs, the constant tossing of the ship—up high on one wave and down on the next—was too heavy to allow for printing. Bob and Al had to tie off all the bottles and loose articles in the darkroom to stop them from being smashed in the rolls.

Tired of having nothing to do other than calculate the power of the next wave, Bob decided to print up some pictures, regardless of the water shortage, making one hundred and fifty prints, which he laid out to dry on the floor in Al's room.

Monday and Tuesday—August 3rd and 4th—there was lot of rain throughout the day, so things were relatively quiet. The night of the 4th, Bob stole another hot bath in Al's room and then went up on deck for some planned stargazing with the third mate—to see the Southern Cross and Milky Way.

The chain-of-command on the *Alva* was:

Willie K. Vanderbilt, *captain.*

Reddington R. Robbins, *first mate (previously second mate)*, a New England man who'd been with Mr. Vanderbilt for eight years.

Louis Evans, *second mate*, who was quickly becoming part of the old gang after the night he and Bob had pillaged the kitchens.

William Quinton, *third mate*, whose hours usually ran through the middle of the night.

Following down the chain of command, the boatswain, Heinrich Hamann, and the chief engineer, Benson C. Martin, both had considerable authority, after which Bob's gang of the electrician, first engineer, artist, taxidermist and his own boss, Al Gilks, were lower orders, but generally treated as superior to most of the true lower orderlies—many of whom were German men that had been hired in Kiel.

Louis Evans had taken Reddington R. Robbins' old position as second mate, Reddington having been promoted to first mate on the *Alva*. Evans shared many of the overnight hours with third mate William Quinton—who was becoming something of a stargazer and Bob's best connection among the ship's officers.

"Not a lot of folks get to see the southern constellations. Most people in the world see the northern nighttime sky," Quinton explained. "Down here there's no North Star to guide you. Southern Hemisphere folks, they have their own way of finding south, using the Southern Cross and whatnot, but it's a lot more complicated."

"How do you know so much about this stuff?"

Quinton looked almost embarrassed for a moment. "My dad used to take me star-gazing. Used to make cheap telescopes out of cardboard. It's just a hobby, really."

"So what's the brightest star in the sky?" Bob asked. "The North Star?"

"No, not at all. Sirius is actually the brightest star in the sky. You can't see Sirius now. It might show up later in the night though—right on the horizon. There are a lot of constellations that'll you'll never see if you live far enough north, and vice-versa."

He pointed up into the bright Milky Way—a hazy strip arcing overhead from horizon-to-horizon.

You see the brightest star in that jumble? That's Alpha Centauri—the closest star to the sun." "Alpha Centauri is so bright 'cause it's really close to us, right?" Bob figured, while looking to Quinton for acknowledgement.

"Not exactly. You see that one over there? Down slightly—ya. That one's called Canopus. It's the brightest star in the southern hemisphere. It's really, really far away, but it's also huge. I mean huge! So even though it's far away, its enormous size makes up for it and it shows up in our sky as brighter."

"How far away is Alpha Centauri?" Bob asked.

"Close to four point four light years. So that's about…let me think… something like twenty-five trillion miles."

"Twenty-five 'trillion'?"

"That's right."

Bob suddenly realized that he was beginning to feel quite lonely.

"Wow…I wonder how long would we have to be on this ship to go twenty-five trillion miles?" Bob thought out loud.

"A long time," Quinton replied.

Letters Home

Starting on August 6th, Bob was again writing to his father, a letter that would be continuously added to until it was finally released when the *Alva* reached a mailing point in Tahiti. They were on the leg of the trip that would see them traveling for long stretches, and exploring very remote locations.

They had been at sea for over a week, but were expecting to reach the Marquesas Islands the following night. Unsure how much time he'd have for writing letters once they reached land, Bob decided to start preparing his while he had the opportunity. There was another heavy rain storm outside as he described the previous week's events to his father.

A storm petrel (a small seagull) had caused a lot of commotion a few nights earlier, when it landed aboard the ship in order to duck out of the weather. After some effort, a couple of the crewmen had managed to catch it, holding it for long enough for Bob to get some pictures. The group got a great rush of adrenaline as it tried to sneak up on this little thing that hadn't known better, without scaring it back to sea. A couple of the men eventually managed to throw a net over it (to the bird's great displeasure), but they were careful not to hurt it. They held it until the morning, (against the Commodore's explicit orders), and then let it go. And even in that short time, some of the men had already grown pretty attached to the little thing.

The storm petrel was the smallest of all seabirds, Bob learned from Mac. They avoided land except to breed, even then building and maintaining their nests during the night to avoid detection by predators. They spent most of their life at sea, moving across the surface of the water, sometimes in bounding leaps, as Bob witnessed first-hand upon the tiny gull's release.

Other than that, days were slow, and Bob spent considerable time on the forecastle deck sunbathing. He knew that he had to be careful about stealing too many baths, as it would still be another month before they could replenish their stores of fresh water. And although they could bathe in the sea, it wasn't always safe or practical given both the strengths of the current and the presence, albeit sporadically, of various types of sharks.

Nearby on the quarterdeck, some of the crew were painting and touching up. It was mostly the German men whose work seemed to never end, always about doing this-and-that. Some of the upper class were also scattered about various decks, under umbrellas mostly, or in other shaded areas.

Bob laid back and shut his eyes, knowing by now that he was just about the most invisible person on board. Even though he could always find something to do, he'd frankly rather just lie out and relax, since he could, and nothing would come of it.

* * *

The *Alva* entered the Haava strait, between Hiva Oa and Tahuata, and was soon under the lee of Hiva Oa, heading northward along its western shore, passing the East and West Sentinel Islands while moving along at half speed.

Unable to dock due to the weather, it wasn't until Sunday, August 9th, that they finally went to shore at Hay Bay, far up the northwestern coast. Learning that Al had gone down with a stomach ache, Bob cursed out the steward for giving them the food they were eating, sure that the growing discontent among the crew was bound to get to the Commodore soon. For now, with Al sick, all the camera duties were left to Bob.

In the bay, there was a soft rolling current at the base of lofty peaks and coconut palms. Bob brought the still and 16mm cameras along, going it alone since Al was sick. He didn't get a lot of shooting done, but did manage to trade three cigarettes for three dozen lemons, feeling very free and independent until he got drenched to the skin on his run back to the ship. But something about these raw experiences was invigorating and, truth be told, he didn't much mind getting wet.

Later, as the Commodore returned to the *Alva*, hurriedly hauling back a sack of various artifacts, Michelle, Consuelo, Pierre, and Earl went

High clouds over the Marquesas.

back to climbing the mountain at the far side of the mission. In the end, Consuelo returned within an hour, unable to handle the mud. Michelle and Pierre also changed their minds shortly afterwards, and went back to the church instead of trying to climb around the mountain. The enthusiastic party of five was quickly reduced to just Earl, and by eleven o'clock, they were all back on board. They departed at 1:30 p.m., aggressively sounding the sirens to let those still on shore know that they were about to leave.

The *Alva* dropped anchor again later that night, out from a little village made up of four men, three women, four kids, and fifty dogs. The natives were mostly dressed in European clothes, cast off by past visitors to the island. There was one big fellow who stood as the chief of the village and bossed the rest of them. Bob got to asking him how they made fire without matches. (Apparently, the only ones the Marquesans ever received came from the schooners, and they could visit the area anywhere from once every six months to once every five years.) It took about a half-hour of signs before Bob got his message across—the chief eventually explaining how they had rubbed wood together until it burst into flame.

On a whim, Bob had brought the phonograph along and everyone was glad that he did. The music provided a welcome relief from the work of exploring and cataloguing, and the Marquesans proved to be wild about music. Bob was ready with his cameras to capture everything that went on, and it was some time before the party settled and everyone considered turning in.

The following day, the natives came aboard the boat for a visit, bringing coconuts and bananas as gifts. The ship's crew came forward and offered up its old clothes, cigarettes, or anything—"Change for Change" as the Commodore described it.

Later that afternoon, Bob went ashore again with Quinton tagging along to help him with the equipment since Al was still under the weather. Within minutes on the way in, their skiff was hit by a wave and the equipment got drenched. In desperation, Bob and Quinton jumped into the water and swam, wading along while holding the equipment steady.

On shore, drenched through and through, they got to explore the many cliffs, valleys, and peaks, having to beat their own paths through vines and brush. For the first time, Bob got to feel like the leader, with Quinton following his example. And they were rewarded with the most beautiful scene yet: spires rising one thousand feet into the air, full of color—the *Alva* laying in a little cove away down below; clouds riding the tops of the peaks, and a real cool breeze blowing at their backs.

After their work was done, they headed back to the beach, stripped down, and went in for a swim in the crisp salt water.

That night, the usual gang enjoyed a night of grapefruit, bottles of beer and a party on the quiet deck. Bob brought some of the concoction down to Al who was glad to eat and drink for a change. (The doctor hadn't let him eat anything but soup and water for three days.)

* * *

Moving among the islands, by Tuesday they were anchored at Na Pon Island, with peaks reaching four thousand five hundred feet, far above the clouds. They went up to the Flying Bridge to shoot 16mm and 35mm stills. Al was still too weak to work, but since the scenery was decidedly beautiful, the gang dragged him along for one outing before they left the island chain.

Anchored in Viao Bay, Bob was anxious to explore, shoot, fish, swim… but the Commodore always seemed to be in a hurry. Although they caught all kinds of tropical fish—squids, octopus, blowfish, and parasites—by about two in the afternoon, he was ready to go ashore with Earl, Merillon, and Evans. The little party went exploring along the beach, finding more shells to add to its collection. Bob was brought along to maintain a chronology of events. Everyone got wet, but this time Bob managed to keep the cameras dry.

Following a stream that ran about a mile inland, they found an old rock foundation and what looked to be a feasting ground. They wondered if it might have belonged to cannibals that inhabited the islands fifty years before. Only half a century before, the cannibal inhabitants of these primitive islands had numbered almost one hundred and fifty thousand—their ancestors now reduced to a mere few thousand after several decades of exposure to the modern world.

The more time he spent banging through brush—over hills, along paths, beside streams and down beaches—the more Bob found himself completely letting go. Before long the group had forgotten about shells entirely. Driven on by Bob's contagious enthusiasm, the men instead got to picking up coconuts, drinking the milk on the beach, and swimming in the marvelous water. The Commodore's body language almost insisted that he was not embarrassed to see his crew swimming naked, but was obviously opposed to joining them. He smiled, almost as if they were children, in a very similar manner to how the crew had smiled at the Marquesans. Bob saw more and more clearly now that true evolution was freedom—the freedom to choose how you lived, down to what you wore on a day-to-day basis. And Bob had decided that out here, mosquitoes and prickly vines accounted for, he'd rather wear nothing at all.

While being slightly reckless, Bob slipped and fell hard on some rocks, drawing some brief concern from Mr. Vanderbilt and the officers, in such a way as people tend to react when a naked man goes crashing down on sharp rocks. But Bob shrugged it off, and he was soon back to clambering about, his bruised knee doing nothing to dampen his mood.

Bob's letter to his father had stretched to fourteen pages by then, and he joked about having it bound in book form.

He had developed all the negatives shot in the past few days and (even in his highly critical opinion) they had all turned out very good. His eye was developing, his craft improving. They were using all kinds of filters to bring the clouds and green hills out in the pictures. When two Graflexes appeared damaged (malfunctioning, probably due to the water exposure), Bob took them apart to see what made them tick. In this way he was becoming self-educated. And the Graflexes were working as well as ever by the time he was finished with them.

Tahiti

"Father Simeon Delmas is known as a 'living saint'. With a title like that we simply had to pay him a visit."

"How did everyone ultimately manage, then? I heard the walk was rather difficult, as I'd suggested it would be," said Dr. Lane.

"When it comes to the Marquesan hills, I've just written an assessment in my journal: 'The bare high crags of the Marquesas are like titan teeth—sharp and terrible'. But, to your question—not particularly. The hike was not that arduous—as long as we kept to the well-beaten path."

"And the Christian Mission there was well-established?"

"The natives seem to be taking to Jesus Christ rather half-heartedly," said Dr. Lane, laughing.

"Quaint, is the word I suppose best describes it. But the Father, Delmas, has been there for decades. In 1888, he met the author Robert Louis Stevenson, who was researching his novel *In the South Seas*. That's—forty-three years ago. Upon reflection, that doesn't surprise me.

"When our group approached, we encountered a crumbling stone wall, covered in climbing plants, and then passed through a little gate surmounted by a cross. After that a winding path led us to the church as well as a coral structure overlaid with this yellowish stucco, all mottled by erosion. Father Simeon made his appearance: an elderly gentleman wearing a soutane and cross, with brown eyes, a hoary beard and thick whiskers."

"And what did he have to say?"

"As you'd expect: he recounted some of the lore he had gathered during his study of Marquesan culture, and he showed us a substantial collection of treasures. When I saw them, I immediately explained to him how our voyage is scientific in nature, and that many of his artifacts could be of substantial scientific value. He was weary at first, but he eventually decided to donate several duplicate items from his collection of rare archeological relics, as well as part of a collection of shells native to the Marquesas."

"A great addition to the museum," the Commodore proudly proclaimed.

* * *

Later that week, in Papeete, another dinner and dancing party in native style was planned. Once prepared, Bob went ashore to Punaauia Pass, on the north end of the island, and set up to shoot the native feast and dance. Bob was becoming quite entranced with Tahitian culture. Being among the people of the islands was tantalizing. The music was like nothing he had heard before, and somehow, that much more interesting—as if the story behind it was richer. The food was incredible too; the Islanders knew how to cook fish like no one else could, and he gorged on the unfamiliar flavors and textures that danced and flamed on his tongue.

He didn't get back to the *Alva* until 2:00 that night, and barely slept either. The excitement of the evening had his ears ringing. He tossed about for three hours and was out on the peninsula again at seven. He had pictures to develop and more to take.

Bob went swimming that evening in a native *paru* (or loincloth), off a shore where the light caught the bottom of the seabed, even at depths of up to six feet. On nights like these, when he didn't belong to the *Alva* or the Commodore, or even to his father, he was the closest to being really, truly free. Although he missed his father more than anything else, and still saw his adventures as inherently selfish, he couldn't help but feel a need to escape. The funny stories he shared, they were all offerings to his father, fashioned with anticipation of antagonism and resentment, but every day, Bob was moving further away from his home.

Monday August 17th

Up at 5 A.M. and reloaded film. Ashore at [s]even and went out to the peninsular[sic]. Very beautiful scenery. Got a good native girl to dance under the cocoanut[sic] palms. All good shots. Back aboard at 3. P.M. and boxed up the film for shipment, then dove of[f] the yard … and cooled off, then got shaved, dressed and went back to

Punarum[1]. Saw the U.S.C. girls—two of them making a three year trip around the world. Some nerve, I call it. We had a very nice evening and went in swimming again in a native Paru, (loin cloth). The moon was so bright we could see bottom at six feet. So back aboard.

What Bob didn't tell his father was perhaps the most thrilling aspect of his work yet. Among the natives, of course, were women, men, boys and girls, many of whom were completely naked most of the time. Several of the women, titillated by Al and his strange sense of humor, had offered themselves as models. Bob realized pretty quickly that he was going to dabble in the art of nude photography for much of the rest of the journey, growing sharply self-conscious and blushing from ear to ear the first time, when a crowd of native women came forward to see the camera equipment. Al had better luck maintaining his professionalism. He looked over and smiled to see Bob so rattled. The young man seemed so together in general, but they'd already been in a couple of odd situations, with naked women—many attractive ones, too—vying for his attention. A wave of giggles distracted them both, Al seeing that the women had sensed Bob's unease. One benefit of Bob's discomfort was that the girls were all the more relaxed around them, and began teasing him, trying to force him to look at them with wiliness and laughter.

Eventually, Bob got a native girl to dance under the coconut palms and captured various shots of her as she smiled and giggled. She had originally worn western clothes, but had agreed to don "traditional" native garb.

"Over by the tree, here. Yes, this tree." *Bob pats the trunk of a tree overhanging the bay.* "Come over here. Yes, right." *Bob runs over to the Graflex, mounted twenty yards away.*

"No, no, without the top—native dress. You understood didn't you?"

The girl doesn't understand.

"The top, yes." *Bob mimes removing a shirt.*

The girl understands and takes off her thin, strapped top. She smiles broadly and leans back on the tree.

"Yes, right. Good." *Bob looks through the lens. He looks up quickly, then back through the lens; then he steps back.*

---

1. Sic: By Punanum, Bob likely meant Punaauia, a town south of Papeete.

"How about—put your arm up over your head. Arm," Bob *grabs his right arm*, "yes." "Over your head—like this."

"Yes. Right."

The bare-breasted girl, stretching on the tips of her toes and leaning back against the tree, looks straight ahead, shifting occasionally, but never looking toward Bob and the camera.

The *Alva* left Papeete harbor the next morning and arrived at Huahina Island by the mid-afternoon. Huahina was a small village, with a few more natives than Papeete, but little else of note. There was an old 1915 Model T Ford on the island, literally the only car there.

Distracted with his work for the time being, Bob stayed on board while the Commodore took other members of the crew ashore. Exploration parties were a part of the routine now, but Bob had negatives to develop and was feeling increasingly independent of the group, especially after his most recent escapades with the natives. The Commodore's style of enthusiasm gave him a knack for making a tour through even the most surrealistic natural environment seem almost sterile. His glowing smile, with the tinge of condescension, left Bob feeling like he was back in Long Island at *Eagle's Nest*, traipsing through another one of the Commodore's exhibits. Bob now preferred his own approach to experiencing things, so while many of his gang were off gallivanting on new shores with the senior crew, Bob decided to stay behind and develop some negatives.

He ran a movie for an hour or so after that, as if to make it up to his employer, quintupling up as the projectionist, assistant cameraman, still-man, developer and printer. He could hardly be accused of evading his responsibilities for he was all of the above, while Al laid low. He was so far behind in the developing and printing he couldn't see his way to ever catching up. The runs were getting shorter—down to one- or two-day hops—and as soon as they docked, he had to go ashore and shoot the stuff.

As they were running the pictures that night, the natives came around in their outriggers and tried to stand up in them so that they could see the show. While many of them had some kind of clothing, there were still a number of them—adults and children—who clung to the old ways, the traditions of the island. Watching the two men at work, the latest group of natives was jabbering among themselves, and seemed tickled. It must have been quite a novelty to them. He wished he could have had them on board to show them the reels. Bob and Al had had fun seeing their eyes pop out at the pictures.

94　MR. VANDERBILT'S PHOTOGRAPHER

Papeete, Tahiti (a-d)

Robert met a young girl (center) in Papeete, who agreed to dance on the beach for him. While she was originally dressed in casual western clothes, she agreed to don "traditional clothes" and appeared on the beach bare-breasted.

Papeete, Tahiti.

Papeete, Tahiti.

Papeete, Tahiti.

Papeete, Tahiti.

Sunset in Tahiti.

The Commodore had Bob run the picture he made on his last cruise for a point of reference. It was interesting, but of very poor quality.

They had pulled into Fare Harbor at three o'clock in the afternoon on the 18th, with no pilot on hand. The pass was only one hundred fifty yards wide, which made it somewhat precarious to navigate. The only beacon guide had apparently been destroyed at some point since the Commodore's last visit, and it was necessary to steer by eye, with the color of the water as the only decent indicator.

Inside the harbor, they dropped anchor and it wasn't long before Mr. Capela, the administrator of the Leeward Group of the Society Islands, and other French officials, came aboard with the port doctor and a priest from the Catholic mission.

Bob stayed on the *Alva* to clean equipment, but still planned on shooting some scenes as the Commodore and his party caught fish that afternoon. But, when it came time to set out, the motor in the boat wouldn't turn over, so they had to call it off. Instead, he and Al had lunch

Fisherman at Punaruu beach, Papeete, Tahiti.

Willie K. wrote: "We got out of the car at Punaruu beach. Some fishermen in canoes offered to paddle us out into the lagoon. Carved from single logs of the breadfruit tree, these canoes are buoyant and seaworthy. They balance nicely and stand much pounding. No metal is used in their construction or in their rigging. The struts sporting the outrigger are lashed with sennit. The current was strong, the water so clear that we could look down through it and see traces of multicolor corals which, like a brilliant carpet, cover the floor of the lagoon. Fish of striking colors and various sizes swam among them. Our skillful fisherman threw their sharp-pointed grains at fish that were not even perceptible to us and invariably speared them. They were surprised at our admiration of their inviting aim." ("*West Made East with the Loss of a Day*," pg. 116)

and then went to a little village up the bay near the entrance, by themselves. It struck Bob as a real native village, too, with its fifteen thatched roof huts lining the shore, and the couple of Chinese stores on the outskirts. The men and women wore *parus*, and the kids ran around naked. For four francs, he had got some shells made into a necklace.

The Huahine were much like the Tahitians, of the same race and speaking the same language. Bartering for shell *leis* in exchange for old shirts, alarm clocks, mirrors, and thermos bottles, they found they had much to learn about the relative value of commodities of exchange—old shirts were at a premium, while other items were considerably less desirable.

The scenes they shot were like most of the others they had seen of late: remarkably picturesque and entirely removed from what they knew as everyday life. Many of the natives smelled as if they hadn't had a bath in years, or perhaps their entire life. It was lucky, he joked, that he was not making "smell-O-tone" pictures. The pigs were running in the houses (which were usually just roofs set up on four poles and a dirt floor) with land-crab holes all around.

On their return, they stopped at Haavai Bay, known as "Cook's Inlet," which extended about a mile inward from the southern pass of Fare Harbor. The water was shallow, and along its edge there were native huts built on stilts, their sides made with thin and loosely pendant fibers.

The natives were visible along the shore, dressed in tattered, unbecoming clothes that clearly showed the influence of missionaries. The boys still ran around without pants, but they had shirts and the girls obviously pulled at their clothes, which didn't exactly suit the climate. Women wore dresses passed to them by the Ladies' Aid Society: the whole thing made for a very odd spectacle. Bob wasn't about to adopt the native style of dress himself, but he had begun to see something questionable in cultures that were not exactly settled and comfortable in their own skin.

The Merillons were accompanied by the French officials to the north side of Huahine, while Rose, Consuelo, and the Commodore set off to the south side, to Port Bourayne. The Commodore was later absorbed in thinking about how it would be an excellent port, a welcome harbor, safe in any weather, even for larger ships.

Another night of entertainment followed an afternoon of swimming in the *Alva's* nets. The natives dressed in their best, and their floors were cleaned with coconut oil that left a sickly, sweetish odor. Everyone danced about. The Polynesians even appeared to know ballroom dances from the West, dancing on until midnight as they played along with the *Alva's* band.

The next morning, they raised anchor and went to sea again, leaving Fare Bay, Huahina and heading for Raiatea, about thirty miles away. It was a dangerous passage, although a short one; the horns extending out from the reef on both sides of the little channel. But by 9:00 a.m. they were clear of it.

Raiatea was quite a large town, at least compared with the other locations they had visited. They generated electricity by a motor run on gas, produced by coconut palms.

Bob got a small grass skirt and tapa cloth top for fifteen francs, the equivalent of about sixty cents. He then spent the day preparing equipment to shoot scenes of another native dance. The event was on the other side of the island, and they had to leave the following morning at eight. They spent most of the day trekking. Once there, Bob took some black-and-white stills and 16mm shots. Al concentrated on the multi-colors. They didn't make it to bed until late again, with all the singing and dancing.

The following day, they stopped at a little village and walked inland to an old sacrificial altar of the Ancient Tahitians; by then little more than a jumble of rocks that lay in ruins. After digging around a little bit, Bob

Sunset over Moorea Island as seen from Punaruu Beach. The Commodore would write: "Sunsets in Tahiti were glorious. Earth and air became suffused with golden-yellow. Mountain peaks were silhouetted against gilded clouds, while above the sun hung fleece like clouds of lavender. Gold changed to rose, and blue to purple. But twilight in the tropics is of short duration." (*West Made East with the Loss of a Day,*" pg. 127)

Willie K. wrote: "We returned to the beach. A delicious feeling of laziness came over us on this warm, languorous island. Hurry, bustle, rush—these words are unknown in the Tahitian's Vocabulary." (*West Made East with the Loss of a Day,* pg. 117)

discovered a bone, a shin bone probably, from one of the victims. The natives who escorted them there showed them the measuring stone, some eight feet high, which was used to select the victims. Those who could reach the top were sacrificed, by being crushed by large rocks. The site was about a hundred years old but it still made Bob nervous. He felt the history of the place—very real physical and emotional pain—that lingered still in the rocks and dust and ashes.

That evening, the entire troupe from the *Alva* started for the village, where more dancing was going to take place. Bob and Al headed off as soon as they had sufficiently appreciated the ruins, getting something of a head start. The performance was to be put on by the French governor of the islands, specifically for the Commodore. They had to carry equipment over muddy paths to the village about a mile distant. It started to rain at first, but stopped as they arrived. The schoolhouse had been made into a feasting hall about fifty feet long and forty feet wide. The floor was grass and the ceiling was put together with bamboo leaves, woven into squares that made it look like parquet, only it sprang when it was walked on.

The natives offered them a real Tahitian dinner, consisting of about fifteen courses, including wine, poi, tara, lobster, clam, salad, and coffee. The poi was very good and tasted like coconut candy—soft and mushy. As they were all savoring the tastes, it suddenly started to rain cats and dogs. However, the thatched roof of coconut branches, impressively, kept the rain out.

During the celebrations, Bob was busy testing his abilities as a cameraman, imagining himself back in California on a very elaborate Hollywood movie set as he filmed the dancing—the *hori hori* as it was called in native tongue.

After the rain let up slightly, they went outside and held the dance of about forty natives, girls and boys, starting it off. They were dressed in grass skirts and performed something that looked like the *hula hula*, only faster. They sang and grunted as they danced to the music; the orchestra consisting of a piece of bamboo about two feet long, with a slot cut at about half the length, that they hit with a stick to keep time. The drum consisted of a piece of coconut trunk with gut stretched over it, and a guitar. During the slack spells, they got a few shots of the dances. Bob again shot the black-and-whites, while Al shot the multicolor.

They feasted on poi and clams the next morning, sitting on the ground on large, round leaf trays. The natives squatted in double file and ate with their fingers. "It sure smelled like the devil, too," Bob wrote to his father.

Bob and Al took the speed boat back to the ship and reloaded, bringing flares for yet another dance that night. The natives got a great kick out of seeing it go through the water at forty miles an hour. It was perhaps the first one they had ever seen, and an equal exchange for the entertainment that was to follow.

Eventually, they met with the boat, but had to wait for the pilot to go into the village to pick up a few of the guests who had stayed overnight. They raised anchor at nine, heading for Tahaa Island. Fifty ensuing outriggers staged a race for everyone, which Al and Bob got on both cameras, marveling at how the natives were able to handle the sailboats. The outriggers had a front bar that came clear across and stuck out equally on either side. When they wanted to turn around in the wind, the three or four natives standing on the bar would run over to the other side, just as the boat was starting to tip.

Bora Bora

THEY HAD raised anchor at ten that morning, leaving Bob stumbling down in the darkroom. After days and days of feasting and dancing, the *Alva* was en route to Bora Bora, where F.W. Murnau had recently filmed his epic picture *"Tabu"*, which depicted life in the South Seas. Bob hadn't seen it, as the film had only very recently been released back home, but he'd heard about the production long before his departure from MGM.

August 23rd—Bob was busy putting film in the desiccators. He used calcium chloride to dry the moisture out of the film, and then added dry black paper, canning them and taping them up. He put clear lacquer on the tape and put that in another can. It was a long, drawn-out process, but it had to be done. The moisture would spoil a photographed image, causing it to fade away in no time. The surrounding saltwater was eighty-five degrees; good for swimming but not for film. The air was too humid. Everyone and everything was either sweating or rusting.

He had to use acetic acid, sulphite, and alum-hypo bath to harden the negatives so that the emulsion wouldn't get soft and run into the washing water. The wash bath was around ninety degrees all the time. This fixing bath was the only one he could use with any great success. It produced a real hard negative that the warm water wouldn't soften.

He'd had considerable success thus far using a borax developer. The temperature of the developer and hypo had to be nearly the same as the water in which it was washed. Development time varied according to the temperature. Four and a half to five minutes was the normal development time at eighty degrees, using an eight-minute borax developer.

He'd been using Super-Sensitive Pan stock, Eastman and Dupont, because they gave a greater range of exposure using filters. He was, humbly, becoming a great practitioner of both the science and the art of film development, and as his skills increased, his passion grew. As he became more engrossed in his work, he grew more at odds with the abrasive shore-leave parties, preferring the days where he could wander idly, looking to set up that one great shot. The passion driven by idle fascination and the self-aggrandizement that followed the Commodore's entourage lacked substance. Bob was striving for something real. Real craftsmanship, real vision, which handshakes with governors and staged native scenes failed to offer.

Bob and Al went up and shot the rugged scenery from the flying bridge in multicolor for a change. The entrance to the village was about fifty yards wide and there were coral reefs on both sides. In fact, every island seemed to be surrounded by coral atolls, with only a narrow strip for boats to enter.

They couldn't travel at night anymore. The night before, they'd run into a reef with the fishing launch as they were returning with equipment. The only thing that saved the equipment was the automatic pump. They had hit the reef with a *bang* and had visions of sleeping with the sharks. Bob worked on the film until 11:30 or so, and was having a hard time catching up on sleep.

Bora Bora, where they arrived by August 24th, was little more than a single village sitting at the bottom of a towering, one thousand foot cliff. Bob bought a grass skirt and a *poi poi* pounder made of stone, quite a steal for twenty francs (or eighty cents). Bob could see why Murnau had chosen Bora Bora: it had some very fine specimens of natives, both men and women. They shot more photographs briefly in the afternoon but, due to very bad weather, they had to turn in. They had dinner and made some prints.

That night, the natives were having another 'hori hori'—singing and dancing wildly. When Bob and Al returned ashore to photograph the dances, actress Patsy Ruth Miller and actor Barry Norton were there, along with another couple, just arrived from Papeete in time to see the dances staged for the Commodore. Bob joined them all for dinner, as they swapped travel stories. It seemed odd to meet familiar people so far from home. There were some disconcerting moments when it was clear that their perspectives on things clashed heavily with the Commodore's. As they all watched the rituals, Willie K. commented on how he couldn't really abide disorder, the appearance of it, or excesses of emotion; it was proper for these things to be contained. He maintained that sophistication was a universal standard, and that Western culture, the culture of Europe and America, was absolutely superior to all others. Ironically, the one thing the Commodore definitely was not, and could not be, was an adventurer.

The San Franciscans didn't directly involve themselves in any of the activities either, but followed the proceedings with wide-eyed expressions: like children visiting a zoo. Bob felt that the dances and music were the best of any of the islands so far. These natives, more than any so far, had no notion of chastity or modesty, and their dances proved it. They were wild and excited, arms and legs and heads swirling and twirling in all directions. It was yet another contrast, and a powerful one, to the world Bob had known and understood most of his life.

"As long as you give them a drink they will sing and dance," Bob wrote to his father while sitting and watching the routine. Under the bright moon, everything looked very wild and barbaric. All the islanders asked for, in order to continue, were cigarettes and drinks. A dog fight nearly broke up the dance, as two men charged after them, right through the party. It was a kind of existence governed entirely by raw emotions.

Gazing upward at the sky, Bob thought about how far away his life was from anything he had known. He bought a grass skirt, headband, and an ancient *poi* grinder made of stone—all of this for twenty francs, which seemed an incredible bargain. He didn't feel the need for these things, but at some point, if he was to hold on to this part of his life, mementos would hopefully help him remember the days and nights on the far side of the world, watching dances by moonlight and listening to natives chant magical incantations.

The more he saw, the more he felt himself becoming all the more open-minded about the world. The natives there looked healthier than any others he'd seen so far, and he wondered whether it was because they couldn't get any liquor to drink (the authorities were trying to dry up the island as much as possible). He wondered whether he too should 'dry up'—put a stop to even his occasional drinking. Clarity seemed the virtue when alcohol was removed from the equation. Lucidity of thought brought a different kind of happiness—less jovial and more serene.

After an early night, Bob woke up around 6:00 and set off with the Commodore's party—hiking five miles up the coast. The natives put on another stone-fishing show for the two of them, and they got a number of good pictures, with several multicoloreds of six hundred or so natives, who formed a semi-circle from a point on the shore, swinging out about a quarter-mile into the shallow water—only about five feet deep.

BORA BORA

The waves pounded on the reefs outside the harbor, as clear as glass as Bob looked down into the waters. He and Al had been catching all kinds of beautifully colored fish—small and large—and would soon be going out to shoot scenes of stone fishing at the Commodore's behest.

They were very close together and started beating the water with stones tied to a rope. Gradually, they closed in, driving the fish toward shore with coconut-palm leaf nets, making a solid wall from shore to shore. When the circle closed, the fish were gradually run up onto the beach. They got quite a nice haul and the Commodore speared several. For a short time the natives and the visitors were all of the same people, with the same motivations and feelings, the same lust for life, for fun, and for laughter.

Samoa

Futina, Samoa, was about sixty miles from Apia and about ten from Pago Pago. On first impression, Futina consisted of another small native village, a scene that Bob was now familiar with. As the ship docked and Bob and Al headed out, the natives quickly gathered about the boat to trade. They never wanted money for their wares. They wanted shirts and hats, Western novelties that also protected them from the heat and the glare of the sun. The ship's crew immediately set about trading its old clothing for *tapa* cloth and other items. Bob traded a dirty shirt and undershirts for two large *tapa* cloths and plate pads.

Although it was an attractive place, Futina was nothing in comparison with the beauty of the Tahitian ports. The reefs of Tahiti showed up from great distances as a very light luminous green against the deep blue of the open ocean. They were about four feet deep and mostly coral-based. Bob told his father how, when scratched with coral, the scrape wouldn't heal up if you kept exposing it to salt water. The reefs in Samoa, however, were just moldy and looked more like shoals rather than coral beds. The land itself was beautiful, with cocoa berries, coconut trees, and plenty of tropical jungle life to draw their attention: vines and huge trees grew with root systems half above the ground.

The natives wore what looked like bed sheets wrapped around their torsos, held in place by belts—not drawn up between the legs like a *paru*, but worn hanging straight down to the ankles. The Samoans were the "true Polynesians," Bob decided, probably the finest physical specimens of the race. Their skin was a light, reddish-brown copper color. They were well-formed, usually erect in bearing with handsome rugged features. Their faces had many of the distinctive markings of the European. The nose was straight and slightly flat; the chin was firm and strong;

The *Alva*, port side, taken at Samoa.

the cheekbones were rather prominent, and the forehead was high. Hair was black, soft, and wavy. The men were tall and proud, very muscular but seldom corpulent. In American Samoa, the natives were also Christians—more so than in British Samoa. Each village had a church or two. The more they saw of the island, the more Bob realized the natives were, in fact, very religious, but with a different way of expressing their faith.

The islands of Samoa, originally dubbed the *Navigators Islands* by Captain Cook, were organized into two groups: American Samoa and British Samoa. The islands known as American Samoa were Olosega, Tan and Rose; British Samoa included the islands of Upolu and Savaii, and several small, surrounding islands. The two groups were disconnected by about a sixty-mile stretch of ocean.

All the islands were originally volcanic—surrounded, in most cases by coral reefs, within which the harbors were located. Apia, on the Upolu

The *Alva* glistens a brilliant white while tied up at dock in Samoa. Reefs appeared as a luminescent green against the dark blue of the adjacent, deeper waters. The wreck of the *Adler*, sunk in 1889, was still visible, having washed up on the reef outside the harbor.

Islands, furnished the boat anchorage in British Samoa. The islands were very mountainous, but the valleys and plateaus were also extremely fertile, and completely covered with a luxuriant tropical growth.

The climate was tropical, with cool southeastern winds in the summer months. This was where Robert Louis Stevenson made his home in the South Seas. The house was now used by the Governor General of the islands in British Samoa. Stevenson's grave was on a mountaintop, a half-hour walk from the house.

The natives' huts consisted of a bamboo floor with poles all around the sides, holding up the round, thatched roofs. In clear weather, these were open on all sides to allow the breezes to blow through; there was nothing at all to stop or keep others out.

In case of rain, they put down bamboo mats, which were rolled up in clear weather. The natives reclined on these soft bamboo floors. Each member of the house had his or her own appointed place or corner and was not allowed to trespass to another spot in the house unless invited.

Apia, Samoa. A war canoe escorting a chieftain to the *Alva*. They came bearing gifts and began the traditional *kava* ceremony. As the bowl was passed, a germaphobic Willie K. feared for his health.

The men usually had tattooing from the stomach down to the knees, one solid mass of tattoos, created by using a fish bone and a small tapper or hammer. Given the method, it took a strong and brave man to get a tattoo. In that time he suffered great tortures, no sleep and he had to stand up nearly all the time.

The government had schools there and a good many of the natives spoke English. They were not as sociable as the Tahitians, more reserved and proud. They didn't much like the New Zealand government that was established in the islands in 1916, feeling much the same way about the Kiwi government as they had about the German rule before that.

The town of Apia was particularly inviting. Al and Bob went ashore at three, and drove out past the native village of about fifty or so huts. They drove up to what was called the sliding rock, in one of the few cars to be found on the island. They had to walk about a mile through the dense jungle undergrowth to get to it. They shot a couple of pictures and then

Apia, Samoa.
The native huts consisted of thatched roofs supported by bark—stripped or hewn trunks of small trees. Vanderbilt was surprised at the relative neatness and cleanliness. He found the countryside to be beautiful; Consuelo compared it to Newport.

slid down the rock into a fresh water pool to cool off. The slide was about twenty-five feet in length and it ran straight down, almost vertically.

On August 31st, Bob woke early and went ashore to explore again, having breakfast at a casino: papayas, eggs, bacon, coffee, and bananas. With Al, he went back out to the villages to shoot scenes of the everyday life. The particular need to preserve a record of life in the South Pacific seemed clear to them, since all of the islands they'd visited seemed to be changing rapidly. Western influence had long, long preceded their arrival, and by now its effects were omnipresent. Still, many things remained deliciously simple. In the village school—a small hut—children sat on the floor as a teacher wrote a word on the small slate. The kids started by all yelling the word at once. Bob and Al stayed at the school until lunch time, taking pictures, and afterward, allowing the children to congregate around the camera. When he picked it up and started to carry it, the children started to laugh and run after him.

At the Commodore's invitation, the crew danced and celebrated, communicating with the natives as best they could. When the dancing quieted down, the natives sat on the floor at one side of a large hut while the Commodore and his party arranged themselves on the far side. They were preparing for a special ceremony. The talking man of the village—the man responsible for all the official 'talking' on behalf of the chief—started to yell at the top of his voice, announcing in native tongue that the dance was staged for the visitors. Then another man dipped a coconut cup into a bowl—a *kava bowl*—and gave one drink to the Commodore, another to Rose, and then another to each member of the group. It tasted like hubs and was made of the roots of a tree—ground and strained. The drink left a dry feeling in the mouth, but that was soon forgotten. Bob looked over to see the Commodore flinch at the sight of those around him eating—Vanderbilt had a particular weakness when it came to foods being prepared in what might be perceived as unsanitary conditions. In fact, uncleanliness in general was always an issue for him (hence the 24-hour shifts of the deck hands). However insignificant this little quirk might be in New York society, out here it became the overriding essence of the man—germaphobic. The Samoans simply did not understand—assuming instead that he was sick.

After drinks, the native dance began—the '*siva siva*'. The dance itself wasn't as flamboyant as some others they'd seen, though it was very graceful. It was performed mostly while standing in one spot, with movement of the hands and feet. It looked enough like the Charleston, Bob thought, that perhaps it was where the Americans got the idea in the first place—many of the steps were similar.

Seeing the natives together in a large group for the first time, Bob observed that most of them past the age of twenty-five were very fat and healthy. He told his father later that it was evidence, above all else, of the easy life they lived there on the island—peaceful, unencumbered.

There was only one old lady there, of medium build. The young men were very well built, though; very supple and muscular. The chief of the village came out and gave an exhibit of singing and spectacle. He even juggled with a big *bolo* knife—a machete weighing about eight pounds—working so fast with it that the blade seemed to spin around like an electric fan. In the end, he hit himself with the flat of the knife so hard, if he had missed, he easily would have lost an arm or a leg.

Pago Pago

Bob felt that Pago Pago was "by far the best" harbor in the South Seas. The grounds of the naval base were very well kept; almost as well-manicured as a Hollywood back-lot, Bob thought. There were no stores, except a government commissary. There was a radio station, a hydroelectric generator and an ice plant. There was even a small golf course.

The island's government maintained a native police force similar to the Marines. There were no real U.S. Marines there, of course, but the natives had their police duties and the island was under the command of a four-stripe Captain of the Navy. Each of the sailors deployed there stayed for eighteen months before they were replaced. It was a relief to be among them for a while and to hear English spoken, seeing all-around that the native life on the island was much more Americanized than it had been on Apia, or on most of the other islands they had visited so far.

He thought about home a little more each day and the strange things that he missed: the tastes of certain foods, the smells of the street around near where he lived with his father. He even missed the gas stations and the bitter taste of poorly made coffee from the local diner. These were things from a world he was so far removed from that he sometimes wondered whether it even existed in his absence. Rationally he knew it did, but it was hard to feel life back home going on as usual while he was not a part of it. And he was changing—it now seemed natural for his skin to be tanned. The hardness of the skin on his hands, the lean muscles he'd developed, and the scent of salt that seemed to linger. All of these now seemed normal.

Pago Pago was not one of the most refined of island villages—as island villages went—and Bob was now finding himself feeling qualified to draw conclusions on the quality of native homes. The road paralleling the south coast of Tutuila, running twelve miles east of Pago Pago and ten miles west, wasn't at all built for speed and was hardly useful anymore. Trying to drive a vehicle on it wasn't particularly safe.

Although they were friendly enough, the natives of the island were, frankly, lazy. They moved about less: they rarely seemed busy with working the land or fishing, all of those basic but profound things he had seen other native peoples doing. In fact, the Pago Pago natives seemed particularly shiftless, all except the police and Marines at the naval base. The outlying villages were particularly unsanitary—as if people cared less the further away you were from the influence of the Americans. Bob wondered whether the laziness was out of spite—perhaps the only effective means of protest in a world where they were treated as second-class citizens in their own land.

The Samoans would present gifts to the Commodore, but beyond that, beyond conformity to the Samoan etiquette of gift giving, they did very little. In fact, even the giving of gifts seemed an empty gesture. Bob watched as the Commodore smiled and nodded. He didn't accept the gifts, though. To do so, he would have had to produce something of equal value in return and, as experience told him, the Samoans were experts at bargaining.

One of the few things the natives would not barter was a type of antique mat—they were the most cherished of heirlooms that were passed down from one generation to another. There were even some mats that possessed a kind of legendary quality, and they were known all over the island. There was one that went by the name of 'Moe-e-Fui-Fui', which translated roughly as: "the mat that slept among the creepers." It was rumored to have been hidden away for almost three hundred years in the wild convolvulus—a flowering plant that grew along the shore line.

Their drive around the island on September 2nd changed Vanderbilt's opinion of the place somewhat. They were confronted by ugly shacks and the poor roads. He was treated to a particularly exotic dance while visiting another village, this one discreetly tucked away, which involved several native girls wearing *lava-lavas*, dancing about in a rhythmic fashion, clapping their hands and singing loud staccato notes. With each movement and sound telling part of a story, the entire dance was apparently an effort to reveal some ancient secret.

On Pago Pago, it was clear that Vanderbilt had noticed the change in the behavior of the natives and he quickly chalked it up to a conclusion about native peoples in general. The Commodore always had his own unique perspective, wherever in the world they went. Bob knew that the Commodore was not an unkind man. And he was not uneducated, but he was staunch in his ways, and he struggled to embrace the world around him. He avoided many foods. He always spoke to the natives through a representative foreigner—the diplomatic consortiums that invariably stepped out to welcome the arrival of Mr. Vanderbilt. He always watched as the other men and women danced, frolicked, swam, and raced up and down the beach. He was an older man, perhaps even starting to feel the weight of his years, isolated from those young men in his service. But it was difficult to even imagine the Commodore as young. Bob tried to refrain from judgment, except he couldn't help but feel something inherently tragic about the idea of not being able to run—or swim.

Governor Lincoln's party drew alongside the *Alva* in a navy boat manned by members of the native guard, known as *fita-fitas*. These men offered a particularly brilliant spectacle, with their coxswain standing up in the stern sheets, tall and very powerfully built. He waved a head-knife in a menacing manner. Another man of similarly impressive build stood up in the bow as the oarsmen rowed and sang rhythmically, their red turbans and short-sleeved white cotton shingles and blue *lava lavas* adding to the generally exotic nature of the scene. The *lava lavas* had a trim around the lower edge of two white stripes, half an inch wide, and a white cartridge belt holding the whole ensemble together. It was all something of a ceremonial undertaking, as the Governor and his wife treated them with the same esteem they would have shown to a visiting native chieftain or a high European official.

When Americans took control of Eastern Samoa in 1900, the Navy Department was assigned the task of ruling the island, administering the control the United States had so far only theoretically established. The Navy promptly authorized the formation of the native guard, with duties, terms, and pay the same as any other enlistment in the U.S. Navy. The only provision in the terms of service was that the natives enlisted would not be asked to serve outside of American Samoa as a condition of their service. It wasn't necessarily a reflection of their issue with the possibility of such a request (they were not, in any sense, particularly quarrelsome), but it was clearly a condition of service that allowed them to feel even greater pride and dignity in their work.

Prior to foreign control, the history of Samoa was riddled with feuds and wars that had torn villages and districts. The warrior maintained a high place in native esteem, and the assignments to the native guard carried not only a sizeable income, with the pay being a dollar a day (a small fortune when converted into Samoan currency), but also a considerable social prestige. These jobs were held at a premium. The system for achieving such assignments was necessarily complex. The candidates were nominated by chiefs and native officials at special meetings, or *fonos*, held by the leading men in each village. Most of the men listed were from notably influential families, and this was somewhat of a reflection of the nature of the nomination process.

Governor Lincoln's entourage of *fita-fita* somewhat outshone the able seamen in *Alva* uniforms as they went for dinner at Government House. The uniform was another privilege of being in the native guard. The Navy Department had designed and approved the design of the uniform. It was all very colorful and liberal-minded. Bob heard something of the details himself as he traveled with Al about the town and naval base with camera in hand. These were, after all, the kinds of details that would fill in the narrative, that helped to explain the odd sights and sounds all about them; the faces of the people and their mode of interaction, how they related one to the other, and to the foreigners that visited their islands. Bob wasn't quite sure how he felt about efforts to make the natives of these islands part and parcel of the modern world, but he knew judgment now was irrelevant—their world was already fading away.

Consuelo and Earl Depart; Others Follow Suit

On September 3rd, a clear morning after a rainy night, Willie K. Vanderbilt and his wife were preparing to bid farewell to Consuelo and Earl, who would sail that evening aboard the *Ventura* for Honolulu.

In order to make the most of the morning, the Vanderbilts drove to the west side of Tutuila. There a traditional village ceremony was performed for them with children standing on the rocks and singing. A shark and a turtle were supposed to respond to a song of supplication by appearing on the surface of the water. The children waved their hands, but not in the direction of the shark and turtle. As the legend went: a boy and girl were parted, but still very much in love. In despair, the girl jumped into the sea. The boy followed her into the water and both drowned. The gods, however, turned them into a shark and a turtle. After several minutes, although the shark stayed away, the turtles appeared.

Lunch was served on the quarter-deck, which had been temporarily transformed into a department store of sorts. The Commodore and his party had spent much of their time buying items from the natives—local wares, such as musical instruments and other exotic tools, and ceremonial items.

As they ate lunch, several of the natives aboard the ship took the opportunity to sort through some of their new-found treasures. One began playing a musical instrument and several of the Samoan girls began dancing, anointed in coconut oil and turmeric, which gave their bodies a kind of surreal, unearthly yellow glow. It rained hard during the entire performance, which reminded the visiting foreigners that they were in the harbor that had been the locale of the play *Rain*. The harbor was also a center for death.

CONSUELO AND EARL DEPART; OTHERS FOLLOW SUIT 117

At five o'clock, Consuelo and Earl prepared to depart. All those who called the *Alva* their temporary home gathered around the dock to bid them a festive farewell. The graceful Consuelo was touched by the display, her lips upturned in a pleasant smile. Vanderbilt took her hand in his and she thanked her father for a delightful trip. They exchanged a warm hug and kisses on the cheek. Vanderbilt shook Earl's hand cordially. Though Consuelo had enjoyed her visit, she was very much ready to leave. She gave her husband a look, saying as much.

The Captain of the *Ventura* stepped onto the dock. Consuelo looked at Earl as if to say she was ready to leave. Servants picked up their suitcases and started walking towards the Captain when suddenly a loud "STOP" was cried out. Everyone froze in their place, looking around for the source. After a few seconds, Bob noticed the Captain of the *Ventura* waving his arms. Mr. Vanderbilt looked at the man quizzically, but the Captain motioned for him not to approach. "There's been an outbreak of influenza," the man cried, "we have one man dead and six others infected."

The effect of this news on the gathered crowd was severe. The buzz of gossip erupted immediately, spreading the news throughout the crew. Mr. Vanderbilt, with his intense fear of sickness, had the most visceral reaction. As soon as the news registered, all pleasant expression drained from his face. He instantly stepped back several feet, taking an embroidered handkerchief from his blazer and covering his nose and mouth with it. He gave orders for everyone to get back on the *Alva*.

No one was allowed to go aboard the ship at first, but after a period of impatience, Consuelo prevailed on her father to help remedy the situation. Vanderbilt was appalled by the idea of tempting the outbreak of plague, but his daughter's pleading eyes convinced him to allow a few of the stevedores to enter the infested ship on one condition—gas masks. Though somewhat cumbersome, it was a necessary precaution.

Bob helped Morton hand out the gas masks to the unlucky stevedores. About half-a-dozen men were selected for the dreary task. One by one, they filed by with long expressions, preparing for the worst. "Damn. They look like they're heading to the trenches," Morton observed.

Mr. Vanderbilt seemed on edge the whole time. Bob noticed that he washed his hands more than usual—which meant he was within sight of a sink the entire afternoon.

After three hours, the stevedores returned. They weren't permitted to board the *Alva*, but messengers were sent to retrieve the report. All sick personnel had been removed from the ship. The ship's doctor had examined all those remaining and declared them healthy. This news was not quite enough to satisfy Vanderbilt, but Consuelo was quite willing to take the risk. She and Earl gathered their servants and trunks and boarded the *Ventura*. Vanderbilt saw them off with an expression which showed he wouldn't board that ship to save his life.

The *Ventura* departed at eight o'clock. Other than Vanderbilt's disgruntled expression, a few whispers amongst the crew, and a slightly darker sky, there was little evidence of the three-hour delay. The Governor's band played farewell music. Many were on the verge of tears as the whistle blew.

"God bless you, and a safe voyage," the Commodore and Rose called out, as the *Ventura* faded into darkness and the sad party returned to the *Alva*. Shortly thereafter, they were maneuvering into the vacated slot at the dock, to replenish the water tanks with two hundred and ten tons of water. Talk of hot showers brightened everyone's mood.

* * *

The weather was fierce in the harbor that night. A torrential downpour flooded the decks, forcing everyone to spend the night on board. Bob and his usual troop of misfits were drinking a few beers, playing a game of poker to pass the time. The stakes were low, as was the general mood.

Anton, as usual, kept raising everyone's bets, bluffing every turn. Occasionally he would get lucky and win the pot, which would keep him in the game a little longer. Bob wasn't that kind of player; he would usually sit out each round until he got a good enough hand. After a while, his patience paid off: he was dealt double aces. Keeping his smile to himself, Bob met the initial bets. No one seemed to notice that he was playing after sitting out for a while, or they were too drunk to care. The focus was on Anton, who was telling a rather belligerent tale about some girl back home: "She had it for me, I tell you. And she weren't no homely gal neither, her bosoms was like two sacks a' sugar. Tasted like it too."

Bob decided to tune this out. When he was playing, he liked to block out all the noise and just focus. He made his bets, drawing his three new cards. Everyone went around the table, meeting the bet or folding. When it was Bob's turn, he decided to play hardball: "Raise ten."

The banter around the table stopped and everyone looked at Bob in surprise. Not only had Bob barely bet all night, few had made a bet of such substance all night. One by one, the others around the table folded their hands—all except Anton.

"I don't buy it. You're bluffin'." Anton bellowed. Bob shrugged his shoulders, not indicating one way or the other. "I'll meet your bet," Anton drunkenly slurred, "and I'll raise ya two bucks."

Bob added another two dollars to the pot and waited. Anton was eyeing him, trying to see if he could detect anything in Bob's eyes to suggest he had been bluffing, but the latter just sat calmly, waiting for his cue to show his hand.

"Alright then," Morton interjected, "on the count of three. One—two—three."

Both men revealed their hands. Anton sat back in his chair and took a large swig of his beer. Al slapped Bob on the back and the winner finally allowed his lips to show a smile. He reached forward and collected his bounty.

"Well done," Al was saying, but Bob wasn't listening. Over Al's shoulder, he saw two crewmen trying to open the door out onto the deck. The wind was so strong that the young men were having some trouble. Bob recognized them as the two scrawny boys they'd taken on board with them in Panama.

"Hey," Bob called as he stood up from the table, "What are you doing?"

The two Panamanians froze. One of them looked at Bob in horror; the other kept desperately trying to push the door open.

"It's practically a monsoon out there. You've got to be nuts to try to go out." Bob approached the two boys who didn't look a day over twenty. The one with the terrified expression was holding a large sack over his shoulder. "You sure you want to go out in this?"

The frightened one continued to stare blankly while the other one kept desperately pushing on the door. Bob remembered that neither of them spoke much English.

"Well alright then, but you're both crazy." Bob pushed against the door, fighting with the wind to get it open. The timid one didn't ask any questions, but joined in the pushing and after a few seconds, the three of them managed to get it open. The two Panamanians slipped out of the door, which immediately smacked shut behind them when only Bob remained holding it.

The anchors of the *Alva* were aweigh at seven the following morning. As they moved past the harbor, the ship ran into another severe squall, with torrents of rain and fog that blocked sight of anything more than a few hundred feet ahead. When it finally cleared, the wind was coming calmly out of the East. There were suddenly smooth seas as they headed for Apia.

They didn't get very far: a new drama was unfolding. The Commodore received a wire from the port they had left that morning. Two men were found on the island, just a few miles inland from the harbor. Apparently determined to create trouble, the deserters had trumped up a charge against the ship's crew and the Commodore in particular.

"This is ridiculous!" Vanderbilt railed, "Indentured servitude? Do you hear this nonsense? They're claiming I forced them on board; captured them in Panama and made them work for me! I've never heard such drivel in my life!"

"Well, what does it matter?" Pierre inquired.

"Besides it being an outrageous insult, you mean?" replied the Commodore, bitingly. "We'll have to return to port and appear in front of a judge to answer the charges!"

Vanderbilt barked orders for the ship to about-face and head back toward the harbor. Given the identity of the defendant, the judge was willing to make the court date for later that afternoon. A rather incensed Willie K. argued his case, trying his upmost to be polite while emphasizing his desire to leave the island as quickly as possible.

Eventually, the case was dismissed. The men had to appear at the police station one hour before the *Alva* was due to set sail, at two o'clock. Still, the crew of the *Alva* had to get involved, providing clothing for the two men to appear in court, and Vanderbilt had to ensure that all their wages were paid up until August 31st. After an apology to the Commodore, the men were temporarily left to their devices, but ordered to return to the ship before it departed. It was all a great nuisance to the Commodore and most of the rest of the crew couldn't help but wonder what had possessed the two young stewards to make such bold and brash decisions—not only leaving the ship for what would most likely be a life on the run from the authorities that policed those islands, but also, when caught, turning against the Commodore and the rest of the crew in an attempt to undermine them.

The Panamanians were not an enigma. The crew represented an eclectic assemblage of men, some who were seasoned sailors, others members of the construction team that had built the *Alva* in Germany. All but a few were unified by one common thread: the world had turned sour, and no man could walk away from a meal ticket. Some accepted the voyage as a respite from the struggle they experienced at home, others found the obscene riches of the Vanderbilts to be at the level of insult.

For all present, the *Alva* represented a rich man's toy. For some it was transportation from one place to the next, perhaps a bridge from one day when they struggled to feed themselves to another, a way of getting through the challenges that the Great Depression had laid before them. To others, like the stewards who abandoned the ship, it was a chance to escape from one hell hole and go to better pastures. All aboard had their reasons, most often it was a necessity and not a luxury, except for a chosen few.

Pago Pago and Apia

As the drama of the stewards unfolded for Mr. Vanderbilt, Bob and the rest of the crew set about their usual routine. Every island, in fact, was subject to the same general routine. Most of the crew rushed ashore at the first opportunity to raid the local stores. Bob was no exception; he hurried off with Al in tow to procure camera supplies and materials to print the photographs.

Regardless of having been initially unimpressed with Pago Pago, Bob was still inclined to do more exploring, mostly in a bid to get some decent pictures. He and Al rented a car and drove away from the main village, searching for some secluded area that might offer more in the way of natural beauty. Sure enough, the exploration showed that the island, away from the dirty, rundown homes, was quite a beautiful place overall, with a magnificent coastline and rocky rising shorelines. The rocks formed into cliffs against the hillside, reaching back into the mass of tropical vegetation. Vines that crawled up one tree would swing down from several others. Plenty of bananas, coconuts, taro, and other edible plants surrounded them. Bob had, more or less accidentally, learned a lot about ferns, fan palms, elephant ear leaves, and all sorts of other exotic plants. Another thing he noticed as he looked around were the rotting coconuts. (Coconuts and copra were so cheap in Pago Pago that many were simply left in the trees.) The young guide ran up a tree and tossed down a couple of the furry round fruits. Although they were far from fresh, the coconut milk was as refreshing as any other they had drunk—appearances weren't everything in the natural world.

The following day, Friday September 4th, the *Alva* raised anchor at seven in the morning—pulling out of Pago Pago and heading for

Apia, British Samoa. The day before, they had also received word on the wireless that the Panamanians who had deserted had been arrested by the authorities and put under police surveillance—at least that was the rumor going around the crew.

Al and Bob were good friends by this point. They had spent enough time together in close quarters to have an understanding that superseded words. They went ashore that night and had a dinner in real native fashion—a meal of taro bread cooked in coconut milk, chicken, fish, and coconut prepared as a sweet delicacy. The meal was served on the floor, spread on large banana leaves. They ate with their fingers and drank kava. Having arrived early, they even got to see how the drink was made. While all this was going on, the chiefs of the island were holding a political conference west of the town. The chieftains wanted to pay their respects to everyone onboard the *Alva*, especially to the Commodore. Arrangements were made for the chiefs to appear at nine the following morning.

On Saturday, the Samoan chiefs came alongside the *Alva* in a cutter boat. Through an interpreter, he set about communicating with his guests. The men answered loudly, but everything they communicated was succinct and to the point. Rose and the Commodore were to be honored with the title of chiefs. As part of the ceremonial effort, the visitors were shown the ship, guided by Vanderbilt. When the small party returned to the promenade deck, more than one hundred and twenty additional native guests had appeared. Everyone took up their place on the deck and the chiefs squatted cross-legged on one side. The dancing girls, who had come on with the last group, arranged themselves in a row opposite the main party. The Commodore and Rose were positioned at the forward end of the ship; at the back was a set of kava bowls set up for the pair to drink from, in compliance with the Samoan custom. The Commodore's germ fear kicked in as soon as the kava-filled coconut was presented to him. He took it, with a sour expression, and drank as little as possible, praying that the germs he swallowed would come to an unexpected death before they could have time to play havoc on his physical condition.

Afterward the chief passed on the title "*Logoiitumua Aumai Tafa Ua Tau.*" Vanderbilt was presented with a magnificent swatter that only the chiefs were allowed to use, its handle made from a turned spindle of a carved chair and its swatter constructed of sisal hemp.

The title of *Gase* was then given to Rose, and after a chieftain had chanted her new title, the ceremonial hostess fastened a bark skirt around

Rose's waist and drank the kava. She and the Commodore expressed their thanks and then the dancing girls began.

The tom-toms, made of hollowed tree trunks, were put on the deck and the drummers struck the inside edges with wooden clubs to produce a thrilling, savage beat that summoned the dancing girls to action.

As Bob watched the girls from the back of the crowd he was suddenly reminded that it was his mother's birthday.

The dancing girls were a wonderful distraction, in their *lava lavas*, with necklaces and anklets, everything decorated with deep fringes and rows of feathers draped up at one side. The dance itself was not at all like the Tahitian manner, but it still told a story. A group of men and women then danced—the men also wearing lava lavas of tapa cloth, longer than the Tahitian *pareos* of printed cotton, and shell leis. They didn't wear head adornments as many others had.

The entertainment lasted for hours, and although the quarter-deck was somewhat overcrowded, the guests enjoyed themselves immensely. Try though they did, Bob and Al couldn't quite capture the sheer wonder plastered across the native's faces with regard to every aspect of the *Alva*. It probably wasn't the first ship they'd seen (foreigners like Mr. Vanderbilt were pretty rare, but they weren't entirely nonexistent) but, undoubtedly, few had ever been invited on board a ship as immense and awing as the *Alva*, with decks large enough to host a party of hundreds.

At around two o'clock, the local authorities were supposed to have delivered the two deserters. Instead, the police arrived to inform the Commodore that both men had disappeared. They asked him to give a bond of two hundred pounds before sailing in order for the authorities to ship the men back to Panama when they were eventually found.

"I'm not responsible," the Commodore fumed. "We have obeyed the instructions of the court, and you were to deliver the men to us today." He decided to postpone the sailing until the next day in the hope that the two boys would soon change their minds.

As dinner time approached, it was evident that they weren't likely to be going anywhere as the Commodore was still battling with the local authorities. The crew had varying reaction to this. There were many comments about wasting time. Many of the crew were getting antsy, ready to move on to the next island. Those of the homesick variety lamented the extra day at sea. Some were unkind in their thoughts.

"With all the money he has, what's two-hundred pounds?" Bob overheard Anton grumble. "Just pay the bond and let's go already."

Bob shrugged it all off and decided to take advantage of the extra day on land. The joy at having the *Alva* stationed in their harbor had not worn off on the natives. They still exchanged excited glances and murmurs every time they saw a member of the crew pass by. Al and Bob enjoyed being among them, exchanging stories and cultural tidbits. Most of the locals didn't speak a word of English, but they managed to communicate with the photographers through the few who did.

"Tell us more about your home," one of the natives requested in highly accented English.

"Is everyone very rich?" the first native translated for a shy girl who had asked then retreated into the crowd.

"Well, some people are," Al began to explain, "and others aren't at all. There are a lot of very poor people nowadays."

The natives didn't seem to be interested in news of the depression; they were much more excited by confirmation of their own dreams of what America was like.

"Do you have big feasts and dances?"

"Well," Bob began, "We do, but they're nothing like the ones you all have here. Ours are much quieter. And the dancing tends to be in partners, rather than in groups."

"Can you show us?" one of the girls asked.

Bob was surprised to meet a woman who spoke English. "Sure." he replied. Al gave him a mischievous look and motioned for him to go forward.

No longer the shy, uncertain boy he was at the start of the trip, Bob confidently walked up to the girl who asked the question and reached out his hand. She looked at it, not sure what to do, then looked back at his face and shrugged her shoulders. Bob's confidence faded a bit, suddenly feeling like the awkward kid at the school dance who had walked all the way across the floor to ask a girl to dance, only to have her friends laugh at him.

After several awkward seconds, Bob reached for the girl's hand. He waited a few seconds to see if she would pull it away, but she seemed to be a willing pupil. He pulled her away from the group a bit so they'd have more room.

"Okay, so, we stand facing each other, like this." He stood facing the native girl, a few inches away from her. She was very curious about what was happening, but wasn't fighting his instructions at all. "You put your hand here," he placed her left hand on his right shoulder. "I put my hand here," he put his right hand on the small of her back. "And we hold hands like this."

He paused for a second to make sure they were in the right configuration. He hadn't done much dancing at home and was copying everything out of what he'd seen in the movies. Slowly, he taught the girl how to do a waltz, all the while counting out loud—"One, two, three, one, two, three…" Their audience was quietly attentive and the girl was a very apt pupil, allowing herself to be moved and quickly catching on to the steps. After a few minutes, he dropped his hands and stepped back.

"And, that's it."

"That's it?" She asked.

"Yeah." Bob replied, though thinking to himself to make sure he had done everything.

The native girl looked back at her friends and they all sort of laughed. "This is how you get a woman to marry you?"

"Well, not quite," Bob answered, slightly embarrassed.

The girls of the group decided to teach Bob and Al how to do one of their dances, but Bob wasn't a very able pupil. He couldn't get his hips to move like theirs did, and after several minutes of laughter (mostly at him rather than with him) he decided to give up and stick to waltzing. Al, on the other hand, didn't seem to mind that he wasn't doing the dance well; he was very much enjoying the fawning and attention of the native girls.

Bob, experienced projectionist that he was, decided he would run a Western picture for the natives. They played a film from 1925: "*Eve's Lover.*" In the exciting bits, the natives went crazy, raising the roof off the place, in a bid to demonstrate their approval. Bob and Al were excited themselves to appreciate how very far filmmaking had come in roughly a decade.

The natives constantly asked questions.

"*Does all of America look like this?*" They would ask.

"Well, no, but some parts do."

"*Do all Americans carry guns?*"

"Not all, no."

"*Do they all wear those big hats?*"

"*How come there are so many more men than women?*"

"*Are all problems solved with gun-fights?*"

Al and Bob spent a lot of the movie explaining the finer details of the Western genre. At first, the natives seemed confused, but eventually they caught on and started to enjoy the eccentricities of the film. The women started mocking the expressions and sighing of the females in the film. The men shot at each other with their fingers, some dying gruesome, painful deaths only to sit up in laughter. All, it seemed, were having a splendid time.

As they were leaving the yacht, they thanked Bob and Al for showing them the movie. "The film," they laughed, "was so bad it was good."

The whooping and howling of the natives tickled both photographers. As they walked to their respective rooms, they reflected on the experience. Audiences in the States had grown to expect the unexpected when they attended a film. The natives could not become conditioned in the same way. To them the rather tame moments of attraction in "Eve's Lover" combined with the Hollywood stars and starlets acting out their respective roles, no matter how badly they did so, stunned them. It was too much stimulus all at once for the Samoan crowd and Al and Bob loved every minute of it.

By Sunday morning, the Commodore had set about obtaining a lawyer. The rest of the crew had been kept in the dark about the situation so far. The official word was only now getting out: that the men were missing and unlikely to be found. By the afternoon, an announcement had been made. The Commodore had to pay the bond for the two men, which he begrudgingly did under much protest, while everyone else smiled and apologized.

The Fiji Islands

News of the desertion continued to spread quickly among the crew that afternoon as the *Alva* set sail for the Fiji Islands. They were now twenty-four hours behind schedule. No one knew for sure, but it appeared the two stewards were still somewhere on the island, waiting for the *Alva* to depart without them.

The *Alva* was headed for Suva, Fiji. At twenty-five minutes past nine that night, September 6th, they crossed the International Date Line, the place fixed by international agreement where midnight of any given day first begins. It was Wednesday in Suva and Tuesday aboard the ship. Bob tried to explain it to his dad—"today is yesterday and tomorrow will be today." When it was Tuesday on ship, it was Wednesday in Fiji. They would go to bed on Tuesday night and wake up on a Thursday.

The line itself coincided approximately with the 180th meridian, but between the 5th degree and 51st degree south latitudes it was deflected eastwards so that the islands that were close together in that area could have the same date.

"West made east with the loss of a day," Bob chuckled.

He thought about Jules Verne and his hero, Phileas Fogg, in *Around the World in Eighty Days*. With his faithful servant Passepartout in tow, he had arrived in London five minutes behind, thinking he had lost his wager that he could circumnavigate the globe in eighty days. But it was Passepartout who, when he was sent out on an errand, discovered that the following day, that he believed was Sunday, was in fact Saturday. Passepartout's watch, a family heirloom, had kept London time for the entire trip, with everyone, Fogg included, clinging relentlessly to their faithful belief in the watch, despite the reality that all timepieces are set to correspond to standard time.

They passed the native Kingdom of Tonga the next morning—the island known as Niuafou. After deciding to land, the Commodore soon realized that the lava cliffs surrounding the island made the whole enterprise rather difficult. There was no safe point of anchorage for any large vessel. The island consisted of about thirty craters, which measured only three and a half miles north to south and three miles east to west. At the center of the island, there was a lake formed from a particularly large, old crater. The volcanoes on the island were generally dormant but occasionally showed signs of life which shook the souls of the island's few thousand inhabitants. In the between times, the soil on the island's surface was fertile, the houses and gardens inviting. Steamers used to leave mail there by simply throwing it overboard in tin cans, which would eventually drift shoreward. Natives would swim out to retrieve the cans—the practice continued until one of the natives was attacked by a shark.

Although it was sparsely populated, the island boasted an observatory—the United States Naval Observatory Eclipse Expedition was where astronomers had enjoyed excellent observations of the total eclipse of the sun on October 21st, 1930. This was rare luck since, in this part of the world, the sun was usually obscured by the clouds throughout the afternoon.

They pulled up to Ovalau Island and waited for developments until a rowboat with a British flag displayed aft appeared, the yellow bunting flapping in the breeze as they approached.

"What ship?" they called.

"American yacht, *Alva*," came the reply.

Such formalities were expected, and the Commodore prepared to explain where they had come from in preparation for landing.

"Where from?"

"Apia, Samoa."

The response from the British official was definitely unexpected.

"You cannot land here!" The explanation—"You have the rhinoceros beetle aboard!"

"I beg your pardon," the Commodore fumed. "We have nothing of the sort!" he exclaimed, wondering what on earth the men were even referring to. The other members of his crew looked just as confused.

The official explained that they would have to go to Suva to be fumigated. He had strict orders not to allow the ship to land and there was no way around it. The informant was diplomatic about the whole process and so the Commodore could not, despite his frustration, take much offense.

Through the megaphone, he called out to the Levuka official: "Will you be kind enough to notify the authorities at Suva of our predicament and tell them we will be there before sunset?"

The British officials agreed and set off to do that as the *Alva* moved off.

From *Alva's* deck they saw the wooden houses and the corrugated iron roofs. Lekuva didn't seem to boast sophisticated living conditions by any standard, but as the palms and other tropical foliage swayed to the trades above the scattered motor cars parked along the waterfront, they were sorry to trade any sort of cosmopolitan feel for more sea.

Suva was the capital of Fiji, on the southeastern coast of Viti Levu, the largest of the Fiji Islands. The *Alva* anchored into the well-protected Suva harbor. The authorities wasted little time in coming aboard. The entire crew was mustered and presented on the quarterdeck for inspection, as a doctor carefully examined each one of them. The customs inspector forced every one of the crew members to give up all of their souvenirs from Samoa. Bob saw the grass skirts and such as they were taken ashore and fumigated. The rhinoceros beetle would cause the devastation of the island's coconut crop if they were allowed to spread.

Bob had been collecting a few more souvenirs for himself: some shell necklaces and war clubs and two small miniature outriggers. For most of them, he had given up little more than a dirty shirt, undershirt or tie. Natives in the South Pacific wouldn't even accept money; it was barter or nothing. They would often wear the articles they'd traded for until they got so dirty and rotten that they fell off. Some wore coats that were in absolute rags—torn up the back, and the sleeves worn down to the lining. Bob had had to suppress a laugh when he traded an old shirt, for a grass skirt and a piece of *tapa* cloth, to a big fat native, twice his size. When the man put the shirt on it gave everyone a big laugh to see the shirt sleeves only coming to his elbows. He was so large across the chest he couldn't come close to buttoning it, but he was determined to regardless. He expanded his chest as though it would stretch the cloth, until the thing ripped up at the back. That seemed to satisfy him, and he buttoned up the shirt, grinning at Bob, greatly pleased with both the shirt and himself. He was so tall he couldn't tuck the tails inside the old torn rag pants he had on, but that made no difference to him—he simply left the tails loose and swaying.

After going through everything aboard the ship, the customs officials decided not to seal up supplies other than those brought over from the Suma Islands group.

Vanderbilt breathed a sigh of relief and bore a smug smile on his lips as if to say, 'My ship could *never* be infected.'

The two hundred fifty islands that made up the Fiji group formed a crown colony that belonged to Great Britain. The hot seasons lasted from December to April, while in February and March the rain fell brutally and continuously. Most of the islands had a scorched appearance on the north side and luxuriant vegetation of the south side, which was the recipient of showers brought by the southeast trade winds.

Seen from the water, the waterfront promenades and houses were surrounded by foliage, though the business section of the town appeared to lack any particular charm. Everyone had gone ashore early to visit the famous Fijians that they had previously only seen in Barnum & Bailey's sideshows. They found a fine landing stage with a gaudily bedecked Indian police officer who opened and closed the motor cars. In Suva, the Victory Parade was the main thoroughfare at the center of the town, with a well-paved promenade section and a string of small, one-story wooden shops to hold the interest of tourists: the Indians, Fijians, Chinese, half-castes, and Europeans who rubbed shoulders in those regions. There were modern elevators, banks, and theaters in the museums. The splendid *Grand Pacific Hotel* faced the sea. The government house on the crest of the hill was surrounded by a beautiful lawn, and large trees, and guarded by sentries at the gate. The botanical garden contained all kinds of examples of the luxuriant flora that was found throughout the South Seas.

Unlike several of the other areas they had visited, Suva and its suburbs, with a population of around thirteen thousand, had well-surfaced roads that led deep into the country. There was even a race track, a golf course, and reservoir with excellent drinking water. Fijians of fine physique, with bushy hair, were to be seen all about. Many tinted their hair with lime to give it a kind of curious reddish color. They drove about in Fords and other modern cars, and maintained an overall westernized attitude.

Suva, and its suburbs, was home to roughly one thousand eight hundred Europeans.

The English, who controlled the island, were a very sociable lot. One of them gave Bob letters of introduction and descriptive articles about

New Hebrides, New Caledonia and the Solomon Islands. The *Alva* would ultimately be avoiding the Solomons as they were rumored to be fever-ridden and plagued with malaria.

Things were especially interesting after meeting a British man at the *Grand Pacific Hotel* by the name of Ashley who had connections with the Marvis Hedstrom Company. He had plenty of means to entertain them. This company seemed to more or less run the islands, being the agents for all shipping needs. They had stores and trading posts even in the smallest, most outlying islands of the South Seas.

Among other topics, they discussed the case of the rhinoceros beetle that had forced the Commodore to change his plans so dramatically. Seeing the Commodore flustered reminded Bob of how his father would get when he was angered by what he perceived as another's incompetence. It was a very controlled, very contained kind of anger; it was bottled, but it was there.

The Fijians usually stay in their villages, while the public servants and men-servants were Hindus whom, as a general rule there, were well-educated and spoke very good English. Their Indian driver insisted on calling Al "Master" which made Bob chuckle more each time. As they clambered about the hills, covered with soapstones, Al almost slipped. At this the driver turned abruptly and said: "Oh, Master! Do be careful," after which Bob almost slipped himself, cackling hysterically.

The less educated Hindus generally waited on the tables and the like, usually dressed in long smocks with turbans wrapped around their heads, although some of them wore a small round Toppen hat. They always stood by watching, springing forward at the slightest sign of need.

The Hindu women were loaded down with cheap jewelry and wore all kinds of arm bracelets and leg bands, and round buttons that were pushed tight into the sides of their noses. They wore long dresses and light flimsy veils over their heads and face. The Hindus in Suva were about sixty thousand strong—previously "the untouchables" of India.

At the market that afternoon, the Commodore and his party saw natives in spirited banter, and admired the Fijian belles of ample figure and lime-bleached hair who were shrewdly bargaining with a shrill voice over their provisions.

The Fijians did not make much *tapa*. Street wear for women was typically cotton dresses. But for traditional dances, men continued to wear *tapa* neck ornaments and skirts, while the women wore *tapa* shirtwaists and skirts.

Fijians were very adept at climbing coconut trees. They grasped the trees with their feet and hands and climbed without support, no matter what the angle, without using bands to brace the feet.

As they continued their tour of the island, the Commodore and his party also enjoyed the sights and sounds of native Fijian feasts—a tremendous affair. Pigs, yams, taro root, bananas, and other edibles were assembled in enormous quantities. Invited to participate in a feast themselves, the Commodore watched as a fire was laid in a pit and covered with leaves, then hot embers, and finally with a layer of earth. The food remained in the ground oven for several hours and when uncovered, emerged well-done and savory.

When the Fijians had held cannibalistic feasts, summonses were pounded out on wooden drums to bring everyone to attention. These same drums were still used to call people to tribal gatherings or to church. They were made of logs four to six feet long and hollowed out to form a trough, sharply squared at the edges. The inner edge was also struck with wooden clubs, and the boom, when the drum was struck, rang very powerfully. From the *Alva's* deck, they could hear the continuous pounding, followed by short pauses and then more pounding.

The Commodore was quick to point out the impracticality of the Fijian houses. There was one opening—a door that was usually so low that everyone had to stoop in order to enter. The foundations of the houses were slightly elevated above the ground, the purpose of this being to keep the interior dry. But the floor was bare earth and the walls were constructed of mud and grass, lashed with thin saplings. The roofs were made from palm leaves, thatched and pitched at an extreme angle, usually from a high rooftree. The roofs extended at the end to form a kind of cable. Cooking was usually done inside the houses, even though the smoke could only escape through the low doorway. It inevitably pervaded the whole interior; the rafters, thatch, and household paraphernalia were covered in soot and ash every time a fire was lit.

Mr. Belanske, while accompanying the Vanderbilts on an island tour, found the top mast of an old canoe in one of the huts they visited. He added the mast into the museum collection, discussing with the

A grass hut, Lautoka, Fiji. Woven carefully as a staple of island architecture, Robert was surprised to find them water tight and impeccably neat.

Commodore the absurdity of the Fijian housing structures, how ridiculous it was that people should ever build houses that had no charm and no ventilation. They kept no order within their houses, nor did they decorate the outside like the Samoans. The houses of chiefs or prominent people were larger, with openings for ventilation, and also tended to be adorned with fine mats and tapas that hung from the rafters. The tapa cloth was of a finer texture than the Samoan, and richly decorated with a whole variety of geometric patterns, often in black and white. The material was surprisingly pliable and cloth-like.

In most villages, houses were laid out in rows. The streets, or paths, were made of soil packed hard by the tread of many feet. To scare away the rats and mice (with which these huts were infested), the Fijians, in the old days, would hang carvings from the rafters, some of them with human shapes. The effigies were designed to frighten away the rodents, but they rarely had any effect at all. If they were undeterred, as indeed most were, the rodents would then encounter wooden disks with food suspended on the underside as a distraction.

The Commodore collected two of the hangers to add to the museum collection. He also obtained several wooden neck rests that the Fijians used to elevate their heads and prevent their hair from touching the ground while they were asleep. Their sleeping mats were woven from palm-leaf fibers. They were also developing a new custom in introducing the use of highly colored aniline-dyed woolen fringes on mats—a custom that had spread from Fiji to Samoa.

With an English-speaking Fijian as his guide, Mr. Belanske went on a tour of the villages to hunt for artifacts for the Commodore. The Fijian man had graduated from the government school and developed a certain intelligence, helpful for liaising with white men. Although the Commodore could not conceal his dislike for such men—colored men—he at least appreciated the man's talent when the artifacts were presented for his collection.

For his part, Bob was gaining a vast practical knowledge of all the difficulties with photography in tropical climates. He experimented with various chemical mixtures; his own ideas for retaining negatives that would otherwise fade due to the heat, moisture, and so on. And in this fact, he had a great means of connection to the people around him. What better way to get to know someone than to be together on a desert island? With Al leaving him to his own devices, at any given time there was only a person or a place, and himself, with a camera lens between them. To capture a moment, one must learn to cut out everything else.

On Saturday, September 12th, the Suva harbor was filling up. Three steamers had found their way into the dock and at about 2 pm, the crew of the *Alva* joined the crews from these ships in filling up their water tanks. The water was carried in pipes from a watershed in the mountains some twenty-five miles off. It was of excellent quality, which perhaps explained why the people traveled so far to get it.

Suva had considerable dockage for boats going from one island to another. From his high vantage point, the Commodore watched people embarking and disembarking, loading on native products and unloading other supplies for the island. It was hard to believe that the place had once been a haven for cannibalism, although there was still some evidence of it in certain areas around the island.

Bukula Creek, a river that ran through Suva to the ocean, was also a crowded water route, popular with Fijians and foreigners looking to load

The Fijians were renowned cannibals. Villagers were summoned to the feasts by beats sounded on a log; four to six feet long, hollowed out to form a trough and then squared off at the ends. By striking the inner edge of the ends with a wooden club, a large booming sound was created. Bob (shown here with life-sized statue) couldn't help but be disconcerted by the resounding sounds of villagers being called to gather.

and unload taro roots, bananas, coconuts, and other tropical products. The native market on the banks of the creek was a busy one.

Native cultural objects were extremely rare. Young Fijians were more interested in rugby and cricket. The so-called white men's utensils—pots and pans, for instance—were rapidly displacing native articles.

There was a rumor that in some shed remained an old double-deck Fijian war canoe, more than fifty feet long. It was said to be well-preserved and for sale, but the price was prohibitive, even for the Commodore, who claimed that the item truly wasn't worth the asking price. Modern sailing canoes, for instance, although they were nowhere near as impressive as their ancient counterparts, carried a lateen sail, usually woven of palm-leaf fiber. The Fijian canoe, like others in the South Seas, also had an outrigger, and often the struts supporting the outrigger were overlaid with a platform of some kind where produce and fishing gear could be carried. Essentially, the older crafts were not as functional and not as well-designed for modern convenience, even if they were attractive, sturdy and of historic value.

Together with Al, Bob made one independent trip into the interior of Suva, where he got some notable shots of local women diving to the bottom of the river for clams. Some were up on the beach around a fire. Others were in the water with baskets. They would dive to the bottom and completely fill their baskets with clams before coming back up to the surface. And they were swimming absolutely naked. The ones at the fire had just a thin skirt around them, which they would put on after they came out of the water.

Bob still wasn't quite used to seeing the women walk around naked or topless. They, of course, didn't mind, but Bob felt somewhat like a voyeur. He found himself averting his eyes, trying not to look where he shouldn't. When speaking to them, he would look into their eyes to avoid looking anywhere else, to make sure they knew he wasn't looking. He considered himself to be a good man, or at least he tried to be, and he felt like he was taking advantage of them in some way if he ogled their bare skin. But sometimes, when he saw a particularly beautiful woman, he couldn't help but sneak a glance at her bosom or admire the curve of her buttocks. Why not? They were right there, out in the open! Clearly the woman didn't mind. She wasn't ashamed. Hell, she was the one not wearing any clothes. But despite these assurances he would repeat to himself, Bob still felt ashamed. He would divert his eyes and feel a familiar reddening in his cheeks. Some cultural conditioning never goes away.

That evening, a message came through the wireless about the two deserters. They'd been found; their arrest even made the local Suva paper.

"That'll teach those bastards to desert," Anton mused to a captive audience. "Six months of prison and hard labor? Should have been six years, the trouble those kids caused."

Bob, meanwhile, was below decks trying to process his latest case of being short changed at the exchange. He had gone to the bank to exchange some money and found the rate was $4.46 to the pound. In other words he was due one pound, two shillings and three pence for $5.00, whereas the stores gave one pound for $5.00 and no more. At the bank, they knew the value of the American money and they could gain quite a bit by going there instead of the stores. He continued to exchange dollars for pounds when he discovered that the prices for apparel were very reasonable compared to the States.

He also took the time to write to his father.

> Sunday, Sept. 13, 1931. Maybe it's Saturday or Monday. I'll have to find out later.

Enroute to Lautoka.

I am sorry I can't send pictures of each place, but when in Port I am kept pretty busy shooting pictures and can only develop them at sea, as we are too busy in each Port, then again, it often happens the Sea is too rough, and I can't fill the Soup-pot for the rolling of the ship will splash it all over. In Port we are always on the alert for good shots and don't want to miss any. …

Oh gosh, I just found out; it's Sunday here and Saturday where you are. But I'll begin to think it's First of April if they keep kidding about it much more, but when we get ashore I'll make it my business to find out WHAT day it is. …

In closing I will say: I am gaining a great knowledge of the world in general; an education in itself, that no one can take away from me. And especially so, of photographic knowledge of the difficulties and experiences of photography in Tropical countries by experimenting with various chemical mixtures along my own ideas, for the purpose of retaining on the negatives the subjects shot due to the tropical conditions of the weather, heat, moisture and so on, and its detrimental effect on the negatives, (Stills and Motion Pictures), and with such a knowledge I feel I will, when I return, be capable of mastering any situations that may arise, for it all has been the best school of instruction possible to attain anywhere…. "The school of (forced) experience." …

From your Sea and SEE-going son,
With love,
Bob

Viti Levu

THE FOLLOWING morning, the *Alva* sailed for Lautoka Harbor, the principal port on the northwest coast of the Viti Levu. Al and Bob would have liked to stay in Suva for another two weeks or so. The rainstorms were making things particularly difficult. Every time they left a port, they felt as if there had been a better story to tell.

Number 5 loaded with sugar cane cars.

Lautoka was Fiji's "sugar city." Little number "5" sported six drivers but would have been dwarfed by the "Mountains" that hauled Bronner from L.A. to Chicago.

Driving on Monday, Bob and Al passed mile after mile of sugar plantations being cut by Indians and the natives. That afternoon they stopped in a village called Vanassi and talked with some disconcerting Fijian folk who, although very courteous, swung Bolo knives about in a wild and reckless fashion that put them both on edge. Flying knives aside, they were shown a *kava* bowl that was at least sixty years old, and a stone axe that the early Fijians had used to chop trees and carve out canoes. The stone axe was deceptively simple—just a hard, oval piece of stone, about eight inches long. Vanassi was also notable as the first landing of the Fijians after they migrated from the Samoan Islands, a promising stop in the search for relics. Although the chief's house was partly wrecked by a hurricane the previous February, he was now in the process of building a new wood-framed European-style house.

Bob had just finished reading a book by Martin Johnson, *Cannibal Island*, about his trip with cameras around the New Hebrides. It contained

Bob, wearing the safari hat much like the one he had tried but failed to purchase in New York, poses next to little number 5 as she pulls a laden sugar cane train.

all sorts of pictures of head hunters and cannibals and had Bob nearly burst with enthusiasm to see what he could capture with his own camera. Bob and Al had been given many letters of introduction to the white traders in New Hebrides from people they had met in Suva, and had been told they would be treated properly. The photographers decided not to get the Commodore's permission to set out.

Dredging

Passing the southwesternmost point of Fiji, the *Alva* headed for New Hebrides, leaving the Fiji Islands for good. It was a fine day with a strong wind from the southeast. They would pass the forty mountainous islands governed jointly by France and Great Britain sometime the following day, wishing they could visit but dissuaded by reports passed to them over the wireless of a raging fever spreading across the islands. A stop there would mean facing quarantine and a delay reaching Australia as scheduled. They would have to content themselves with a distant glimpse, all their letters of introduction for naught. In the cool morning they caught sight of Futana, then Aneityum, some sixty miles in the distance.

Under the lee of Aneityum they were ready to begin dredging. The Commodore considered this not only a sport, but also a test of seamanship. When skill was lacking, dredging could involve the loss of ponderous and expensive gear. With the dredge suspended from the end of the twenty-foot boom at right angles to the ship and parallel to the sea, it was then rigged up forward to enable the Commodore to watch the cable that connected the dredge to the drum. The electric drum was itself capable of hoisting up five tons and had, coiled about it, some three miles of cable, a quarter-inch thick. An officer was specifically set in charge of the drum, responsible for paying it out slowly so that the net could not foul the iron frame. He ensured that the amount paid out was referenced to dials on one of the three blocks used as leads. The cable was usually released two and one-half times the depth of the sea. A typical ocean dredging depth might be one hundred fathoms, with two hundred fifty fathoms of cable released to drag the dredge over the ocean floor.

As the ship moved along, never at more than two knots, the current was taken into careful consideration. There was just enough steerageway for careful maneuvering, and as the dredge led out forward from the starboard side, the Commodore maintained his control of the ship by running the port engines only, limiting the ship's speed as much as he could to make the exploration all the more effective.

The cables had to be kept well clear of the propellers as it continued on its way. Any large obstruction created a heavy strain on the drum and the officer in charge, to allay any problem, was to immediately release the brakes and pay out more cable. An obdurate obstruction warranted rather elaborate maneuvers, pulling the dredge free of it by retracting the cable. The *Alva* would have to be maneuvered to allow this, but carefully enough to avoid losing a dredge in the process. A single dredging took about two hours to complete. It took a considerable amount of time just for the dredge to descend to the bottom of the sea. Hauling the dredge was a faster process, particularly when the main cable was taken in. An adjustable lead forward of the drum caused the cable to rewind in even layers and it could be controlled by one man alone.

Bob managed to observe the whole escapade from the lower deck while the Commodore stood at his raised perch, observing the affair and celebrating the results of his efforts. The Commodore had become increasingly determined to spend more time dredging. Sometimes the net came up fairly full. Other times, it took time to discover what, if anything, had been brought up. The whole crew was often involved in sifting through the contents of a net when those contents were numerous and could not easily be identified. There were many who outright thought that the Commodore was crazy, and voiced it, but everyone on board was nonetheless interested in what the net would capture, the secrets it might divulge as its contents were examined.

Mr. Belanske, the chief artist-scientist of the ship, transferred specimens to the aquariums, which had been put in place on deck to make the job easier. Unfortunately, and despite their best efforts, a dredge to some five hundred fathoms often brought up nothing at all that could contribute to the advancement of science—nothing except really small shrimp and the like.

Yet the Commodore persisted in his pursuit of immortality. If he could locate a new species, through its naming he would become indelibly remembered. It would be Belanske's task to memorialize the find when and if it would come. Bob would photograph and Belanske would paint. Vanderbilt would reach deep into the ocean to find his immortality, but the task was more difficult than he knew. A new species of insect was to be found in every tropical jungle. But Vanderbilt was intent on identifying something worthy, a vertebrate that no one had previously described. He would be working against the odds: new species of vertebrates were not found easily.

Bob could not wrap himself around the pursuit of glory that seemed to encompass Vanderbilt. There was a day to live every morning; to live for something that might never happen seemed out of place.

Noumea Harbor

TAKING SOME time to explore alone, Bob found himself in what seemed to be a typically French town. The island's capital was a little disappointing, with dusty streets and a quay along the waterside lacking in cleanliness. Noumea was mostly the home of the Javanese, with many small Javanese women employed as servants and nursemaids in French households, wearing gaily colored batik sarongs and bright jackets. The sight of the white, heavily powdered faces of the Javanese contrasted starkly with their black glossy hair. They had an almost masklike expression.

Anamese men were seen walking about in glazed silk pantaloons, jackets and turban-like headdresses. Their hair was also held high by gaudy-style ribbons, wound around the head. Their complexions were deep brown with frizzy black hair, which was often dyed.

Noumea was one of the first places without the faintest trace of the old native civilization. There had been a gradual progression from the isolated Marquesas Islands, to laid-back Samoa, to the motorcar-laden streets of urban Fiji, and finally, as the European influence swept eastward, to westernized New Caledonia.

Their journey took them to the mountains. Hunting there was supposed to be particularly good, with deer in abundance, wild boars, and many colorful birds. Shooting deer was allowed throughout the year—they were considered destructive. They were not native to the land, which made them all the more dangerous to the balance of the natural habitat.

Then there were the fish. A great variety populated the waters around the reefs. According to the law of the colony, only live fish could be sold at market.

At the end of the wharf, there was a forty-year-old English yacht, formerly owned by the bride of the British governor of the New Hebrides. A fish dealer, an intermediary who bought and sold the daily catches from the locals, had acquired it. He put the fish in traps moored to the bulwarks of his yacht and floating on the surface of the water. Many came from the deep sea rather than the reef and created a veritable rainbow of color. The Commodore inspected many of them and set about acquiring some for his collection.

By that evening, they were watching the French fete, true to tradition, with its catch-penny devices, wheels of fortune, and shooting galleries.

Clouds had collected at the tops of the mountains, and it was beginning to rain as the two men set about exploring Noumea, a busy mining town with lots of smoke and few natives. There was an epidemic of black fever and dysentery so the Commodore put contagion screens in all the companionways. One screen had been put up right in Al's stairway, and it remained until the Commodore heard about it and came down to apologize and have it removed.

Bob went ashore with Al and together they drove out to the village of St Louis. There was a mission church, built in 1865, made of the wood collected around the islands with a high-vaulted ceiling and steeple and a silver cross perched on top. Their primary role was to convert a populace they openly considered to be a bunch of cannibals and savages.

The mission grounds and buildings housed a printing shop that published their weekly paper. There was also a saw mill, run by a water wheel, that provided power, a battery station to give electric lights, a blacksmith's shop, stables, and a school.

Bob stayed aboard the ship that night, changing the Bell & Howell camera to Multicolor and taking the whole thing apart in the process. Writing to his father, he thought later about an old dollar Ingersoll he had taken apart once when he was a kid, just to see what made it go and to find the ticks. It had been a Christmas present, and he remembered how his father had sat beside him with a long grin on his face as he tried to put it together again with about one hundred forty-four parts left over and a main spring that seemed a mile long.

After receiving orders from the Commodore, Al and Bob went out to shoot some horse races. It was Grand Prix day in Noumea. The races

There was much to pray for in Noumea, New Caledonia—an epidemic was raging in the town.

took place on a six-kilometer track at the edge of town. They were neither good horses, nor particularly good races, but the Frenchmen and natives got a big kick out of watching them and betting on their favorites. The Commodore was particularly tickled with the whole racing experience.

"I was tempted to put money on the very horse that emerged a winner—number six. The jeers of our companions restrained me though."

Vanderbilt wrote of his experience in Noumea. His party visited Noumea prison where Vanderbilt wrote:

"Two old fellows were in cells. One has been there for thirty-three years, poor devil. He looked out of the window and talked to us, complaining about a pain in his leg. His gray hair and long scraggly beard set off a face that seemed kindly and sad. "He goes crazy," said our guide, "and becomes violent when released from confinement." The other, a Javanese murderer who killed two men, is to be guillotined as soon as instructions come from Paris. The execution will probably take place next week."

Across from the harbor, Noumea was mainly deserted, with lots of smoke and not many natives in town.

"We returned to the launch and sailed over to where the main group of prisoners was confined in the old days. We saw cells where men had been shackled to their beds or to the walls, and cells where no light or air could penetrate, in which men were kept for days at a time. Some, we were told, were shackled to balls that they had to carry around with them. Now all is peaceful. Only walls remain as evidence of those tragic days. We were saddened by what we had seen. Still we felt that the prisoners of today are well treated. The sanitary conditions and housing facilities might be better, yet these prisoners live to a ripe old age and enjoy the best of health while in confinement. Some of the *libres*, old and broken, make a sorry living in Noumea, whatever way they can, awaiting the day when their wretched existence on this earth will be terminated."

The Commodore, in search of his own happiness, had been confronted by a prisoner who had found himself in confinement. It was an existential challenge that Vanderbilt was not capable of confronting.

To Australia

They couldn't see New Caledonia anymore, even though they were only a few miles off the island. Another destination behind them that Bob felt he hadn't had ample time to appreciate. If they were truly going to see all these places properly, they would have to be away from home for several years, not just the eight months they planned.

With no notice whatsoever, they were all given a great shock—the largest whale the Commodore (and most of his crew) had ever seen. Bob was the first to acknowledge it. The whale broke water and jumped thirty feet in the air, landing with a fearful noise, as if the *Woolworth Tower* had suddenly toppled into New York's North River.

"Hard over right rudder!" the Commodore ordered, not believing his eyes.

To their great relief they spotted a huge shoal ahead with the ninety-foot whale still hot on their tail. Twenty minutes later, when everyone had finally caught their breath, the steam pilot boat was alongside the *Alva* to pilot the vessel.

In Moreton Bay, there were many lights and gas buoys. They passed through the ever-shifting shoals, and an hour later, had entered the mouth of the Brisbane River. The city of Brisbane was situated on the banks of the river, about fourteen miles farther up.

"It's the funniest place," the Commodore said to the pilot. "This part of the world, everything is different. Your spring is just starting at the end of September, when, in our country, we look forward to winter. At Christmas, you go bathing, whereas we go shopping. The glass goes down for a northerly wind, whereas in our country, it goes up. And your trees," he added, "do not lose their leaves but shed their bark. You drive to the left, have mosquitoes when we have snow, and call squalls 'busters'."

The pilot smiled broadly and nodded.

Rumor had it that the *Alva* was going into dry-dock here to have the moss and barnacles scraped off of its bottom. They expected to remain in Brisbane about a week in total, and there was also talk that Bob and Al might drive down to Sydney. The mail wasn't due to arrive at Brisbane until October, so Bob was holding a letter to his father until then. He expected some mail in Brisbane. He read all of his father's letters over again the night before. He'd gotten a hold of a good coconut wood cane for his father, and couldn't wait to get it to him, but couldn't risk mailing it. He also had a kava bowl from Samoa to use as a fruit tray.

They were traveling quite a bit below the equator; the air was cool and invigorating. Bob now needed a sweater when up on deck, as did most everyone else. He also needed a new diary—the one his father had given him was already full.

They finally entered Brisbane at 5:30 p.m. and tried to get into dry-dock, but the dock was only made to accommodate vessels up to fifteen feet in draft. At nineteen feet, they were out of luck and instead were directed, just before dark, to an obscure wharf owned by a flour-milling company, close to a large bridge that spanned the river in the heart of Brisbane.

The *Alva*'s crew was besieged by newspaper reporters as soon as it landed, interrupting the process of its departure into the city in order to photograph everyone. The Commodore said a few words for the *Fox Movietime News*.

Vanderbilt wrote of the experience: "A mob of reporters interviewed and photographed us. We posed and talked for Fox Movietone. We were asked to stand, sit, talk, and walk. Mr. Gilks, master of our own movies, looked on with envy. I wondered what he would think up for the rest of the trip."

The Movietone cameraman took everyone to lunch as thanks for what they did for him.

The mail was pouring in: telegram after telegram arriving and people all over requesting the Commodore to speak to them about his adventures. What did he think of Australia? Would he say something about the unemployment? Did he care to express his opinions on the financial debacle? What did the *Alva* cost him? Did Mrs. Vanderbilt ever get seasick? What was the purpose of their visit to Australia in the first place?

Brisbane was in a very depressed state. Bob had women approach him the first night as they came out from dinner at the *Lennon Hotel*. The *Lennon* was a very high-class sort of place and it was drawing attention to him. He hadn't seen a good-looking girl in Brisbane yet, only sour-faced ones, and the men went about shabbily dressed, a drawn look upon their faces. Everything was far worse there than in Hollywood or any part of the U.S. Bob knew of.

After dinner, he exchanged some U.S. currency at a Brisbane bank. He got one pound, four shillings and sixpence for a five. The value of the pound was down. Bob made a dollar on the exchange, but the eight pounds, twelve shillings and 13 pence in his pockets felt like eight pounds of dead weight.

Bob weighed himself at ten stone. So he weighed one-hundred and forty pounds, and the funny part of it was that he had had a dinner of four pounds and he was still the same weight. Then there was the eight pounds in English money in his pocket. There was something wrong with the scales, he decided, another matter for the complaint department of the union local 659.

Brisbane

THE MORE Bob saw of Brisbane, the more convinced he was that it looked a good deal like a Mississippi River city. The city was, after all, situated about thirty miles up a river and had a kind of depressed border-town feel to it. It was a little seedy, obviously fun-loving, and the prices of materials were very low since no one could sell anything for close to its actual value. The modern buildings were spread over a big area. The city hall was imposing, costing something in the region of £800,000. The place boasted considerable traffic congestion and all the drama of traffic lights and one-way streets could throw off even the most capable and experienced of drivers. There was even something familiar about the bustle of Brisbane—the same vibrations of Manhattan transplanted to the Australian coast. The people also had mannerisms similar to New Englanders, sanguine people in a young country.

The Commodore said goodbye to his two principal companions, Michelle and Pierre, who had left for Sydney and Melbourne. He was now wrapped up in his own private entertainments. He was collecting again, as much as possible, and recording in his journal. The officials had not been at all disagreeable. They were, in fact, most courteous. They had been particularly thorough; so much so that at the end of thirty-six hours, the Commodore had a better inventory of the ship's content than he had ever expected to have. Yet, it was not possible to eat food aboard the ship, smoke the ship's cigarettes or cigars, or even drink their own milk brought from the States. Nothing on the ship, from engine room parts to the stores' contents, could be replaced without taxes being paid. They even had to pay a tax for running auxiliaries and for oil consumed.

Despite the customs laws, the Australians were an interesting lot. The Commodore was invited to morning teas and regattas, and to deliver lectures. He was asked to purchase various rare objects, whole valuable collections in some instances. It was even propositioned to open his yacht up to public viewing, an offer he flatly rejected. They offered theater seats for free, put the Commodore and his party up at clubs, and gave numerous other courtesies. Entertaining the crew was just another one of these benefits.

On Saturday, Bob headed out with Al and a small gang to a local scene—the *Carlton cabaret*. Fun was very much in the cards now that the *Alva* had arrived in a place somewhat resembling something familiar to the crew. Brisbane wasn't exactly an American town, but it had enough in common that they felt comfortable with letting loose. They had a very nice dinner and danced at the party, a veritable spectacle.

Men and women were arrayed in the usual format: guys in clusters afraid to cross the abyss and mix with the girls, girls in groups gathering the courage to find themselves some company. But the standoff didn't last for long.

For the first time in a while, Bob found himself confronted by attractive women. He danced his "fool head off," he joked to his father, after meeting *quite* an English girl who kept his attention for most of the evening. Everything fell into a kind of haziness by the late night, though, so it was hard to determine precisely how much fun he had actually had.

Sunday, he found himself playing ball in the morning, working on stills in the afternoon, and down for a private showing of some MGM pictures in the evening. They saw *Politics* with Marie Dressler and Polly Moran and faced a bombardment of questions from other audience members—Australian ones—as soon as it became clear that Bob and Al were from Hollywood.

Bob felt like a minor celebrity. He was not accustomed to all that attention. The Aussies wanted to know if he had ever seen some of the big stars. He was embarrassed and felt that Al Gilks should field the questions. But it wasn't a controlled situation, certainly not a press conference, and given a few beers he would have complied. Al seemed to be comfortable with the questions and offered a polite smile and said that he had seen many stars. But instead of providing a list, he volunteered that most of them were nice people, not that different from Mr. Vanderbilt.

There was something in the air in Brisbane, something about the place that made him tingle. Perhaps it was the women all around. He wasn't exactly on the market yet, but some clearly saw him as something of a catch.

Taking time to explore the land, Bob drove out into the bush with the Commodore and his party, a beautiful drive through eucalyptus trees, pines, and figs. Around every corner, there seemed to be a fine view worth appreciating, and in clearings, every so often, there were farms and sleek cattle that fed in the fields. As hard as they searched, though, they could find no underbrush. As they learned later, the chauffer referred to the virgin timber as brush. Such small, nuanced differences in language were hard to pick up on.

The Carlton Cabaret

THE NEXT DAY, stiff from a baseball game and late night partying, Bob could hardly crawl out of bed. He had every intention of spending the night in, but Al and the boys dragged him to the Carlton Cabaret. At first, he resented the need to dress presentably, but the energy at the cabaret soon put him in a better mood. Surrounded by the girls of Brisbane, he spent several hours dancing and admiring the local beauties.

Anton seemed to think that being a foreigner made him as valuable as gold, which was mostly true. In the face of the world depression, everyone was seeking an escape from their gloomy lives. He was a man who came from far away and had seen much of the world, which made him quite attractive, as can be imagined. But Anton took this to his head, assuming all women were just dying for a chance at him.

The guys stood around, watching Anton chat up the locals, mostly too shy or embarrassed to do any talking themselves. Anton set his eyes on one Australian girl, a beautiful specimen with an attractive, womanly figure. She stood several inches above the other girls. Though naturally tall, she still wore two-inch heels. Her smile dazzled as she laughed with her friends, who danced in a circle, unaware of the predator who watched them.

"Hey dolls," Anton called to get the girls' attention. They paused and looked at him, wondering why someone had addressed them. "My name's Anton. I've come all the way here from the good ol' U.S. of A. with my lads here." He motioned behind him. Most of the guys were intrigued by Anton's brazenness, but Bob was looking off in the distance, slightly embarrassed by his friend's shamelessness.

Anton focused on the girl he'd been admiring before. "You wan' a dance?"

"With who?" She replied coyly.

"Me," he replied, as if it was to an audience.

"Oh no, thank you, but I don't think so."

The guys were taken aback by her response and started laughing at Anton's rejection. His pride hurt, the man bellowed, "Well, why the hell not?"

"I'd rather dance with him."

It took Bob several seconds to realize that all eyes were now on him. Anton was giving him a dirty look, but he looked past his friend at the beautiful woman whose eyes were now looking in his direction. One side of her lips turned up in a lopsided smirk.

"Well, what do you say?" She asked, one hand on her hip, daring him to say yes.

"Sure," he shrugged.

Before he knew it, the dame was gliding over to him and sliding her arm around his. "If you'll excuse us, gents." She guided Bob further into the crowd, away from his friends. He heard jeers and hoots behind him. He wished he had seen Anton's expression, but then he gazed at his new dancing partner, and suddenly everything else was unimportant.

She was beautiful in that one of a kind way; it was clear there was no one else like her in the world. She looked nothing like Ginger Rogers, Bette Davis, or any of the other movie stars men fawned over. Her beauty was her own—unique and timeless. Her hair barely covered her slender neck, which led seamlessly to her shoulders. Bob watched her collarbone poke out as the dance caused her to move her shoulders. With his eyes, he followed her plump arms all the way down to her short fingers. Her hands looked like doll's hands—minuscule in his awkward, giant hands which wrapped around hers and made them disappear. But inside his palms, he felt the warmth of her stodgy fingers and held them even tighter.

He desperately wanted to peak at her bosom. He could tell her breasts weren't large, but they seemed the perfect size: apples that he could hold in his hands. He thought of the many native girls he had seen naked, and suddenly felt embarrassed for thinking of this beautiful woman in such a way.

Instead, he looked at her eyes; and in them he gleaned the stars. Her eyes shone with the sparkle of passion, the sign of someone who loved fiercely. Someone who was stubborn and occasionally given to foul moods. Her eyes shone of an inner wisdom, as well as an innate youthful curiosity.

Suddenly he realized that he was not the only voyeur: she was looking in his eyes just as he was looking at hers. He suddenly felt awkward, like he'd been caught doing something wrong. She smiled at him, showing teeth that were just a bit too pointy but seemed to reflect her zesty personality.

Her name was Jo. They had dinner together and danced the night away, smiling and laughing as if they were old friends. In the back of his mind was the idea that perhaps this vivacious, enticing, ambitious young woman might be the person he was destined to love. She could be his true love, fulfilling all of those childhood dreams for such a thing. Still, he kept telling himself not to get too wrapped up with anything on his travels. He was working, after all, and he had to return home to a life totally removed from the *Alva* and the Commodore, from Australia and every other place they had been or would visit. And what hope did he have that any woman would drop everything suddenly to be with him, away from her home and family?

There was something about Jo, though. She had something so easy-going about her, something so vibrant. He had a hard time keeping his head from the second he'd met her. Even after only so short an acquaintance, he started to see her and him together years into the future, happy and laughing as they had that night.

Bob excitedly wrote his father about the fact that he'd met "a very nice English girl" who was "a very good dancer." But he decided to "keep the rest to [him]self, for daddies mustn't know too much."

They were going out again for dinner and dancing, alone this time, and unencumbered by Al and his daydreaming of his wife. The more Bob thought about Al and his wife, the more he was thinking about Jo for himself. She was so excited to hear about his life and so open to talking about her own: her family, work, friends, and beyond that, the things she wanted from life. She loved to hear his stories as much as he loved to tell them, but not in an obsequious way. She was a good dancer, and Bob discovered he loved to dance. He was inspired by all the native dances he had seen over the past weeks and by the need to let off some steam after being cooped up on the *Alva* for a couple of days straight.

Jo wasn't like the other young women in the town—latching on to sailors and other foreign, working men, in the hope of finding an easy husband, and a quickie wedding to follow. It was an age-old story and he knew it. No, Jo wasn't like that, just like the Commodore's second wife hadn't turned out as Bob had imagined her: a latching, gold-digging woman as you might expect. Lady Rose was sensible, and very obviously, genuinely in love with her husband. He trusted her, one of the few people he trusted explicitly. And Jo seemed at least as trustworthy to Bob. She was working and she had goals for herself that didn't involve having a man on her arm. She was training to be a nurse and working part-time to help support her family. She wanted to travel someday soon, which explained her particular interest in him, and she hoped most particularly to travel to America someday to see New York and Hollywood and the bay of San Francisco everyone said was so spectacular.

When Jo talked about her dreams and hopes for the future, her eyes lit up. Her smile was electric, and it told him that he might stay in Australia for good. Give it all up.

On seeing the state of things in Brisbane, Bob also felt the need to spend as much money as he could. The taxis there were so cheap it paid to ride in them instead of streetcars. He took Jo home in a cab and then drove about ten miles back to the ship. The whole evening cost him only $3 when, in the States, the same kind of night out would set him back about $50 even before the good beers and wines for himself and his guest. It all seemed quite ridiculous, really.

The next day they went ashore again and had lunch with one of the leading photographers of Brisbane. It was something to take Bob's mind off of Jo. He was already thinking of taking her out again, going to dinner and the works. The photographer had lots of questions and was very interested in all of the equipment Al and Bob had to show him. Bob helped him with panchromatic stock. The stuff had just been introduced into the country.

Back aboard the *Alva* at three, Bob got to writing postcards and letters, distracting himself from thoughts of Jo. He'd called her to set a date for eight at the same club. Bob was trying to nap as someone came hurtling down the hallway. Morton came crashing through the door so hard, tumbling over himself, that Bob almost punched him in the nose—he'd given him such a fright.

"This you're never going to believe. Never, I tell you."

"What, that you brought the blond home? You're right, I don't believe you."

"No, no, listen to this. So yesterday the Commodore calls on the American consul, right, a Mr. A.R. Preston, and drives to Southport. They go lunching at this fancy hotel. Him, Rose, Lane, and the consul and his wife—silver spoons and all. So, while they're adding up the bill for their meal, they hear this scratching and shuffling, and when they finally look up, the Commodore almost falls backwards out of his chair. Rose—she jumps to her feet, damn hysterical. She's screaming in fright and everyone else is just stunned and cowering."

"So, what was it?" Bob asked, admittedly intrigued.

"A bear."

"A what?"

"A bear, in the hotel dining room."

"Like a rug? One of Belanske's jobs then?"

"No, like a bear—a black bear."

Bob stared, confused, then thought for a second.

"Are there even black bears in Australia?"

Morton apparently hadn't considered it.

"I don't think so—koalas."

"So, you're pulling my leg."

"I'm telling you—a black bear in the dining room looking for a fancy meal. The thing stands up on its hind feet right in front of Mrs. Vanderbilt, face right up close to hers, and she goes white as a sheet. The bear is startled by all the woman's shrieks, grabs a hold of Doctor Lane's arm with his paws, and he goes white, too. This waiter reacts quickly, though. He stands up, taking a table cloth, and throws it around the bear's neck like he's Tarzan. Another waiter grabs a hold of a second table cloth and throws it around the bear's head. They dragged it right out into the ante room, and it bites the cashier. By now everyone's screaming to shoot the thing, but these Australian blokes aren't afraid of some damn bear. They drag the thing right back to the adjacent zoo and then just get back to pouring drinks like nothing's happened."

"So, how did the Commodore react?"

"Well, everyone was shaken up, obviously. Apparently the Commodore was quick to joke that they had had many such sorts of experiences in dining rooms. The word is that the same dining room apparently saw a woman bitten by a leopard, so if anything they got lucky."

"That's the craziest story I ever heard," Bob exclaimed, flatly.

"I know, right? I told you, you wouldn't believe me. I'm telling you—Australia…"

It was the kind of story that Bob wanted to share. He thought of telling Jo to get an Australian viewpoint.

Doctor Lane stayed in Brisbane to mind the ship while Rose and the Commodore headed to Sydney by train with Bob in tow to record it all. They left at a quarter to ten, with the roadbed proving not at all as bad as they thought. They crossed through a mountain range and then descended from that at Casino. It was an overnight trip, yet everyone seemed to shout along the route. Even the track gangs shouted, and when, at Grafton, they took a ferry across the river, the Commodore and Rose considered it a definite relief that they might rest their ears.

By Monday morning, they were fifty miles from Sydney. They arrived at eight and checked into the *Australia Hotel*, where they planned to spend the rest of their time. They gave little thought to the *Alva's* crew back in Brisbane from then on, concentrating instead on taking in everything that Sydney had to offer: streetcars, motors, parks, museums, and theaters, again reminiscent of an American city, but certainly grander and more refined than Brisbane.

The Sydney Harbor Bridge was almost completed and had the world's next-to-largest span. It was among the greatest works of its kind and a must-see attraction. There was a tragedy manifest in it though, since it was being constructed under heavy losses to the steel company. The construction costs were running way above what was projected, and everyone was teetering on the brink of nervous collapse and exhaustion as a result of the financial strain. Bob thought romantically about crossing the bridge with Jo when it was finished. It was so grand; it would make a fine climb someday.

They drove to Sydney Head that afternoon, and later motored to the suburbs, throwing boomerangs and visiting the zoo and beaches. Vanderbilt insisted that they stop to visit the monuments built to two other great explorers—La Perouse and Cook—before movies and a cabaret completed the day.

Another month was drawing to a close. The Commodore and his wife had returned from their adventure in Sydney and everyone on the crew had suddenly stepped up, and cleaned themselves up so as not to give too much away about what they had been doing, or not doing, over the last several days. Back in Brisbane, Bob stayed aboard all day, making enlargements for the Commodore. He didn't want to, but he had his orders. He showed his work to Mr. Thiel, the photographer who had such a renowned reputation in Brisbane. Bob was tickled that the man had learned a few things from him, just watching his routine work. Thiel was supposed to be the best in Brisbane.

The end of the month brought more time with Jo. They made a plan to meet in front of the *Carlton*. They went for a drive together and then headed upstairs at the hotel. Jo settled on a chair by the window, looking at the Brisbane skyline.

"Would you like some wine?" Bob asked, trying to be the gracious host.

"Isn't it inappropriate enough that I'm in your hotel room?" Jo quipped.

"Touché," Bob replied with a smile. He sat down beside her and looked out at the view. He pretended to be preoccupied with what he was seeing, but really he was thinking about how close Jo was, but how he wanted her to be closer. She reached over and laced her fingers with his, not even looking in his direction. Her fingers felt so small that he worried about crushing them. He held her hand as if it were something very precious.

After several minutes, Jo broke the silence: "Isn't life strange?"

"How do you mean?"

"Just how everything works. Either everything is this big accident or it's all fate. It can't be anything in between. But think of all the accidents that had to happen exactly as they did in order for us to meet. I had to choose that night to go with my girlfriends to the *Carlton*. And you and your friends had to choose that exact night as well. Of all the places we could have gone in Brisbane, we had to choose that exact one. On the same night, no less. And you had to be chosen to work on this cruise. And our parents had to meet in a similar precise manner in order to give birth to us. And if my ancestors hadn't moved to Australia, I wouldn't have been here. Likewise with yours in America. And if any of the choices we made in our life, or any of the choices any of our ancestors made for generations and generations, had been any different, we never would have met." She paused, letting her thoughts digest. "It makes me feel small, really."

"It makes you almost believe in fate, doesn't it?" Bob responded. He pulled her onto his lap and caressed her cheek. He thought to himself that she was the most beautiful woman he had ever met, but he didn't want to say it; as if her beauty were some great secret that only he was privy to. But he didn't need to say it; she could see it in his eyes.

She leaned over and pressed her lips briefly against his. She pulled away just enough so that they were no longer touching, but not too much that they didn't feel a pull of energy towards each other. They felt each other's breath on their lips. With both of their eyes still closed, she whispered, "I love you, Robert Bronner."

His eyes shot open. Hers were still closed as if she were embarrassed by what she had said and didn't want to see the effect. He smiled and placed both his palms on her cheeks; her tiny face was swallowed by his hands. She opened her eyes cautiously, but smiled when she saw the grin on his lips. He wrapped his arms around her, pulling her as close as he could, and kissed her with all the passion he could muster.

It was all he could do not to betray his own feelings and ask her to meet him in Europe in a few months time.

After lunch he played some ball, enough to get his arm sore again. He was having trouble clearing his mind. He was going to meet Jo's parents that night—attending some family event as Jo's date. He was still enjoying her company, of course, but he was weary of how everything felt. He knew he would be leaving Brisbane soon. He wasn't about to desert like those two Panamanians back in Fiji. He couldn't if he wanted to. It crushed him even to think about deserting. There was the Commodore, and his own father, too, and the implications that a move like that would inevitably have. These concepts remained in a fog for him, but he struggled with the idea nonetheless.

Bob met Jo's parents and the rest of their family. He complimented them about their house and their daughter, smiled and joked. He entertained everyone with tales of his adventures aboard the *Alva*. He talked about the Commodore, fondly describing the man's idiosyncrasies. Everyone was fascinated by the idea of the Vanderbilt fortune. The story about the bear put them all in hysterics.

Bob made his excuses soon afterward, before the party was even in full swing. Foremost in his mind was creating a good impression. He was dreaming again about a future, his family and hers sitting around a table somewhere. He had to clear his mind. Like the moon tugged at the tide, Jo pulled on him.

The next day they were raising anchor at 5:30 p.m., heading out of the river towards the channel that would take them far away from Brisbane. The more he thought about it, even as he drifted away, he realized how little he could do to change things regardless of how much he hated to leave so soon. Jo had cried at the news, but she hadn't asked for anything, or proposed any solution. She just broke down and cried as he got into the cab.

Alone in the World

A MUSEUM VISIT had generated a particular amount of talk since it included a very particular exhibit on the aboriginal implements of war. The Commodore was so keen on the display he felt inclined to review the many pictures Bob and Al collected from the Fiji islands and others. He spent an hour or so down in the development room, having Bob rummage through the files to pull out every shot he could find of the natives and their weaponry. Bob handed his prints over to the Commodore and basked in the older man's praise for a short while. They were set to arrive at the Percy Islands at five that evening, planning to drop anchor overnight. There were three islands in the group to be photographed—about five miles overall. The praise was nice—not unusual, even—but it was given with the expectation that Bob would run back to his work.

There was North Island to photograph, which was separated from the mainland by a narrow channel. Another channel separated North Island from Middle Island and then a third narrow channel surrounded South-East Island. All three thrust abruptly out of the sea—about 250 ft high—and sported rolling hills and very sparse vegetation. Just inside the reef, the sea was calm as a mill pond. They carried a pilot all the way along the reef up to Thursday Island at the northernmost point. Bob didn't see why they needed him, though, since they were anchoring every night, sailing only by day.

At night, the boss' pantry boy still persisted in bringing large plates full of ice cream to Al and Bob on a regular basis. It had become a sort of nighttime ritual to enjoy the Commodore's unwitting hospitality before bed.

Time was beginning to move quickly as the *Alva* prepared to finish its journey around the coast of Australia. Bob, for one, no longer felt as if he were heading out on a great journey. Instead he was being pulled back home, toward his father and his life in California. Jo was a memory now, and one that held him back perhaps more than he had allowed himself to realize. He had been awkward, even deceptive, but so was the way of it. No liaison thousands of miles away from home could please his old father. To be in love with a woman from a different country—that was the kind of problem the soldiers had dealt with after the war, their sweethearts in France or England. Men, sometimes with wives already, returned home to find that the place had lost its meaning. But Bob was no soldier. He traveled in unusual, almost surreal comfort; he couldn't deny it. But still, it seemed everyone had the same problems. It was the beginning of October, too. Bewilderment and loss—they were undoubtedly consistent with the season itself, even if the seasons in the southern hemisphere had everything in reverse.

There was decent food again. Back in Brisbane the ship had been supplied with two hundred tons of diesel oil and the water tanks were filled. Able-bodied men had hurried back and forth, in and out of the ship's larder, carrying boxes of vegetables, milk, butter, beef, and eggs.

Rumors were beginning to circulate about the Commodore's finances. Back home his fortune was apparently being slowly eaten away by the flagging markets—the Vanderbilt inheritance was being wasted with his absence. Round-the-world cruises surely cost a fortune. Bob hadn't thought about the adventure in quite those terms yet—"A venture that simply cost too much, that brought little value, no return on investment," Anton explained. "You ask around and folks'll tell you that the ship's not sinking, but think again."

The more they moved through the same scenery, seeing the same thing over and over again, capturing the same shots over and over, the more it seemed that they were alone in the world. As if the world itself was transient, and places no longer existed as soon as they'd left them.

Bob thought about Jo, alone in Brisbane, or perhaps not alone, and the thoughts drove him to distraction. What was it about this existence that seemed to lend such an illusion of freedom?

The air was cool and the wind was slowly dying. The *Alva's* anchor was tied up to the dock at the Townsville harbor instead of being dropped into the water as it usually was. Bob set out quickly for the shore, as usual, but after dinner played ball with the second mate Evans, looking over the small rural town rather quickly, deciding that he'd learned to spot when a place was worth visiting and when it wasn't. After the game, though, he wound his way around the town to the *Flying Squadron Hall*, a boat club set up near the harbor, where a little music and drunken German seamen provided ample entertainment.

Despite the excitement of a fight and loud, excited talk with some of the other crew members, Bob was slowly feeling overcome with the loneliness that had plagued him quietly for a long time before Brisbane. It was worse now that he had met Jo and lost her; when the fuss had died down, he was alone wondering about another strange place.

When he got back to his bunk, he pulled out a piece of paper and scribbled a letter to her. He had no idea whether he would get a reply, whether it would even be possible for a letter to reach him from Australia, but he would try. He wrote honestly that he loved her and asked her to consider meeting him somewhere, anywhere—Europe, America, wherever. If she loved him, he said, she should meet him, drop everything and meet him, or tell him to do the same. One word, he said, would convince him. He signed the letter and tucked it into an envelope, thinking perhaps he would send it soon.

Townsville was the trading center for Queensland, the export and import center for the tropical region, and a place where one could easily find finished articles of commerce received from all around the world: great stores of merino wool, beef, raw sugar, and lead and silver, stocks of which were shipped out from Townsville and sent to other parts of Australia. The cleanliness and modern appearance of Townsville was refreshing, particularly along the main streets, with their shrubs at the center and the low buildings, which seemed rather uncharacteristic for the region. Hospitals, banks, hotels, and theaters seemed to make the place something of a thriving tourist destination, although there had been little evidence at sea of the popularity of that particular stretch of the region. A bathing pavilion was surrounded by shark-proof nets as if to offer a clue about the scarcity of people. In Sydney, the Commodore had heard reports of a girl being carried away by a shark while hundreds of people looked on helplessly, unable to do anything to help. In Melbourne, there was a story that a man had been carried away. Still more had been badly mauled and attacked, and others were always being killed. In Townsville, the record confirmed several deaths from recent shark attacks.

The greatest menace, however, was the lack of rain. There had been no rain for twelve months and the cattle and horses were literally dying on the plains. People were out of work and the mosquitoes and flies were hard to keep at bay, threatening disease all the while—tropical fever and dengue.

Despite its dangers, Townsville was a picturesque location. Built on the flats, it offered an excellent view of the surrounding countryside and the harbor, particularly from the vantage point of one or other of the small hills on the outskirts of the town.

Early in the morning on October 7th, the Commodore had called upon the chief of police in Townsville to get permission to visit the Palm Isles, about twenty islands and rocks lying off Halifax Bay, some fifteen miles from the coast of Queensland. The *Alva* was clear of the dock at 11:30 a.m., and by 12:10 p.m., the river pilot was over the side. The Barrier Reef pilots' licenses didn't include harbors, so whenever they entered a port, they had to take on a local pilot—another expense to consider, along with the port, lighthouse, and doctor's fees.

The last several days, after continued efforts to break his thoughts away from Jo, Bob had been finding as many opportunities as he could, any opportunity, to lose himself in his work. He was beginning to see himself moving through the last weeks and days of his journey, the last days on the *Alva*. He felt himself on the verge of the inevitably painful realization that he was far from being a man: aware of and connected to what he wanted and needed in life. He touched the letter in his pocket, and got back to tossing through prints.

Heading on a course that took them through Steamer Passage, they began to sail in a kind of leisurely, vacant, and dreamlike sea. All of the islands were wooded and the timber was standing out in noble relief on the hills. Mount Bentley rose to some one thousand eight hundred and eighteen feet above the shores and was wooded even at the apex. Forest fires were raging on several of the smaller islands, although the fires were already behind when they spotted them, and they could hardly go all the way back to extinguish them. There were fires on the mainland, too, but still nothing for which to give up time and man hours. There was little sign of human existence anyway, just a few insignificant looking buildings, not worth the trouble.

There was no pier on a small island they wished to explore, and the waters were rather shallow, so they put off for the beach in the launch, wading ashore for the last fifty yards through the mud and silt. Although

The aborigines of Palm Island were encouraged to shed their warring and cannibalistic past to embrace the ways of the missionaries who struggled to convert them.

there was little sign of human life, the island was in fact home to a group of Australian Bushmen known for troublesome disputes with other tribes and bloody altercations with their neighbors. The tribe wasn't native to the island. As punishment for their crimes, the Bushmen had been deported there by the Australian authorities.

The Commodore had never exhibited any such stab of conscience about the hierarchy of power as it existed in such places. He greeted the black tribesmen friendly enough, smiling and taking in the expressions of excitement and astonishment on their faces. He was a bit uncomfortable, though, and frankly the tribesmen seemed to share that sentiment. They seemed particularly put off by Pierre who stood nearby in bright red swimming trunks, seemingly unaware. The Commodore asked to speak with the superintendent, Mr. Cornell, who was apparently at the tennis courts. The words "tennis courts" were repeated back quizzically a few times by members of the *Alva* crew.

Mr. Cornell was an excellent player and the Commodore and his party witnessed a rather good game of doubles, with hard serving and swift rallying that proved decidedly entertaining. Pierre, however, had a rather odd dilemma when Mr. Cornell, finally distracted from the tennis match, informed the Commodore that one of his guests was not properly dressed, indicating Pierre.

Mr. Cornell and the chief of police told them a story that explained something of the awkwardness of the aborigines on the Great Palm Island and shed some light on his own misgivings. The Queensland government, in 1921, had sent an Australian man named Robert Curry to Great Palm Island to be the superintendent. His wife and two children, along with a Doctor Maitland Pattison and his wife, had accompanied him. The four adults had previously done a great deal of work educating and caring for the aborigines, according to the reports, and the government charged them to try and work their magic on the Palm Islanders.

The Commodore commented on how he thought this Curry to be a particularly interesting fellow, apparently very much in keeping with his own conception of what a gentleman should be: handsome, redheaded, and tall. He was also college-educated and a sportsman, talented both academically and athletically. As he did, the chief warned him to reserve judgment.

In World War I, he earned a citation for bravery, but a new philosophy on life was opened up for him when he met his future wife, who advised him not to measure his strengths according to physical feats but according to his social value. Curry began to rethink his life entirely. With his wife at his side, he began teaching aborigines, first on the mainland and then on Great Palm Island. They stayed there for ten years, but when his wife died, in May of 1931, the man who was so gentle and apparently wise by nature went mad. He suddenly believed everyone around him was hostile, so he put on the bright red swimming trunks he had worn on his first day on the island—the day he proved that he could swim, leap, and wrestle better than the natives, a distinction that earned him the status of a god. He went to the infirmary and returned with a hypodermic needle, injecting both his children with fatal doses of morphine before placing bombs under their beds and cans of gasoline in the school house and infirmary, lighting wads of paper under the buildings to set about killing everyone in his path.

Doctor Pattison, who apparently tried to intervene, realizing that his friend and long-time associate had been entirely lost, was shot through

An aboriginal man throws a boomerang on Palm Island, Australia.

the thigh, his own wife killed as well. And then Curry and his abject worshipper, a native called Mad Jack, jumped aboard a speedboat, heading out of the dock, throwing sticks of dynamite into a larger speed boat that also stood in the harbor, perhaps the last line of escape for anyone who might almost have survived the explosions and the fires. They shot at anything and everything in sight.

Hardly able to move, Pattison found himself demanding that the aborigines shoot at the man they had worshiped as a god. Only the threat of being shot themselves was sufficient for them to overcome their fears.

Seeing Pierre standing there in red trunks, they'd thought that Curry had returned. The tragedy had taken place not six months before, and it was barely acceptable for the chief of police to mention it. But he had no choice, and the discomfort clearly showed in his face.

The island tribe had something of a sinister history to explain, even beyond this particular tragic tale. The Commodore did his best to draw attention from Pierre by discussing the history of the aborigines with the chief of police and quietly sending Pierre off to change. By all accounts, the tribe had been moved to Great Palm Island as an initial punishment for the tribal disputes they caused on the mainland, but they continued to make trouble: raiding the black settlements on neighboring islands, and sometimes even some of the white settlements on the mainland. They had become reconciled in recent years, and there were arrangements that allowed some of the men to return to Queensland for work, with the support of the government: mostly clearing the jungle, building roads, schools, and warehouses—heavy labor. They were sometimes allowed to visit Townsville as well. But they were so easily spotted with their strong, muscular physiques, thick lips, wide noses, and frizzy hair, as the Commodore noted, it would have to be almost as awkward for them as when Pierre presented himself to the small army of aborigines still haunted by the image of Curry.

When Pierre had changed out of the offending red garment, his mistake was quickly excused and the natives there were very quick to decide that they would stage a dance for the visitors the following morning. Bob changed the film in the Bell & Howell back to black-and-white so that he and Al could shoot both black-and-white and multicolor images the next day, weather permitting. At the very least, they hoped to capture a few shots of the terns that had been following the boat for two days. Most of the crew had gone around calling them gulls, seagulls, of course, but the Commodore was most insistent. He was an expert on such things. They were pesky birds in any case, fluttering around the yardarm and antennae, being a nuisance.

Bob was feeling sort of restless that night, and went out on deck a few times to enjoy what proved to be a cloudless sky and a beautiful sunset. His thoughts were drifting, but nowhere in particular. He thought about his father and his brother, and Jo, again. He was still unclear how he might ever reconcile the life he was living to the one he had back home, whatever home actually meant. It seemed odd to be wandering the ship alone and it might well have been frowned upon, so he headed back to his bunk. The *Alva* might have been one of the most luxurious vessels in the world—perhaps it was, perhaps it wasn't—but for Bob, there were still rules, and he didn't want to risk losing the Commodore's fondness for him.

One particular night, Bob had returned to his bunk with a cup of coffee and a piece of ripe Camembert cheese that he put on the chest of the second mate while he was asleep. He smelt like a skunk when he got up in the morning and that was the idea. Bob and his roommate Mac had locked the door to their cabin that night only to wake up to the second mate banging wildly on it until there was nothing for them to do but throw water through the ventilators and hope he might see the wisdom in not waking the Commodore. It was the usual gag when the ship was in port—that whenever one of the boys comes aboard late—he went around to all the rooms and woke everyone up. He turned on all the lights and pulled the bed covers off. Any clothes lying around were thrown on the bed. Bob had an empty beer bottle that he kept in back of his bunk for such use; it scared some of the boys out when he'd wield it, half asleep and not caring who he conked with it. Still, that was the night, after Bob had fallen asleep finally, that the second mate, as payback for the cheese, found the bottle and took it. The rest of the guys in the dorm promptly threw all of the dirty clothes at Bob and pulled the covers off the bed in revenge for all the head conks. It was another hour before all scores were settled and everyone was ready to return to bed.

The Crash

THE COMMODORE returned to the *Alva* that night to read the news from New York. It was the market quotations, mostly, that forecast a considerable disruption in his affairs. The turmoil in the city was discouraging and although he could communicate by the sophisticated radio set, it was perhaps something of a relief not to be dealing with it directly.

By the morning, the *Alva Daily News* was abuzz with word spreading among the crew that the bottom had continued to drop out of the stock market, most importantly in New York Central stock, the primary holdings of the Vanderbilts. The Commodore's concern was obvious and there was a buzz among the men that the plans were going to be changed. He was going to be hitting the high spots only from then on—in a hurry to get home. They were eleven thousand miles out from New York, but still not yet at the halfway point, which would be in Singapore.

The news had Bob thinking, too. It was unlikely a man like Vanderbilt would suddenly be unable to support his crew. It wasn't that bad. But finding work in dire conditions, that was going to be difficult. The letter to Jo was still in his pocket, and the increasingly alarming news from New York further disturbed any hope he had. How could he offer anything to her if the future of his country, the world, was so uncertain? He hoped it would be better when he returned, or that he'd at least be able to leverage his experience to find work as soon as possible; right away, he hoped. He still had to support his father.

He went ashore after lunch to shoot some pictures of the aboriginal war dance performance put on for the Commodore. The natives were dancing out on the open rugby field, the most popular sport there.

One will never know how much the tribal customs displayed on Willie's behalf were authentic or showmanship to appease the wealthy foreigner.

Bob made note of their faces painted with some sort of whitewash, spotted about the body and hideously marked on the face. They danced to the time of two boomerangs being hit together rather fast. Bob saw the dance as a series of gestures, grunts and barks—very much like a pack of dogs all growling at once. Between that noise and the boomerangs whizzing around, and the sounds of the aboriginal dancers, the performance was easily one of the most frightening they'd seen. The goal of the war dance was to menace and, regardless of the act, hostile intent seemed to burn in their eyes.

The tribe made its way down to one end of the field with spears—pieces of bamboo about three inches in diameter and four feet long. As soon as the camera was in place, the natives let all the spears fly at once, and the ground around the stick they aimed for suddenly looked as if it were surrounded by porcupine quills—about sixty spears sticking in the ground, none more than ten feet away from the stake.

On the Commodore's behalf, the Palm Island aborigines gathered to put on a show. They remained deeply connected to a culture deemed repugnant by the westerners who sought to convert them.

Al had wanted to set the camera up near the stake.

"Oh, yeah!" Bob laughed, and they were both glad they had changed their minds about that. "We would have lost the cameras and maybe ourselves to boot."

The *Alva* was making its way out of the Pacific. The agenda for the next day included an excursion to Kuranda, some one thousand eighty feet up in the mountains. The Commodore and his party ascended the mountain by railroad on a special train designed to handle the steep gradients and to cope with the loops and horseshoe curves of the tracks necessary to navigate the lay of the mountain. Al and Bob were taken along on that trip, with Al in charge of the moving pictures: skirting the bluffs and hanging over the sheer precipices, over the valleys and gorges, enjoying the tangles of trees and matted scrub, fields of grass, orchards of mangos and oranges, mandarins, bananas, and pineapples. This was a rich country compared to what they had seen of late along the coast line. Bob and Al's ride was considerably less comfortable than the Commodore's. They were set up in a trailer on the end, the train being little more than a gasoline motor coach. It was a very bumpy road, and thirty miles worth of it. Shooting the scenes of the Barron Falls through dense forest, posed enough of a challenge to keep them occupied.

At Kuranda, a charming mountain resort, the party saw the well-kept railway station and took photos of the collection of flowers in profusion there. Orchids hung from the eaves in painted gasoline cans.

They visited a private collector in the area, one Mr. Dodd, who had a tremendous exhibit of butterflies and moths representing his life's work in the tropical bush of North Australia. They then continued on with the Commodore to a maze made of fan palms and ferns. They were allowed to have lunch in the Commodore's company (just about anyway—inside of the hotel) but the journey back was no better than the trip there, leaving Bob bumped and bruised. They got back to the *Alva* by five and Bob was desperate to sleep, but for the seven o'clock show he was expected to attend with Al to get the required number of shots. In the end, it was midnight before he got to rest.

Cairns and a Cuckoo

SATURDAY, OCTOBER 10th, was an unusual and busy day. The first event was the discovery of a stowaway. Twenty-five years of age, the young Russian man was hidden in the engine compartment of the ship's speedboat and hoping to get a free passage to Europe. He had apparently been rowed out during the night by a friend who was never discovered. He had concealed himself well enough under the hatch while the boat lay alongside the *Alva*, but was discovered later in the morning as others started to go about their duties. The Commodore wasted no time in calling the authorities, who put him ashore.

By 10:00 a.m., they moved to the dock and filled their tanks with ninety tons of the best spring water in Australia. By 10:30 a.m., the port doctor had mustered the crew a second time, for a final examination; they were now eighteen days away from Noumea, New Caledonia, but still being cautious. By lunch, they left by motor to Lake Barrine, some forty miles away and some two thousand six hundred and fifty-five feet above sea level. When the Commodore and his party reached the foot of the precipitous mountain, they were stopped by town traffic before beginning their ascent. The road was one-way for twelve miles, from the Bottom Gate to the Top Gate, and it offered no less than six hundred and two curves in one nine-mile stretch. The road overlooked a spectacular river and various gorges, making the vertigo worthwhile.

The soil of the surrounding land was volcanic and extremely fertile. On the summit were Lakes Barrine and Eacham, sheets of quiet water contained in two old craters and surrounded by dense tropical jungle. As they drove along, it wasn't just the vegetation that drew their attention. The Commodore was determined to return home with an Australian bird or two to feature in his museum exhibitions. Before departing from

New York, he had become engaged in a rather lengthy exchange with the Australian authorities in order to obtain a permit to carry and shoot a gun. Therefore, he felt a somewhat overwhelming sense of needing to fire the weapon at least once after all the effort he had made to procure the permit. With the jungle thick on both sides of the road, it was nearly impossible to retrieve a bird that fell on either side. Only when he saw one flying directly overhead did the Commodore decide it was appropriate to shoot, which he did quickly, the bird dropping instantly, and all form of congratulations followed.

The chauffeur retrieved the bird, and in doing so suddenly looked worried.

"My God," he cried. "You have shot a cuckoo."

Trying to contain his surprise, the Commodore stepped closer to examine the creature. Rose and Dr. Lane stepped forward too, Rose resting her hand on her husband's arm.

"Poor thing," she said, looking at the bird as if its death was now entirely unjustified.

"That cuckoo should have stayed in his clock," Willie joked.

"Are you sure you want to bring it back to the ship?" asked Dr. Lane. "It might not be the best thing to do."

Whatever appearance of confidence he was trying to maintain, it didn't take much for the Commodore to give it up along with his prize. The bird was buried quickly in a shallow grave.

The Top Gate opened at four every evening for the downward flowing traffic, so in any case, they had to head back to the car to make their descent. By six, they were back on the *Alva* and there was no need to think too much more about the cuckoo and their possible brush with the law.

Bob was particularly amused to find that the Australians knew nothing of baseball. They drew crowds of onlookers every time the crew stirred up a game. Some bystanders even jumped in and tried to throw or catch the baseball, but were generally too clumsy. Others interrupted the game with questions—all kinds of odd questions probably in reference to cricket which, in turn, no one on the *Alva* knew a thing about.

At 6 am the shackle broke on the port bow anchor. By seven, they had sent for the diver and an outfit to get a line on the thing. The crew was prepared this time after the debacle in the Galapagos, and many jumped in to help. There would be definite advantages to whoever

Barron Falls, Cairns, Australia.

found the thing, not least that the Commodore would be mighty pleased. Frankly, if they didn't help, they may well have been called on anyway. In that case, the Commodore would be annoyed, and it wasn't worth the risk. Although he was still a very mild-mannered man, particularly around his crew, there were some signs that the stress of the market struggles were beginning to get to the Commodore. His temper was definitely shorter.

Watching the anchor being heaved up that morning, Vanderbilt's face most definitely dropped when he saw the thing break, the chain flinging aboard with its grinding clanks and the anchor dropping back into the water. He dropped the other bow anchor without a moment's thought. Unsure how long it would be before the diver arrived, the first mate was out dragging for the anchor from the lifeboat. It was muddy at the bottom of the water, and that was hindering his efforts. Clearly, there was not much hope of finding the anchor until the diver arrived and, just their luck, it was a Sunday.

Cairns, Australia
For the second time in the voyage, the *Alva* lost anchor.

Not until 9 did the man arrive with his crew, pump, hose, and helmet. It was a rather elaborate procedure, very technical, to lower a man deep into the sea. The tide was ebbing, and the current quickly became too strong for the operations. They had no choice but to wait until eleven, when the tide and current finally slacked.

By noon, they had the chain and anchor back on board. The diver had found them relatively quickly, even in the mud. The ship was back under way at 1 p.m. after the diver was paid and duly thanked. It was another expense, though, and again that look of ever-so-mild annoyance and concern crossed the Commodore's face.

They started out on the dredge channel a second time, ready to enjoy the brightness of the afternoon and the smooth sea. Their new course would take them past a mountainous coast devoid of habitation. After a day of trials, they finally, and ironically, anchored in Weary Bay, just north of the Cape of Tribulation—a namesake omen from the logs of Captain Cook.

Earlier in the day, they passed a group of islands at which they were supposed to have stopped. But, perhaps because they were slightly behind schedule already, or because the Commodore was worrying about money, they did not. Bob, who was excused from much of the activity that morning, had lain in his bunk reading. He fell asleep after an hour or so. When he woke up again at 4:30 p.m., he found a message from Al summoning him to meet with the Commodore on deck to hand him the prints of the aboriginal dance.

Heading to the darkroom first, he fumbled through his makeshift filing system to find the best of the pictures he had developed from that day. He was glad that he had worked to develop the film so quickly. The backlog had encouraged him to get on top of it and he ended up getting through the lot, now planning to develop as many of the negatives as he could within a day or two of taking the pictures.

Bob carried his little portfolio up to the deck and asked one of the crew where the Commodore was—"Up on the bridge." He headed up there, warding off the curious glances from the other officers. He was relieved to see the Commodore recognize him and step forward.

"Bob," he smiled, taking the portfolio to review the pictures, very much pleased with what he saw and anxious to have enlargements of most of them.

"You know Bob," The Commodore started to say, "I've been thinking, we've caught so many fish and photographed them out of the water. Belanske sketches them and you photograph them, and later Belanske taxidermies them. You saw my exhibits where I attempted to recreate the undersea environment, but I don't actually have any real footage of it. So what do you think?"

Bob paused, trying to understand what the Commodore was asking. "Sir?"

"Bob, I think it's time for some underwater footage."

Around 2 pm on Monday, the *Alva* dropped anchor on the north side of a sandy beach, close to a detached coral shoal that formed a natural overlapping breakwater. Bob, along with Al, put on *Dunn* diving helmets at that point and they descended below the surface, taking the electrically operated submarine movie camera. The smoothness of the water was a relief and made the filming that much easier. His head enclosed in the helmet, it was as if he was trapped in a kind of bubble. The helmet was heavy, shifting his entire body out of balance, but swimming through the water—wading, more like—he managed to be dexterous enough.

The nine feet of water wasn't quite clear enough for the best sorts of pictures. The experience might have been better if he hadn't had a touch of ptomaine poisoning the night before, leaving his stomach sore through a sleepless night.

They kept up the effort for almost two hours, but realized the work wasn't going to pay off as they'd hoped. The Commodore was busy prying loose a number of good specimens of variegated coral, the amount, color, and design of which was quite impressive. Blasts of dynamite brought about twenty new specimens of fish to the surface, captured for inclusion in the Northport museum.

When the diving effort was finally ended, the Commodore headed to the beach to collect bird specimens. Bob was much relieved to be allowed out of the water. He hadn't had anything to eat all day, only managing a cup of tea. He made his excuses after drying off and went to bed early, sensing an early morning due to the crew members' ongoing antics. Lying in bed, Bob ruffled inside the pockets of his shorts. It seemed an age now since they had been in Brisbane, but Bob was still looking for Jo's face in crowds and carried his hopeless love letter. He planned on sending it several times a day only to always find reasons not to.

Exactly as he'd guessed, some of the boys woke Bob up in the morning before six, charging into the room and banging on whatever they could find. Bob groaned but made a show of getting up, pretending that he was going to be unable to go back to sleep after all that. He waited for them to leave, and lay back down, hoping to steal a short snooze before the troublemakers returned. He laid in wait for a good ten minutes, but they came back—one, anyway—with a flashlight that he shone into the room hoping to catch anyone sleeping. Bob threw a glass of ice cold water in the man's face and called it a morning. He lay in another half hour or so after that and then got up.

The Commodore was already up and about by the time Bob made his appearance on deck. Not that he was required to be there, but there was an air of concern as he looked over his charts. Vanderbilt made some remark about the date and the numbering of the chart in a technical jargon that Bob couldn't follow. He did catch that it was also the thirteenth. The Commodore, being a superstitious man, was more than a little unnerved.

They would stay on course that day, keeping to the deepest waters and avoiding any detours from the well-charted track. All measures of safety precautions were going to be used that day. Although they were sailing along serenely, there was no advantage to risking fate so far from home.

They dropped anchor just after dark at the Piper Islands and even in the darkness they could take note of how the country had changed. It was now flat around them with sandy spots of chalky whiteness still vaguely visible. A lazy calm had come over much of the crew, officers included, and that was how most everyone passed that day and evening, without much objection from superiors. There had previously been talk about taking the underwater camera equipment out for another go, but the Commodore insisted that there had not been a suitable place to stop and shoot underwater pictures that day, saying that someone could have been bitten by a shark or had some other sort of accident.

The following morning, the Commodore was his usual self, giving orders and ready to brave the waters, even though the wind had sprung up during the night and caused considerable choppiness compared with the norm for the protected waters of the barrier reef. For a while, caught unaware as they were by the weather, they shipped several seas through the starboard ports before they could close them and seal off the ship from a further deluge.

The *Alva* definitely wasn't prone to sinking: she had sixteen water tight compartments, with two that could flood, but everyone felt it prudent to err on the side of caution. Regardless, the staterooms ended up waterlogged and were apparently damp and uncomfortable for a time. Bob had awakened just in time to close the porthole of his room. It was right at his side and the noise of the wind coming through the screen woke him. Just as he closed it, another gust came through—the biggest yet—and he thought the glass might give way.

By 12:30 p.m. that afternoon, they were off Cape York—the northeasternmost extremity of Australia. They drank to the health of the Pacific, and moved on swiftly to the Torres Straits. There, very strong currents and tides made problems. Sometimes the water rose as the tide ebbed. Other times it fell. Still other times, the direction of the current was entirely opposite to what was expected.

Further on, they nearly ran into Hammond Rock, as it appeared to be moving past them in the opposite direction, with a bone in its teeth, so to speak, and leaving a long wake astern. The rock was light, though, and they thankfully missed their target; but land went by as if the *Alva* were a train instead of a ship. The officers were thankful to throw down anchor anywhere after the kind of chaotic vortex they'd encountered at the Pacific Ocean's end. Thursday Island was where they'd stop to breathe, with many of the crew disappointed that all the excitement was over.

With a particularly important position on the map, Thursday Island was a spot from which pilots were often engaged to take ships down inside the Great Barrier Reef, or were otherwise dropped from ships that had recently passed through it. The reefs were undoubtedly treacherous without the assistance of someone experienced at navigating them, and they took a pilot aboard just for that reason. Many ships had wrecked on the Barrier Reef, even in the hands of experienced pilots.

Timor

THE COMMODORE was busy giving out directions, confounded by the wind, which seemed to be specifically surrounding the vessels on the water. The locals laughed off their ordeal as was typical. In such seas as they had had, it would have been impossible for the spear fishermen to carry on at all, even with their well-built schooners. The town on Thursday Island was intriguing and rather reminiscent of Western frontier towns, drawing the line between familiar land and the other: the wilderness and vast crossing that lead to the next signs of real civilization. Small wooden shacks with thin tin roofs dotted the shore, backyards overrun by chickens.

The backyards seemed to compromise the space set aside for banged-up vehicles—Fords mostly—that carried supplies and passengers along the broad dirt roads. Try though he might, the Commodore was unable to conceive of the island's poetical aspects. It seemed such a seedy place, the kind people could not wait to leave one way or the other, and in which people had a propensity to simply abandon things—vehicles and property—that were of little value to them. The day saw two steamers stop by the island. One was bound swiftly for Sydney, the other for Singapore.

The *Alva* saw the arrival of customs officers that afternoon as well, and they set about breaking the seals on the supplies cordoned off in storage. The officers inspected the ship's supplies and imposed the duty tax, handing the Commodore his bill with a kind of satisfaction that he considered intolerable. Nevertheless, Willie smiled. They had been in Australia since September 24th and the visit had been mostly positive, instructive and enjoyable. But Bob still didn't receive his cigarettes back until morning.

They were headed to the Arafura Sea as Bob worked on developing his negatives below deck. Except for the noise, he was rather oblivious to the wind. By evening, he was comfortably in his bunk reading. There was some possibility of fun, too. Their time at sea that night might offer the perfect opportunity to get even with some of the boys. He had a stock of rolled tape and rubber bands hidden along the side of his bed. He took them all by surprise. When the time was right, he heated a few and snuck them into the bunks of the second mate, the third mate, his roommate, Morton, McGuire, an oiler named Patrick Rooney, and Belanske, sending temporary hysteria throughout the ship as they popped and smelled.

On open water the next day, still in the Arafura Sea, they were rolling ever so slightly when Bob finally awoke. Finally hitting his roommates and lower cabin mates with his tape was all Bob had looked forward to for a while. Looking around his cabin from his cot and seeing that he was the only one still snoozing made him feel lazy, but he wasn't sure what to do with himself.

He tossed over abruptly as he heard the call that land was sighted.

Approaching Timor from the east, all they could see was wilderness. It was hot and uninviting, to say the least, although moving along the northern shore revealed the existence of mountains. Mount Name was clearly visible in a cloudless atmosphere. The highest peak in Timor was Mount Ramelan, many miles westward, and although the mountain itself could be spotted from aboard the *Alva*, the peak wasn't visible at all. The coast, from what they could see, was barren and brownish. There were few trees and the settlements widely separated. Timor was two hundred and fifty-five miles long, with the eastern end under Portuguese control and the western end controlled by the Dutch.

The harbor was nothing more than a small reef harbor. From the bridge, it looked restricted and the Commodore considered whether it wasn't better to anchor outside of the harbor, even though they weren't used to anchoring in such depths. If they did anchor outside, it was going to be difficult to make contact with the shore in the smaller boats due to the wind. However, in the harbor, the only safe anchorage was beside a five thousand ton steamer, which was bound to cause problems. But when the pilot came aboard with an interpreter and explained that there was plenty of room, everything was settled rather quickly. They entered the harbor and slowly passed the steamer. Everything was going well until they entered the restricted water and the pilot seemed to lose his nerve.

"It's too small," he decided.

The pilot shouted and the interpreter determined they should, "Let go the anchor." Suddenly, they were positioned close to two reefs with the giant steamer practically alongside them. The Commodore had to take great care to move the ship about, swinging it, since they had dropped the hook on a running chain to try to avoid hitting the steamer.

When they finally had the ship positioned, a doctor came aboard to inspect the crew. With him came the captain of the port, who struck up a conversation with the Commodore rather promptly, revealing that he could speak both French and English, and that, in his opinion, the *Alva* was very safe where she was. Still, the Commodore was adamant that the ship be relocated. They needed to move farther in, he insisted, because they were close to the back of the inner reef and the moor was within the dock. The ship's position, he maintained, was a dangerous one if there was a change in the direction of the wind.

"The wind never changes in this port," the captain of the port said, adding that the commander of the "man-of-war" ought to know that well enough. There was only one other passenger ship in port and what looked like an overgrown New York Harbor tug, which appeared to be the ship the captain was referring to.

"Another man-of-war is due in the morning," the officer added, "and will lie alongside the dock."

The Commodore announced that they would leave by daylight to avoid being sandwiched any further in what was already a tight situation. And beyond that, he picked up the anchor and moved into a secure berth, let go two bower anchors, and ran the ship's stern line to the dock.

The Javanese were very shy. The boys tried for five minutes to coax a few girls to stand for a picture before they finally succeeded in convincing them.

The town was clean, but low and susceptible to malaria. The Commodore was driven into town over a mountain road, built several hundred kilometers along the northern coast, with Rose, Dr. Lane, and Bob in tow with the Graflex. The lowlands were rich, and along the shore were some of the finest banyan trees the Commodore remembered seeing. The trees grew more sparsely higher up, but produced a fine quality of coffee. The largest plantations were owned by the Sociedade Agricola Patria e

A Javanese woman reluctantly poses for Bob.

Trabahlho, which employed nearly four thousand laborers year round, and double that in harvest time. Most of the coffee was shipped to Hamburg, Germany.

The natives of Timor belonged to the Papuan race, but they were distinct from the tribes of New Guinea. They were peaceable, but still dressed in their native style; many wore only loincloths.

"Extremely primitive," Bob heard the Commodore call out through the wind.

Towards the evening, the party observed groups of natives about fires, surrounded by water sacks and all their worldly goods. They also saw prisoners at work, standing at attention as the visitors passed by in their car. (About fifteen miles north, on Kambing Island, there was a prison to which certain revolutionists of Madeira were committed.) The natives were otherwise chewing betel nuts outside of their huts, although many lived wholly on their canoes, which were generally elaborately designed.

The hulls of the canoes were carved out of one enormous piece of wood, ornaments rising sometimes two feet above the deck, with outrigger supports of bamboo and large bamboo floats attached to them, giving the crafts extraordinary stability. Platforms built partly over the outrigger struts were designed to hold household utensils: fishing gear, nets, booms, and sails which were woven matting.

The Javanese they saw that day were very erect in bearing and the girls were all small. Bob stood beside some to have a picture taken in which he seemed remarkably tall. A few Chinese roamed the island, too, although none could speak English.

Passing one Chinese hut, they heard a phonograph playing *Aloha Oa* with the singing in English. Perhaps they didn't know what it meant, but they did like the sound of it.

The ship's departure was something that Bob might have missed, but the boys insisted on waking him up, along with his roommates, who were particularly obnoxious and persistent this time. He promised he would pay them back while they were sleeping that very night.

Up on the deck, the Commodore spoke to Reddington, Pierre Merillon and Dr. Lane. He told them how that morning he'd looked over toward the steamer and felt a great sense of justice. "…a sense of satisfaction that she was indeed tailing out to sea with a land-driven breeze. It pays to be stubborn," he smiled. "We passed 'the successor' in the anchorage—a Portuguese man-of-war that was truly no more than an old tramp, but nonetheless flew her ensign proudly from the mainmast gaff."

It was a beautiful day, "perfect for yachting" Dr. Lane pointed out. They sailed along under a mackerel sky and over the smooth sea, capturing the wind "of cat's paw force" that towed them, ever so gently, off on the right course. Thousands of flying fish darted about from beneath the bow, and that was deemed reason enough to call Al and Bob to the deck to observe and photograph as best they could.

Then there was a succession of islands to observe, large and small: Kambing, Alor, Treweng, Pantar, Rusa, and Lomblem. The Commodore named each as Bob captured shots of all of them and took notes. Most of the islands had rather high peaks, but surprisingly little vegetation. They were the sort of islands that Bob now tended to consider unappealing, not the sort of place he'd like to find himself trapped. He wondered what kind of natives inhabited them. The Commodore wondered whether they would be amenable to European civilization, as much as it could exist in such a place. Although they were stopping in fewer places than before, avoiding any serious delays in their travel, the places they did stop introduced them to rather kind and obliging locals, the sort that had a history of being ruled by white people with what the Commodore considered to be "results extraordinary, perhaps indicative of their potential."

By three that afternoon, they were closing in on the shores of Lomblem. Smoke rose from the Mount Lewotolo and, on one side of the crater, there was a whitish substance that appeared to be ashes or sulfur. On the islands, there was a handful of very small villages scattered about. Farther up the slopes there was a brownish sort of soil that afforded little vegetation yet, up toward the crest of the lower hills, there was a forest.

Although they were several miles off, they also got a good view of the village of Lamararap, which was built partly on the beach and partly on the rocks. They could just make out the grass huts, the council house, canoes, and a gathering of several hundred people on the beach. One

They dropped anchor in the Solor Straits near the Adunara Island later that afternoon, and the Commodore gave the quartermaster a shotgun to hold while on watch on the bridge. The Commodore was taking an increasingly cautious stance—odd, Bob felt, since as far as he'd seen these islands were some of the most friendly yet.

They were followed by a crowd of kids, mostly naked and dirty.

sailing outrigger canoe made for the *Alva*. The boat was hewn from a very large log, and had quite an interesting design. The prow and stern, which rose high, were decoratively carved and hung with shells "for good luck." There was also a large grass-mat sail set on a huge bamboo mast that tugged her away by embracing a southerly wind, toward the village. The trawling lines extended from two sets of lashed bamboo outriggers that dragged into the boat's wake. The boat's fifteen occupants were a real spectacle—naked except for loincloths and oddly shaped hats.

"Can you see their funny little mushroom hats?" the Commodore pointed out to a gathering by the side rail.

Their brown skin shone in the sun, and they rose to their feet to give a kind of lusty cheer to the *Alva's* crew. All around the little boat the sea was alive with fish, and the men had clearly been celebrating a spectacular catch. Bob captured the exchange on camera as best he could, and smiled to hear the Commodore's stories as he described what he had read about the island men.

The following morning, trying to keep a low profile, Al and Bob went ashore to a little village in the afternoon and got some shots, including one of a crowd of kids—mostly naked and dirty—that had followed them all over. Since it was very hot in the village, and there was no wind, the children, who smelled rather bad, were something of an unwelcome distraction.

The Commodore had planned to go to Komodo Island, to get a specimen of the ten-foot lizards, but they were refused permission from the Dutch. The lizards were apparently getting scarce. Vanderbilt was not pleased.

That very night, Bob attacked his fellow crewmen. The purpose: a fundamental and primitive one—to assert his territory and to defend it. Bob had found a couple of slices of bread and a chop bone in his pocket, put there by the second mate, so he was going to get even.

Below deck, Bob and Mac together drowned second mate Evans with glass after glass of water. Mac then held him while Bob shaved the hair off the man's chest. The only downside was that they ended up making so much noise they woke up the chief officer.

Bima

THE *Alva* sailed through the night on the Flores Sea. Thirty-five miles to the north were the Tiger Islands and twenty miles to the south were the Celebes. Picturesque as those places were, the *Alva* would not stop to delve into their mysteries. The economic conditions in the United States were worsening, and there was a sense that the Commodore could not afford to spend much more on the trip. A stop would also have necessitated several hours of delay and accumulated expenses. It was raining anyway.

They decided to head for Bima on the north coast of Sumbawa. By the morning, they could see Komodo Island, home of large lizards and deer. Lizard hunting was forbidden and they had no interest in deer. They passed in near darkness.

The harbor in Bima Bay was one of the finest in the Dutch East Indies. It was spacious, which was a relief, and it was also well-protected. They let the hook drop about half an hour after their arrival and found themselves opposite the little island of Kimbing, where native chiefs were buried—a sacred ground where visitors were allowed to venture.

The town of Bima was barely visible from where the *Alva* was positioned. It was built on a flat and would often become swamped during the northwest monsoon. Fever was a common problem, in several forms, and when present, tended to affect the population en masse.

In the harbor was a fleet of schooners that looked as if they were cut out of cardboard and stuck up on a comic-operetta stage for a fifteenth-century play.

The island of Sumbawa was one of the Lesser Sunda Islands of the Dutch East Indies. It lay between Lombok and Flores and was both mountainous and volcanic. Mount Tambora had a gigantic crater some five miles wide—its eruption in 1815 had killed twelve thousand people and still haunted the inhabitants.

On the north coast there were many bays and a few stretches of alluvial land, while the southern shore had a great depth of water that reached out to the Indian Ocean. The island was almost cut in two by Saleh Bay, which cut deep and wide to the north coast, and the smaller Chempi Bay to the south.

With his wife and small party in tow, the Commodore went ashore and noted a pole on the wharf that had a lantern on the end of it—a large ship's lantern.

"Kerosene-burning, a fixed red light, visible at two miles," the Commodore said, demonstrating his knowledge to his entourage.

Bima was very hot when the party arrived there, and they started on a tour almost immediately in two American motorcars. They set off first along the highway, passing houses raised on posts about twelve feet above the ground. Several were storehouses, they learned, holding grain, rice and other products. For the most part, they were constructed of wood, with roofs built from thatched palm leaves. The two principal rafters were crossed at each end at the ridge pole and then rose above it. The dwellings were also generally raised above the ground, but only to four feet or so. They were loosely built, which permitted a circulation of air. Above or below the intersection of the principal rafters, one could usually spot a carved wooden figure, somewhat grotesque, representing a given animal. Bob could not figure out if they were of religious importance, to ward away spirits or something like that, or just decorative. One side of the roof extended downwards and out of the eaves to form a porch-like covering, and ladders were positioned to lead up to the lower doors. Many of the houses were surrounded by split-bamboo picket fences.

As the party continued along the drive, it saw the men hanging up corn husks under the eaves of many of the houses and spreading bunches of bananas on the roofs to ripen more effectively. Some others were carrying water from the river in half-moon-shaped, accordion-pleated baskets that were hung from yokes to make the burden palatable.

Women were also about, preparing rice for cooking by pounding it with wooden pestles in wooden troughs. Girls were busy swinging pestles, while the boys were free to play about.

The downside, as the Commodore pointed out, was the dirt and the accompanying flies that were everywhere. Around the compound there were chickens and doves and even water buffalo. The Commodore immediately wanted pictures of the diminutive ponies that were a feature of the area. The old two-wheeled carts that had once been common in America and in Europe but had disappeared at the advent of the motorcar, were still used in Sumbawa, harnesses and all, pulled by undersized horses.

Vanderbilt was quick to point out that many of the natives seemed as if they hadn't bathed in years. When they got downwind of a bunch of them, the smell was fierce. Even Rose couldn't hide her foul expression.

When it was normal not to bathe, there was little to be done.

Bob and Al decided to get shots of the natives' homes and market places. Few spoke English, so it was difficult to communicate. They had to resort to a universal language of signing what they wanted in a charades-like manner, at which they were becoming increasingly better.

The only real export from the island, Bob learned, was onions—very good onions, but onions all the same.

The people of Sumbawa, despite their limited access to the world, were gregarious and talkative by nature. They dressed in Malayan styles and the men tended to wear black velvet visorless caps and sarongs tucked in around their waists. Many also had short coats. The women wore dresses that hung from their shoulders. Most of the children went without clothes. Along the wayside, the Commodore and his party noted the cerise, green, blue, and yellow garments on display. The locals loved multicolored clothing.

Another great highlight was that the locals tended to carry everything on the top of their heads. The women would drape a folded cloth around the crown of their heads for protection, on which were placed a large tray or basin to hold whatever it was they were carrying—bottles, bowls of rice, vegetables, fruit, or masses of banana leaves that were often used as a kind of wrapping paper.

The tour took them through the rice and onion fields, into the mountains, and over a road that was full of hairpin turns, but was otherwise quite acceptable. Acres and acres of ground were covered with onions. Big jabbering monkeys, hanging about the fields, scampered away at the first sign of something approaching. One group the Commodore's car chased off included at least eight monkeys. The bravest of them ventured within about ten feet, looking at them with a kind of comical curiosity before it was shooed away.

The Commodore and Mr. van Duir, an assistant resident and the foremost Dutch official on the island, were to meet the Sultan of Bima. They went to van Duir's house first, met his family, and then the whole party rode to the palace in cars that the sultan had put at his guests' disposal. He was expecting their arrival around five that afternoon, and when they entered the gates of the palace, they saw the troops that guarded the entrance readying to welcome the sultan's guests. The sultan was waiting with his minister and aide.

The sultan's wife joined their party and the whole group sat in a circle on a large veranda. Although it was a charming setting, the conversation was not easy. The sultan spoke Sumbawa and only a little Malay. He had to speak to his minister, who translated the Sumbawa to Malay. Mr. van Duir then translated the Malay to French for the Commodore and his party to process.

After the audience with the sultan, the Commodore and his party were given a tour of the palace and shown the throne that was being prepared for the marriage of the sultan's daughter to the son of the Sultan of Labuan Balat. The bridegroom would arrive by boat with roughly three hundred attendants, including dancing girls, officials, and servants. Feasting and dancing were the mainstay for the wedding ceremony itself. The party would last for three days in Bima, before moving over to Labuan Balat and continue on for several more days. For six days and nights, the bride and groom would sit on the throne that had been specially prepared for them. People would come in to look at them—to stare, and then leave. Some would offer presents. When they were finally allowed to retire to the bridal chamber, they would have the luxury of an American brass bed covered with lace and ribbon. Four old ladies would sit on the floor in front of the bed to keep evil spirits away.

The sultan's treasures included jewels, swords, knives, spears, and silver on display, true relics indicative of the power of the sultan and his family who had ruled Bima for five centuries.

Returning to the veranda to say their farewells at last, the Commodore was offered soda water to drink, which, as usual, he tried to avoid, concerned about malaria. He had watched rather apprehensively for malaria mosquitoes that might be attracted by the lights of the Sultan's new electrical plant. He was burning the plant perhaps more out of pride

Willie K. attended the lavish wedding of the Sultan of Bima's daughter, to the son of the Sultan of Labuan Balat. Despite the setting, Willie's mind wandered nervously at the presence of mosquitoes.

of possession than necessity, the Commodore suggested, but there was something to be said about being prepared for the dark.

When a drum roll suddenly called out from the piazza above the entrance gate, the Sumbawans came to attention and the Commodore and his party said goodbye. Taking his helmet down from the peg on the wall, where it had hung since his arrival, the Commodore noted a lizard jumping out and rushing off into the darkness, making a kind of clucking noise that unnerved everyone.

The Commodore's Birthday

Bob and the rest of the crew had a day or so to themselves while the Commodore made social calls. At least, they almost did. They were keen to explore and be free from the encumbrance of their boss, in any case. Although he was very kind, the Commodore was also rather particular about what he wanted, yet not necessarily the best judge of how to capture the true art. Bob had wandered the local village and rented a car with Al to get about, following in the Commodore's trail to an extent, but running off the beaten path more than the Commodore would ever have condoned. His fear of bugs was beginning to become something of a joke, given that he chose to visit places that tended to be riddled with disease.

The next morning, October 24th, Bob was up early and set up in the darkroom to print the more than two hundred pictures he had taken the previous day. When he went back to his room that afternoon, feeling that he had really done his duty in working for the morning, he found his room in total chaos. It was as if a typhoon had hit it—his clothes, and bedding suitcases were all over the floor. The chairs had been put on the bunk. It was funny to see, but the finger of suspicion had to be pointed. Yet both the second mate and MacDonald swore they hadn't done it. They even offered to help put things back in order, maybe as a kind of ruse. Either one could look you straight in the eye and swear they weren't responsible, that they wouldn't even have considered it. They were particularly talented liars.

There seemed no doubt that one of them did it and they were keeping their rooms locked when absent precisely to prevent any efforts to level the score.

The Commodore was sleeping soundly until early morning, resting after a particularly busy day. He had another full agenda and sent word to Bob and Al to expect to have the day to explore the island themselves, visiting the relevant spots that he had listed for them. It was a particularly warm and pleasant morning. They would probably be in Bali the following afternoon, and they would have to load everything up to be ready to leave. That was the other half of their orders from the Commodore, who was getting ready with his wife and fellow social lot to head out on their next excursion.

Aside from anything else, he was behaving rather distractedly because of the area that they were navigating. Not a hundred years ago, the waters were infested with pirates, and it seemed that they may still have been lingering there. The Commodore was abuzz with reports of ships being attacked going north into the China Sea. No doubt he would be arming the watch with a shotgun or two, as he had occasionally done as protection against the natives.

While he was in Singapore in 1929, there had been a tramp steamer in port that had been attacked; the captain and some of the crew were killed in the skirmish. There was nothing romantic about that prospect, and the notion of venturing into such dangerous waters had many of the officers anxious. For the first time, the Commodore seemed to be thinking about home in a positive light. He had thought about the markets enough and felt more than ever that he ought to be back in New York to deal with personal affairs. He came from a long line of successful businessmen, and he was aware of what he should be doing to be both responsible and practical in regards to his financial well-being.

Bali was perhaps the most interesting place that they had seen on the whole trip. The island had only four hundred white men, all of them Europeans. Some were Dutch government officials overseeing the highly religious natives who would group into processions of eight or ten and walk along the road to make an offering at the temple with a kind of obsessive devotion. One of the girls in the lead appeared to have about one hundred and twenty-five pounds of fruit on her head, piled in a cylindrical shape about four feet high, with a fan decoration of gold on top. The others had fish and pigs to offer, which Bob thought was something of a waste considering the lack of variety in his diet over the last few months. The worst part was having to run ahead of the procession to get pictures. Bob was sinking to the ground and then sprinting ahead, positioning

Bob found Bali to be the most interesting of all the islands, off the track of tourists until only three years before. He found the native girls who wore only a sarong around their waists "almost erotic."

himself as quickly as he could to get the best shot and then running off again.

When the procession finally made it to the temple, Bob had something of a reprieve. They weren't permitted inside—even the Commodore's sense of propriety would not have permitted it—but Bob was to stand outside to get as many pictures as possible. The natives were wearing only a sarong around their waists and nothing to cover either the breasts of the women or chests of the men. The girls were very well-formed and the people carried themselves in a strong, upright manner. It was another of those experiences that was almost erotic. But now a seasoned photographer and traveler, Bob didn't feel the least bit embarrassed. It was something he was vaguely used to, although he couldn't resist looking to the Commodore to see what his reaction would be. Charming and refined though he was, Vanderbilt found primitive displays unnerving.

Only about four hundred white men lived on unspoiled Bali. The natives, highly religious, made temple offerings with obsessive devotion. This woman carried a four-foot stack of some one hundred and twenty-five pounds of fruits on her head for this purpose.

When the festival was finally underway, they saw a procession of four hundred worshipers circling the walls of the temple beside the sea. The women, clad as they were, appeared very statuesque and graceful. They could carry bundles on their heads that weighed more than one hundred and fifty pounds.

Not wishing to intrude on the ceremony itself, the Commodore observed the priests in their resplendent robes carrying their ceremonial umbrellas. They watched the spear carriers come after that, and the girls with their offerings, and then they left, picked up by a car at Buleleng and drove off towards a region that had a far more European vibe.

There were uniformed police officers about and a tourist steamer anchored in the roadstead. There was a tourist headquarters, where a crowd of American, French, English, and Dutch travelers—perspiring terribly—waited to get more information about the right places to visit on the island. Although it was a far from welcoming scene, the tourists looking as irritated as they did, it was nice to see people from home again.

THE COMMODORE'S BIRTHDAY

The Commodore's birthday was an excuse for revelry. Robert found a personal means of celebration, by waking early and heading ashore.

October 26th was the Commodore's birthday, and for the first time in weeks, there was little sign of his concern about the markets. He was congratulated by everyone, of course. Reaching the age of fifty-three was quite something.

"I wonder whether I look as old as I am, or whether I feel as old as I look," he said in his acceptance speech to a bunch of reveling well-wishers. Rose had brought along a fine present for her husband—a piece from Cartier of New York. Doctor Lane also presented him with a fine set of operating knives. They were used by naval surgeons years before and were quite valuable.

Bob had been asked, along with the rest of the crew, to sign a parchment wishing the Commodore happiness and long life, and that ended up being the extent of his participation. He was simply too tired that evening. The entire day's events had been skillfully executed by Mr. Belanske, who was also in charge of the card and responsible for overseeing the efforts of the chef and the cooks, who produced a cake and patisserie for the dinner table that night.

Since celebrating other holidays was a bit of a challenge so far away from home, celebrating the Commodore's birthday was an opportunity for everyone to have fun in a way they were familiar with, and in luxury at that. The dinner table decorations were quite spectacular that evening, thanks to the crew. As they sailed away from Bali that evening, with the full moon gazing down upon them, everyone onboard felt like a millionaire.

Bob had distanced himself from the celebrations and was one of the few to wake up early the next day, heading to shore. He had gotten some interesting shots earlier in the day, before the rest of the crew had even started packing to leave, until he was ordered to spend most of the day shooting the processions and temples. He had recorded men weaving, the silversmiths, and a handful of other day-to-day activities that had been going on around the island. In a way, he decided later, it was his silent birthday present to a man much like his father, whose orders were dangerous to question.

A Javanese man is either unaware of, or not particularly pleased with, being photographed.

Vanderbilt had opened the door to an entirely new world for a group of people who might never have seen such things any other way, at any other time in their lives. And at the same time that he opened the door, he did so without any real intention of following through, of providing any one of those boys with a way of coping. They would go back to their lives in America as if nothing had changed. Back to the ordinary, coping with monotony, maybe wiser, maybe not, maybe knowing that home was where they belonged, maybe not.

For Bob, that was the feeling about the Commodore that had him conflicted. He admired the man, but he also knew, somehow, that he was not the kind of father figure he presented himself to be. He was the man in charge. Perhaps Bob could go to him for a job when he returned to America. But more likely, the very attempt to do so would be perceived as wrong somehow, against the code. Upon returning, Mr. Vanderbilt had security, Bob did not. And Bob was beginning to realize that.

The grace and charm of Bali captivated master and crew alike. Vanderbilt would later write that the days in Bali were some of his happiest.

Wearing the pith helmet he had searched for but failed to purchase in New York, Bob takes a ride on a cow sculpture at a Buddhist temple in Borobudur. Once buried to conceal its presence, the fabulous monument, built between 750-850 C.E., had been overgrown by jungle brush. Sir Stamford Raffles, once governor of Dutch East India, set out to uncover the ruins in 1814. The temple contained some one thousand three hundred sculptures, but Al and Robert, accompanied by their cameras, were denied entry. Instead they contented themselves with a cow ride outside.

That day he felt the need to work hard, and work alone. Serving the Commodore had both offered and withdrawn the possibility of a stable future: a future with Jo. The letter was still in his pocket. He began to doubt he would ever send it. He wondered if there was any point at all in dreaming big.

Michelle and Pierre motored down to the south side of the island while Rose and Doctor Lane traveled with the Commodore along the north shore. The end of the day brought them all through the Balinese landscape, like a vast mural painting with luxuriant vegetation and peaceful, leisurely people that huddled by their carven temples and thatched-roof bamboo villages. They spotted the water buffalo wandering about, grazing and paying little attention to them. They headed west later, and left the coastal road to climb into the hills. In the village of Moedoek, they heard the music of a *gamelan*. The time in Bali had been two of the happiest days in their journey.

Surabaya

THEY REACHED Surabaya by two o'clock in the afternoon and went ashore a couple of hours later to enjoy the town. The crew had plenty of time to enjoy themselves. Bob had dinner at the *Orange Hotel* and later explored the town a little. He had fun trying to get the taxi drivers to take him back to the docks. He gave directions as best he could, using the kind of sign language he had perfected in the other places they had visited where few people spoke English.

The Javanese got the equivalent of only thirty-five cents American for working an eight-and-one-half-hour day in the boiling sun. It was a small wonder, the Commodore noted, that Java was creating such competition in the world of commerce. Not only did the place have an excellent harbor and thus a means of importing and exporting with convenience, but it also had modern facilities and good transportation systems from the field to the ship.

The afternoon of their arrival was full of activity: they all went up the river in the launch and got some good shots of native river boats and bathing scenes. Bob spent the rest of the evening preparing equipment to leave on a three-day trip with the Commodore into the back country.

Leaving the *Alva* far behind, they had traversed all sorts of farming lands and every inch of land seemed to be planted, or was otherwise being used in some way. Taking in so much detail was exhausting. One place had rice fields, another had tobacco, and then there were the flooded rice paddies underneath where the tobacco *kapok* trees blossomed.

The next day, they had lunch at the village of Solo before heading off over perfect roads that ran from Surabaya to Djokja. The party dressed for dinner and prepared to go off and see a dance. Al and Bob were invited along for that particular occasion, with Al as the master of ceremonies.

Bob's style is captured in this reflective still under a dock in Java. Al and Bob believed the Javanese to be an industrious people, always chewing betel nuts much the way Americans chewed tobacco.

The gamelan included a variety of instruments, styled like xylophones. The Javanese dancers were also impressive to watch, although rather more like actors than dancers. The women, like many of the other natives they had seen on the trip, wore interesting selections of jewelry and clothes—tight bodices, waistbands, and long flowing sarongs, all vividly colored. The men wore short trousers and sarongs, had long hair, and decorated their ear lobes with elaborate pendants.

After the dance, just as the sun was setting, they made a visit to the massive ruins of the *Water Castle*, which was built in 1758 under the aegis of the first Sultan of Djocjakarata, and then destroyed in an earthquake. Those that saw the sundown from the castle thought it rather gloomy. The Commodore was obviously uneasy; mosquitoes had been found breeding around a large pool of stagnant water and he did not care to linger. He began making his excuses to move inside and back to the hotel as quickly as possible. Following behind the Commodore and his party, Bob

Buddhist Mandoet Temple—Java
The Javanese dancers were impressive to watch, although more like actors than dancers. Here, a legendary drama was played out in pantomime.

was already fading as he and Al continued to snap shots. Thankfully, the Commodore pulled through, and they returned not much later.

That evening, Bob wandered aimlessly around town before retiring to a double room that was larger than his apartment in Hollywood. Jo was still in his thoughts, but he was not aching for her as much. What he felt was more a distant longing; he dreamed of her but she was not near him anymore.

On shore all morning, Bob was excited to finally be able to get his checks cashed. It was nice to have some money in his back pocket again.

Djokja was some two hundred miles inland from the seaport and the scenes were truly some of the most wonderful in the world. The many Hindu temples all around (and there seemed to be thousands of them) were breathtaking. Bob excitedly jogged around, shooting pictures of the temples, but, as he would tell his father, it was "as hot as Hades." All he wore was a shirt, khaki short pants, and a sun helmet.

Djocja was even noisier than Havana; they were surrounded by activity of the liveliest and most colorful sort. They saw a procession of about fifteen decked carriages as the sultan and his entourage were going to the horse races, which started at 8:30 a.m., because of the midday heat. Six horses pulled the sultan and, on the rear board, men stood dressed in red with krisses stuck into their waistbands. Outriders and cavalry also attended him. The sultan himself was dressed in a white uniform. White seemed to be the best color to wear in the heat, but lugging the many medals about his neck, he still looked hot. His wife was on his right as well as an accompaniment of several concubines all dressed alike and sitting very quietly. Bob heard the sultan had something in the region of forty concubines and seventy-two children, which made him wonder how exactly a man could manage such a handful of women at once. The occupants of the other carriages looked rather bored, though they appeared to be dressed in the height of fashion. They glared out at the crowds with what the crew interpreted as blank, almost disdainful, expressions.

After the parade, the Commodore, accompanied by Rose and Doctor Lane, set out to see one of the finest monuments in Java—a stupendous product of the Middle Ages known as the *Borobudur*. A magnificent Buddhist temple built between 750 and 850 C.E. When the Buddhists were driven out of the Java by the Muslims, the priests in charge of the temple had covered it with earth. As years passed, the jungle had also helped to conceal the temple itself, until Sir Stamford Raffles, governor general of what had been Dutch East India, set about uncovering the ruins with a formal excavation in 1814. Just before the First World War, the Dutch had taken to restoring the temple to its former splendor.

Built on a hilltop, the temple took the form of a *stupa* (or *tope*). It was almost prismatic in its lower parts and then cylindrical in the upper portion. The structure featured nine terraces—six in the upper section of the building that were designed in squares and three in the lower section that were circular. It covered an area of three hundred ninety-four square feet and stood one hundred and fifteen feet high. It contained about one thousand three hundred sculptures and various Buddhist relics of which the Commodore would have liked to have a record. Unfortunately, it was hardly considered respectful to take the cameras inside.

While the Commodore and his party explored the Buddhist temple at Borobudur, Bob and Al made the most of things, shooting the statuary in the Mendota Temple, two miles east.

After taking some pictures of the outside, Bob and Al followed the Commodore in to get a look at some of the sculptures, which told a story of the life of Buddha.

Climbing the steps for a closer look at the temple itself, Doctor Lane and the Commodore trailed behind somewhat as Rose led the way up a steep pathway. Just before reaching the second terrace, where there were yet more sculptures to examine, the doctor slipped and fell backwards rather dramatically, frightening everyone, not the least himself. He looked like a rubber ball, bouncing down the steps and ricocheting off a side wall before finally disappearing over what seemed from their vantage point to be an outright precipice. There was a moment where it seemed likely he could have died right before their eyes, until a head appeared and a cheery but rather shaken expression accompanied a true declaration of health. "Heigh-ho-the-fox," he smiled.

Al and Bob were prohibited from taking photos inside temples, a denial that at times was more of a blessing than a curse.

Rose, of course, had raced down the stairs to his aid, and her husband, determined not to play the shrinking violet, had stood his ground and simply looked to see that the Doctor was indeed alright. Bob and Al stepped forward to help the doctor back to the motorcar, on what appeared to be a sprained ankle.

An x-ray at the hospital in Djocja an hour or so later confirmed the bone to be intact and the doctor was quite ready to get on with his day. The Vanderbilts, however, insisted that he return to the hotel. There was little point in prolonging a visit after such drama.

The sultan and his retinue were making their way back to the palace just as the Vanderbilts and their party arrived at the hotel. Deciding a journey back to Surabaya by automobile might be overly strenuous for the doctor, shaken as he was, Willie K. booked seats on the express train for that afternoon.

Far East

Back in Surabaya, the new month—November—brought with it a slew of responsibilities. The Commodore had bills to pay before the *Alva* could continue the rest of its journey toward home. The cost of day-to-day affairs was no longer being viewed as entirely trivial. By noon that Sunday morning, the ship was heading out of the Surabaya harbor onto a smooth, welcoming sea. They had been on land for what seemed an age. They hadn't been so long on the shore since Brisbane and they had begun to feel out of place by the end of it. Everyone missed the rocking of the sea; sometimes they still felt it onshore, like a recorded sensation.

They were passing through the shallow Java Sea, some twenty to thirty fathoms deep. They had a pilot aboard again and others had informed the Commodore of the need to note the one-knot current, which was sweeping the ship up the coast in a somewhat westerly direction. The Commodore made the point that there had been predictions such as these offered in similar instances only to be later disproved.

They passed many fishing boats and some under sail. Others had drift nets out. They really wanted to gaze upon Java's high mountains, but the best they could do was catch a short glimpse or two through the clouds.

By seven that morning, the tall lighthouse of the flat Boomjes Island came into view. By three that afternoon, they would reach the Batavi Harbor.

The Hindu temples were "the most marvelous of sights," Bob wrote to his father; they were built roof upon roof, glittering in gold against the sun.

They took many pictures of them and at one place they got into a Buddhist temple and shot a picture of the largest Buddha they had yet seen, carved of solid rock and over three hundred years old. It was one of the most difficult shots Bob had ever attempted. It was all dark except for a small ray of light coming through a tiny door. He had to stoop way down to get inside the gap, propping the Graflex up on a couple of rocks and giving it a good time exposure along with hope and patience. He just had to get a good picture of it, because there had been very few ever taken, and those with only flash lights.

When the Commodore was given an enlargement of that Buddha picture, he was ecstatic. He shouted praises, calling the Buddha as well as the portraits of Javanese and Balinese girls, "Splendid, marvelous, beautiful! Beautiful, Bob." It was high praise indeed and Bob was delighted.

The more he saw of the countryside in Java, the more he decided that there could hardly be more than ten feet of vacant ground in the whole country. Every foot had rice fields, kapok groves, tobacco, bananas, coconuts, sugar or something else. No matter which direction they looked, they could see the Javanese working these fields or walking along the roads with heavy loads on their heads. Paddy field guards manipulated strings attached to bells designed to frighten away the menacing birds. There were plenty of Chinese there, too.

The land was divided up by many rivers and, as in most tropical islands, they overflowed into swollen streams during the rainy seasons. During the dry seasons, however, they often dried up completely. The dry season was from May to October. Everybody was happy when the rains came in November, except the tourists, and the natives celebrated with a jubilee for the rain that made everything grow and look beautiful.

The Javanese themselves were industrious and constantly chewing betel-nut just as Americans chewed tobacco. Young Javanese seemed to have a particular inclination towards education. Many spoke English well enough, at least enough to understand the requests of tourists.

Visiting the market with Al in tow, Bob bought some more *batik*, the native-made cloth that, if for nothing else, was useful as a form of attire in the heat. He found several good pieces, a cross, and a native royal dagger to go with his father's own collection of Japanese swords. A carved bird of ox horn was the most expensive item he bought there, costing seventy-five Dutch cents, which ran to the equivalent, he guessed, of about thirty-five cents in American money.

Admiring the real estate of Batavia, which was owned, for the most part, by the Chinese and Arabs, the Commodore was quick to admire how so many had set up businesses by leasing their properties in the city to earn a decent return. The Chinese also capitalized on the city's need for reliable transport. They owned most of the local buses, competing rather effectively with the railroads in Java, as the buses were beginning to do in the United States, to the great chagrin of the Vanderbilt line.

Motor vehicles in general were proving quite popular in Batavia, but the government had imposed a heavy tax on them. The Commodore preferred the railroads, which were relatively well-maintained, with good facilities and equipment. When he spoke to Doctor Lane on the subject, the latter was quite impressed at the depth of the Commodore's understanding and enthusiastic talk about the fine details of the railroads. Knowing only pieces of the family history and recognizing only elements of the Commodore's character, Bob could never be quite sure how much of his history he carried with him.

They moved about the city, which was clean, healthy, and well laid out, observing the many attractive residences, boulevards and public parks. The canals were also of interest, crowded as they were with a colorful shipping industry.

By Tuesday November 3rd, after a day in Buitenzorg (a town whose name meant carefree), a torrential downpour quickly killed much of the party's enthusiasm for the place and the Commodore sent word to the crew that they would be leaving Batavia the next morning. The Dutch, being effective colonizers, had a talent for making just about any atmosphere temporarily bearable, the Commodore joked. It was far better to enjoy another night in a relatively good hotel, surrounded by all of the modern conveniences of railroads, electricity, highways, automobiles, and wireless telegraphy, rather than venturing out in less than favorable weather conditions.

While the Commodore was entertaining himself and his party, Bob had been busy experiencing some of the benefits of Batavia for himself. He had, amidst the calm waters, managed to catch up with his still developing work, and felt rather proud for sticking to his resolution to avoid any serious backup again. He had another ten dozen stills to be developed that day in the darkroom. This was better than when they were out at sea where, only weather permitting, could he ever keep a steady hand.

There were also certain advantages to the work that were becoming increasingly obvious now that the Commodore wanted everything to

Bob had an eye for capturing people at work. Here a Balinese girl works a loom.

move at a faster pace: Al and Bob were frankly seeing more of the world than most of those on board. Although the work was hard, it was all worth it on that basis alone. They flew between the ports and the interiors, cameras in tow, capturing far more in days, sometimes hours, than the ordinary tourist would see in a month. On one trip, two hundred miles into the interior and all over the native sections of Surabaya, Solo, Dejokja and Batavia, they managed to wrap up most of their work in just four days.

They planned to head towards Europe relatively soon, and Al was abuzz with news that his wife was going to be able to meet them in Marseille, France. Everyone was very aware by now of how much Al missed home. Bob wrote to his father about how much he wanted to see him, how he wished they could meet in France as well, and tour Europe together.

Muntok

Posting the latest letter to his father, Bob prepared for the *Alva's* departure that night. The news had spread as effectively as ever that they would soon be gone from Batavia. The next stop was Sumatra and then Singapore. Bob rushed to mail his letter so it would catch a steamer for the States, or some European port, and in a moment of rare determination, he posted the letter to Jo with a second note telling her of the *Alva's* plans for the next several weeks. What compelled him to take action, he could not be sure, but he had felt himself growing up as the *Alva* set on a course increasingly driven back towards New York. He mailed the letter with hope and left it at that.

Along the Sumatran coast, they could see enormous tree stumps and other vegetation that had been carried out to sea. The helmsman was kept busy watching out for similar flotsam in the water and calls of "Hard over right!" and "Hard over left!" were sounding out for quite some time as they sought to dodge the larger obstructions that might damage the propellers.

The following morning, they were underway again, headed to Muntok, the capital of Banka Island, which rested at the northerly entrance to the strait. With clearer skies now, they could see the Sumatran coast close by, running low and flat, dominated by swamps that forced the villagers to build their homes on stilts in the shallow water to escape the damp and the risk of disease. The shore was not entirely flat, but dotted with low hills. The Banka Strait, for the most part, was well-marked with lighthouses and gas buoys, positioned by the Dutch "in a bid to be useful to the travelers that visited them," as Vanderbilt proclaimed. The port was hardly difficult to sail through, particularly with all of the portholes open, but navigation was beginning to become a problem: the four magnetic compasses were causing them trouble due to the large quantities of iron and electrical instrument on board. The Commodore had to check their accuracy regularly. At Surabaya, the Commodore had even moved one of the compasses to the top of the after-house, where a stand was erected for it. It stood up like a lighthouse, but its new position seemed to solve the problem; it experienced less than one degree of deviation from then on.

By 1:30 p.m. that afternoon, they had bearings for Muntok again and were passing over nearby shoals. Twenty minutes later they were anchored in deep water two miles from the town, a speedboat ready to put them to shore. They were back to dealing with papers and officials. The Commodore had another American motorcar made available so he and the members of his party could drive into the town, basking in its shaded, tree-lined streets. The town had a population of five thousand. The Chinese predominated in business affairs, with Chinese signs over almost every store they saw. There were also numerous roads and railroad businesses thriving in the region, primarily under Chinese management.

The drive took them some twenty kilometers through a rolling countryside, past impenetrable jungle just off the edge of the road. They passed another village in which the houses were on stilts again, built in rows, with leaf-thatched roofs and matted sides held in place by bamboo poles. The people living in those houses looked particularly unhealthy, convincing the Commodore that disease was prevalent.

* * *

It was not long before the *Alva* entered the China Sea. They were headed for Singapore at last, choosing the Strait of Durian, which looked to be the easiest of the various deep-water channels that might be used. The weather was warm, and the sail was pleasant. It probably would have been whichever passage they'd chosen. Another dredging exercise in the afternoon brought trouble—a headache of sorts for the Commodore, who was hardly looking to take on the additional expense of something even as minor as the loss of a dredge. Nevertheless, lose a dredge they did. As the *Alva* moved through the Malakka Strait, reaching to the sea bed with four hundred meters of cable supporting it, the dredge got caught on some large obstruction. The cable had been on the drum for five years, and had been used on Vanderbilt's earlier yacht *Ara*. The use of a brand-new cable seemed to mark the end of an era. Nothing they did, no day at sea, went without exorbitant expense; even the luxurious *Alva* was not infallible.

Singapore was one of the busiest harbors the Commodore had ever seen, comparable even to New York. It was a strategic spot, important to many of the world's trade routes. Although it continued to rain hard that afternoon, the Commodore and his wife found themselves stuck in the launch, the water crammed with lighters by the hundreds alongside a variety of Chinese craft.

In Singapore, domestic life was definitely more colorful than sanitary. The stench was particularly unnerving, enough to nearly bowl them over, they had to cover their noses with handkerchiefs, ignoring the surprised looks of the many people.

The gang went ashore and waited at the wharf for more motorcars, hackney carriages, and rickshaws. In the heart of the city, there was also a conglomeration of fascinating faces: natives, Malays from Sumatra, and a considerable number of Chinese. There were also Japanese, Indians, Javanese, Arabs, and Europeans detected in the crowds, along with sailors from all variety of maritime countries.

Color was everywhere: on the boats, the houses, the costumes, the sea, and even the vegetation, all of it startling. The Chinese and the Indian bazaars were particularly exciting places, defined by their turmoil and bustle, the sort of energy that was difficult to find anywhere else. In Singapore, it was possible to buy just about anything: from Malay-made sarongs, to Malakka canes, baskets and other rattan ware. Models of native boats and imported jewelry were also significant, with all kinds of imported curios. In the European quarter, there were fine British department stores. Outside the main commercial centers, small shops were dotted all around the city. Chinese, Hindu, and Confucian temples were to be found all over; Jewish synagogues alongside Christian cathedrals and churches. They took in as much of the scenery as they could: all the modern structures alongside historical relics.

The first full day in Singapore afforded the opportunity to drive about the town, taking in yet more diverse scenery. The foreign groups, although living under British rule there, had preserved their own religion and customs rather well. The city existed as relatively segregated sections: a Malay city, then English, and then a Chinese. The European quarter was decidedly clean and defined by its wide boulevards and harbor view.

It was also apparent, without much exploration, that everyone besides the Europeans and a few of the Chinese was living in slums.

Traffic officers controlled the mixed menagerie of vehicles, contending with speeding motorcars as well as lumbering ox-drawn carts. They maintained control by turning their backs to the traffic they wanted to stop, and exposing wings strapped to their shoulders, five feet across and about six inches deep. Near both ends, there were strips of red glass reflective disks, fixed for use at night.

Bob and Al started their shore leave by shipping fourteen thousand feet of film back home. They then set a camera up in the back of the car, cruising around the native Chinese and Malay streets, getting pictures in the afternoon. Although it rained hard most of the morning, Bob certainly didn't want to walk down some of the narrow, dirty alleys after dark. The European and business districts were rather beautiful—festooned with parks and white buildings—but the native sections were made up of narrow alleys from which the Chinese, Malays and Hindus stared for long hours, out of dark windows.

The crowded harbors of Singapore

Pierre and Michelle arrived by steamer from Batavia, having been motored through Java since the *Alva's* arrival there some time ago.

Bob spent most of his day observing men at work and in their small living quarters, usually two stories high and closely crammed together with hardly any breathing space. There were coolies cooking their rice on the floor of their homes and men that smelled of refuse and rotten fish. All the larger boats had to be loaded, coaled, or unloaded while at anchor in the harbor, and junks crowded around them loading the ships' goods in them to be taken ashore. He captured images of the clothes hanging out from the windows on long sticks, the chickens running in the streets, the rickshaws, and flying restaurants, and Hindus sitting or squatting on their haunches in small, dark doorways.

Penang

It seemed everyone was on holiday in Singapore. For the first two days of their visit, every store was closed. It was a half holiday on Sunday and then all the English ports closed down for another holiday on Monday. Armistice Day was on Wednesday.

On Armistice Day, the *Alva* raised anchor for a final time, departing Singapore for the Straits of Malacea and then Penang at Cape Rachado.

The bustling streets of Penang.

They took advantage of a strong westerly breeze. It sprang up in the morning and prompted clear skies in the afternoon as they sailed up the coast of the Malay Peninsula, the land constantly before the ship on its starboard side, wafting fragrances of the tropics into the air.

Working in the darkroom most of the day, developing negatives and taking advantage of the ship's relative steadiness, Bob kept a weather eye on progress, noting their entry to the twenty-mile channel to Penang at about 5:30 p.m., with anchorage at 7:30 pm. He also watched the skies. He was brooding about his future, along with most everyone else, and he missed his father and wondered about the differences between the sky he was seeing and the one his father looked upon.

Accompanying Al, who was in desperate need of distraction, Bob went off to the *Runnymeade Hotel* to send off Christmas cards. The mail moved so slowly that mid-November was the last time at which they could credibly mail the cards and have some hope of them arriving on time. Few cared much about the precise timing of the messages' arrival, but it seemed nice to at least try and coordinate their greetings with the familiar Christmas celebrations. Years of Christmas were beginning to

A forest of masts creates a memorable silhouette in the port of Penang.

haunt Bob. He remembered the unspoken tensions between his brother and his father—the quiet and still painful thought that his mother was gone, never returning. He never understood the circumstances of her passing. With the cards sent off, the Christmas duty was all but fulfilled.

The next stop was the city itself, following in the footsteps of the Commodore, who had planned to wander the streets a bit; as much as his nose and his fear of disease would allow.

Wandering off the main streets, cameras in hand, Bob and Al quickly realized that the most dramatic record they could make of the place depended on whether they could capture the vast variety of smells produced all around. The roads were adorned with beautiful flowers and shrubs, tree ferns, and tall, feathery plants, each of which produced a particular odor. Then there were the spices, the smells of food cooking in the houses, and the bath houses which lent a certain quality to the air's humidity.

The Commodore was somewhat afraid of snakes, but sent Bob and Al to photograph the scene nonetheless. There were snakes everywhere—slithering and sliding—sleeping in whatever position the cool air of dawn happened to find them—on top of pictures, in lattice work, and perched on top of Buddhas.

Willie K. had grown squeamish as he aged. Needless to say, the inhabitants of the Buddhist snake temple of Penang must have sent shivers through the millionaire.

Bob set a camera up in the back of a rented car and drove through the streets of Georgetown, photographing the scenes they had spotted on foot. He and Al stopped off at the Chinese snake temple, at the Commodore's behest. There were snakes slithering all over the place, sleeping in the day time in whatever position the dawn happened to come down on them—on top of pictures, in lattice work, or perched on top of Buddhas, or small trees. Bob took several pictures and made a number of movies. He and Al smiled to think of how nervous the Commodore had been in making the request, suggesting that they might even want to delay their visit a day, given that it was the 13th and there was certainly no predicting what might happen around such potentially dangerous animals.

They attempted to visit another large Chinese temple as well, but the rain drove them away. They were in the mountains and the clouds seemed to split open when they hit the hills. Trying to dodge the rain, Bob

Bob found this Buddhist temple in Penang to be a particularly beautiful place with a spectacular interior.

directed their driver to take them over to another large Buddhist temple in Penang. The interior was spectacular. Bob and Al had to take off their shoes before they were permitted to traverse the floor of the worship room. Bob occupied himself by collecting time exposures for most of the interesting design features. A very beautiful Italian white marble statue of Buddha and the disciples posed a particular challenge; there was no good light, but Bob was able to get the pictures just the same.

After lunch, Bob and Al again met with the Commodore, preparing to motor up through the hills and visit the Ayer Itam Chinese temple, also known as the Temple of the Thousand Steps. The Commodore and his group had gone to the Oriental quarter, visiting Hindu temples with their towers, niches, and polychrome decorations. He also visited the Chinese temples, with their gates of deep vermilion green or black, flanked by dragons to keep away evil spirits.

In the Chinese residential section, they found one villa, and then another, decorated with the same great wealth of ornament: dragons on roofs, china and pottery figures in niches, and pictures in panels on the outsides of walls. In this case, the European part of the city was decidedly colorless and unimaginative.

On Friday the 13th, Bob noted that there was hardly anyone around. The temple facades, rambling roofs, and raking gables were very impressive. Its shrines, jars, gongs, and shining brass were also stunning. At least Bob thought so as he looked over them, preparing to take stills to test the light for the possibility of filming some moving pictures later. On the lowest tier of steps, there was a pool for sacred turtles and above that a pool for goldfish. A third pool contained an assortment of colored fish, surrounded by marigolds, roses, and chrysanthemums. There were statues of the gods all around: amiable ones and more hideous ones, the kind that might have terrified those with more fertile imaginations. Perhaps if Bob hadn't seen the pits once used by cannibals—the stones used when people had once been brutally executed—he might have felt more in awe of man's image of the gods brought to life so vividly. The *God of Mirth* and the *Gods of the Four Winds* drew the Commodore's attention, and he asked Bob to get whatever shots of them he could.

While Bob and Al finished their work inside the temple, Rose and Willie set off on the walk back down the hill to the car. It was a long walk, and they were more than a little nervous for fear of falling, again given the date and the all too recent experience of watching Doctor Lane tumble down a similar flight of stairs. The Doctor's incredible luck in being unharmed was too remarkable to believe that that kind of fortune could be repeated.

As they progressed down the pathway, a danger of a different sort confronted them. Not really a danger, so much, as a distraction—in the form of a Hindu vendor selling small, precious stones.

"Very fine," he said, in English. He opened a small piece of paper and revealed two fairly large and well-cut yellow diamonds. "No business for ten days, Mister," he said, proving his English even better than might have been expected. "Only eight dollars," he insisted. "Straits money. Have been asking sixteen."

Vanderbilt wasn't interested and began to grow impatient as the man continued to follow them rather closely. "No, go away!" he said sharply, attempting to protect Rose from the peddling nuisance. He was trying to catch her eye with the jewels even though he was addressing Willie K. with his bargaining.

"Oh, please Mister, look, look!" He opened a second parcel to reveal two light blue sapphires. "Same price," he added, having finally irritated Willie enough that spending money seemed the better option. They had, after all, a considerable way to go down the hill, and Bob and Al were now in pursuit, carrying heavy and expensive camera equipment.

"All right, two dollars for the diamonds," the Commodore bellowed, making his authority quite clear, while indicating that he had no intention of being pestered much longer. The sapphires were acquired for one guilder, Dutch money, and ten cents Straits—local currencies were rather confused and often used together.

Driving again to the *Snake Temple*, the Commodore wondered for a minute if he had been bamboozled in regards to the place. On his first visit, he had imagined a series of crypts with dangerous, hissing snakes everywhere around, kept there as a kind of menace against unwelcomed visitors. He had been disappointed on that first trip, as he explained to Bob and Al: "The snakes were coiled on branches of trees and stuck in vases. They were also rather inactive and as such, hardly dangerous."

As they entered, they were at the back of the altar, with a big old-fashioned New England clock ticking away. A few worshipers were present, burning joss sticks, but the atmosphere did not impress the group as being particularly religious.

"Definitely disappointing," the Commodore reaffirmed.

That night, Bob took the opportunity to tell Al about his letter to Jo. He confided in his friend—the first and only person he was likely to tell—the plan for her to meet him somewhere: Europe or Los Angeles. And like a limpet, Al jumped onto the long-term consequences and launched a barrage of questions—Was he proposing marriage? Where would they live? What about her family? What about his father? How would he support her? Bob, of course, had no answers to any of these questions.

Ceylon

WITH THE thirteenth of the month overcome, the following morning showed the beginnings of a beautiful day, fairly cool and surrounded by a smooth sea. The *Alva* raised anchor at 10:30 a.m., underway for the island of Sabang—another Dutch island where they would be spending guilders—it was really hard to keep the currencies straight.

Ceylon was perhaps the most beautiful place in the world.

A calm sea allowed them to work, and Bob and Al set about developing all of the interior pictures from the day before. Despite the challenges of the light, all of the pictures came out very well, surprising since you couldn't buy a decent picture of the interiors. Bob wondered: if he were a photographer out of the region, could he have cornered the market? No one else seemed to have the ambition to produce interior pictures properly.

By four that afternoon, there were more photographs to be taken. There was an extraordinary rock—known as the Pulo Perak—which appeared abeam a little over a mile away. It was steep, gray and tall, supporting no vegetation. Countless birds made their home there, along with the rats that swarmed the shores.

The next three days would see the *Alva* at sea, passing through the Bay of Bengal, bound for Ceylon. A new moon greeted them on the first night, as they sailed over placid waters. At daybreak, they were close to the harbor of Sabang: one of the northwest extremities of Sumatra. The Commodore's last world cruise had involved them anchoring in roughly the same spot. Their second night was not as pleasant. They had been lucky to escape the violent southwest wind in the Malakka Strait, but a change of weather came up rather unexpectedly, as it often did at that time of year, and blew at force eight from about seven in the evening until midnight, bringing with it thunder, rain, and lightning to set everyone ill at ease. The Commodore managed to retain his wits and directed the crew to shore up the ship to avoid any unnecessary dampness. Cleaning out the staterooms after the last deluge had not been fun at all.

By noon, the weather had changed again. Several hundred miles from Penang, the sea was smooth except for one deep, old swell that was coming in from the southwest. Since there were no signs of further rain-squalls, the Commodore set all hands to painting the ship, as he deemed that it was in need of some basic maintenance. Bob and Al were exempt from such work, along with one or two of the other skilled professionals, but they could hardly remain below deck lounging around while everyone else worked. The Commodore expected prints, and if prints were unavailable, he wanted to see that his photographers were at work and that his dollar was being put to good use. They photographed the men at work painting, as well as performing other maintenance, all to keep the photographic records as accurate and comprehensive as they could be.

Port scene. Colombo, Ceylon.

Another day at sea and the *Alva* finally arrived in Colombo. A trip had been planned that would take the main party into the interior of the city. Bob and Al were charged with shooting as much of the harbor and the city as they could before setting off.

Ceylon was part of a British crown colony and perhaps, from what they saw, one of the loveliest places in the world. The plantations, farms, and forests embroidered the plains, hills, and valleys, while the central and southern regions boasted high mountain peaks. The harbor of Colombo was magnificent and the environment was tropical. Kandy, on the other hand, at a height of one thousand six hundred feet, had a mean annual temperature of seventy-six degrees; it was restful and cool at night. Nuwara Eliya ran to six thousand five hundred feet, an exhilarating elevation with frigid nights. In the hot months, Nuwara Eliya was the official residence of the Governor of Ceylon.

Throughout history, powerful dynasties had risen and fallen in Ceylon. In addition to Aryans in the fifth century B.C.E. and Tamils in the

Colombo, Ceylon Customs House.
 Colombo was both the capital of Ceylon and a key harbor.

third century B.C.E., the Portuguese, the Dutch, and the British all made conquests there in 1507, 1665, and 1796, respectively. Only the British, however, were particularly successful in penetrating the great variety of races and nationalities, including the Singhalese, Veddahs, Tamils, Moors, Malays, and Parsis.

After the final trip arrangements were made, and the last of the provisions loaded, they departed in the car via roads that cut through jungle, passing coconut, teak, tea, cocoa, and rubber plantations. The island had a total area of twenty-five thousand, three hundred and thirty-two square miles, and although it was only six degrees north of the equator, three distinct climates could be experienced in a matter of a few hours.

They arrived in Kandy, some ninety miles from the ship, at five that evening. Kandy was like many other places in the region: a very beautiful city in the mountains, bordering a sizeable lake. While the

Kandy, Ceylon. The only obstacles their driver treated with caution were the elephants.

Commodore toured the town, revisiting spots he remembered from his previous trips, Bob and Al rented a car and set up a camera in the back to capture a moving picture of their adventures.

By eleven, they had joined the Commodore again for a larger excursion out through the jungles. Bob found a challenge in trying to capture the most amusing images of the monkeys. It was also difficult to get clear pictures of the jackals, but the Commodore wanted a record of them, too. The journey was far from smooth as they traveled along narrow roads through a dense jungle. Monkeys and jackals were certainly not the only animals the driver had to be aware of. There were wild boars in the area that might suddenly leap out of the vegetation and damage the cars.

After making it through the jungle in one piece, the party moved on, under the Commodore's direction, to visit some of the old Buddhist temples. Such temples had become the main highlight of the trip, and the principal reason for stopping in the places they did. There were many elaborate ruins, many built of solid rock and several hundreds to thousands of years old.

They spent a good amount of time photographing the *Temple of the Tooth* at Kandy.

They stopped at a rest house for a time and everyone caught their breath while the Commodore noted the lack of sanitary fixtures. The pail and sawdust were not visible at first, or at least they were not noted either for their particular nature or function. The Commodore promptly made his exit from the rest house when everything became clear. Bob and Al were eventually left alone in the place, trying not to laugh too hard from recalling their employer's expression. They were somewhat used to that expression which signaled his extreme disgust and discomfort being in the vicinity of anyone or anything that was less than appropriately hygienic.

The people of Ceylon fascinated the Commodore and Rose, who dutifully followed her husband's lead in such things. Bob was not oblivious to the people's particular charm, either. They were turbaned Afghans and Malays, in some areas, dressed in round chintz caps. Others were Hindus with tonsured heads. Then there were the Moors, drawing attention with their tall brimless hats.

The *Rock Temple* was an interesting spot, cut into the summit of a barren rock and rising sharply out of the surrounding countryside as if to make as dramatic a statement as possible about its existence and purpose.

On the trip to Kandy, Al and Bob were able to capture many images of the people and places.

The climb to reach the temple was particularly arduous, and somewhat reminiscent of the stairs leading up to the temple where Doctor Lane had fallen. The memory of that scare continued to make it difficult for the members of the upper class to keep their heads. On such excursions, Rose had been rather like a school girl on an adventure up until then, but lately her demeanor was decidedly different. This particular climb was not to be recommended to anyone but the very young or those who were relentless about exercise, without objection to the discomfort of high humidity. It was rather like a Turkish bath for all the perspiration it produced.

Seeing such places over and over, Bob was struck by how, all over the world, so many people sought isolation. They hid away from the world, maybe for some spiritual reason that the artist could perhaps understand better than any other sort. Bob thought he felt it, too. In the jungles (as opposed to on some tropical island) there was a cooler, almost richer, experience to be had. They appeared as life forces unto themselves, as the very center—the cradle—of life. The green vegetation and colorful flowers enriched the whole area with their beauty and vibrancy. Whatever it was that a man looked for in such places, solitude was found to have an inherent value in and of itself.

The Commodore regretted sending Mr. Gilks and Bob off in the opposite direction at their leisure, but they were resourceful and enjoyed being among the native peoples perhaps more than any others in the crew. They had left in an instant. Bob, particularly, was becoming bolder and, at the same time, more withdrawn.

Trapped in monsoon weather, they faced clouds and nearly relentless rain—Bob began to despair of ever taking decent photographs in that particular spot. For all the freedom he and Al were given, the Commodore made his rounds of the classic tourist destinations in the area leaving lesser locations to the two photographers.

Bob left the hotel that morning at 8:00 and headed toward the coast amid plenty of tropical rain. He stopped at Puttalam, and then to Chilaw and Negombo, where he and Al shot scenes of native fishermen and old sailboats—more whimsical romantic images to feed the soul—as the wind and rain beat down on them. They wandered around and talked about everything, and nothing, like they always did. Al was still waiting to see his wife, and Bob had his own romance to consider. He had not heard anything from Jo, but he was hopeful that he might. Most of all, he thought about dancing with her. He'd felt a special connection as they touched. The letter had probably reached her by now. She was now perhaps considering how to respond.

It was quite an experience driving along the narrow, winding roads on a rainy night, enough to distract him from the prospect of his *amore*. The road was so narrow they had to stop, turn off their lights, and creep slowly ahead—fearful of running into other motorcars and causing what would undoubtedly have been a devastating accident. They spent much of the ride home turning the headlights on and off at intervals, as cars came toward them and wound down in the same manner, so each driver had a little time to see the road before the lights were turned on again.

Saturday, November 21st, brought the Commodore and his party to Mount Lavinia, strolling through the town and driving through the mountains, seven miles south of Colombo. They passed fishermen's homes that stood among palm trees that lined the sandy beaches where outrigger canoes were lying rather unceremoniously, their sails bellying on the breeze.

The stern of a ship in Colombo beckons from a lost era of wooden ships.

The weather had been cloudy nearly every day of late and it was again raining by noon, especially in the hills. Atop Mount Lavinia, a charming coastal resort of sorts (and the headquarters of several jewel merchants), the Commodore found himself and his wife the subject of considerable censure because they refused to buy any worthwhile products from the locals. They retaliated as best they could, but the natives had the last word and pushed them persistently until the party was ready to leave again for Colombo.

As they went ashore again for dinner that night, their last in Colombo, the greater impressions of Ceylon were foremost on their minds: the Hindus trying to persuade them to buy in their stores, walking along streets, passed by half a dozen rickshaws and others walking alongside, whispering propositions to take them about town. Bob ignored them, but they still followed him, incessantly, and talked and talked until he got really mad and shouted, just about knocking them down before they finally went away. It was all that roaming through narrow, beautiful roads that made Bob wonder whether the images they had taken were enough to capture it all. In any case, it was too late to do anything more.

This transfixing pose was captured at Lavinia Beach, Ceylon. At Lavinia, the Commodore suffered a dose of censure because he refused to purchase anything from the many merchants. The merchants were so insistent that the party quickly left the village.

On the 22nd, the *Alva* left Colombo and headed for Adeu, some two thousand one hundred miles west. The rain-squalls and the northeast winds bombarded them as they headed for the entrance to the Red Sea, the southernmost point of Arabia and yet another new world. They crossed an unusually rough sea. The ship rolled around so much, Bob found he could not work in the dark room at all. He spent his time on deck instead, taking in a truly beautiful tropical sunset. He thought of Jo, and his father. Two people on opposite sides of the world he cared about so much. It seemed almost unreal they could be so close to him and yet so far away. And as he moved closer to one, he moved further away from the other.

Since leaving Colombo, the Commodore had been steering a true course again, 270 degrees. That morning, however, November 24th, the course changed at last, to 290 degrees; it was a little after 4 am when the Commodore marked the change in his diary.

Colombo, Ceylon. Two bullock bandies are drawn by a donkey breed known as "trotters."
   Willie K. would write, "Ceylon is immeasurably far from the hustle, bustle and worries of the occidental world. Why do we continue to live in New York where there are elevated railroads, street cars, gasoline fumes, noise, and an eighteenth Amendment to help make life unbearable?"

"Such little details appeal to him," Bob heard from Louis Evans. "Minor course corrections and knowing the Hydrographic Office chart of the Indian Ocean for the month of November."

Bob managed to print most of the morning, but he had been nervous and preoccupied since the week before, which made focusing even more difficult. Try as he might, he couldn't seem to define his feelings. He was falling into moody spells that were hard to break, and all he wanted to do was be by himself, which he of course found near impossible. He silently bemoaned the monotony of the six days of steady traveling. He had homesickness, which he found himself thinking of more often than anything else. He worried about whether his Dad was happy lately, or not. He would be glad when he got home, and could put everything about Jo out of his mind.

Bob wasn't the only one feeling down that day. Word was that the Commodore was devastated by the news on the wireless that the markets had dropped again. The stock of the New York Central had reached 35, which seemed to be an all-time low.

"A blessing and a burden to be forever in touch with the world," he proclaimed.

The day was warm, and that was a blessing. By noon, they had traveled some three hundred fifty-six miles, making as steady progress as ever. Thanksgiving Day would take place on the Arabian Sea that year, and a nice turkey dinner awaited everyone on board. The crew celebrated with a big feast at luncheon, with many turkeys and a great deal of beer. Although the turkeys were put on board in New York, they were good enough to remind everyone of home and a certain solemnity and thankfulness overcame everyone under the warm sun.

A strong westerly current pushed the *Alva* onto the coast and they had to change course against it to stay on track. The crew sighted a *felucca* with the foot of its lateen sail hauled up. She put out a boat with three men in it, one waving a flag, to get the Commodore's attention. Shifting the *Alva's* direction once again, he called for his megaphone and prepared to make contact. The men in the boat held up an empty goat skin. They claimed to have no water. The *Alva* waited until the men had paddled up on the side of the *Alva*. The men in the boat held to a rope while two men in the crew filled three goatskins with water and gathered some provisions for the men aboard the *felucca*.

The three men came over wearing shirts and trousers, but their ten shipmates on the *felucca* were naked except for a stalwart Arab, standing aft, enveloped in a burnoose. They spoke no language that anyone aboard the *Alva* could understand, languages not being one of the crew's particular strengths: it wasn't something the Commodore had looked for in any of his crewmen, officers, or sundry crew.

By five, the *Alva* was underway again, the drama of their little encounter all but forgotten. The coast of Sokotra—the eastern end—became visible in all its desolation, and the north side thereafter, with its large quantities of white sand piled up against the hills as if it had been rather carelessly dumped there; the high mountains revealing a peculiar stratification. It was a beautiful, cool night. The sea was smooth as they sped on, everyone feeling more and more that they were on course for home.

Canals and Cairo

ARRIVING IN Aden, Bob went ashore with an outfit and rode up to the town, which was situated in the crater of an extinct volcano about three miles from the seaport. This small Arabian town controlled the southern entrance to the Red Sea. Surrounded by rocky hills, Aden was well-fortified and under British control. The town itself was decidedly quaint—a mass of camel carts and rides for sale; the natives used camels as work animals. They tied them to two-wheeled carts, while packing their backs as well. There were goats by the hundreds, lying all about in the narrow streets. A strong wind blew in off of the Arabian Desert as groups of kids ran and shouted after Bob and Al as they set about taking pictures.

Aden was equipped with large tanks with which to catch the rain water and store it for the drought season. Sometimes they had plenty of water and other times not enough, all according to how hard it rained during that season.

Aden was, the Commodore concluded, somewhat improved from his last visit. The Roman reservoirs and tanks had been abandoned. The water was obtained from artesian wells now, some of which were driven two thousand feet into the ground. Pierre took Michelle to see one of the old reservoirs at the Commodore's recommendation.

Rose and the Commodore drove to the town alone for a change, experiencing the same things they had seen before. The camels were particularly amusing, with all the colored trappings, as was the jabber of the drivers. There were many broken down cars of ancient vintage, an almost charming touch. The crowded sidewalks were reminiscent of New York, but Aden was far more congested. There were not only hoards of people,

Al Gilks on a railway cart near Aden, Arabia. The town was decidedly quaint.

but dogs, goats, chickens, camels, cats, babies, children, sleeping Arabs, beggars, women veiled and unveiled, men of the desert, and at least one horse. The beggars were generally surrounded by swarms of flies that would slow their buzzing and eye the Commodore whenever he and his wife stopped to look at something.

The local smells were rich and overpowering. Vendors of pots and pans, shoes, baskets, water pipes, and jewelry were all standing about. Fortunately, no one approached the couple to solicit trade as they mounted up.

On what seemed like an otherwise perfect day in paradise, the *Alva Daily News*—the wireless aboard the ship—picked up the announcement that New York Central stock was selling at 28 a share.

A sickening feeling passed through the crew. Bob thought of the many Americans he'd seen in rags while he rode on that train from Los

Angeles to New York. He thought of the bread lines and the squalor he'd witnessed in the Big Apple. Could it get much worse? Was there really nothing that could be done?

Rose came rushing to her husband, delicately wrapping her arms around his neck. In her refined manner, she ordered the crew to return to their positions. She saw to it the rest of the afternoon that the Commodore was occupied.

Everyone was struggling with the heat. The showers were being run constantly, and were now being shut off intermittently. Bob was talking to Quinton and Evans in a shaded part of the starboard promenade when Reddington Robbins walked toward them.

"It's your shift Louis," he told the second mate.

"Oh, grand," Evans replied.

"It's not so bad up there. The Commodore has fans set up."

Evans stood up to leave.

"Couldn't we set up a pool on deck somehow? That would be perfect," the second mate suggested.

"Some boys tried that on the *Ara*. Damn near flooded half the living quarters when their contraption broke apart—water ankle-deep. Fresh water, so they'd collected it when it rained. And they all ran off as it happened, too. Never did figure out who was responsible."

Bob thought he knew who had done it, but he didn't say anything.

The heat didn't last for long. As they continued through the Red Sea, Bob noticed the climate getting dramatically cooler the further they went. They were traveling due north, and were now having to take sweaters and coats with them on deck. The crew was abuzz with news that they would soon be stopping in Cairo. Writing to his father, Bob tried to sound enthusiastic about all of the wonders he was still experiencing.

"We are now traveling so fast we keep ahead of the mail boats, so I'll keep this until we make good mailing connections instead of mailing it here," he said, optimistic that his letters might otherwise reach his father promptly.

During the last several days, Bob had decided on his future—well, at least for the next few months. Instead of leaving the ship at France, he would remain on board until they reached Miami, Florida. He told his father, and himself, that it was for the best. He would like to tour about France, but he thought it best to stick to the *Alva* and save the difference for now. That way he could continue to do some more experimental work, too. The *Alva* would be in Miami in the beginning of February, but they expected to reach Monte Carlo and Cannes by Christmas—well ahead of schedule—and there was talk of remaining there until Jan 4th or 5th.

By chance, Bob received a radiogram from his father the next morning at breakfast—a sort of early Christmas present and a nice one. He didn't want to make too much of a big deal about it, being that he was one of the only guys on board to get a present, it seemed, and as such he had followed the example of Al and others in being discreet about it. He hadn't sent anything over to his father. He had a ton of gifts, but he would bring them home with him to save on the postage. Saving as much money as possible out of his pay was the priority. He was buying fewer and fewer souvenirs lately, too.

They would reach the Suez soon and there was more mail to collect when they reached Egypt. He hoped there would be more from his father. He hoped there would be a ton of mail, in fact.

In the meantime, Doctor Lane did a ship inspection. He asked Bob all sorts of questions about the water in the dark room: if it had sediment in it; how they were disposing of it, and so on. The doctor knew all about his own line of work, and pretended to know a little about photography as well. He asked about the chemicals Bob had been using: their purpose and the precautions they'd been taking with them. Apparently the doctor had been very pessimistic at the start of the cruise with regard as to how the film would handle at high temperatures, but he had since changed his mind. He and Bob had quite a good talk every so often, and regardless how he occasionally pushed in on his work, Bob had gotten to like him. The doctor had been a captain of medicine and surgery at *Annapolis;* he was retired now, having left the Navy only one step from an Admiral.

They reached the Port of Ibrahim just after eight that morning. Bob and Al went ashore at 10:00 a.m. with all the equipment and loaded it all in a large touring car. After mailing letters at the post office, they started for Cairo, ninety miles across the desert, tacking along behind the Commodore and his first-class crew. It was quite windy and a rough road to travel: rather well policed as far as roads in that area went, though uninteresting.

The party arrived in Cairo just after midday. It was like being lost in the desert, but with all the benefits of near first-class accommodation. Bob had been far more interested in the desert than his employer, who consistently reaffirmed that he hardly had any time to stop and take in the

244 MR. VANDERBILT'S PHOTOGRAPHER

An anchor seems out of place as it remains upturned in the rigging of a boat along the Egyptian seafront.

The policeman escorting the Vanderbilts struck a posture of dignity and pride.

details given how he was now urgently needed back in New York. And, frankly, he had seen everything before.

On the Nile, Bob and Al got some good pictures of sailboats they found to be rather picturesque, with their bows raised out of the water in a circular line and with high triangular sails.

As they had through the centuries, Bedouins clustered at the fringes of Cairo and the margins of the desert.

Cairo was a city of sights with over five hundred alabaster mosques placed here and there throughout the maze of city streets. After sundown, they drove down many small, narrow alleys, bazaars lining each side, with native Egyptians sitting by smoking pipes called *Hubble Bubbles*; similar to the Turkish pipe, it had a long hose to draw the smoke through and a tall bottle on the ground before them. It was what they called "long distance smoking."

Cairo, Egypt. High in the bow, with eye spots to ward away evil, this Nile cruiser awaits its next task.

As they had through the centuries, Bedouins clustered at the fringes of Cairo and the margins of the desert.

The car finally came to a stop before a narrow lane not wide enough to drive through. They left it, while the guide lead them down many more narrow lanes, among shop-keepers all trying to persuade them to look at their wares. The Egyptians wore the *fez* hat, its real name being *tarboosh*.

Monski was the main street in the Arab quarter of Cairo. It had people of every nationality, all in their native dress. The quarter was dense with bazaars and every type of store—crowded with people, narrow streets and stands jutting right out onto the sidewalks, donkeys and camels passing amid milling crowds of men, women and children. It was a Babylon of noises: the barking dogs, the moans of the camels, the braying of the donkeys, shouts of men at the animals, and the shouts of the shopkeepers, calling attention to their endless bargains. The shopkeepers also had a rather disconcerting habit of walking right up to them, forcing them to stop by standing in front of them to display their goods. Then there were the yelps of mothers at their children, yelps of the children running from their mothers. All of this occurred in dozens of languages spoken at once.

Camels hobbled so that they could not trouble their masters.

As Bob and Al meandered about, children started walking alongside of them shouting *"Baksheesh! Baksheesh!"*, and holding their little hands out for money. It seemed begging was one of the arts taught to children as soon as they were able to walk—the old trends faced new demands in an Egypt that was being stripped of all its best resources.

Tourists were still relatively rare in Cairo, but the *Shepherd Hotel* maintained its standing as one of the world's best-known hostelries, with less than a hundred guests at any given time. But rather than lounge in the hotel, Bob spent as much time as he dared wandering about. There was only so much he could take at a time, so when he found that he couldn't bear the chaos any longer, he tucked himself into a sufficiently appealing shop and hid away for a while.

Bob had tucked himself into a large, warehouse-like store, stocked from floor to ceiling with Persian rugs. Al appeared behind him, having followed him some distance, pursuing some of his own interests, but also quite convinced of "safety in numbers." Seeing the two men together—sharply dressed and carrying expensive camera equipment—the owner suddenly appeared from behind one of the rugs. He enthusiastically asked them in rather broken English if they would accept his hospitality by having tea with him. Tea turned out to include a showing of a variety of rugs of very rare Persian makes. In the end, it even seemed as if the show itself was all that the owner wanted from them. But the owner let them leave without pressuring them too severely to buy even one of the smaller rugs as a souvenir.

They headed next into a perfume store several blocks down. The oils themselves were collected from flowers grown in an oasis out in the desert and as such were apparently extremely rare and valuable. The scents made them feel as if they were walking through a tremendous tropical garden, or through the wild jungles of the East. Bob thought about Jo for an instant and tried to resist the urge to think of the perfume she had worn; it was much less overpowering, but somehow even more distinct in his mind. He decided to buy ambergris in the end, as Al picked out a perfume for his wife. The Egyptians use the grease for a tonic. Al and Bob had been

A merchant in a market in Cairo.

drinking the stuff in the tea they were served at breakfast. It seemed as if it only perfumed the tea, though: it had a very sweet scent but a bland, oily taste to it.

Laden down with wares, and at last free of the attentions of the sellers—assumedly since vendors saw it as hardly likely that they could carry anything more—Bob and Al headed back to the hotel for dinner and then together set out to see the sights of the city by night—an Egyptian cabaret being one of the more entertaining aspects, with a mass of red *fezzes* to dazzle the audience and hardly any ladies inside at all. The men sat about at little tables, drinking their wines and whiskeys, while on the stage a dozen men were crooning in song to one girl in front of them. The girl left after a few minutes and others came out, ornamented with silver lace, and danced, to the great delight of the men in the audience. Al was beaming from ear to ear. Bob enjoyed himself enough, but the prospect

A crowded street in very crowded Cairo.

of pyramids was vastly more enthusing and perhaps, before the morning, some stargazing under the desert sky.

Bob walked home alone and thought about Jo again, how they might have spent time together in such a place as this, thoughts that were cocooning him from the future. But if the Commodore wasn't immune to it—a man like that—then there was little hope for anyone else with lesser means and far less hope of understanding the world.

Making the most of their time before visiting the pyramids, Bob and Al were assigned camels in order to be able to shift positions relatively quickly, and planned a good set-up for the cameras with a bit of persistence. While the Commodore and his wife retraced the steps of their last trip, Bob and Al took pictures of the Pyramids of Giza—a little way outside of Cairo—dating back to 3,000 B.C.E. All three structures, which rose to a height of approximately four hundred and fifty feet, were built of more than two million stone blocks weighing more than two and a half tons each. As he angled for each shot, Bob couldn't help but wonder how they had been constructed in the first place; block upon block, to such a height, all by hand. Though it was a mystery how the pyramids

Bob on a camel. He and Al were provided camels to enable them to position themselves for the best shots.

were made, Bob guessed that they must have used trestle work or props of some sort, although the Commodore and their guide said different. It would have taken them an hour to climb to the summit of any one of the pyramids, which would have been discouraging in and of itself, although they would have had a wonderful view of the Nile Valley.

On leaving the pyramids and the Sphinx, their next stop was the Citadel (or *Alabaster Mosque*): a landmark of Cairo. It was built on a high bluff in the year 1166. The whole panorama of Cairo and a portion of the Nile were visible from its highest point, the Pyramids and Sphinx dotting the skyline. The *Alabaster Mosque* had five round domes, with two thin minarets rising nearly two hundred feet from ground level. Cairo—with its many mosques with golden domes, lit up under the sun in a golden sky—absolutely radiated.

The photo session completed, the word from Mr. Vanderbilt was that they couldn't lose much time any more. They wouldn't be visiting the Holy Land, but instead would go straight to Greece. The whole adventure seemed to be ending too soon. The Commodore was already talking about his plans to visit family in Newport when he was back in Long

Bob uses a combination of light and shadow to give the pyramids a sense of definition. The textured planes speak of thousands of years of erosion.

Island and New York. Al was apparently using his wife as an intermediary to set up new jobs for himself back in California. All this talk made Bob uneasy. He'd given a lot of thought to what he'd do when he returned, but apparently much less so than others. Was he being irresponsible in not actively preparing for the next step? But the next step seemed like a step backwards, and frankly, he'd come to really appreciate a world without assistant directors.

Their next port of call was Ismailia. Conveniently situated on Lake Timsah, it was the central station on the Suez Canal and a transportation hub connecting the Suez to Port Said and Cairo. The *Alva* had started through the Suez Canal at eight o'clock on the morning of the 5th and Bob had been set up on the flying bridge to capture it all on film. There was nothing on its banks but a long flat vista of desert sand as far

Cairo, Egypt. The Citadel (or Alabaster Mosque) built on a high bluff in 1166. Five round domes, with two thin minarets rising nearly two hundred feet.

as the eye could see in either direction. It also appeared very narrow, only about fifty yards wide. All vessels were forced to equip themselves with a searchlight suspended over the bow during the darker hours. When ships passed each other, one of the ships had to tie up to one of the many posts that lined the banks. Usually the vessel heading into the current tied up to prevent the tide from swinging it about. It took all of twelve hours to traverse the Canal.

The proximity did not undercut the relative desolation. Even aboard the *Alva*, surrounded by water, Bob felt he was traveling across the desert for real now. Hot though it was, lonely too, it was breathtakingly beautiful to look in the far distance, across the desert, toward the setting sun where the silhouette of caravans of a few roaming tribes with their camels showed up against the sunrise. Once in a while people would appear, often alone, emerging right out of the open desert toward the shore. They would stop dead, and stare quizzically at the *Alva*, all the while practically naked and bearing the oppressive heat with such an absurd level of nonchalance that those hanging out by the rails would stare back with utter disbelief.

The *Alva*, barreling toward Athens. With a voyage fast drawing to a close, the *Alva* pressed through the Aegean Sea leaving hundreds of small islands in her wake.

Greece

It was colder than ever as the *Alva* anchored in Port Said on December 7th. Bob felt that he was perhaps feeling the cold more after being in the tropics for so long, perspiration having thinned him out, like most of the rest of the crew. Still, there had been a sudden change of temperature in just one week's time.

As they entered Suez, the crew also changed its uniforms. They had been wearing white so far on the trip. Now that the weather had changed and the *Alva was* headed toward Europe and home—colder climates in both cases—the crew changed to blues and overcoats, heavy ones at that.

Later that night, they raised anchor again and moved out of the port into a very heavy sea. They battened down the ship, finishing just as the wind blew a heavy cold rain at them, but only for a few minutes. They were doing a bit of pitching and taking spray over the bow. Several of the boys were seasick, although Bob himself hadn't missed a meal yet. They had just finished dinner as he stepped out onto the deck, and this time he did feel a little bit queasy, but decided to work through it. *To hell with the weather—after one year at sea, one should be able to hold one's dinner.* Seasickness wasn't as bad now as it had been in the heat, anyhow.

Despite the pitching and the wet wind, Bob felt an urge to brave the deck. Instead of returning to hide in his bunk after dinner, he changed his mind abruptly and wandered down the portside promenade toward the stern. He had been one of the last ones to leave the mess hall, and the decks were entirely abandoned. By now, every seasoned *Alva* crew member had long abandoned romantic notions of standing out on slippery decks braving stormy weather. But this time—maybe for the last time—Bob wanted to feel the water on his skin. He didn't remember the last time he'd had a reprieve from the stagnant heat—they hadn't had a cold rain in forever.

He was having trouble seeing as he approached the open area by the stern, hugging the portside rail. The *Alva* rocked like an enormous baby's cradle each time an errant wave slammed into her hull. The wind howled in bursts and trailing whistles, lulling, followed by a soft breeze, a cold wind smothered like a blanket, a deafening whistling would fill the air then lull off again, accompanied by blinding gusts of stinging, saltwater raindrops.

The wind had calmed, longer than usual this time, and Bob leaned out over the port railing, holding tight, feeling the *Alva* supporting him as she bobbed roughly on the waves.

"*She walks the waters like a thing of life: And seems to dare the elements to strife.*"

Bob swung around, startled. Someone whom Bob hadn't seen before was standing, facing off the stern on the starboard side, hidden beneath a rain hood. Bob's first thought was that it was Earl Smith, who used to stand out in the rainy weather more often than most, but he knew almost right away that it wasn't Earl because he and Consuelo had left them months ago.

"Byron," the man said. "Have you heard of Lord Byron?"

"No," Bob replied. "I haven't."

"A poet—one of my favorites."

Bob didn't reply. Between the wind and the water, he still couldn't tell who he was talking to.

"I had to see this view again. Be damned with the weather!"

Bob knew who it was now. It wasn't Earl, or anyone he might have expected. He was talking to the Commodore.

"I remember the last time I was in this spot. I had completed my first circumnavigation of the globe. It was my lifelong ambition to circumnavigate the globe, and now here I am, and I've done it twice. In a way it's right what they say: it's often better to want something than to have it. I remember looking at this very same view as my crew celebrated the accomplishment, toasting their glasses to our great success. I looked at those shores and you know what I thought to myself?"

Bob shook his head no, but with the rain and the dark the Commodore probably didn't see it. Not that it mattered; he was in his own world.

"I thought to myself, 'what's next?' Strange, don't you think? I had accomplished something which few men have ever achieved: a life-long dream. But did I feel proud? Did I feel any sense of triumph? No. I simply wondered to myself: what on earth would I do next? What would be the next obsession to distract me for a time?"

The two were silent for a bit as each reflected on what was said. "Sometimes I feel as if there has always been so little in this life that I found a challenge, so little in the world that truly engaged me. Captaining was one of those things. Yet here I am and it's just like it was years ago, after accomplishing the same feat. Though I've been getting endless congratulations, day in and out, I fail to see what real achievement I have to celebrate. Now that I'm here, all I really think about is how little I've done in the interim. I'm no closer at all to knowing what my true purpose is in this world."

"Well, your science. Your museums and collections," Bob suggested.

"Will they last long after I'm gone? Perhaps," the Commodore mused.

"If your collections are going to the Museum of Natural History then they'll last for—who knows how long," Bob said optimistically.

"They no longer want collections from my museum," the Commodore informed the young man. "I have argued with them, but they are, apparently, no longer interested in the *Alva's* brand of science." Bob wondered if Belanske knew, the fellow who constantly reminded everyone to work at the highest standards in the name of science.

"Well then they'll be in your own museum," Bob told him.

The Commodore looked back out over the stern and continued talking. "I remember my decision to build a unique museum of the sea, styled after a church I'd seen in Guatemala—something that captured more of the true essence of the ocean, its spirit, rather than a bare, theoretical nature of species and environment. So I hired Mr. Belanske. I've made many attempts, throughout my life, to live a life of passion. I tried my hand at business, but all of them failed in the bank crash of '07. I tried my hand as a sportsman, racing yachts and cars. I've been a family man; a husband, for a time, and a father. But I've always felt this need to build something, to leave behind something substantial. Like my great-grandfather, the real commodore. People respected him. They remember him still. He left behind a fortune which has lasted generations. What will I leave behind? Surely not a fortune; I'm too old to start more businesses and the railroad is dying. Everything I've tried to build has crumbled. They'll probably tear down my museum to build a golf club or some such depressing nonsense."

"But you don't need to hear all this. You're young, everything is ahead of you."

"I don't feel that way," Bob told him.

"Neither did I," Vanderbilt replied, as a large gust of wind shrieked across the hull.

"That was the last one," the Commodore claimed.

"How do you know?" Bob asked him.

"I'm a Captain. I know these things," the Commodore said.

* * *

At midnight they sighted a light that marked Cyprus, but they would not be stopping. The *Alva* drove onwards to Rhodes, which appeared around three in the afternoon. There was no protection for a good anchorage, and again they did not stop. It seemed every day they sailed, they sailed faster. They were on their way to Athens, through the numerous small islands of the Aegean Sea—passing them all without stopping. The *Alva* cleared the labyrinth of small islands before nightfall, and entered the main strait, which was better equipped with guiding lights.

Bob Bronner poses at the Parthenon with the Graphlex. The photo was likely taken by Al Gilks on the smaller format film camera. In later photos, Bob's expression and posture trend toward stoicism and professionalism.

While Robert captured this image, Willie and Rose bantered about the "crowds and chaos" that had become Athens.

The following morning, they dropped anchor at Piraeus, the harbor to the city of Athens. The hills were hidden by low hanging clouds and more rain squalls. Across the world, ancient civilizations were almost synchronously failing to survive the grip of the modern, western world. The process by which an ancient culture was displaced was never simple. Athens, though, was an example of an ancient culture whose spirit still endured.

Bob and Al rose early and went through customs with their equipment, ready to take in the sights of the town. In the back of his mind, as Bob went through the tedious process of checking and customs, was the realization that Jo had not responded to his letter. He had no word from her at all, and it was hard to imagine that the *Alva's* progress was so impossible to track. She had chosen not to respond.

Bob tried to distract himself from thoughts of Jo with their busy sightseeing schedule. Once they were through customs, he and Al went directly to the *Acropolis*, the hill on which the ruins of the *Parthenon* still stood, following the Commodore's car in one of their own. Bob saw magnificent structures that had survived thousands of years. They stayed around the *Acropolis* all morning, trying to get pictures with the few seconds of sunlight that occasionally broke through the dark rain clouds. The view from the hills was breathtakingly beautiful even in rainy weather—overlooking the town of Athens, with the stadiums, theaters, and *Temples of Hephaestus* and *Olympian Zeus* below. Nearly a mile away was the Monastery of *Saint John*, sitting on top of a sheer bluff. He marveled at everything he was seeing, how the ancient Athenians moved all the marble and terra-cotta up the precipice to build their magnificent structures. And if done by the slaves of those times, "then all the more credit to them," he would write to his father.

From the *Acropolis*, Bob and Al followed the Commodore to a church built of terra-cotta sometime in the twelfth century. The dome was still in a very good state of preservation. Some of the mosaics still clung to the walls, regardless of the many small earthquakes in the past centuries. A few of the stones had been crushed and dislodged, but very few considering.

The realization that it was likely the first and last time Bob would see any of these wonders was slowly seeping into his conscious thought. The marvelous beauties of the old world were scattered all about, some in ruins, others still standing intact in all their splendor. In many ways,

The Monastery of St. John looms over Athens.

The Parthenon was the crown jewel of the Acropolis. As tourists always did and continue to do, Bob marveled at the fluted columns that continue to carry the load of centuries of plenty and plight. The day was cloudy and rainy; Bob and Al struggled to capture it on film.

structures that had been destroyed spoke more than those that remained largely intact. Perhaps there was beauty in destruction; perhaps Bob was becoming a pessimist. Perhaps pessimists were right. Perhaps the visions of untainted theaters and columned temples were more of a fanciful dream. He knew that was probably true.

 As they drove back toward the city, Bob wondered at their having seen so much on their voyage and yet they could travel about for months, years, forever… and not see it all. Because if they went everywhere and if they'd finally been to every village, city, roadway, plantation, jungle, desert, mountain, valley, beach, cove, volcano, forest, cave, tundra, and section of open ocean—they would return home to find that home itself (and most every other place) would have changed beyond recognition.

An Unexpected Realization

TIME WAS of the essence as they approached mainland Greece. Bob and Al hoped the cloudy, heavy overcast sky might break and allow them to take some better pictures before the ship moved on.

Loaded in a boat, Bob was sent ashore to chance the weather the following morning with a trip to Delphi, a few miles into the hills. But no sooner did they leave the *Alva* and get the equipment ashore, than it started to rain. The equipment was returned to the ship immediately and everyone waited below deck for better weather.

Bob and Al dropped the equipment back in the darkroom and made their way to the empty crew lounge, collapsing into two cozy chairs to the sound of the rain beating down against the steel hull. There was little to be heard save the rain, as most of the crew huddled in their bunks or, in the case of the guests and officers, hid in their personal quarters. Bob and Al took turns catching their breath, which led to several minutes of silence and staring at the raindrops streaking against the window glass.

"How did Mr. Vanderbilt get the title *'Commodore'*?" Bob asked, a question he'd wondered about for weeks and weeks.

"Ah, it's an honorary title, as far as I understand," Gilks replied. "From his yachting club on Long Island."

"But wasn't he in the Navy?" Bob responded, confused.

"Rumor has it he was rejected from service during the Spanish-American War due to a heart condition. But he served during the Great War. He's legitimately a Lieutenant Commander with a license to pilot ships of all sizes and a retired Navy officer if that's what's bothering you."

"No, no, I was just…wondering. I still don't really know much about him. I knew that his great-grandfather was called *the Commodore*, and it got me thinking, that's all."

"What did we talk about back on the train in New York?" Gilks asked, rolling his eyes up and to the left, trying to remember.

"You talked about Cornelius—the original Commodore—and the railroad empire, and our Commodore's father, I think. William Kissam I," Bob recalled. "But you must know all the ins and outs by now, with all the time you've spent around him and Mrs. Vanderbilt."

Al smiled. "Sure, I could tell you a few stories. For instance, do you know who this ship is named after?"

Bob thought hard for a second. "His mother."

"That's right. Well, William Kissam Sr., and the Kissam branch of the family, owes much of its success to Alva Vanderbilt. The Commodore's mother was a very formidable entity in New York and Newport society. The Vanderbilts were still considered 'new money' and she bemoaned the fact that people in her social circle were snubbing her for marrying a man whose grandfather had peddled vegetables. She worked fiercely to establish the Vanderbilts' place within the ranks of New York's elite families.

"You didn't hear it from me, but I think that woman was nothing more than a bully. I mean, I'm sure the Commodore's childhood was anything but average. He was exposed to the kind of luxury that people like us could only dream of: spending summers abroad in the south of France and the like, educated at the best of schools all the while."

"Didn't he go to Harvard?" Bob suddenly remembered.

"Yeah, but I think he dropped out," Al affirmed, slightly thrown off by being interrupted, and paused to remember his train of thought.

"So, Vanderbilt's mother controlled every aspect of her children's lives. I've heard the most unbelievable things about this woman. Did you hear what happened to Mr. Vanderbilt's sister?"

Bob shook his head 'no'.

"Alva faked a heart attack to get her to marry some Duke. Poor girl was heart-broken about it. She was in love with someone else, if you can believe it. It was all over the papers. But Alva decided her daughter having a title was more important than whether or not she was happy. They're divorced now, alright. Special dispensation from the Pope and everything."

"Well that seems… unmotherly." Bob wasn't quite sure how to respond. What kind of mother sells off her daughter like that in this day and age?

"You know, Vanderbilt travelled regularly with his family as a child. It's my opinion that his love and longing for freedom on the open waters

AN UNEXPECTED REALIZATION

The Vanderbilt family cruising the Nile on the *Prince Abbas* in 1887. Alva and her husband found family cruises much to their preference. Left to Right: Oliver Hazard Perry Belmont (OHP, family friend who later became the second husband of Alva Vanderbilt), Wiliam Kissam Vanderbilt I (Willie K's father), Willie's older sister Consuelo, M. Kulp (standing), Captain Henry Morrison (background), F.D. Beach (front and center), Willie K. Vanderbilt II (age 9), Dr. Francis Johnson, a servant (background), Alva Vanderbilt, and William S. Hoyt. (Courtesy of the Suffolk County Vanderbilt Museum.)

became rooted in this childhood contentment—before his family was divided."

"What do you mean?" Bob asked.

"Alva left Mr. Vanderbilt's father for O.H.P. Belmont. But of course she accused him of adultery to get the divorce."

"A real charmer, huh?" Bob quipped.

"Alva?" Al quipped back, "I wouldn't know."

"Why is he always so concerned about the stock market?" Bob asked. "Doesn't he have enough money to last him?"

"Rich is... relative when you're one of the wealthiest people in the world. Mr. Vanderbilt has made some serious errors in judgment while

Willie K. Vanderbilt II. Until his passing in 1920, William Kissam I never relinquished either his fortune or what little remained of the railroad leadership to his son.

trying to maintain his family's falling status. Belanske told me part of why Vanderbilt separated from his first wife. Get this, it was 1908, just one year after bank failures caused his business to go bankrupt. He didn't inherit any money until his father died in 1920. The man was completely broke! To bail himself out, he tried to sell off his wife's real estate holdings in San Francisco. They separated shortly after."

"But 1920 was just a bit over a decade ago. Mr. Vanderbilt would have been, what, forty-two?" Bob calculated.

Gilks nodded in affirmation.

"So for the first forty-two years of his life he was on his own, and then all of a sudden he was heir to a fortune?" Bob imagined a younger Willie K. An inheritor that found himself alone in a world he neither built nor, in all likelihood, really understood. The photographer felt he finally somewhat understood the enigma that he worked for. "It's not an easy thing for a man to be suddenly laden with large responsibilities, and the high expectations of others, when he is well past his prime."

Bob leaned back in his chair to let this new enlightenment roll over him. It was all too clear now: after a dozen ports, and weeks of adventure-leisure, Mr. Vanderbilt, to some degree, enjoyed playing a part. He made records of places he had been and things he had seen, but there was a disparity between life and the way he seemed to recall it. Calls at port were usually brief. His occasional snobbery was perhaps worse, because he knew now that he could have been something more if he had wanted. Experiences were almost superficial. The ship itself was home: a haven that was literally and physically transported with them from one location to the next.

Bob had managed to idealize the man right up until the end, but looking closely, he realized everything was all about Mr. Vanderbilt and his comfort. The call 'in the name of science' was nothing more than a rich man's vain attempt at justifying his lavish expenses and months of purposeless wandering. When the Commodore spoke, Bob had always been stung with a certain apprehension—wondering when the man's accounts crossed the line between reality and fantasy, or if that line even existed. And when Bob considered a middle-aged Willie K. Vanderbilt II, burdened with the torch of his namesakes, Bob thought of his father, and Christmases in Brooklyn. And he wondered what was better—the fantasy or the reality.

Delphi and Naples

WHEN THE rain stopped, it was still very cold, with snow visible on top of the hills. Taking only a small amount of equipment, Bob and Al joined the Commodore's party for a visit to an ancient Greek amphitheater and a temple at Delphi. Near the temple were two very picturesque villages nestling on the edge of precipices, which Bob had even been able to spot from the ship.

Wandering about alone, Bob noticed that the locals still wore the traditional clothing—shirts and vests with tassels around their knees—and wished he could photograph it for his own sake.

Delphi was the most famous of the mythological shrines. The temple had been erected in ancient times in a town on the slopes of the Parnassus, which became the seat of the oracle of Apollo. Prophecies were given by the rustling of laurel leaves, later to be pronounced by a woman who drank from the nearby stream and, chewing the leaves, would offer divine wisdom.

Above the site of the temple was a theater, and higher up, a stadium. From the town itself, the Emperor Nero had removed some five hundred bronze statues and later, Constantine the Great had removed the sacred tripod upon which the oracle sat.

Visiting the museum next to the temple, which contained many other ancient relics, Bob was in awe of the small collection of items still in place there.

"Many things have been lost," the Commodore insisted, as he reviewed the visitors' book for 1907, which contained his name, inscribed there on his last visit to the museum twenty-five years before.

While the Commodore headed back to the ship to review the travel plans for the next several days, Bob took in the last views of the magnificent town: the rich valley of olive trees and the little hamlets hidden amongst the bare mountains and across the slopes of the valley. In the heart of the town, Bob exchanged ten dollars for seven hundred and seventy-five Greek drachmas, and couldn't help grinning at the prospect of being so seemingly wealthy. It really did seem like a lot of money; at least until he spent two hundred and twenty-five on dinner, and then one hundred, and another, and it soon all went. He found that wherever he went buying with his American money, the people were anxious and happy to receive it. Its value seemed to stay at relatively the same rate of exchange, while currency from other countries fluctuated almost all the time. It seemed almost impossible to even give away the English pound sterling, which had gone to $3.29 that day, as Bob and Al tried to use up all of their money before leaving port. They never knew how much they would lose on exchange.

On the thirteenth day of the month, the *Alva* departed from the Gulf of Corinth and entered the Gulf of Patras, rolling and tossing along the way, into the harbor of Patras, where the ship finally tied off behind the breakwater. The wind blew and sent the spray flying from the crests of the waves.

Patras was the second largest seaport in Greece (Athens' harbor, Piraeus, being the largest), yet most of the population had turned out to see the *Alva* tied up and tossing about in its particularly cramped and exposed slot. They were lining the low pier until the wind and spray drove them to cover.

The water in the harbor was turbulent, lifting up into the air and carried along by the wind as a white squall. It was no sea for a boat of the *Alva's* size. With the weather bureaus reporting full gales and very heavy seas all over the Mediterranean, the only sensible choice was to wait out the storm.

Suspicious as he was, the Commodore took it as a sign that the pilot in the harbor had positioned the ship in the worst possible location: two anchors out with sixty fathoms of chain on each. The stern was moored to a quay, exposed to the harbor entrance and the northeast wind despite the Commodore's rather vehement suggestion that they should have been set up on the other side of the quay beside a five-thousand-ton tramp steamer. The Commodore disappeared for a while to fume in the privacy of his own stateroom, as the gale continued into the night. Finally, there was word that he had been compelled to break his gentlemanly habit. Vanderbilt went ashore to insist upon a change of location, talking to the yacht agent in an uncharacteristically insistent manner, wondering why they had been positioned in such a location in the first place. No one aboard the ship could stand by that point, so heading back to the *Alva*, Vanderbilt sounded three whistles—the pilot call—and waited for the man to appear on the quayside.

"I'm so glad you blew the whistle," the pilot claimed.

Offering no apology for his inconsistency, the pilot smiled and, with the kind of soft-spoken urbanity that the Commodore considered typical of Orientals, helped the *Alva* change positions.

"Now that you are settled," he said, "I shall be able to sleep. If you had not moved, I should have worried all night."

The wind howled through the night and tossed the ship about into the early hours of the morning, albeit with less force than before. At least everyone could more or less stand.

The winds died down by morning and the *Alva* was ready to depart the harbor by eight, not wishing to be the focus of any further drama. The Commodore said that he had enough memories of Patras and felt no particular need to revisit the place. It was, he said, "rather clean for a Greek port, but there was nothing else particularly notable about it." Bob thought it looked vibrant, full of life, with a brass band helping to enliven the crowd.

By noon, to the Commodore's dismay, the sea and weather became worse again and the *Alva* was once again anchored, this time in a snug harbor at Vardiani on Cephalonia, a final landfall en route to Italy.

Heading for the town of Argostoli, the Commodore and his wife had quickly sought to escape the rocking of the boat and visit the water wheel on the island, which they had first seen in 1927. "How much seems to have happened since then," he laughed, as if it was almost painful to say so.

The water wheel stood idle. No ice was needed in winter, after all, the leafless trees and deserted streets confirmed the change of the seasons. Fifteen feet in diameter, the structure was decidedly impressive and turned by a small fall of water passing from the Mediterranean Sea through a canal on a porous and rocky part of the earth. On so many levels it seemed ingenious in its simplicity: sleek and reliable, a drop of five or six feet creating enough momentum for the water to hit the wheel and force it to turn. The pressure brought to bear on the paddles by the fall was sufficient to generate a small ice plant. Where the water disappeared to, no one was quite sure. It was enough to interest geologists and other scientists, who had hunted for an outlet by pouring oil into the water, but had found nothing.

The sea started to show signs of improving the following morning, after everyone had enjoyed a relatively quiet night. The Commodore was eager to move on, and raised anchor at eight to continue en route to the Straits of Messina, two hundred fifty miles west of their current position.

Looking out of the window of his cabin, Bob was relieved to see for himself that the storm had died down and that the sea was fairly smooth. After so many days of rain, it was such a welcome change that many of the crew spent an extra hour or two on deck in order to watch the Italian coast come slowly into view. Cape Spartivento appeared at around midnight, and brought the distinct sensation to all that they were, truly and finally, on their way home.

The following morning, navigating the narrow straits of Messina, the Commodore felt as though he were passing up the Hudson, with thousands of electric lights lining each shore. They passed Messina and continued their straight run to Naples, up along the Italian coast, with the weather seeming to get a little warmer every few hours.

Many of the men instantly fell in love with the Italian hills, but the Commodore was anxious about navigating the coastal waters, which offered up "a tremendous breeze, whirlpools, and currents of up to five knots most of the year around." But they found the journey to be pleasant enough, and the *Alva* made her way through the strait unscathed.

Bob and Al took as many pictures as possible in what was close to being their last few days together. But the young photographer was starting to find his mentor's company tiresome. In between talks about how much he missed his wife, and how much he would enjoy showing her France, Al had complained about her letters—her frustration that she had not heard from him more often—her reports of tiffs with friends and family over Al's extended absence—how she could tolerate it, how she coped with things that were so bad back home. Every worry, every doubt, took its toll and mingled misery with happiness, dissatisfaction with contentment.

Al was set to meet his wife in France, and was all abuzz—planning the trip they were to make around the country; daring to ask the Commodore for suggestions on places to visit when his courage rose and the mood struck. Despite the general elation rising in the crew in regards to the Mediterranean, the Commodore was rather more concerned about the coastline, and when Al approached, he described the efforts of the Italian government to make the stretch safer for visiting sailors.

The mountains in the background were of more interest to Bob, who had tried to keep his nose out of Al's business, but had still heard all of the details of the pending trip at least twice. The hills rose high, riddled with villages and rivers, railroads and viaducts all around the Bay of Naples. The snow caps lent a certain charm to the place, in deep contrast to the steep cliffs of Capri Island off in the distance, and the smoke pouring from Mount Vesuvius. With a calm sea and generally fine weather, broken only by a few showers, Bob kept himself busy with plenty of opportunity to capture breathtaking views.

Setting the clock back one hour after lunch, the *Alva* stopped outside of the break water of Naples to take stock of the harbor and explore the city. The harbor was full of life, with battleships, cruisers, and destroyers lining the quay, and overhead, a slew of aircraft demonstrated the skill of Italian aviators, the air humming with motors.

The Commodore went ashore with his wife to roam the streets and stretch their legs for an hour or two, but they returned early and collapsed in front of the fire that burned on the hearth of the *Alva's* living room.

Bob wanted more time to explore alone—to walk and think. Being in Europe, his confidence was all the greater—he felt as if he were among people that were not in the least bit different; they had, for the most part, a common culture and identity, even if the particulars weren't quite the same. He was in the modern world again, the world that was slowly wearing away the ancient cultures of distant islands.

Naples was a very picturesque city. Part of its allure was its age, its charming, but somewhat decrepit state. Riding in a carriage from the harbor, they passed a medieval castle that was mostly in ruins. The outer walls had partly fallen away and the huge arches of the interior were exposed. They walked up narrow side streets, built on the sides of hills, with bumpy stones stepped up every fifteen feet and small shops alongside, then went back down to Via Roma, the main business street.

At the *Gumbrinos* Restaurant, they stopped for a sumptuous and very Italian dinner of spaghetti, chicken, and Chianti. Al couldn't stop talking about the taste of Italy back home, and how somehow, the two experiences just couldn't have been more different.

Merchants swarm the *Alva* in Naples in hopes of selling their wares. The city reeked charm with a combination of old buildings, narrow streets, medieval ruins and, at times, decrepit architecture.

Needing some time alone, Bob decided to stay in town a little longer and visit the *Trocadero* for a little dancing and music. He found that the Italian women were surprisingly similar to the Australians—women among whom Jo had stood out so starkly—girls chasing down military men and other tourists looking for a good time.

Bob did his best to smile and laugh, even to charm one or two of the local women who showed an interest, but he felt that he was untouchable now—maybe that was what made it easier. Dancing and music was for pretending; it was a surreal experience and good only so far as it helped him forget what he'd had before.

The next morning, the Commodore organized an expedition to see Mount Vesuvius up close, crossing the bay and climbing the treacherous sides of the mountain towards the smoldering crater. As Bob looked down into the bay, he thought about the degree of total and absolute

Naples was, foremost, a port city. Here, Bob captures a touch of the old and new shipping assets with the harbor police in the foreground.

devastation its eruption had caused all those centuries ago. He wondered if the suddenness had mitigated the panic and pain of the victims. Was their suffering reduced by not understanding their impending fate?

By mid-morning, another adventure was over and everyone was back aboard the ship to greet the Crown Prince Umberto. The Prince and Princess of Piedmont, as they were known, came aboard with their aide, equerry, and a lady in waiting, posing for photographs and accepting, rather gleefully, the requisite tour of the ship. Bob watched from a distance, continuously looking up to Vesuvius, realizing how fleeting these moments were, toward the end of what would likely be the greatest journey of his life.

Monte Carlo

On Friday, December 18th, they were anchored in the harbor of Villefranche—a point between Nice and Monte Carlo—with the promise that they would be able to anchor in Monte Carlo first thing in the morning. By noon that day, the *Alva* had completed her first trip around the world, touching back to the same meridian as Kiel, Germany, where she had been launched last March. It was a day of milestones and, finally, they were in France.

Al had been packing up expectantly and would be ready to leave the ship as soon as it docked in Monte Carlo. Bob would stay with the *Alva*. The final word was that they would be docked until the New Year. The downside of arriving at last in a place so longed for, was having no one there to greet him. In the back of his mind, Bob still had hoped for Jo—for her to suddenly appear before him in Monte Carlo as she had appeared in Brisbane, which seemed like ages ago. Maybe he'd even dare to venture back to the South Seas if she was with him. He imagined them becoming gypsies—wild and untamed, like the remotest islands and jungles he had seen.

The Commodore was among the crew, for once, after the celebration of the *Alva's* crossing of the meridian, which came with a hearty toast and celebratory meal at lunch time.

That evening, the ship's orchestra was playing in the mess room, livening things up to mark many partings of ways.

It will be much quieter in the morning, Bob told himself. He thought of what he might do to pass the time—run up to Nice and get some printing paper, perhaps. He also had to find out what was waiting at the American consulate. Then he would have to see at least a little of France—especially

Al Gilks anxiously anticipated meeting his wife at the end of the voyage. In the last few days, his feelings became so evident that it made Bob feel quite alone.

Paris—while he was free to do so. Even if he was alone, at least he would see it.

A number of the crew were leaving to head back to Germany and the Commodore was politely wishing them a farewell. His guests—Michelle, Pierre, and Dr. Lane—were also leaving, the Merillons on the 19th and Dr. Lane on the 20th.

The fateful morning came. The *Alva* raised anchor from Villefranche to travel to Monaco, passing along a beautiful, rugged coastline, with little coves and anchorages below the rolling hills and homes built into the sides of the palisades, right up to the water's edge. Where there was a stone wall, or breakwater right in front, the waves pounded only twenty feet below the houses themselves.

Monaco was breathtaking, and a great relief. The casino of Monte Carlo and the homes creeping up the sides of the hills provided the perfect picture to set the final scene of their final chapter. Red tile roofs on white buildings were candy to Bob's artistic imagination, set up as a beautiful panorama around the small "u-shaped" yacht anchorage.

Al Gilks (left) and Mr. Vanderbilt (right), probably in Monaco, separated by the instrument that brought them together: the motion picture camera. Al would lead a most successful career in the film business, culminated in 1952 by an Oscar for 'Best Cinematography, color' for *American in Paris* (1951) shared with John Alton.

Everyone was desperate to get to shore, more so than ever, and there was a great fuss as the Merillons' baggage was removed from the ship: people chaotically stepping over one another where they would have usually first ceded way to the upper-classes. The stewards were kept busy battling the chaos of crowds and cries that ensued.

The Commodore and his wife were leaving as well. They would dine on shore that night, and make their final preparations to leave for

Monte Carlo, Monaco, was "breathtaking." There were two *Alva*s in port that day: one Willie's yacht, and the second his mother for whom the former was named.

Paris. Alva Vanderbilt, the namesake of the mighty ship, awaited her son and daughter-in-law in her European hideaway, planning to entertain them over Christmas, assumedly with her usual brand of extravagance and splendor.

The senior crew couldn't leave without a final celebration of what had been accomplished on the voyage. Assembling on the deck, the Commodore, his wife, Dr. Lane, and many crewmen, sat back to watch an array of movies and stills from the voyage. They had accumulated roughly eight thousand six hundred ninety six feet of colored film and more than ten thousand feet of 16-millimeter film. Bob, as he oversaw the showing of the stills and movies, realized he now had almost one hundred fifty negatives to work his way through. They had been piling up since the *Alva* left Aden, as he had become increasingly focused on taking in rather than churning out.

The *Alva* draped in flags at the yacht berth in Monte Carlo, Monaco. Vanderbilt must have delighted in drawing attention to his own yacht.

Bob headed by bus to Nice, and went directly to the American consulate to pick up his mail. He went alone, making his way in a somber, reflective state. Awaiting him was a pair of binoculars his father had sent—*never too late*. And a letter. He anxiously opened the letter that would likely be the last from his father before he returned to Los Angeles—but this one was not from his father. Bob stood right outside the doorway of the American consulate and read his final letter –

> Bob,
> I hear this (France) is your last stop before you're back in America. You must be tired of sailing by now. Or maybe not. I hope you're still in one piece, at least—not kidnapped by pirates, or the like. And that you still have your job when you get back. Maybe Vanderbilt will hire you.

Al and the Mrs. in Nice, France. Al grew anxious to see his wife as the long voyage drew to a close.

> Everything is O.K. here. The economy and such is as bad as it was when you left, so no changes there. The girls love the sailors more than ever—makes me jealous to think of it!
>
> Did you see the Pyramids? Must have been incredible. And hot!
>
> I don't know when I'll see you again, but take care of yourself, and get home safe.
>
> - George

As he re-read the letter and examined the package from his father, Bob couldn't avoid a pang of disappointment at the fact that Jo had sent him no word. He had no hope now, and truth was he never really did. He'd known all along that, at this point, the dream would be over. How could she have written to him, though, really? Would she have been able to even if she had wanted to? She knew the name of the ship and his name, of course, and had a vague notion of where they were traveling, and when. Maybe there was confusion? Or maybe great romantic feats were

MONTE CARLO

Bronner, who would spend the rest of his life in the motion picture industry, here does a study of motion, in this and the photograph that follows. The place was the port of Monte Carlo, the subject billowing steam.

only for the movies. Instead, he had something that he was going to have to live with for the rest of his life.

Bob put the letter in his pocket. He left the post office, leaving behind his hope of hearing from Jo. His imagined future with her had been a fantasy. It was time to accept reality.

Bob gave himself completely to the last weeks of the adventure. He decided to buy a Leica camera in town for sixty-eight dollars, remembering that they cost close to one hundred and ten dollars in America.

He made rush prints for the Commodore to take to Paris and, with Al leaving in two days and a roommate headed to New York on a faster boat, he did what he could to be social and cheery.

The season at Monte Carlo would not begin until the end of January. The promenade was empty most of the day and night, like the set of some heart-wrenching romance. The climate, too, was unusual, with a sharp, cold breeze blowing in all the time, reminding everyone that it was indeed Christmas, with the New Year around the corner. The days were getting

Steam from a passing ship, framed by the superstructure of the *Alva*, appears to blend with the billowing silhouettes of trees.

shorter, with the bugle sounding for sunrise at a little after seven, and for sunset around four.

* * *

Bob finally settled into the life of the truly independent traveler. Now realizing the distance to Paris, he remolded his expectations toward experiencing and appreciating the Côte d'Azur.

Cannes was a much larger city, with quite a number of English and American yachts, and numerous smaller sailboats of various designs lining the harbor. There was a fair going on as Bob arrived, reminding him of a little California beach resort where all the concessions were run in the same way, but in this case with a French atmosphere.

Walking along the sidewalks, people either had to walk single file or have someone walk in the road. A great number of shops were still open, despite the fair, so Bob indulged in a bit of window shopping to pass the time.

Alva's funnel at Monte Carlo.

He traveled with the second mate to Menton, on the Italian border—a very picturesque town with narrow lanes and white plastered buildings—and then along a road built on the rim of the mountains by the early Roman conquerors. On one side, he could see the blue Mediterranean, and to the right the caps of the Alps, rolling through little villages nestling on the tops of steep cliffs.

As the New Year began, the Commodore made his appearance back aboard the *Alva*. His Christmas had been extravagant and vibrant, with the usual group of friends and family, with resentments well-concealed beneath the surface splendor.

Aboard a much quieter, calmer ship, with a mostly new crew, the *Alva* left Monte Carlo on January 2nd and headed for Marseille. It seemed to Bob, fresh from days of freedom, somewhat of a pity.

Aboard the *Alva* the crew gathers for a formal photo in Monte Carlo. Navy blues have been substituted for whites in tune with the cooler weather. Much of the crew would soon depart and return to Germany.

They came out of dry-dock at Marseille and the Commodore announced that they were headed back to Villafranche, a favorite anchorage for U.S. Navy ships. Bob listened to the crew try to out-think the Commodore as to when and where they would go next. But being one of the crew veterans now, he'd had too much experience with rumors to get caught buying into them.

Bob thought of home—thought of his father. He tried not to think of Jo—and the women of Monte Carlo provided a fair distraction. They reminded him that the future was always full of possibilities. He had hope left still, even if he never saw the world again. Even if he had truly lost himself somewhere in the South Seas.

Hovering around Villefranche, the Commodore still had plenty to cope with. He had battled his whole life with what it meant to be a Vanderbilt. And as he showed his mother about the ship he had

Willie K. strikes a military pose while in the port of Marseille, France.

commissioned, with a tone of nonchalance but a posture that still desperately sought approval, Bob, for the first time, saw a type of hopelessness that he did not envy.

Alva Vanderbilt—aged, but still fashionably dressed—a woman capable of drawing all eyes toward her, gave every appearance of admiring and approving of her son, but there was something haunting about the interaction. Every exchange was tenuous. She, too, had escaped to Europe.

The final end to it all was more abrupt than Bob had expected. One day he was watching the celebrities that were the Vanderbilt family—interacting, laughing, feeding on the luxury of their wealth—and the next, suddenly understanding the Commodore really had no idea of when he would return home. The Commodore announced that he was headed to Paris again—for a week, or ten days, there was no telling. Then, like a breath of fresh air, Vanderbilt announced he would be detained indefinitely in Europe. Bob prepared to make his own way, leaving the Commodore and the *Alva* for good, and taking the *President Harrison*—a steamer—home instead.

Bob would sail from Marseille on the 20th of January. The *Alva*, anchored at a little fishing village called Sète on the Gulf of Lyon, would not return to Long Island anytime soon.

 The photographer sat in the darkroom and quietly processed the news. The Commodore was leaving for Paris again and it was a final farewell on that count, too.

Before he left, however, the graying, formal figure had materialized suddenly and, glad to find Bob alone, said he was more than satisfied with all the work and the results. Grateful for the praise, Bob grinned and shook the hand of his employer. He thanked him for the experience of a lifetime. The Commodore, still dressed like a sea captain, had already given way to the social demands of Europe. Willie and Rose would celebrate their urbanity, their sophistication, and regale their friends with the wildest tales of their adventures.

When the *Alva* would finally return home, whenever that might be, the Commodore had decided that she should have what he called "a period of quiet." It was unnatural, he said, for a ship to be so active since the day of her launching. What seemed more unnatural to Bob, however, was that she would suddenly and almost inexplicably become inactive. After weathering the seas around the world—exploring, adventuring, discovering—the ship was destined for a kind of sudden death. The adventures could never be relived or repeated.

Epilogue

"(T)o those who travel onward(s) toward the enlightenment of mankind comes the satisfaction of duty well done, of effort well expended. Nothing can bring more comfort to the heart of man than devotion to the cause of science."

Charles Francis Adams, Secretary of the Navy, as written in the introduction to William Vanderbilt's *Alva* memoirs.

Neither Bob Bronner nor Willie K. Vanderbilt II ever circled the globe again.

In May, 1932, two years after the launch of the ship he had named for her, Willie K's mother suffered a paralytic stroke that left her bedridden and weak. She died on January 26th, 1933. Her final decline came too suddenly for either of her sons—Willie K. or his brother, Harold—to make it to her side to say their goodbyes.

At her funeral, the Commodore was visibly grief-stricken. He departed on yet another cruise almost immediately after the event, heading for Europe, this time with his son and his wife's children, as well as several friends.

On November 8th, 1933, the *Alva* returned to the Vanderbilt Florida estate—Fisher's Island. In Florida, the Commodore spent time with his wife and his son, William Vanderbilt III. The ship was originally to proceed to New York with all aboard, but young Vanderbilt still did not have his father's sea legs and decided to drive back to New York. Willie K. III was intent on seeing his mother, Virginia Graham Fair Vanderbilt, with whom he had maintained a close relationship. At twenty-six he had spent much of his life with his mother. There was no way to prepare for the next tragedy.

Willie K. III adored speed and, like his father, he loved it most from behind the wheel of an auto. On a long straight section of road north of Ridgeland, South Carolina, he struck a vegetable truck which was parked on the side of the road with a flat tire. Young Willie, traveling seventy-five miles an hour at impact, was thrown clear of the vehicle and landed hard on his back on the concrete. He died within ten minutes.

Ensconced in a silver coffin under a blanket of spring flowers, the body of the Commodore's son was laid to rest. His father was motionless through the brief service and, in the presence of hundreds, sat at the foot of the coffin wrapped in grief. Like other Vanderbilts, the young man was interred in the New Dorp Mausoleum on Staten Island.

The death of a parent, especially one held closely, is a blow. However, nothing can compare to the loss of a child. After this second family tragedy in the same year, the Commodore hardly spoke a word about his loss. It wasn't the Vanderbilt way.

Instead he built an edifice: the third expansion of *Eagle's Nest*. It was profoundly expressive and personal: it became known as the Memorial Wing and it closed in the last open side of the courtyard. Willie chose one brief period in his son's life to memorialize, remembering his son as "The Great White Hunter." He created a trophy room consisting of the bounty of one six-week trip to the Sudan the young man had taken in 1931. Central to the memorial was a victory photo of Willie K. III, with his heavily armed cadre of native hunters, standing over an elephant that had unluckily crossed their path—converted into a large mural. The room was filled with trophies, from a stuffed alligator to hollowed-out elephant's feet, and in it a grieving father would stand and wonder what might have become of his son.

The death of Virginia, the Commodore's first wife and mother of his children, was the third blow. Virginia never recovered, neither emotionally nor physically, from her grief over the death of her only son. She went into shock in November 1933, just days after the death of young Willie K., and died the following year on July 7th, naming her ex-husband as her executor, referring to him as "the father of my three children."

The rest of the Memorial Wing provided an exhibit space on the first floor for marine and ethnographic collections. On the second floor, a separate bedroom suite was constructed for Rosamund, with a long hallway separating her room from her husband's. The reasons behind this particular design feature are ultimately unclear. One theory is that Willie K.'s rapid decline in health put too great a strain on his marriage. By 1936, Willie K., who had lived his whole life with a heart ailment, required a nurse almost full-time. No doubt, the recent family tragedies added to his condition.

When his strength recovered slightly, Willie took another stab at immortality and produced *Over the Seven Seas*, a movie of the 1931 trip that soon appeared at Loew's Ziegfeld Theaters. One can only wonder if Al and Bob saw the film and how they reacted to it.

At the declaration of World War II, Vanderbilt donated his beloved *Alva* to the war effort and she was promptly refitted armed and renamed the *USS Plymouth*. In August 1943, the *Plymouth* was on a routine escort of a convoy from New York to the South, ninety miles east of Elizabeth City, North Carolina. She made contact with an unknown sonar target later determined to be the German submarine U-566. As she swung to port, she was struck behind the bridge by a torpedo. The explosion lifted the ship out of the water, and when she settled into the sea she was gone within two minutes. The waters were shark-infested. The commander in charge left his ship last, and lost his leg. There were many casualties. Ironically, both the *Alva* and the torpedoes that sunk her were built at the same German shipyard—Krupp Germaniawerft in Kiel.

Hearing the news, Willie K. was heartbroken at the loss of his beloved *Alva*.

Willie's heart finally gave out and he died January 8th, 1944 at 12:32 a.m. in his Park Avenue home.

Although he had lived on for another eleven years, the spate of family tragedies took an immeasurable toll on Willie K. Vanderbilt II. And try though he might, after the *Alva*, the Commodore was never again able to enjoy captaining a ship. In essence, he was lost, not in the South Seas, like Bob, but in a permanent limbo of his own slow, methodical creation.

* * *

After leaving the *Alva* and the Commodore in Europe, Bob returned home to his father and reunited with Al Gilks at MGM. He went on to enjoy a stellar career, first as an assistant and later as a principle camera man and director of photography on several films. He eventually married and raised a family with his wife, settling down to enjoy the American dream. He longed for adventure the rest of his life. He dreamed of the South Seas, where he felt so strongly that he had discovered himself. He felt guilty for having left his father and perhaps allowed that guilt to grow over time into a sense of hopelessness.

Despite his wealth of experience and his artistic talent, Bob always felt second rate because of his lack of education. And although he liked and respected the Commodore, he never tried to get in touch with him after his return. He did not feel it was proper.

In the mid 1930s, he made one attempt to go back to sea, whaling off of California's Channel Islands. He killed a ninety to one hundred foot blue whale, and pulling it in between a pair of cruisers. The ships started to move, and to save himself from being crushed between them, Bob (who was in a small boat at the time) had to make for open sea. He was seasick on the first leg of the journey, and downright miserable in his efforts to try and recreate the feelings of joy and freedom he had experienced aboard the *Alva*.

Several decades later, heart disease also claimed the life of Bob Bronner. His memories of the Commodore and the *Alva* haunting him to the last. He remembered the greatness of the man along with his weaknesses. He remembered the man's kindness and his charisma; he remembered his insecurities and veiled disgust toward some of the more uncivilized cultures they had visited. He remembered the man for all he was and longed to be like him or better, becoming increasingly aware that he could never be such a man and would probably never meet anyone like him again.

The frailty of life was what inevitably haunted Bronner for the rest of his life. He had seen cultures, whole civilizations, disintegrating in many of the places he'd visited. And although he longed to see those places again, he knew it was hopeless. As hopeless and futile as spending every day in a dream.

Index

A

Abbas, Prince, 263
aborigines, 167-70
Acropolis, 258-60
Aden, 240-1, 276
Adunara Island, 189
Aegean Sea, 253, 257
Africa, 48
Alabaster Mosque, 251-2
Alton, John, 275
Alva, 30-3, 35-9, 44-5, 56-8, 62-4, 68-71, 73-7, 84-7, 120-5, 128-30, 174-7, 182-6, 252-5, 261-3, 267-71
  anchor, 164
  arrival, 220
  band, 98
  base, 46
  cost, 150
  crew, viii, 26, 28-9, 31-3, 37, 39, 40-1, 50, 56, 58-61, 66, 68-9, 71, 74, 76, 84, 93, 119, 120-5, 127-30, 150, 160, 165, 167, 176-81, 190, 201-3, 218, 239, 241-2, 254-5, 276, 281-3
  Daily News, 172, 241
  deck, 130, 133
  departure, 216
  first-class, 243
  luxury, 76
  nets, 98
  size, 267
  uniforms, 115
American Automobile Association, vii
American Consul, 158, 273, 277
American Samoa, 107, 114
American War, 261
Americans, 54, 62, 111, 113-14, 126, 207, 213, 241
  wealthy, 30, 49
Anamese, 145
anchor, 35-6, 38, 72-4, 120, 178-9, 185-6, 220, 244, 267, 273
  bower, 186
  down, 183
  lost, 179
Athenians, 259
Aneityum, 142
Annapolis, 243
Antarctic, 73
Anton, 46-7, 51-4, 58, 79-81, 118-19, 137, 155-6, 164
Apia Samoa, 106-7, 109, 110, 112, 120-23, 129
Apollo, 266
Ara, vii, 70, 74, 217, 242
Arabia, 237, 240-1
Arabian Sea, 239
Arabs, 213, 218, 241
Arafura Sea, 185
Argostoli, 268

289

Armistice Day, 221
Around the World in Eighty Days, Jules Verne, 128
Aryans, 230
Ashley, 132
Athens, 253, 257-9, 267
Australia, 61, 142, 149-50, 153, 157-9, 161, 163, 165, 169, 176, 178-9, 182, 184
Australians, 153, 168, 177, 271
  authorities, 167, 177
  viewpoint, 159
Azur, 280

B

Baksheesh, 247
Balboa, 64-6
Bali, 198-9, 200, 202-3, 205
Balinese girls, 213, 215
Banka Island, 216
Banka Strait, 216
Barnum & Bailey, 131
Batavia, 212-16, 220
Beebe, William, 69
Belanske, William, 32, 41-3, 51-2, 54, 70, 77, 133, 135, 143, 159, 180, 185, 201, 256, 264
Belanske's taxidermist assistant, 51
Bell and Howell camera, 146, 170
Belmont, Oliver Hazard Perry, 263
Bengal, Bay of, 229
Benson, 81-2
Berangaria, 31
Bima, 192-3, 195-6
Black Fever, 146
blatherskite, 15
Boomjes Island, 212
Bora Bora, 102-4
Borobudur, 209-10
Brisbane, 61, 68, 149-55, 158, 160-2, 164-5, 181, 212, 273
British Samoa, 107-8, 123

Bronner, Jack, 5, 7, 10
Bronner, Robert (Bob), vii, 1-33, 35-89, 91-4, 98-104, 109-15, 117-20, 122-8, 134-41, 149-66, 180-2, 184-91, 201, 204, 206-16, 222-7, 232-43, 247-74, 279, 285, 288
  amusement, 12
  anxiousness, 36
  attention, 74
  confidence, 125
  expression, 257
  eyes, 23, 119
  family's south Brooklyn home, 10
  father, 3, 7-9, 11, 15-16, 30-1, 36, 89-92, 146, 150, 212-13, 215-16, 222-3, 242-3, 277-8, 286-8
  friend, 5
  grieving, 286
  haunted, 288
  letters, 131
  roommate, 51
  style, 207
Brooklyn, 3, 11, 36, 265
brother, 7, 11, 79, 170, 223, 285
Buddhas, 210, 213, 223-5
Buddhist Mandoet Temple, 208
Buddhist snake temple of Penang, 224, 225
Buddhist temple in Penang, 225
Buddhists, 209
Buitenzorg, 214
Bukula Creek, 135
Buleleng, 200
bullock bandies, 238
Bushmen, 167
Byron, 255

C

Cabaret, Carlton, 153, 155
Cairns, 176, 178-9
Cairo, 240, 242-3, 245-52
calcium chloride, 102

INDEX

California, 3, 8, 31, 46, 101, 164, 252
camels, 240-1, 246-7, 250, 253
Camembert, 170
cameras, 3, 38, 43, 51, 59, 66, 70-1, 85, 87-8, 92-3, 111, 115, 140-1, 173-4, 182, 215, 219, 223-4, 227, 248
  format film, 257
  motion picture, 275
  moving picture, 28
Canadians, 62
Canal Zone, 65
canals, 37, 58, 63-5, 67, 214, 240, 253, 268
Canary Bay, 71
Cannes, 243, 280
Cannibal Island, 140
cannibals, 88, 135-6, 141, 146, 226
Canopus, 83
Cape Canaveral, 44
Cape Hatteras, 43
Cape of Tribulation, 179
Cape Rachado, 221
Cape Spartivento, 269
Cape York, 182
Capela, 96
Capes, Virginia, 35
Capri Island, 270
captain, 16, 78, 82, 117, 186, 198, 243, 257
  four-stripe, 112
Captain Cook, 107, 179
Captain Henry Morrison, 263
Captain Nemo, 21
Carlton, 161
Cartier of New York, 201
Catholic mission, 96
Centerport harbor, 3, 17, 25, 30-1
Century Club, 67
Cephalonia, 268
Ceylon, 228-33, 236-8
Ceylon Customs House, 231
Channel Islands, 288
Charles Francis Adams, 285
Charleston, 111

Chempi Bay, 193
Chianti, 270
Chicago, 8-11, 140
Chicago and New York, 7
China Sea, 198, 217
Chinese, 131, 213-14, 217-19, 225
  craft, 218
  hut, 188
  management, 217
  temples, 225
Christian cathedrals, 218
Christian Mission, 90
Christmas, 146, 149, 222, 243, 265, 276, 279, 281
  cards, 222
  celebrations, 222
Chrysler building, 37-8
Church, Frederic Cameron, 21
Citadel Mosque, 251
Colombo, 230-1, 235-8
Colón, 36, 57, 59
commissary, 65
Commo, 159
Commodore (William K. Vanderbilt II), 18, 43, 66-76, 78-81, 123-4, 132-6, 146-50, 157-60, 165-72, 174-82, 184-200, 205-10, 212-14, 239-43, 255-9, 265-71, 283-8
  attention, 226, 239
  behest, 105, 224
  birthday, 197, 201-2
  body language, 88
  character, 214
  childhood, 262
  daughter, 37, 65
  dismay, 268
  entourage, 103
  father, 262
  finances, 164
  germ fear, 123
  mother, 262
  party, 105, 266
  son, 286

stories, 190
style of enthusiasm, 93
Confucian temples, 218
Constantine, 266
Continental Divide, 64
Cook's Inlet, 98
cormorants, 73
Cornell, 167-8
Cristobol harbor, 64
Crown Prince Umberto, 272
Cuba, 36
Cuban 53-4
Cuban pesos, 51
Culebra excavated, 63
currencies, 151, 228, 267
  dollars, 138
  exchange, 97-8, 137, 151, 177, 190, 267, 284
Curry, Robert, 168-70
Cyprus, 257

D

Dahlonega, 2
dances, 91-2, 94, 101, 103-4, 111, 113, 124-6, 156-7, 170, 173, 206-7
  aboriginal, 180
  ballroom, 98
  exotic, 113
  native, 99, 111, 157
  traditional, 133
  war, 173
darkroom, 28, 45-6, 48, 55, 81, 102, 180, 197, 214, 222, 237, 243, 261, 284
Darwin, Charles, 69
daughter-in-law, 276
Davis, Bette, 156
deck, 27-9, 32, 36, 38, 40, 56-9, 78, 82, 85, 118-19, 123-4, 180-1, 188, 242, 254
  forward, 68
  lounging, 229
  lower, 37, 39, 63, 143

main, 39-40
starboard, 47
upper, 55
Dejokja, 215
Delmas, 90
Delphi, 261, 266
desert, 137, 162, 241, 243, 245-6, 248, 253, 260
deserters, 120, 124, 137
Diamond Shoal Light Vessel, 43
dignity, 114, 244
dioramas, 24
discontent, growing, 85
diver, 177-9
diving effort, 181
divorce, 70, 263
Djocja, 206, 208, 209, 211
Djocjakarata, 207
Doctor Lane, 69, 159, 160, 201, 205, 209-10, 214, 226, 234, 243
Dodd, 175
dreams, 4, 14, 55, 125, 158, 256, 262, 278, 288
  childhood, 157
  fanciful, 260
  shared, 35
dredging, 27-8, 72, 142-3, 217
  channel 179
  equipment aboard, 27
  exercise, 217
  process, 27
  single, 143
Dressler, Marie, 153
Duke, 262
Dupont, 102
Durian, 217
Dutch East India, 192, 204, 209
Dutch
  government officials, 198
  island, 228
  money, 227
  travelers, 200
Dutchmen, 62

INDEX

E

eagle, 17-18
Eagle's Nest, 15, 17-19, 30-1, 93, 286
   transformed, 19
Earl, 37, 63, 67, 69, 73-4, 76-7, 85-6, 88, 116-18, 255
East and West Sentinel Islands, 85
East River, 36
Eastern Samoa, 114
eccentricities, 127
Ecuador, 70
Egypt, 243, 245, 247, 252
Egyptian Cabaret, 249
Egyptian seafront, 244
Egyptians, 245-8
Emperor Nero, 266
Empire State building, 36
enchanted isles, 74
engine compartment, 176
engine room, 27, 80
engine-room revolution counters, 27
engine-room telegraph, 35
engineer, 50, 52
   first, 82
   first assistant, 46
   third assistant, 81
engines, main, 36
English, 49, 109, 119, 125, 131, 186, 188, 194, 200, 206, 213, 218, 226, 240
   girl, 153, 157
   money, 151
   ports, 221
   pound sterling, 267
   protectorate, 56
   yacht, 146, 280
Englishmen, 62
epidemic, 146-7
equator, 37, 65, 70, 150, 231
Europe, 103, 162, 165, 176, 194, 215, 227, 254, 270, 284-5, 287
European 131, 198, 218-19
   civilization, 188
   clothes, 86
   influence swept eastward, 145
   port, 216
   quarter, 218
Evans, Louis, 62, 75, 82, 88, 238, 242
Eve's Lover, 126-7
expense, 166, 179, 192, 217-8, 265

F

Far East, 212
Fare Harbor, 96, 98
Father Simeon, 90
Fawkes Island, 72
felucca, 239
Fernanda, 54
Fernandina Island, 75-6
fez, 246, 249
Fiji, 128, 130, 134-5, 140, 142, 162
Fiji Islands, 128, 130, 142, 163
Fijian belles, 132
Fijian canoe, 136
Fijian housing structures, 134
Fijian war canoe, 136
Fijians, 131-6, 140
   early, 140
film, 4, 6, 33, 38, 46, 50, 57, 66, 102-3, 126-7, 170, 243, 252, 260, 287
   16-millimeter, 276
   cans, 5
   colored, 276
   reloaded, 91
   storage chamber, 28, 40
financial well-being, 198
World War I, 209
fish, 19, 24, 28, 30, 61, 63, 69, 71, 88, 96-7, 104-5, 145-6, 180-1, 190, 198
   blue water, 43
   colored, 105, 226
   devil, 21
   flying, 188
   tropical, 43, 88
fish taxidermies, 32

fisherman, 97, 184, 235
Fisher's Island, 45-7, 285
Flores Sea, 192
Florida, 21, 46, 242, 285
Florida coast, 21, 47
Fogg, Phileas, 128
Fords, 93, 131, 184
fortune, 16, 146, 164, 226, 256, 264
Fox Movietone, 150
France, 31, 164, 215, 242, 262, 269, 273, 277-8, 283
Franciscans, San, 104
Frying Pan Shoal Light Vessel, 43
Futana, 142
Futina, 106

G

Gaillard Cut, 63
Galapagos Islands, 24, 37, 41, 65-6, 68-9, 70-2, 74, 76, 177
  fairytale, 73
Gase, 123
Gastleman, 25
Gatum, 65
Gatun Lake, 63
Georgetown, 224
German 62, 80
  crewmen, 40, 53, 63, 81
  quartermaster, 25
  seamen, 165
  shipyard, 287
Germany, 25-6, 121, 187, 273-4, 282
germaphobic Willie, 109, 111
Giant Manta Ray, 21
Gilks, Alfred, vii-viii, 14-18, 20-2, 25, 31, 33, 36-8, 42, 51-2, 55-6, 150, 153, 261-2, 264, 274-5
girls, 53-4, 92, 98, 101, 116, 118, 124-6, 153, 155-6, 188, 193, 198-200, 249, 262
  chasing, 271

dancing, 123-4, 195
good-looking, 151
love, 278
shy, 125
Giza, 250
God, 53, 177
God bless, 118
God of Mirth, 226
gods, 116, 226
Gorgas, William Grawford, 67
governor, 103, 114, 204, 209
Governor General, 108
Governor Lincoln, 115
Governor of Ceylon, 230
Governors Island, 36
Graflex, 89, 92, 186, 213, 257
Grafton, 160
Grand Central Terminal, 10, 12-13
  old, 18
Grand Pacific Hotel, 131-2
Grand Prix, 146
Great Barrier Reef, 183
Great Britain, 131
Great Depression, 1, 121
Great Palm Island, 168, 170
Great War, 261
Great White, 24
Great White Hunter, 286
Greece, 251, 254, 258, 261, 267
Greek Amphitheater, 266
Greek Drachmas, 267
Greek port, 268
Greenlawn, 33
Greenlawn station, 17
gringos, 54
Guatemala, 256
Gulf of Corinth, 267
Gulf of Lyon, 284
Gulf of Patras, 267
Gulf Stream, 45-6
Gumbrinos Restaurant, 270
Gustave, 62

INDEX

H

Haava strait, 85
Haavai Bay, 98
Habitat, 23
Halifax Bay, 166
Hamann, 63
Hamburg, 62, 187
Hamburg American, 31
Hammond Rock, 182
happiness, 104, 148, 201, 269
Harmon, 10, 12, 14
Harold, 79, 285
Harvard, 262
Havana, 36, 45, 47-50, 52, 55, 57-9, 66-7, 209
Hay Bay, 85
head chef, 29
heart, 13, 150, 218, 267, 285
   ailment, 287
   attack, 262
   condition, 261
   disease, 288
heartbroken, 287
heat, 2, 47, 51, 61, 73, 106, 135, 138, 209, 213, 242, 254
   lightning, 56
   midday, 209
   oppressive, 3, 253, 255
   tropical, 69
heavy seas, 57, 254, 267
Heggs, 56
Heigh-ho-the-fox, 210
Hamann Heinrich, 40, 82
Hephaestus, 259
Hindu 132, 218-20, 233, 236
   educated, 132
   temples, 208, 212, 225
   women, 132
Hiva Oa and Tahuata, 85
Hollywood, 65, 151, 153, 158, 208
   back-lot, 112

movie set, 101
movie stars, 30, 127
Holy Land, 251
Honolulu, 116
hopelessness, 284, 288
Hori Hori, 101, 103
Hotel, Lennon, 151
Hotel Washington, 59
Hoyt, William S., 263
Huahina Island, 93, 97-8
Hubble Bubbles, 245
Hudson, 269
Hula Hula, 101
Humbolt Current, 73
Hydrographic Office, 238

I

Idle Hour, 24
iguanas, 60-1
India, 132
Indian bazaars, 218
Indian driver, 132
Indian Ocean, 193, 238
Indiana, 9
Indians, 131, 140, 218
Influenza, 117
Ingersoll, old Dollar, 146
inspector, 56, 130-1, 184
Isabella Island, 73
Isle de France, 31
Ismailia, 252
Italian aviators, 270
Italy, 268, 270

J

jackals, 232
jai-alai fronton, 66
Jamaica, 55-6, 67
Jamaicans, 56
Japanese swords, 213

Japanese territories, 48
Java, 206-9, 212-14, 220
Java Sea, shallow, 212
Javanese, 145, 186, 188, 202, 206-7, 213, 218
   dancers, 207-8
   murderer, 147
   woman, 187
Jesus Christ, 90
Jewish synagogues, 218
Jo, 156-8, 160-2, 164-6, 170, 172, 205, 208, 235, 237-8, 248, 250, 258, 271, 273, 278-9
   close, 161
   date, 162
   home, 158
   parents, 162
   telling, 159
Johnson, Francis, 263
Johnson, Martin, 140
journal, 30, 90, 152

K

Kambing Island, 187-8
Kandy, 230-4
Kava, 109
kava bowls set, 123
Kenneth G, 25
Kiel, 25-6, 82, 273
Kimbing, 192
Kingston, 55-8, 61
Kingston harbor, 56
Kissel, 3-4
Kiwi government, 109
Komodo Island, 191-2
Krupp-Diesel engines, 25
Krupp Germaniawerft in Kiel, 25-6, 287
Kuranda, 174-5

L

La Perouse and Cook, 160
Labuan Balat, 195-6

Ladies' Aid Society, 98
Lake Barrine, 176
Lake Champlain, 2
Lake Crystal, 2
Lake Timsah, 252
Lakes Barrine and Eacham, 176
Lane, 37, 47, 77, 90, 158, 177, 186, 188, 274, 276
Lautoka, 134, 138, 140
Lautoka Harbor, 139
Lavinia, 235, 237
Leeward Group, 96
Leica camera, 279
Lekuva, 130
Lennon, 151
Lesser Sunda Islands, 192
letters, 31, 56-8, 64, 84, 89, 141-2, 150, 158, 165-6, 172, 216, 227, 235, 242, 277-9
   father's, 150
   final, 277
   mailing, 243
   writing, 84
Levuka, 130
Lexington Avenue, 14
Lieutenant Commander Vanderbilt, 261
Lincoln Town Car, 17
lizards, 191
   dodging, 59
   large, 192
   ten-foot, 191
Loew's Ziegfeld Theaters, 287
Logoiitumua Aumai Tafa Ua Tau, 123
Lomblem, 188-9
Lombok, 192
Long Island, 13, 15, 30, 33, 43, 93, 251, 261, 284
Long Island Railroad, 17
Long Island Sound, 35
Long Island waterfowl, 24
Los Angeles, 1, 5, 7, 17, 227, 277
Los Angeles Limited, 1-2, 8
Louis, 62

INDEX

love, 8, 65-7, 70, 116, 138, 157-8, 164, 262-3, 269
   gentle, vii
   new-found, 35
love letter, 181
lovers, 70, 126

M

Mac, 52-4, 77, 79, 84, 191
Mad Jack, 169
Madeira, 187
Maguire, Walter, 51
Maine, 17
Malacea, 221
Malakka canes, 218
Malakka Strait, 217, 229
malaria, 132, 186, 195
Malay city, 218-19
Malay Peninsula, 222
Malays, 195, 218-19, 231, 233
Malecẋn, 49
man-of-war, 186
Manhattan, 13, 69, 152
manta ray, 69, 71, 75
   captured, 20
Marquesans, 86-8
Marquesas Islands, 75, 84, 86, 90-1
Marseille, 215, 281, 283-4
Martin, 81-2
Marvis Hedstrom Company, 132
Masonboro Inlet, 43
mate
   first, 41, 50, 60, 74, 82, 178
   second, 62, 75, 82, 170-1, 185, 191, 197, 242, 281
   third, 82, 185
McGuire, 185
Medieval-styled four-storey boathouse, 19
Mediterranean, 267-68, 270
   blue, 281
Melbourne, 152, 165
Mendota Temple, 210

Menton, 281
Merillon, Pierre 37, 41-3, 67, 76-8, 88, 98, 188, 274-5
merino wool, 165
Messina, 269
Metro-Goldwyn-Mayer, 4-6, 24, 102, 153, 287
Miami, 45, 47, 242-3
Miami estate, 55
Michelle, 37, 85-6, 152, 220, 240, 274
Michigan Avenue, 9
Middle Ages, 209
Middle Island, 163
Midtown, 14
Milky Way, 83
Miller, Patsy Ruth, 103
Minarets, 251-2
Miraflores Lake, 64
Miramar, 49-50, 52
Mississippi River, 152
Moe-e-Fui-Fui, 113
Moedoek, 205
Mohawk, 12
Mojave, 8
Monaco, 274-7
money, 2-3, 15-16, 32, 106, 125, 130, 137, 147, 158, 180, 208, 227, 243, 247, 262-4, 267
Monski, 246
Monte Carlo, 243, 273-4, 276-7, 279, 281-3
Moorea Island, 99
Moran, Polly, 153
Moreton Bay, 149
Morgan, Henry, 59-60, 64
Moro Castle, 51, 55
Morro stone crabs, 66
Morton, 45-7, 50-2, 54, 62-3, 79-80, 117, 119, 158-9, 185
Morton hand, 117
Mosques, 251
mosquitoes, 88, 149, 166, 196, 207
mother, vii, 7, 21, 223, 246, 262, 276, 283, 285-6

Mount Bentley, 166
Mount Lavinia, 235
Mount Lewotolo, 189
Mount Name, 185
Mount Ramelan, 185
Mount Tambora, 193
Mount Vesuvius, 270-1
mountains, 1, 86, 135, 140, 145-6, 174, 185, 194, 224, 231, 235, 260, 270-1, 281
Movietone cameraman, 150
Movietone news, 150
Muntok, 216-17
Murnau, 102-3
Museum of Natural History, 42, 256
Muslims, 209

N

Na Pon Island, 87
"in the name of science", 265
Naples, 266, 269-72
Naples, Bay of, 270
Narborough Island, 76
native articles, 136
   boats, 218
   cultural objects, 136
   river boats, 206
   royal dagger, 213
   village, 97, 106, 109
natives, 86-7, 90, 92-3, 98, 100-1, 103-9, 111-16, 125-7, 129-30, 132, 147-8, 172-3, 187-8, 194, 198-200
   aboard, 116
   beauty, 122
   habitat, 145
   magical incantations, 104
   religious, 198
Natural History, 42, 256
Naval ships, 283
Navigators Islands, 107
Navy, 35, 112, 114, 243, 261, 285
Navy Department, 114-15
Navy Officer, 261

negatives, 65, 77, 93, 102, 135, 138, 180, 185
   developing, 68, 222
Negombo, 235
Nevada, 8
New Caledonia, 132, 145, 147, 149, 176
New Dorp Mausoleum, 286
New Englanders, 152
New Guinea, 187
New Hebrides, 132, 140-2, 146
New Year, 273, 279, 281
New York, 33
New York and Newport society, 262
New York Central Railway 8, 9, 10, 13, 172, 239, 241
New York City, 12, 17, 36, 41
   left, 11
New York to Chicago route, 9
New York Harbor tug, 186
New York's North River, 149
New Zealand, 109
Newport, 19, 110, 251
Newport News, 32
Nile, 245, 251, 263
Nile cruiser, 245
Nile Valley, 251
Nolando, 2
North Australia, 175
North Carolina, 43, 287
North Island, 163
North Star, 82
Northport, 27
Northport museum, 181
Norton, Barry, 103
Noumea, 145-8, 176
Noumea Harbor, 145
Noumea prison, 147
Nova Scotia, 81
Nuwara Eliya, 230

O

officers, 28, 37, 76, 80, 82, 88, 142-3, 180, 182-4, 186, 198, 200, 239, 261

INDEX

Olosega, 107
Omaha, 8
onboard newspaper, 37
onboard physician, 47
Orange Hotel, 206
Oriental quarter, 225
Orientals, 268
Oscar, 275
outrigger canoes, 93, 97, 101, 136, 188, 190, 235
Ovalau Island, 129

P

Pacific, 65, 174, 182
Pacific Northwest, 6
Pacific Ocean, 64, 183
Pago Pago, 106, 112-13, 122
Palm Beach, 44
Palm Island, 166, 167, 169, 174
Palm Islanders, 168
Panama, 36-7, 57, 59-60, 62-4, 119-20, 124
  left, 68
Panama Canal, 36
Panama cathedrals, 64
Panama City, 64
Panama City and Old Panama, 59
Panamanians, 62, 119, 121, 123, 162
Panchromatic film, 49
Pantar, 188
Papeete, 63-4, 91-5, 97, 103
Papuan race, 187
Paris, 147, 274-5, 279-80, 284
Park Avenue, 14, 287
Parnassus, 266
Parsis, 231
Parthenon, 257-8, 260
Paru, 106
  native, 91-2
Parus, 97
Passepartout, 128
Patras, 267-8

Pattison, Doctor Maitland, 168-69
Pedro Miguel Lock, 64
Penang, 221-2, 225, 229
Pennsylvania, 10
Pennsylvania Railroad, 9, 13
Pennsylvania Station, 13, 17, 33
Percy Islands, 163
Persian rugs, 247
photographers, 3-4, 14, 42, 80, 125, 127, 141, 158, 160, 229, 264, 284
  assistant, 4
  union shop, 5
  well-liked boy, 66
photography, 4, 135, 138, 243, 287
  nude, 92
  studio, 6
photos, 48, 66, 175, 257, 282
  framed, 20
  victory, 286
  well-timed, 44
pictures, 31-2, 47, 49, 55, 71-2, 89, 91, 93, 180-1, 186, 188, 198-9, 210, 212, 223-6
  good, 105, 213, 245
  interior, 229
  moving, 174, 226, 232
  perfect, 274
  shooting, 138, 209
  smell-O-tone, 98
Pierre, 76-7, 85-6, 120, 152, 167-70, 205, 240, 274
Piper Islands, 182
Piraeus, 258
pirates, 64, 198, 277
pith helmets, 32, 204
poi grinder, 104
Poi Poi, 103
Politics, 153
Polynesians, 98
Pope, 262
Port Bourayne, 98
Portuguese, 231
Portuguese control, 185

Portuguese man-of-war, 188
Prado, 49
President Harrison, 284
Preston, 158
pride, 14, 29, 114, 156, 195, 244
Prince and Princess of Piedmont, 272
ptomaine, 181
Pullman sleepers, 2, 10
Pulo Perak, 229
Punaauia, 92
Punaauia Pass, 91
Punanum, 92
Punaruu Beach, 97, 99
Puttalam, 235
Pyramids of Giza, 250-1, 278

Q

Quarto, 48
Qué tomará, 53
Queensland, 165-6, 170
Queensland government, 168
Quinton, third mate William, 82-3, 87, 242

R

Raiatea, 98-9
railroad empire, 16, 217, 262
railroad leadership, 264
railroads, 174, 214, 256, 270
Red Sea, 237, 240, 242
Restaurant de Paris, 66
Ridgeland, 286
RMS Berengaria, 31
Robbins, Reddington, 37, 41, 43, 60, 77, 82, 188, 242
Rock Temple, 233
Rogers, Ginger, 156
Roma, 270
Roman conquerors, early, 281
Roman reservoirs, 240

romance, 67, 235
  heart-wrenching, 279
  true-life Hollywood, 30
roommate, 31, 185, 188, 279
roommate Mac, 171
Rooney, Patrick, 185
Round-the-world cruises, 164
Ruid, 25, 27, 81
Runnymeade Hotel, 222
Rusa, 188
Russian, 176
Russian bank, 79

S

Sabang, 228-9
Saint John, 259
Saleh Bay, 193
Samoa, 106-9, 115, 129-30, 135, 145, 150
  chiefs, 123
  crowd, 127
  currency, 115
  etiquette of gift, 113
  girls, 116
  Islands, 140
Samoans, 106, 111, 113, 123, 134
San Bernadino Valley, 8
San Francisco, 158, 264
Santa Barbara, 63
Sea Bat, 71
second mate Evans, 164
  drowned, 191
Sète, 284
sharks, 24, 75, 85, 103, 116, 129, 165, 182, 287
Shelton, 14, 30-1, 33
Shelton Towers Hotel, 14
Shepherd Hotel, 247
ship, 25-33, 37-41, 53-64, 74-81, 83-5, 116-18, 120-1, 123-4, 128-9, 142-3, 182-3, 185-6, 265-8, 283-5, 287-8

first, 124
lateen, 239
passenger, 186
wooden, 236
shots (photographic), 48, 51, 92, 98-9,
    101, 103, 109, 127, 137, 163-4,
    168-9, 175, 191, 194, 202
  best, 199, 250
  decent, 37
Singapore, 172, 184, 198, 216-18, 221
  crowded harbors of, 219
Singhalese, 231
Sirius, 82
Siva Siva, 111
Smith, Earl, 255
Snake Temple, 227
Sociedade Angricola Patria, 186
Society Islands, 63-4, 96
Sokotra, 239
Solo, 206, 215
Solomon Islands, 132
Solomons, 132
Solor Straits, 189
South American, 41, 69
South Carolina, 286
South East Island, surrounded, 163
South Pacific, 110, 130
South Sea Islands, 42, 63-4
South Seas, 27, 37, 69, 90, 102, 108, 112,
    131-2, 136, 273, 283, 287
Southern California, 74
Southern Cross, 82
Southport, 158
Spanish style, 66
Spanish town, old, 49
Sperry Master, 26
Sphinx, 251
SS Île, 31
SS Imperator, 31
St. John, 259
St. Louis, 146
Stamford Raffles, Sir, 204, 209

Stevenson, Robert Louis, 90, 108
stewards, 61-2, 85, 121-2, 128, 275
stock markets, 6, 172, 263
Strait of Durian, 217
Straits of Malacea, 221
Straits of Messina, 269
Studebaker factory in Elkhart, 9
Sudan, 286
Suez Canal, 243, 252-4
Suffolk County Vanderbilt Museum, viii,
    263
Sultan of Bima, 195-6
Sultan of Labuan Balat, 195-6
Suma Islands, 131
Sumatra, 216, 218, 229
Sumatran coast, 216
Sumbawa, 192, 194-6
superstitious, 181
supplies, 25, 29, 31-2, 47-8, 61, 131, 135,
    184
Surabaya, 206, 211-12, 215, 217
Surabaya harbor, 212
surreal experience, 271
surrealistic, most, 93
Suva, 128-32, 135, 137, 139, 141
Suva and Tuesday aboard ship, 128
Suva harbor, 130, 135
Swedes, 62
Sydney, 150, 152, 160, 165, 184
Sydney Harbor Bridge, 160
Sydney Head, 160

T

Tabu, 102
Tagus Cove, 73-4
Tahaa Island, 101
Tahiti, 41, 63-4, 84, 90, 94-7, 99, 106
Tahitian culture, 91
Tahitian ports, 106
Tahitians, 97, 99, 109, 124
Tamils, 230-1

tapas, 133-4
Tarboosh, 246
taro root, 133
taro bread, 123
taxidermist, 31, 42, 50-1, 74-5, 82
Temple of Tooth, 233
Temples of Hephaestus and Olympian Zeus, 259
Thanksgiving Day, 239
Thiel, 160
thirteenth, 181, 228
Thompson, Charles, 70
Thursday Island, 163, 183-4
Tiger Islands, 192
Timor, 184-5, 187
Tommy guns, 9
Tonga, 129
Tooth, 233
Top Gate, 176-7
Toppen Hat, 132
Torres Straits, 182
Towers, Shelton, 13
Townsville, 165-6, 170
Townsville harbor, 164
Trabahlho, 187
trees, 57, 59, 92-3, 106, 111, 122, 133, 149, 174, 186, 217, 227, 280
  banyan, 186
  breadfruit, 97
  coconut, 106, 133
  eucalyptus, 154
  Kapok, 206
  olive, 267
  palm, 235
Trocadero, 271
Tropical Waters, 45
Tuesday, 30-1, 82, 87, 128, 214
Turkish bath, 234
Turkish pipe, 245
Tutuila, 113, 116
Twentieth Century Limited, 9

U

U-566, 287
underwater pictures, 182
Union Pacific, 2
United States, 62, 114, 192, 214
United States Fleet, 66
United States Naval Observatory Eclipse Expedition, 129
United States Navy in Berlin, 25
unsanitary conditions, 111
Upolu and Savaii Islands, 107
Upper Bay, 36
Urgh, 58
US Treasury, 16
USS Plymouth, 287

V

van Duir's, 195
Vanassi, 140
Vanderbilt, Alva, vii, 262-3, 275, 284
Vanderbilt, Consuelo, 117, 263
Vanderbilt, Cornelius, 9, 13, 15-6, 262
Vanderbilt, Cornelius II, 16
Vanderbilt Estate in Long Island, 14
Vanderbilt family, 284
Vanderbilt family cruising, 263
Vanderbilt family hunting lodges in Canada, 24
Vanderbilt Florida, 285
Vanderbilt fortune, 162
Vanderbilt, George, 66-7
Vanderbilt, Virginia Graham Fair, 285-6
Vanderbilt, William Henry, 15-16
Vanderbilt, William Kissam II (Willie K.), vii-viii, 13, 19, 22, 30, 67, 70, 72, 97, 100, 173, 177, 184, 224, 227, 258, 263-65, 283, 285-7
  bridge-deck cabin, 26
  childhood days in Oakdale, 24
  cigar, 23

cruises, 263
eleventh yacht, 26
estate, 17
explorations, 24
fate, 161
    impending, 272
    risking, 182
father, 263
fortune, 16
heart, 287
history, 214
house, 3
inheritance, 164
love, 19
money, 35
mother, 262
nonchalance, 75
photographer, 3
residences, 18
sister, 262
son, 22
son-in-law, 21
step-children, 22
tragedies, 287
veiled disgust, 288
yacht, 7, 276
Vanderbilt, William Kissam III, 285
    son, 5, 7, 13, 15-16, 22, 31, 39, 43, 138, 195-6, 264, 275, 284-6
    son's life, 286
    young, 3, 5
Vanderbilt, William Kissam Sr, 262
Vardiani, 268
Veddahs, 231
Ventura, 116
Verne, Jules, 128
Vesuvius, 272
Viao Bay, 88
Victory Parade, 131
Villa Franche, 273-4, 283
visceral reaction, most, 117
visions, 103, 260

Viti Levu, 130, 139
volcano, 129, 260
    extinct, 75, 240
voyage, vii-viii, 19, 29, 35, 41, 67-9, 74, 90, 121, 179, 253, 260, 274, 276
    first, 21, 74
    long, 278
    safe, 118

W

war, 6, 115, 163-4, 188
war canoe, 109
war clubs, 130
war effort, 287
Warburton, Barclay, 70
Warburton, Rosamund Lancaster, 21, 37, 67, 70, 286
water buffalo, even, 194
Water Castle, 207
Water-Gordon milk, 29
water shortage, 68, 81
weaknesses, 111, 288
wealth, 15, 30, 284, 288
    great, 225
Weary Bay, 179
West, vii, 2, 11, 97-100, 128
Western, 73
    attitude, 131
    culture, 103
    frontier towns, 184
    influence, 110
    world, 258
whale, 73, 75-6, 149
    blue, 288
    humpback, 75
White Shadow, 66
wife, 25, 114, 116, 157, 159-60, 168-9, 235-6, 248, 250, 252, 268-70, 274-6, 278, 285, 287
    first, 264, 286
    second, 157

Wilgus, 13
wireless, 123, 137, 142, 239
  aboard, 241
  operators, 37
  room, 27
  telegraphy, 214
woman, 30, 125-6, 137, 157, 164, 200, 262, 266, 284
  ambitious young, 157
  gold-digging, 157
  local, 15
  tapa shirtwaists, 133
Woolworth Tower, 149
World War, 168
World War II, 287

Y

yachting club, 261
Yale, 69

About the Authors

STEVEN H. GITTELMAN is a current trustee at the Suffolk County Vanderbilt Museum and has served as president of the Board of Trustees for many years. He is the author of four books on the Vanderbilts and their era. Once again, he partners with his daughter Emily, to live history together.

EMILY GITTELMAN is thrilled to be part of another historical adventure. In addition to writing, Emily has also narrated dozens of audiobooks and is an actress living in Los Angeles, CA.

ANDREW WELLS is from Montreal, Canada. This is his first work of historical nonfiction.